And Nothing But the Truth

Charlie Cochrane

RIPTIDE
PUBLISHING

Riptide Publishing
PO Box 1537
Burnsville, NC 28714
www.riptidepublishing.com

And Nothing But the Truth

Cover art: L.C. Chase, lcchase.com
Editors: Carole-Ann Galloway and Grace Stack
Layout: L.C. Chase, lcchase.com

ISBN: 978-1-62649-996-6

First edition
May, 2024

Also available in ebook:
ISBN: 978-1-62649-995-9

And Nothing But the Truth

Charlie Cochrane

RIPTIDE
PUBLISHING

Table
of Contents

Chapter One

Late spring 2022

Adam Matthews slipped out of bed and headed for the window to have a peek at what the weather was doing. As the BBC had predicted the day before, it was a glorious morning, more flaming June than showery April.

He glanced over his shoulder at where his husband Robin Bright lay in bed, gently snoring and appearing very little older than when they'd first met eight years ago. The odd grey hair had sprouted—generally in his stubble rather than on his head—but he was still as handsome. And still as effective at catching villains and putting them behind bars as he'd been in the murder case which had introduced them, without ever resorting to any of the dodgy tricks so beloved of TV cops.

"Go with the evidence, wherever it leads. Although a touch of copper's instinct never comes amiss," was what Robin said, and his instinct had been proved correct on many occasions.

Adam yawned, stretched, and headed downstairs, to where a canine bladder was no doubt awaiting a chance at relief. He opened the kitchen door, said, "Morning Cam—" and stopped. Funny how he'd managed to avoid using the wrong name for so long, but now he wasn't concentrating, it slipped out. As his mother had told him would no doubt happen.

"Like in the stone age, when we wrote cheques. I'd never get the year wrong on them all through January because I'd be thinking about it, and then I'd find myself writing the incorrect date come February, when my attention had wavered. It'll be the same with the dog."

As so often, she was spot on. "Sorry, Hamish. Old habits. Am I forgiven?"

The Newfoundland bounced up and bestowed a slobbery kiss.

"Thank you. I love you, as well." Maybe not yet as much as he'd loved Campbell, but that would come with time.

"I heard you nearly say the wrong name as I came down the stairs." Robin's voice sounded chirpily as he came into the room. "I'm so pleased, because I made the same mistake yesterday. I could become paranoid that he thinks his name is actually *Cam*, whereas he's a handsome Hamish. Aren't you boy?" Robin gave the dog a good ruffling round his neck, which was received with obvious pleasure, then let him out into the garden.

"Maybe we both need to write out fifty times, 'His name is Hamish,' and hang it up in here." It might have been easier if they'd chosen a different breed, rather than a dog who resembled a younger and smaller version of his predecessor, but they were used to Newfoundlands. Switching to a Labrador or other kind of pooch would have felt treasonous to the big lad's memory.

Robin gave Adam a peck on the cheek. "I think we should. You'd have thought a whole week's holiday away with him would have got us into the habit by now."

"It's being home. We've slipped into very old habits. We never called him *you know what* down in Devon."

A term into his first headship, that break had been needed and a glorious time that had been, with generally bright weather, no murders, and no schoolchildren—none that Adam had to be responsible for, anyway. He'd done a couple of months as acting headteacher the previous year, when Jim Rashford, for whom he'd been deputy at Culdover, got appendicitis, but that didn't bring the same kind of pressure. While it had been great preparation for taking on a similar role, the place he'd been running was someone else's school, and he could eventually give the responsibility back. Like babysitting.

Now Adam was leading the primary school in the large village of Wickley. It was proving similar to the one at Lindenshaw where he'd been employed when he met Robin, with the same links to the local church and the same set of values espoused.

Values that Adam could buy into straight away. Reconciliation, forgiveness, and loving your neighbour as yourself were right up his street, albeit difficult to do on a regular basis.

The job had its challenges, naturally, including a member of staff who wasn't cutting the mustard and who'd need dealing with once the new term was up and running. But Jane could be put out of mind for the moment.

"Wakey wakey, daydreamer," Robin said. "The sun's breaking through."

"Shining on the almost-righteous."

"Days like these make me wish we could win the lottery and be on holiday permanently." Robin put on the kettle while Adam got Hamish's breakfast ready.

"You'd get bored. We both would. Besides, the experience wouldn't feel so good if it wasn't a treat."

"I'd be willing to risk seeing if I could get used to it. In the interests of science. Do you want toast?"

"Nah, just cereal. I think I over-calorified myself when we were away. Anyway, you can't win the lottery because you don't do it. Even my most numerically challenged pupils would realise that if *you ain't in it, you can't win it*. I hope they would, anyway." Adam called a few to mind who might struggle with the concept. The villages of England might be leafy, but they still had children with special needs or parents who didn't quite have a proper grasp of reality.

Robin snorted. "If your pupils grow into some of the people I have to deal with, I wouldn't bank on the fact. Not all villains are sharp. Some are simply lucky, so they get away with things they shouldn't. Then there's the ones who rely on the fact nobody reports them or—if they do—complaints don't get taken seriously enough."

Adam nodded in sympathy. Prior to their holiday, Robin had been dealing with the aftermath of an historic child-abuse case, where the victim had waited so long for justice that he'd taken things into his own hands and beaten seven colours of brick dust out of the choirmaster who'd made his life a misery thirty years previously. Robin only had the assault case to deal with, but the details behind it had got to him. While Robin's own schooldays had hardly been a bundle of joy, they'd been nothing compared to what the man had endured when he was a pupil. At least Adam and Hamish had been there to support and comfort the bloke through the process, with hugs and a wet nose respectively.

Adam fetched Robin's favourite cereal bowl. "I wish all parishes were like Wickley. If Katie Morgan had been the safeguarding officer for that choirmaster's parish, there'd have been no nonsense about sweeping things under the carpet." Katie was one of the foundation governors at Adam's new school, and her opinion on the church's lax handling of abuse cases had been a joy to hear.

"Speaking as a probably-not-very-good Christian, I have to say there's a hell of a lot of muddled thinking around forgiveness. You won't know this yet, boy," Robin said to Hamish, who'd returned from the garden and wanted attention. "Actions can be forgiven but they still have consequences. Life lesson, free and gratis, from your dad."

"If you want to give him life lessons, we should start with training him not to go throwing himself at guns or knives. Like the old boy did."

"Maybe I should train *you* not to get too closely involved with my cases, as well." Robin put the finishing touches to the food he'd laid on the breakfast bar, then perched on a stool.

"Might I remind you," Adam said, wagging a teaspoon at him, "that if you insist on interviewing a murderer in my kitchen, in the vicinity of the lad's Bonios, then you're tempting fate? I'm glad this house is keeping itself a killer-free zone." So far, no trouble had followed Robin home there, and long may that prevail. Adam surreptitiously touched wood but clearly not surreptitiously enough.

"I saw that. Was it your 'please no murders' touching wood?"

"Something like that." It had been over a year since Robin had dealt with a homicide case, if one didn't count a manslaughter due to diminished responsibility, and their luck was due to run out. Murders meant long and unpredictable hours and risked Robin getting stressed or—worse still—relocated for weeks on end.

"If I do get a murder case anytime soon, *he'll* not know what's going on with all the long hours. He'll think I've deserted him." Robin glanced over to where a supremely unbothered Hamish was concentrating on his breakfast.

"He'll learn to cope. Another lesson for life in the Matthews-Bright household." Adam chomped on his granola. "Any chance we can bring him up to think he's a cat? Or another dog breed that doesn't do water rescues?"

"Vain hope. It's inbred. The old lad always liked being in water. Even if we didn't think he had the urge to rescue in him." Robin patted Adam's hand, and they focussed on their food, probably both fighting a lump in the throat.

Late last autumn they'd been out for a walk in a country park, with Campbell off the lead but walking to heel as became his habit as he'd grown older. He'd evidently been the first of the three to see a toddler fall into the lake, at which point some deep-rooted instinct must have kicked in. Before Robin had got to the water's edge, Campbell was already immersed, paddling like mad while taking the child by the back of his jumper and pulling him to the bank.

In the general kerfuffle of administering first aid and calming the child's parents, it had taken Adam and Robin a while to realise that their dog wasn't getting himself up off the ground. A minute or so later, it had all been over.

"Talk to me about something funny," Adam said. "Daft things your newbie coppers have done."

"Nothing to offer, sorry. Our latest recruit—Danielle—is proving far too sensible to provide you with cheering-up fodder." Robin managed a grin. "I think Pru's taken her under her wing, rather like I did Ben when he joined the team. Then I've just this morning heard we've got Ashok relocating from Kinechester, so he's a known quantity."

Adam nodded. Robin had met Ashok when he'd had to take over a murder case from a nearby team which had been struck by Covid. Apparently, the constable had needed the odd rough edge knocked off but was pretty solid underneath. "That's come out of the blue, hasn't it?"

"Yeah. Part of Superintendent Cowdrey getting everything shipshape, I suspect. Played two blinders, because not only did he secure us Ashok, he's also got rid of Gareth. He's the new one we'd been allocated at the same time as Danielle, but he rubbed Cowdrey up the wrong way, so the boss persuaded him that he'd be getting a wider range of experience in the Kinechester team. Which is no word of a lie."

"A very useful lie. What did Gareth make of that? What did *you*?"

"He's delighted. Thinks he's got one over on Danielle. Special treatment and all that." Robin rolled his eyes. "As for me, I wouldn't argue with the boss. He's too astute and has more experience of young guns than I have. Although—and don't quote me on this—I wouldn't be surprised if Gareth ends up in the papers or on the telly one day, and I don't mean him getting the George Cross."

"Potential to be bent?" There'd been plenty of similar stories in the news recently and not confined to the Metropolitan Police. The lad must have been particularly bad for Robin to have formed such an opinion so quickly.

"I don't know. There's something not right about him—in the short time he's been with us, he's said a few things which raise alarm bells, but he may be capable of being converted away from the dark side. I suspect Cowdrey doesn't want his patch soiled at this late stage of his working life, so he's palmed Gareth off on Kinechester."

"What does Denness think?" He was Cowdrey's equivalent at Kinechester, at a not-dissimilar point in his career, so surely wouldn't want to deal with somebody else's issue.

"He's happy, actually, despite the rather frank conversation Cowdrey had with him about his concerns. Denness is regarding Gareth as a challenge. A potential feather in his cap if he works the miracle."

"Like you've done in the past." Adam patted Robin's hand. *He'd* had the Augean stables job given to him and performed it with aplomb. Not something he'd want to do again, though.

Robin pushed his empty plate away, a sign Hamish clearly took to mean his dad was available for making a fuss of him. The Newfoundland bounded over, to be hauled onto Robin's lap. "I know, I know, breaking house rules, but he's still a baby."

"So long as you break him of the habit before he's fully grown, or you'll have flat thighs." Adam watched the pair affectionately. "How's the crown holding up?"

"I'd forgotten about it. Must be a good sign." Robin had been having issues with his molar. The first temporary crown he'd been fitted for had barely lasted forty-eight hours, but this replacement seemed like it would last until the permanent one could be installed, first thing on Thursday. "I had a text from Mum this morning, by the way. She's being rather mysterious. Wants to know if we'd have time to drop in today."

Adam shrugged. "Don't see why not. We don't have much planned for today. Although I bet she only wants to see the boy and spoil him."

"Yeah. No doubt who's her favourite from us three." Robin let Hamish lick his ear. "I'll say we'll pop in for a cuppa this afternoon. She says she wants us to do something for her. Bit of family business, although she's not telling me exactly what."

"Your aunt Clare hasn't given Jeff the push and has a new fancy man needing investigating?"

"I've no idea. Mum will tell us in her own good time. Maybe she's found a black sheep lurking among the Brights, the kind of family member nobody mentions. Everyone's found it safer to ignore their existence in case questions get asked."

Adam snorted. "You've been reading too many books this holiday. They've given you strange ideas. She didn't give you any clues?"

"Not really." Robin retrieved his phone from the worktop where he'd left it, having to reach round Hamish to do so. "She says: *Too complicated to explain by text. Nothing sinister. You could call it a mystery I'd like some advice about clearing up.*"

"We'll definitely go over for an hour or so this afternoon. I'm very curious."

"We could take this boy for a walk along the old railway line near Mum's, then grab lunch at the pub. The one that used to be the stationmaster's house."

"Didn't it used to be a dive, as well?" They'd walked past it before, with Campbell: he'd turned his wet nose up at it despite having been a huge fan of hostelries.

"It's been tarted up, apparently. Mum says it's dog-friendly too." Robin addressed the last part to Hamish, who looked bemused. "I could see if I can book a table in the garden."

"You do that, while I get washed and dressed. It'll be a nice end to the holiday."

While he headed for the bathroom, Adam's thoughts headed off in several directions. He'd heard about people finding an illegitimate child on the family tree, one who'd manifested in the form of a stranger turning up on the doorstep to say, "Halloo. You don't know me but I'm your half brother." There'd been a child born out of wedlock in the Matthews's line, which had only come to light after Adam's great-aunt had warned his cousin Sally not to go investigating family history as she wouldn't like what she found. That had, naturally, made her keener than ever to go delving. It had proved a general letdown that the only blot on the family escutcheon had been something that nobody would bat an eyelid at in modern days. Sally had confessed she'd been hoping for a murderer or bigamist at the very least.

Still, they wouldn't have long to wait to find out what was exercising Mrs. Bright's brain. And no doubt the answer would come with a healthy slice of cake. They'd have to be on the frugal side at lunch to make room for it.

When they got to his mum's house, not only did Mrs. Bright provide refreshments with their mugs of tea, it was Robin's favourite boiled fruit cake. Sweet and moist—as sweet and moist as Adam's lips, he'd once said in a moment of high soppiness— the cake was the perfect crown on a pretty perfect day. The pub garden hadn't been too busy, their lunch sandwiches had been delicious, and the walk had exhausted Hamish, who was sprawled on the rug, probably dreaming about the squirrels he'd not been allowed to chase.

Once they were settled and the food had been given its due attention, Robin said, "You've got us really puzzled with this family business stuff. You're not about to spring a stepfather or half sister on me, are you?" He was only half-joking, having been going through various scenarios in his mind all day.

Mrs. Bright chuckled. "I'm too old for getting wed again, and if you *do* have a half sister, I'd be as surprised as you would be. But I have got something strange that's cropped up, and I need two extra brains and a bit of specialist help to make sense of it. My solicitor's drawn a blank. I think it's to do with your dad being adopted."

Robin cast his husband a puzzled glance. Despite not having known his father-in-law, Adam knew all about the adoption, which had never been kept secret, nor had it seemed a big deal. Robin hadn't speculated that much about his paternal grandparents, not having felt the need of anyone but the elder Brights in his life. "You've lost me already, Mum. Can we start right at the beginning, please?"

"Sorry. I wouldn't make a very good impression in a witness box. You know your father never made a fuss about his background, not like these folk on the telly who want to know exactly where they came from. Your gran and gramps were his parents, full stop, the end. He just accepted that was how it was."

Robin nodded, feeling rather choked. His sexuality was one of the things Mr. Bright senior had readily accepted, and he would have made good friends with Adam, no doubt dragging him down the pub to discuss the test match or Robin's foibles. But his sudden death, from a heart condition he hadn't known he suffered from, meant that could never happen. "Is this to do with his biological parents?"

"It may be. That's the only explanation I can think of. Somebody wants to give us some money. You and me. No, Adam, I'm not falling for a scam." Mrs. Bright broke into a giggly smile, one which took years off her. "It isn't somebody pretending to be a Christian lady whose pastor husband has left a fortune and who needs my bank account's help to access it. My solicitor, Mr. Caswell, has done lots of checks and thinks it's legitimate."

"Who's the benefactor, Alison, and how did they get in touch?" The worried note in Adam's voice and the rare use he'd made of her Christian name showed he was still doubtful, official reassurance notwithstanding.

"Not by email. They wrote air mail, to Mr. Caswell's firm. Another solicitor—somewhere in the Commonwealth, Mr. C says he's not allowed to be any more specific about where and *his* name is Brown, so that's not too helpful—has been looking for a Mr. David Bright, born on the day your father was. I think they managed to track him down through the obituary we put on the local paper's website." She took a sip of tea, or pretended to, as the drink must have been tepid at best. Probably a stalling tactic to allow her to get over memories of Robin's dad's sudden death. "Whoever is behind this has clearly done their research, because they followed the trail from the memorial notice to Mr. C. He's heard on the grapevine they contacted various local firms to try to get a trace on your dad's family. Mr. C didn't get in touch with me until he'd done enough of what he calls 'proper diligence' to be convinced this was real."

"But you're not allowed to know where the money comes from?" Robin asked.

"No, or who sent it. Anonymous bequest. Very *Midsomer Murders*." His mum grinned again.

"Don't you end up as the victim, then." That was only half a joke, as well. "What do you want us to do?"

"Two things. The first is a big favour." Mrs. Bright's fingers twisted round each other. "I hate asking you to do anything that's work connected, Robin, but do you have—I'm not sure what they call them—forensic lawyers, like the forensic accountants you've mentioned?"

"We have people who specialise in fraud and the like. One of them, Henry, probably owes me a good turn, so I'll get him on the case. Check it's all kosher."

"It's not simply a favour for a family member," Adam pointed out. "Proactive policing, to prevent a crime. If it's actually a clever scam, it's unlikely you'd be the only victim."

"Absolutely." Robin's brow crinkled. "Can you also make sure your solicitor has checked this isn't linked to money laundering? That's big business now, and the rules changed not that long ago, so I hope Caswell will be up to speed about what to keep an eye out for. Also get an understanding on your position regarding inheritance tax. You don't want to be landed with a bill down the line because of Double Taxation treaties."

"What the hell are they?" Adam asked.

"No idea, but Henry once mentioned them because they helped him to narrow down which country some dodgy money came from."

"I'll ask about both of those. Thank you." Mrs. Bright patted Robin's hand. "The other thing I need to ask *you* about is a bit silly. I've always wanted to find out about David's family, but I wouldn't have done it when he was alive because he was quite determined not to know. This seems an ideal time, because I can't help feeling that if this inheritance is real, it has to be linked to his birth mother or father. Trouble is, I don't know where to start and when I browse the internet, it's bewildering. I've asked Clare but she's been no help. I know you two are rushed off your feet, though."

"We are but I'm sure we can find time. Maybe if you bribed us by coming over and cooking dinner one night, we could repay you by putting you on the right track. Friday, say?" Robin suggested.

Adam nodded, no doubt keen for another opportunity to sample his mother-in-law's cooking. "Works for me, especially as that'll give us time to think. We must know someone who's into genealogy."

"It's not that I'm struggling with." Mrs. Bright waved her hand so vigorously it dislodged a cushion and woke the pup, who shot her a mortally offended look before going back to sleep. "I know all about places like Ancestry or the other sites where folk put their family trees, but if David was taken off his mother when he was barely a few days old—and he was in the right generation for that to have happened—he may not be listed under the name David, if he's listed at all."

"That's why you need an expert," Robin said. "I used to work with someone who got bitten by the family history bug but was too fond of shortcuts to do things properly. If he saw a Fred Bloggs, he was sure it had to be *his* Fred Bloggs. It usually wasn't."

"Barking up the wrong family tree, was he?" Mrs. Bright giggled, Robin groaned and Hamish woke again, wearing such a disdainful expression that they all ended up laughing.

Robin could only hope they didn't fall into the same trap. Family histories could be labyrinthine at the best of times.

As they drove home, Adam sat in the back with Hamish to keep the Newfoundland happy. Maybe he'd get forty winks, although Robin would probably want to chat.

"I wonder why it's taken Mum so long to get round to this if she's so keen to know the truth," Robin said, when they were barely fifty yards into the journey.

"Probably she felt it was being disloyal to your dad. This inheritance gives her a legitimate excuse. I'm glad you gave her some jobs to get on with for the next few days."

"Few weeks, I'd have said." Robin had suggested his mother start by going up into the loft and going through the papers that had come from his paternal grandparents' house when they'd gone into sheltered accommodation. They'd had no room to take all their old things but had been reluctant to chuck them away. Unfortunately, she couldn't draw on their knowledge, as Mr. Bright senior's memory was no longer reliable and Mrs. Bright senior had gone to her long home. "I wish she'd asked Gran and Gramps about this when they were able to give an answer."

"I've heard that so often. People kick themselves because they didn't ask Aunty Win about Uncle Fred's war record, or why nobody mentions Cousin Danny, when they had the chance. You can fish out marriage certificates and the like, but the stories get lost. Oh, behave. Sorry, not you, the boy with the raspy tongue."

"Dog lick. Delightful." Robin snorted.

"Have you ever wanted to do what she's doing? Trace your biological grandparents?"

"Not really." When they'd started dating seriously, Adam had joked about nicking a sample of hair out of Robin's comb to do a DNA comparison, in case they were actually cousins and were in a relationship that some folk would find too consanguineous. From then on, the adoption had been merely a fact, like a date of birth, to be aware of but not make a fuss over. "Occasionally I've run across a bloke or woman of the right age who bears a familial resemblance to me and wondered if they're the ones, but I'd never ask them. Anyway, I'd be a bit scared of what I'd find out, and Dad was the same. What if he'd been the offspring of an equivalent of Fred and Rosemary West, which meant he'd been removed at birth primarily to protect him? He'd decided he'd rather not know."

"We'll have to hope your mother doesn't turn up anything like that." Adam's voice was light, although he'd no doubt be thinking of the media headlines if it was discovered that Robin was the grandson of a notorious criminal. "However, whatever facts emerge, it's not your fault or your dad's. You can't be held responsible for the sins of your forefathers, irrespective of what they turn out to be."

"Why are you so sensible?" Robin glanced into the rear-view mirror, caught Adam's eye, and smiled. "We'll just have to deal with what comes up, because once Mum's got an idea, she'll pursue it to the bitter end. She won't settle for not knowing."

"Worse than Hamish when he's lost a biscuit. Do you remember *my* great-aunt showing us the Matthews family bible?" Adam asked. "The family tree that seemed like it went back to Noah?"

"Yes. Why?"

"I thought you were taking a surprising interest in all the names. I supposed you were either being polite or so enthralled with me that you hung on my every chromosome. Was it anything to do with the unknown family?"

Robin squinted into the mirror again, shaking his head. "Sorry, no. I'm ashamed to confess it, but I was searching for surnames I might recognise in a work connection. Checking you weren't first cousin to an Abbotston drug baron."

"You sneaky bugger." Adam chuckled. "You'd better watch him, Hamish. He'll be doing all sorts of background checks on *you*."

"There's no pit bull blood in him, I'm sure of that." Robin pulled up at some lights, taking the opportunity to glance over his shoulder at his family. "I wish we had another week of holiday."

"So do I. Hey, the light's gone green."

"Oh, heck." Robin got his attention on the road again, before he got a blast from someone's horn. "Back to the grindstone tomorrow, then."

"Yeah. This is usually the point where one of us inadvertently tempts fate and then has to deliberately untempt it. I'm afraid, Hamish, that often leads to some poor sod being found murdered and your other dad spending all the hours God sends at work. And that's all I'm telling you because you're not to get involved like your predecessor liked to do."

"Too right. While you're at it, can you show Hamish how to keep his paws crossed that nobody decides to commit a serious crime over the next few days?"

"He'll think that's a great game."

Robin left them to it, concentrating on driving. He'd have to ignore the fact that, by the law of averages, his team was probably due another murder.

Chapter Two

Luck ran out on Tuesday lunchtime, when one of the Wickley primary school admin team rang through to Adam's office to inform him that the police were on the phone.

"It's a Chief Inspector Robin Bright calling," she said in a worried voice. "Should I put him through?"

"Yes please, Val, and don't panic. This should be personal, not business."

Although the staff who'd been in post when he'd taken up his job in January were aware of his domestic setup, people like Val who'd only joined the school for the start of this new term wouldn't be in the know. Unless the staffroom gossip machine had informed them. Adam made a note to give both Val and the new maternity-cover teacher the lowdown once the call had ended.

"Hiya." It sounded as though Robin was out in the wilds somewhere. "You can guess why I'm ringing you. May be home late. Suspected murder in the Kings Ride Woods."

"A murder? You've managed to get the news to me before I saw it on the local news page." Or heard it in the staffroom.

"I'm not sure the media will have got wind of it yet. The body was found by a woman out for a run, who's had the sense to keep shtum. Somebody will notice our activity here soon, so I've rung Cowdrey to brief him before the enquiries pour in. I'm still at the scene."

Adam winced. Even at the most difficult of times, like when an Ofsted phone call came, he wouldn't swop his job for his husband's. "I appreciate the heads-up. I know the score by now so, when you can, let me know what to have ready dinner-wise and when."

"You're a legend. I don't need to tell you not to say anything until we break the news."

"Keep quiet and carry on?"

"Something like that. He's been dead at least a couple of days, so we think there's no immediate danger to the public, although we'll issue the usual warning about taking care when you're out alone until we're clearer about what went on. The person who found the body was bright enough not to assume it was a natural death, which proved right when we turned the bloke over and saw the back of his head. You don't want the gruesome details."

"I do not. I'm trying to grab my lunch." Luckily it was a hummus wrap and not a ham sandwich.

"We'll be putting out an identity appeal, as well. Nothing on the victim or with his corpse, apart from a small, empty packet of Party Rings and a few old crumbs. Oh joy."

"Good luck with that. I'll wait to hear from you; otherwise, Hamish and I can have a romantic dinner together."

"Don't nick his Bonios or he'll turn nasty on you. Got to go. Don't forget the milk."

"I won't." He'd never forget that special bit of code, either—although surely the rest of Robin's team had twigged by now that the pair couldn't run out of semi-skimmed so often? Had they guessed it substituted for *I love you*?

He put down the phone, grateful that his role meant he could usually take calls straight away—assuming he wasn't in deep conversation with an irate parent or other person who demanded his entire attention—and not have to wait until lessons were over. A death at Kings Ride wouldn't directly impact the school community at Wickley, given how far away it was, but once the playground chitchat started, people would be unsettled. He'd deal with that when the time came, having had plenty of practice.

Meanwhile, he'd wolf down the last bit of an already delayed lunch, then head to the office, where he could explain to Val exactly *who'd* been on the phone, if not the *why*.

By the end of the school day, the news had broken and was the talk of the staffroom. But while Adam was willing to confirm to his staff that his husband was indeed in charge of establishing what had gone on—it was only a *suspected* murder, after all, and could still turn out to be a freak accident—he made it clear there was no point pumping him for inside information. He wouldn't have had much to share at that point, anyway, even if he'd wanted to. Which he didn't.

The police had put out an appeal in an attempt to identify the victim and said he didn't match any local missing person's reports. That had brought unpleasant echoes of the case Robin had tackled just over a year previously, although that victim had lain undiscovered a lot longer.

"The dead man mustn't have had any ID on him to give them his name," Val said, as she gathered up her things, although she didn't seem ready to leave at present. "Maybe the killer took it."

"A robbery that went too far?" Alice, the deputy head, shrugged. "He might not have been carrying it in the first place. If I go out for a run and I know my husband will be in when I get home, I rarely take anything with me of value. Except my wedding ring, obviously."

"It's pointless speculating." Liam, the year-two teacher, glanced over his shoulder as he wrestled with the tea bag in his mug. "Anyway, the police probably know more than they're letting on."

Not a lot more, Adam guessed, ensuring his face didn't give away his thoughts.

"Whether they do or don't, people can't stop speculating. It's part of how we cope with these awful things," Alice said. "Trying to make some sense of what's senseless. Would that be fair, Adam?"

"It's a valid point. I don't mind you discussing the Kings Ride death in here, so long as it's away from the pupils and doesn't intrude on work." The case would likely be a seven-days wonder, especially if the police made an early arrest, although Adam wasn't getting his hopes up on that front. "What I would suggest is that none of you go running on your own in *any* local woods for a while. And no, I don't have any inside knowledge about whether there's a particular danger out there, although you don't need inside information to know that people can't always go for a walk or a jog in safety, because that's the kind of world we live in. I'm not only thinking of 'stranger danger,' but the standard of driving we have round here. Robin had a case a few years back that hinged on a hit and run."

A sobering reminder that appeared to have the desired effect, given the facial expressions around the room.

Adam gave them all what was hopefully a reassuring smile. "Right, finish off anything you need to do here, then get home at a decent time. Hug your family."

"You too." Alice nodded sympathetically. "Although I suppose your bloke won't be home as early as you will."

Wasn't that the truth?

At Abbotston police station, there was no sign of anyone getting away any time soon. The public response to the media appeal had already resulted in some information which Robin's team was following up, although they'd drawn a blank on identification so far. The Saracens wolfpack T-shirt the victim had been wearing should have helped, it being distinctive and not for a local rugby team, although Sergeant Pru Davis's experience was proving the opposite.

"Another dead end," she announced to those in the incident room, after practically slamming her phone down. "I've just spoken to a Mrs. Gambling, who was sure the dead bloke was her husband, except that when I drilled deeper, he couldn't be. Mr. Gambling's been gone for a month and never supported

Saracens in his life, both of which could be explained away but the mouthful of dentures can't be."

"You were very polite with her," Danielle said, with an air of real respect.

"Probably too polite. I wonder if he's upped sticks and she wanted someone to talk to about it." Pru sighed.

Robin, who'd emerged from his office to give his team an update, suspected she was right. "I know it's frustrating and I hate this 'not knowing' phase as much as any of you, but keep your peckers up. Early stages." Albeit it was an early stage without many of the usual things they'd be doing, like conducting door-to-door interviews or speaking to friends and family. None of that could happen without a name or a place of residence. It also meant that precious time would slip by before they could deal with the obvious suspects in many a case of violence: those who had been closest to the victim. "Unless he was jobless, he must have an employer somewhere trying to get hold of him. It's only a matter of time before they join up the dots."

"Given the fact he'd got nothing in his pocket—not even keys—what are the chances this was a mugging that got out of hand?" Danielle asked.

"A pretty good chance. Which is the worst kind of case, as far as I'm concerned, because—as those of the team who've worked with me before will tell you—I initially focus on people the victim knew." Robin glanced over at an incident board which was horribly short of content. "We've not got the full forensics or postmortem results yet, but you don't need to be a CSI or a doctor to have spotted the blow to the head or the pool of vomit." Analysing the crime scene and searching the wider area was one thing they'd been able to do.

Pru took up the discussion. "We mustn't rule out that the sick belonged to the dead man. Blows to the head with our old friend the blunt instrument can cause nausea. Only he'd have had to have moved after he'd spewed because that vomit was a good two metres away. I know I'm now going to state the obvious, but it could also be the killer's or have come from somebody else who found the corpse and didn't bother reporting it, for whatever reason. Our runner said it isn't hers."

Ben nodded. He'd been with Robin for a while now and had experience of exactly how his teams worked. Robin made sure his officers could air ideas, be open, never be afraid that they'd get the mickey taken out of them for suggesting something a bit off piste. "She must have a strong constitution, then. Not a pretty sight."

Pru let out a snort. "She's a midwife, so it would take a lot to faze her. Talking of constitutions, who wants to attend the PM in half an hour? Danielle, have you been at one before?"

"No. But I'd like to," the constable added, clearly trying hard to hide the fact she didn't. "Got to be done sometime, hasn't it?"

"We can go together," Pru said. "If that's okay, boss?"

"Fine by me. You can always call me down there if anything surprising turns up." Robin smiled his approval. Pru was developing all the skills necessary for the next stage in her career, and part of that was bringing on junior officers. That could be seen in her willingness to support Danielle through what was likely to be an unpleasant experience. "What did this midwife have to say?"

"She—Kathy Hartley—had the sense to make a careful note of what was at the scene, in case it got disturbed while she went off to call us. She doesn't think anything *did* get moved."

"We're sure of that?" Ben asked.

"So Kathy says," Pru replied. "She hung around so she could take us to exactly the right spot and then apologised because she'd not had the sense to take the what3words location, bless her. She said she could have taken pictures of the crime scene but that wouldn't have felt right."

"Can I scroll back a bit, please?" Ashok asked, in a sheepish voice. "I may be being thick, but why did she need to go elsewhere to make a call, sir? Doesn't that seem suspicious?"

"Not to us locals. There's no signal in that part of the woods. One of the many regional blackspots where no provider reaches." Robin jerked his thumb towards the window. "Go out into the wilds and try it sometime. Although you've made a good point." He took another shufti at the board. "We can't ignore the chance that Kathy could have been involved and her discovery of the body was staged. Can we get her name up there, please?"

"Good to have something to fill the gaps," Pru said, as she jotted the midwife's name on the incident board.

Ashok continued. "Would the killer have known there was no signal, sir? That may have been why they chose that spot to biff his victim one, if he couldn't ring for help."

"It could be. That would imply they might be local because, like you, lots of folk who visit the area get a shock when they realise it's like being up a Scottish mountain, rather than sixty odd miles from London." Robin smiled in remembrance of the black spot around Lindenshaw school and its indirect connection to meeting the love of his life. The lack of mobile signal had formed part of the murder investigation in which Adam had been a witness. "Still, let's rule nothing out and nothing in until we have more in the way of facts. Ben, you and Pru stayed at the scene longest—anything to offer us?"

"Not a sausage." Ben moved to the incident board, where Ashok had put up a map pinpointing where the body had been found. "As you can see, the victim . . . Can we give him a name, please, sir? It feels so impersonal to keep calling him *the dead man*."

"Gary," Pru suggested. "He looks like a Gary."

"Okay. Carry on—" Robin was about to say *Constable* in an inadvertent nod to one of his aunt Clare's favourite films, but that felt like an inappropriate note of levity.

"Gary was found here"—Ben indicated the spot—"so the closest houses are right over to the west, a mile off and not near an official access point to the woods. There are several footpath entrances and a couple of car parks, but there were no vehicles left unaccounted for when Pru and I did a sweep of the area on the way back."

Pru joined her colleague at the board. "So, Gary could have lived within jogging distance, maybe at Kings Ride itself, or been dropped off by a mate. Unlikely to have used public transport, especially at a weekend, because the bus to Kinechester comes twice daily on Saturdays and not at all on Sundays."

"He could have brought his own car and whoever killed him nicked his keys and then took *it*," Robin pointed out. "That wouldn't necessarily have been planned, either. We all know how opportunistic thieves can be. Hopefully, our appeal for runners, or anyone else who uses the woods, to come forward might yield results."

"I keep thinking of that Ellen, sir," Ashok said, in an unusually sombre voice. "She lay undiscovered for weeks, but that was in her own home. Why wasn't this bloke—Gary—found if he was near a running route?"

"He wasn't, not really," Pru said. "According to Kathy Hartley, most runners stick to the main paths because there are adders at Kings Ride. A jogger got bitten during lockdown and ended up in hospital with a severe reaction. Folk tend to be wary of going on the smaller paths, but Kathy said she knew you're unlikely to meet a snake at this time of year."

Robin nodded. He'd seen a warning sign about venomous snakes when he'd parked his car.

"There was a flasher up there, as well," Danielle said. "He started during lockdown. They only caught him last September, so it put some women off running in those woods."

"I'd forgotten that." Pru gave the constable an approving nod and then checked her watch. "We'd better get organised and head down for the gruesome bit, Danielle. It'll be marginally better than dealing with people who think Gary's theirs, only to find out that he can't be. All frustration at our end aside, it must be heart breaking for them."

On that sombre note, the team went back to their tasks, still none the wiser as to Gary's actual name.

By the end of the day, Robin and his team had the results of the postmortem, if bugger all else. The autopsy hadn't thrown up anything unusual and a still green-about-the-gills Danielle confessed that she'd struggled to hold it together and not puke. She'd managed to take notes, which she relayed to the rest of the team.

"He died as a result of a blow to the head with a blunt instrument. Something like a smaller version of a baseball bat," the constable said. "If it had been anyone else, they might have survived, but he had quite a thin skull, so probably death followed soon afterwards, although he might have been able to stumble a yard or two."

"Eggshell-skull rule," Ben said. "The killer won't be able to rely on that fact to mitigate their crime."

Danielle nodded. "Another couple of things. The vomit contents at the scene don't seem to match what was in Gary's stomach, and in terms of time of death, he was likely to have been killed somewhere around seventy-two hours previously, so maybe Saturday lunchtime."

Robin noted, with a touch of guilt at the thought, that Gary would have already been dead by the time he was discussing Hamish crossing his paws. If that was the case, had he tempted fate after the event?

Chapter Three

Adam was pleased when Robin arrived home on Tuesday evening at a reasonable time and sympathetic when he confessed he'd rather have been back later and have more to show for it. He briefed Adam—as he always did—on what they'd found out so far, but the process didn't seem to be as fruitful for him as it usually proved. Too early, too few facts. The only positive was that Henry, Robin's contact in the specialist fraud section, had said he'd have a dig into the mysterious inheritance business and hoped to report back by Friday about whether Mrs. Bright was getting into something dodgy. They had an early night in bed, both weary from a busy few days, and woke to a wet Wednesday when their alarms sounded.

While the weather was dreary, the news that Robin received over breakfast clearly wasn't, and it appeared to brighten his mood considerably. The duty sergeant at Abbotston had rung at seven o'clock, apologetic that he was so early, to say he just received a call from a distressed mother confessing that her son and his friend might have some important information about the dead man found in Kings Ride Woods. The sergeant had calmed her down and arranged for them all to come in at nine thirty. Robin thanked him and reassured the officer that ringing so early was never going to be a problem if he was bringing news like that.

"Sounds encouraging," Adam said, once Robin had updated him on the call. "Did she say what this information was?"

"No. She was in too much of a state, apparently. Maybe the lads found the body earlier than our midwife did and have been keeping quiet about it. They're only ten."

"Oh heck." That would mean the usual protocol for child witnesses having to be put in place. "Perhaps they're the ones who nicked whatever he was carrying in his pockets." Adam stared into his tea. Boys that age weren't too young to mug someone.

"I've been having the same thought." Robin crunched away at his granola. "On the positive side, it would mean a chance of getting an ID for the victim and maybe an address, assuming the items haven't already been disposed of."

"I hope this pair aren't any of my pupils. I'll be keeping an eye out for absences today in years five and six." Because that was the way the universe seemed to enjoy working where Robin's murder cases were concerned.

"I think you're okay this time. They're local to Kings Ride, and I don't believe your catchment goes that far?"

"It doesn't and I don't think we've got any families who've moved there and still bring their children back to Wickley." It happened, especially when the pupils only had a year or so left at primary before going up to secondary school. Less disruption to their education and their friendships. "I'll also get Hamish to keep his paws crossed that these lads aren't related to any members of my staff."

Robin snorted. "I wouldn't bother. Crossing his paws didn't work on Sunday, did it?"

By half past nine, Robin knew that if Hamish *had* been crossing his paws, he'd been effective this time. Neither of the boys—Kyle Simmons and Archie Hill—were pupils at any school Adam had been associated with, as he and Pru had discovered when they'd chatted to them as part of putting them at ease. A process not helped by the presence of two livid mothers who evidently wanted to get to the point as soon as possible, although they weren't letting out any hints about what that point was. They'd clearly decided that their sons were going to have to do all the talking.

Once the preliminaries were done, Mrs. Simmons said, "Tell Mr. Bright what you did."

"We were in the Kings Ride Woods on Sunday afternoon." Kyle kept his eyes fixed on his hands. "We weren't supposed to be because we're only allowed to go as far as the play park or the rec."

"Too right you're not to go any farther." Mrs. Simmons shook with anger.

"I'm sure we all did things when we were ten that we shouldn't have done," Robin said, before she could pitch in again. Interviewing children was a delicate business. "Helpful" parents were no help at all. "What happened at the woods?"

"We went for a walk, to see if there were any trees we could go climbing on. We found that dead bloke."

"Okay." Robin nodded. "What time was this?"

Kyle shrugged. "I don't know exactly. In the afternoon. We'd had football in the morning."

"You didn't tell anyone that you'd found him?" Pru asked.

Both boys wagged their heads, Archie adding, "We didn't want to think or talk about him anymore. It was horrible. I was sick."

That probably explained the pile of vomit. Robin assured the lads that lots of people were sick when they saw a body. He got Pru to make a note of what the lad had eaten that day and carried on. "You told us he was dead. Did you know that at the time you found him?"

"Yeah. See, I felt for his pulse and there was none. We learned that at school." At last Kyle looked Robin in the face. "I know he wasn't breathing, either, because we both watched his chest. We'd have gone and got help if we thought it would have saved him."

Mrs. Hill couldn't keep quiet any longer. "Like good little citizens. Then, instead of finding a phone and ringing for an ambulance or the police, you went in his pockets, nicked his wallet and scarpered to leave him for the foxes to eat?" She reached into her handbag and produced a Tupperware box with a mobile phone and wallet in. "You could have made an emergency call from this."

"I told you, Mum, those things weren't in his pockets," Archie protested. "They were lying next to him."

"And then all of a sudden they were in this tub, under your bed?" She slammed the box onto the table, none too gently.

Robin snatched it up before damage could be done to the contents. "We'll take that for our forensic people to go over. We'll have to get all of your fingerprints too, for elimination purposes. Did *you* find this under the bed, Mrs. Hill?"

"No," she conceded. "Archie brought the two items down this morning and told us what had happened. I put them in here to keep them safe."

"I'd heard about that guy on the local news. I had to come clean." Archie avoided Kyle's gaze. Was there some tension between the two—one the instigator and the other the obedient lieutenant? Although if Kyle had been the one doing the egging on, Robin would have expected him to have been the one in possession of the stolen items.

"So, let's get this clear." Robin produced a rough sketch of the scene, which he'd had the foresight to prepare prior to the interview. "If this is the dead man, where exactly were the wallet and the phone?"

Archie indicated a point to the left of the body, then checked with Kyle, who said, "That's right. Archie was sick around here." He pointed to another spot, which matched where they'd found the vomit.

"Could the wallet and phone have fallen out of the dead man's pocket?" Pru asked.

Kyle, who'd probably expected a bollocking, was beginning to blossom, maybe as a result of being taken as a serious witness. "I don't think so. Not unless he'd moved all weird when he fell down on the ground."

Archie nodded. "My dad keeps his wallet and phone in his back pocket so they're safe. This guy was on his back, so they couldn't have fallen out from there."

A decent piece of logic. Could the killer—or another person who'd come across the body—have removed the items? Although, in that case, why rummage them out and not take them?

"Was there anything else lying by the body?" Pru smiled encouragingly. "Every detail you can think of will help us find who killed him."

"No, honest. Apart from one of those little packs of biscuits, like you get in your lunchbox. It looked full, but I didn't want to touch it." Kyle eyed the Tupperware box. "We didn't spend any of the money in that wallet, either. Everything should still be in there."

Robin asked, as gently as he could and aware of their mothers' scowls, "Tell me and Pru why you took the wallet and phone."

"We thought they'd be safer with us," Archie said. "We were going to tell our mums and dads what we found, but then we got scared. We knew we'd get told off for being in the woods and then we were worried that people might think we'd done it."

The explanation could be partially if not the whole truth: the classic situation that the longer you left off doing something the harder it became to do it, although Robin would guess the full story was more complex. Perhaps a dare that had gone too far or a split-second decision that had soon been regretted. Still, the two youngsters had appeared to have done the right thing, albeit a touch late. And if they'd ensured that these personal items had been kept safe, rather than ending up in the possession of someone who *would* have spent the money and sold on the phone, the police should be grateful.

"Did you look in the wallet at all?" Pru asked. "Get us a name for the man?"

"We were going to, then Archie thought about fingerprints. We only opened it, then shut it again. Didn't poke about." Forensics would see if Kyle was telling the truth on that, unless they'd had the sense to wear gloves when they'd done it.

"Okay." Robin nodded. "Did you see anything else that was suspicious when you were in the woods? We're not trying to catch you out. We all want to find who did this and the more reliable information we get, the better."

Kyle shook his head. "There's nothing else. There were some people out jogging and a woman with a dog, but not near where he was."

Mrs. Simmons broke her silence with a curt "*You* shouldn't have been there, either. I've told you about the snakes."

Robin ignored the interruption; that scolding could carry on at home. "And nothing else? Archie?"

"No. Mr. Bright," Archie added, either remembering his manners or deciding he should make a better impression. "I've been thinking about Sunday ever since, and I can't think of any clues. Sorry."

"Did the foxes eat him?" Kyle suddenly asked, referring back to Mrs. Hill's earlier rebuke.

Pru, who'd confessed prior to the interview to being torn between being sympathetic and giving the boys a right royal telling off, said, "Well, he certainly wasn't in pristine condition. Look boys, Mr. Bright and I have decided that we aren't going to punish you, because I'm sure by now you know you've made a lot of wrong choices, but I want you to promise me that when you leave here, you'll think about what I'm going to say. What if that had been your dad or your grandad lying there, and then two people came along and found him, took his stuff, and just went off? How would you feel?"

Robin watched as the chastening words sunk in, both boys' lower lips starting to tremble. "You can go a long way towards making things better by making sure you tell Pru everything you can about what you saw and heard in the woods, like a description of those people jogging and the lady with the dog. Even if you think it's trivial, tell her anyway, because she's really good at picking out what's important. Then we need your fingerprints, as long as your mums say that's okay, and we also need to ask what you were both doing on Saturday." Suspecting he was about to get a blast of maternal anger, he hurried on. "It's nothing but routine. If I didn't ask everybody who's concerned with the case where they were then, my boss would tell me off."

Robin would also be remiss if he didn't consider the possibility of one or both of the boys being the killer. Everyone in the room would have been aware of high-profile cases, like the murder of James Bulger, in which children around Kyle and Archie's age had committed unthinkable acts.

"We were coming home from our holiday," Mrs. Simmons said. "We were late starting, and then the A303 was a nightmare, so we were *very* late getting back, and then we had to be up early on Sunday to get his majesty here off to his football training."

That accorded with Saturday's fatal crash which had made a road that was notoriously prone to delays almost grind to a halt. Adam's mum had been caught up in the tailbacks too. "Thank you. If you could give Pru your holiday details later, we'd be grateful. Mrs. Hill?"

"Archie was out with his dad most of Saturday, fishing, so I could get on with the housework. *He'll* be able to confirm that. Mind you, that'll be the last fishing trip or any other treat for *you* for a while." She shot Archie a withering glance. "I'll be watching you like a hawk."

Both lads fixed their gazes on their hands again; Robin really wouldn't want to be in their shoes for the next few weeks. "Last couple of things. Archie, you said your dad keeps his wallet and phone in his back trouser pockets. Make sure you warn him to keep them buttoned, because there's a lot of thieves out there and you never know when they might strike. Does he also carry his keys with him, when you're out?"

Archie looked up, evidently happier to be addressing the police than his mother. "Yeah. Or else he couldn't drive the car or get in the house. Why?"

"The dead man had no keys on him. Did you see any near his body?"

Archie shook his head, as did Kyle, who then said, "I've been thinking about that. I *have*, Mum," he protested, at a snort from Mrs. Simmons. "Because I want to help, I really do. There weren't any keys. We'd have picked them up if we'd seen them."

"And that leaves just one silly little thing that's bugging us," Pru said. "That packet of biscuits. Party Rings?"

"Yeah, miss." Kyle, frowning, seemed puzzled at the question.

"We won't get angry, whatever the answer is, but are you sure you two didn't eat them?"

Her question made Kyle wince. "Ew. No way. Not from next to a dead bloke."

"I couldn't have eaten anything, because I was being sick," Archie reminded them.

On which intriguing note, Robin left Pru and the family liaison officer who'd been in silent attendance to complete the statement taking and the rest. If the lads hadn't picked up the keys, what had happened to them, and if they'd not eaten those biscuits, who the hell had? And when?

Robin entered the incident room with the Tupperware box in hand.

"Is that your lunch, sir?" Ben quipped.

"Cheeky sod." Robin grinned. "It's Gary's wallet and phone. Those two lads we've been talking to had found him and taken them." He summarised what Kyle and Archie had said, the key bits of which Danielle jotted on the board. "So, still no sign of his keys. Incidentally, the lads say they didn't eat the biscuits, and I'm inclined to believe them. Their mothers are going to have that pair on a very short rein for the foreseeable future, so any further lies and it'll be no treats for months. Hopefully the experience will put them off crime for life."

"That empty packet is bizarre," Ashok said. "If it was full on Sunday afternoon, who ate it in between then and Tuesday? Do you get homeless people living up there, the sort who could be desperate for food?"

Ben shrugged. "It's possible. We do get people camping out in odd places. I can't see the killer revisiting the scene only to eat Party Rings, though, no matter how yummy they are. I could murder a packet now."

"Solve this crime and I'll buy you a big pack of them, not merely a snack size." Robin had a feeling he'd be held to that.

Danielle tapped the incident board. "I'd have my money on these biscuits being a red herring. I've been on the beach and had seagulls open a packet of Iced Gems I left when I'd gone for a paddle. They snaffled the bloody lot. You get gulls everywhere these days and not just on the coast."

"You could be right to put it down to furry or feathered friends. Hopefully forensics might show something up. As they could with this." Robin waggled the box. "Much as I want to peruse those cards and get his name, I'm going to wait. Ashok, can you nip this down now to the clever mob and say it's top priority?"

"Will do."

As Ashok set off, a phone rang and Sunita, one of the civilian support staff, answered it. Immediately she waved her hand, before covering the mouthpiece. "Got someone down in reception who says he thinks he knows who the victim is, although the desk sergeant isn't sure if it's another dead end. He says the witness is called Ryan French and he's recently back from a cruise, where he seems to have caught a dose of verbal diarrhoea."

"Ben," Robin said, "that job sounds right up your street. I'd like to join you, but I've got to give Mr. Cowdrey an update. Danielle, when Pru's finished, can you both get back to Kings Ride and have a shufti round the car parks? Talk to people who walk their dogs there regularly or whatever. You know the score. Don't worry if you haven't got his name by then."

As Robin turned to go to his office, a text came through to inform him that Cowdrey would be delayed by at least half an hour because a big drug raid a bit off their patch was at risk of spilling onto it and he was being briefed on that fast-moving situation.

"It's your lucky day, Ben. We can see this Ryan chap together."

Within a few minutes of meeting him, Robin was wishing he was in the drug briefing, or on a raid, or anywhere else than in the same room as Ryan. Before they'd asked any questions, the witness leaped in.

"I'm afraid I didn't contact you yesterday because I didn't know you'd been making an appeal. You see, I've been on a short cruise to western Europe—into Zeebrugge for Bruges, then St. Peter Port on Guernsey, all very nice—with my great aunt. She was supposed to be going with her friend Anne, but she's been taken ill, so I had to substitute. Internet on the ship was too expensive, and Aunt Josephine wouldn't let me do what she calls 'playing on my phone' too much when we were in port, because it was supposed to be a holiday for both of us. We had a lovely, relaxing time, so when we got in this morning and I read the news, I felt poleaxed. I drove straight up from Southampton." As an explanation it was entirely plausible, if long winded. Over egging the pudding to cover something up or just the bloke's style?

"Who do you think the dead man is and why?" Ben asked. "I'm asking that second bit because we've had too many false starts."

"Mark Bircher. The picture looks right and that's definitely the same T-shirt he has. He got it at one of the Saracens home games before the team slipped into disgrace. Not that it was the players' or fans' fault, but they have to bear the brunt of the stick, don't they? Mark was very upset about it because he's supported them since he was a boy. He *had* supported them, I should say. I can't quite get my head round the fact he may be dead."

Robin took advantage of a momentary pause to dive in. "How did you know him?"

"As a client, initially, although I'd like to think that he became a friend. We got to know each other quite well, despite the fact that I'm a fan of the Mighty Quins, which can lead to a bit of tension, I promise you, especially when it's game day. I've done it again. *Could* lead to a bit of tension. Mark contacted me after his wife died—too young, really—a few months back, which is when he started researching his family history, probably as a reaction to being widowed and needing a project to throw himself into. There were some things he'd wanted cleared up but hadn't had the chance to ask his mother while she was still alive—something he always regretted—and his dad wouldn't or couldn't talk about them. Mark had never had the time to devote properly to the job before, especially with Suzy having apparently been so ill for so long."

Another brief pause for breath, into which Ben leaped. "You said he was your client. What do you do?"

"Silly me, I should have explained." Ryan gave a shamefaced grin. "You see, while I work in IT, I have a side line in helping people discover their family's past, because often they're either too busy or too short of tech knowledge to be able to do it themselves. I only charge a nominal fee because it's a hobby as well as a job."

Robin fleetingly considered whether his mother could make use of Ryan's service, and whether she'd be able to cope with the tone of voice, which was the most monotonous he'd ever come across. The bloke could make a fortune doing tapes for insomniacs. Robin mentally shook himself and refocused before *he* nodded off. "Did Mark have any enemies? I know that sounds dramatic, but we're trying to find out why he was attacked."

"Not that I know of. He told me he didn't get on that well with Suzy's parents, although I wouldn't say they were enemies of his. There were the usual strains that can happen in any family, especially when Suzy was ill. They're into new-age stuff and didn't want her having chemo or anything like that. Crystals and oils are more their line, which is absolutely ridiculous. I mean, they're all right as an adjunct to conventional treatment but not as an alternative. Mark hinted to me that he'd suspected one of the reasons she'd not gone to get a diagnosis from a traditional medic until it was too late was because of family influence, which is awful. Aunt Josephine's had cancer, and she's right as rain now, because—as she says—'You have to catch the bugger early, Ryan.' Mark wished Suzy had got help when she needed it." Despite the loquaciousness and the boring tones in which he spoke, this witness was providing valuable information. "I think he had some stuff off Suzy's phone that backed up this theory about adverse parental influence, but he didn't really want to talk about it. Her death was too painful, still."

"Where did he live?" Ben asked, stifling a yawn as he did so. Ryan's voice was clearly proving soporific to him too. "And did he go to Kings Ride Woods often?"

"He lived in Lindenshaw, which is a very nice village—well, it's a small town now—although, as you'll know, it's a fair way from there to Kings Ride, so it's a mystery why he should have been in those woods at all. He's never mentioned the place, I don't think, and I'm not aware that he was a runner or a jogger or a twitcher or involved in anything that might have taken him there.

He never struck me as the outdoor-type in any way, unless you can count travelling to rugby matches. However, I must point out that I don't know every detail of his life."

Robin caught an eye roll from Ben, which seemed to communicate that a simple *Lindenshaw and no, he didn't*, would have done as an answer.

"Did he have a car?" Robin asked, then immediately added, "Sorry, have to check this," when his message alert went off. "I'm afraid I've got to go and brief my boss. Ben, can you take a proper statement?"

Ben winced, but he managed a polite "Yes, sir."

Robin escaped, grateful to have something concrete to report about the victim, despite how painful it had been to obtain.

Back in the incident room half an hour later, with Cowdrey properly updated, Robin noticed that the name *Mark Bircher* had appeared on the board, next to the picture of the victim. As Ben didn't seem to have returned, that information had surely come from the contents of the wallet, as Ashok soon confirmed. Nothing else of any note had turned up among those contents, which included the bog-standard bank cards, driving licence and a less bog-standard out-of-date EHIC, or whatever they were called now, post-Brexit.

"Maybe he hadn't bothered to update it because he'd not been travelling recently. His wife was very ill and only died a few months back." Robin waved his hand in the vague direction of the interview rooms. "Ryan told us. I'll let Ben update you on the rest when he gets here, only be kind to him. Don't ask."

"I won't." Ashok grinned. "The phone's battery is dead as a dodo, so those two lads mustn't have recharged it. The people in the lab can do that and then we can take it from there. Ben's good at the tech stuff, isn't he?"

"Yep. And he'll deserve a treat when he's finished downstairs. I hate to give people nicknames, but *Ryan nice but deadly boring* gives you the idea." Robin jotted the name—but not the nickname—on the board, near Kathy Hartley's. "Again, not a likely suspect and he's given us a solid alibi."

"I've got some news on Kathy," Pru said. "She's the same, alibi-wise. Been away on a fortnight's holiday in Majorca and only got back on Sunday evening. One of the reasons she was out on a run was to start countering the effect of all the carbs and the piña coladas. Unless she's working in concert with the person who did the killing because they needed to stage the discovery, I think we can count her out as well."

Robin nodded. As far as he was concerned, she'd never really been in the frame but if they weren't thorough, these things could come back to bite them. "He had a driving licence, Ashok, so do we have an address for him and did he keep a car?"

"Tumulus Gardens, Lindenshaw, and according to the licence people, he had a red Yaris, a couple of years old," Ashok said. "I've put out an alert for it."

"Isn't Lindenshaw your old stomping ground, sir?" Pru knew damn well that it was, so the question must have been for the benefit of the others.

"It is. I think Tumulus Gardens is part of a fairly new estate, on the east side. Near where there's some Bronze Age remains, hence the street names featuring things like Tumulus or Flint. The locals call it the Barrows. He can't have lived there longer than three or four years, because it used to be fields." Robin studied Mark's picture again. "Long way to go to Kings Ride when there are perfectly good woods nearer to home. Ryan reckons it wasn't a place Mark habitually went. So, what was he doing there?"

"Meeting his killer, or is that too obvious?" Danielle asked.

"Not too obvious at all," Robin said, glad that she was already feeling confident enough to pitch in. "Never ignore what stares you in the face. Why *there* though? If you had any doubts about the person you were going to meet, wouldn't you choose somewhere safer?"

"Which suggests he knew whoever he was meeting and felt safe with them," Pru said. "It also speaks against this being the kind of attack where a mugger knows their victim uses a certain route at a certain time. If the lack of articles taken hadn't already ruled out a mugging."

Ashok raised his hand. "I wouldn't rule out a random attack, though. Mark's there, waiting for whoever, then somebody comes along and chances their arm, thinking he's an easy target and the location means there'll likely be no witnesses. The mugger hits Mark, he goes down and matey cleans out his pockets. He—or she—gets the fright of his life when he realises he's hit his victim too hard, so he leaves everything, to avoid being connected to the crime scene, and legs it."

"What about his keys, though?" Pru said. "I've been researching bus services, and the Kinechester to Kings Ride route goes nowhere near Lindenshaw. While I wouldn't swear to it, I think you'd have to change at least once to use public transport between the two places, so he'd likely have driven or been given a lift."

Robin nodded. "You can ask about that Yaris when you're lurking in the car parks."

"Is that an unsubtle hint for us to get down there, sir?" Pru quipped, fishing out her own car keys as she did so. "Come on, Danielle."

Before they could leave the incident room, Ben entered it, face as strained as Robin had ever seen it. "Have you told them what Ryan's like, sir?"

"I left that pleasure to you. Anything else emerge after I left?"

"Not really, although I might have missed it, if it did. I kept zoning out." Ben held up what must be the statement. "I got the whole story again, in greater detail, including Aunt Josephine's medical condition."

"Talk the others through the bits about his wife, then get them written on the board. We need to look at family tensions, so contact details and background on both Mark and Suzy Bircher's families are a priority." Robin aimed the last part at Sue and Marcus, the two admin members of the team. "It seems like Ryan had all the info about Suzy secondhand, therefore some direct statements would help get things straight. Oh, and you'll soon have a nice mobile phone to tinker with, Ben. Consider it a reward."

With that, Robin headed to his office, to have a think about how odd it was that his mother and Mark had been in a similar position and whether he could inflict Ryan and his services upon her.

Chapter Four

Adam had a staff meeting after school so wasn't able to get home at a sensible time on Wednesday. Kate, their seemingly superhuman domestic help, said she'd stay on a bit later, ostensibly to make sure a meal was prepared for Adam and Robin, given the latter had a murder to deal with. No doubt that was merely a convenient excuse to spend more time with Hamish. She had been willing to do as many extra hours as needed while the Newfoundland was small—in fact she had often taken him to hers when he was in need of additional care. She doted on the dog and had confessed to dreading the time when he didn't need as much looking after.

Adam had not long been home—and was still lavishing attention on Hamish—when he heard Robin come through the door.

"Hello? Is that a handsome policeman or a bold burglar? I've a dog in here and I'm not afraid to use him. Even if he'd likely only slobber on you."

"Pillock." Robin came into the kitchen, then gave Adam a kiss and Hamish a pat. "I'll go back to work, shall I?"

"You'll go and get your tie off while I get this heated. Smells like there's curry in the pot." Adam lifted the lid, taking an appreciative sniff. "One of Kate's specials. Naan breads on the side."

"Perfect to discuss a murder over. I have a name for the victim and plenty else you'll be interested in." Robin backed out of the door, Hamish in tow, no doubt in search of the clean top he always liked to change into after work. Maybe he felt he was casting off the atmosphere of the police station as he did so. Adam, grinning, heard him talking to the dog as he made his way up the stairs, telling him how Hamish would be learning all about his first serious case and that there were many puppies who never got a chance to have the inside information straight from the police.

"Bonkers, but I love him," Adam told the curry as he stirred it, acknowledging that he was pretty bonkers himself for doing so.

Once they were settled over dinner, with a bottle of beer each as a treat, Robin said, "The victim was called Mark Bircher. I wanted to see if that name rang any bells, because he lived in Lindenshaw. Tumulus Gardens, on that new estate, round the back of the Esso petrol station."

Adam shook his head. "Nope. Name doesn't mean anything to me. Did he have any children I might have run across?"

"No, so be thankful that potential connection isn't there."

"I am. You've traced his family?"

"Not entirely. Although we'd not long released the name to the media when his wife's parents gave us a call, for which I'm grateful, because it makes our lives easier and the information will get to me quicker."

"I hope it's as reliable as it's quick," Adam said.

"Indeed. We've had nothing from Mark's side, yet, assuming he had anyone close still alive."

"Where did he live previously? The Barrows hasn't been up that long."

"Kings Ride. We've heard that he and his wife moved away from there supposedly because they liked the new builds, or so the in-laws say, although I wouldn't be surprised if the real reason was to get away from *them*. Suzy's parents have a smallholding on the Kinechester Road, a couple of miles out. Not a nice story, there, if what we've been told is correct, Hamish." The dog had placed himself at Robin's feet and kept looking up adoringly. "I'm seeing them tomorrow so I can assess things firsthand, rather than from hearsay. I'll give you the full story when I've heard the other side."

"I'll be patient." Adam scooped up another mouthful of the excellent curry. "It's a shame I don't keep up with the

Lindenshaw gossip network anymore. Neil might have known the dead man—given that he seemed to have a clerical finger in many a pie—although I think that ship's sailed." Neil had been the vicar at Lindenshaw when they'd lived there, but he'd now been promoted to a key diocese job somewhere well north of the Watford Gap so wasn't easily available for a pint and a natter. "I'm pretty sure Christine Probert moved to that new estate, although it's going to seem odd contacting her out of the blue. I mean, we've already thanked her for the card she sent for our wedding."

Robin's nose wrinkled in its usual attractive way. "Keep her—and anyone else we used to know at Lindenshaw—on the subs bench in case we draw a blank elsewhere. Though from what I remember of Christine, she'd have been a sympathetic ear for anyone with family tensions."

"A confidential one too." Christine had been the first of the Lindenshaw parents who'd known about the blossoming Matthews-Bright romance. At Wickley, the board of governors all knew that Adam was married to a copper—a male one—and several of them had confessed to being delighted at the fact, partly because it gave them one up on their rivals in the neighbouring village, who thought themselves very trendy but weren't. "Still, it sounds like you've made a lot of progress today."

"We have. Starting with the call that came this morning." Robin launched into the tale of the two lads he'd interviewed. He finished with, "In your professional opinion, does their explanation seem likely?"

Adam nodded. "Absolutely. I mean, you can't discard the possibility they did it, but their story's not implausible. Boys of that age don't always act in a logical fashion. It could have started as a bit of a dare, taking the wallet and phone, and then they found themselves in over their heads."

"I think that's very likely. And we didn't automatically discount them—we made sure we asked where they were when Bircher was killed on Saturday." Robin loaded the last serving of curry onto his plate. "Those alibis check out. We've got a mystery, though, because they say they didn't see any keys on him and he *did* have a car. That seems to have disappeared, so if he used it to get to Kings Ride Woods, then someone's had it away. Pru and Danielle were down there today talking to regular visitors, but we've drawn a blank. Nobody claims to have seen him or his Yaris."

"You think he might have been killed to get hold of the car or was that a corollary? Seems odd to nick his keys and not his wallet or phone."

"Agreed. We don't think whoever took them wanted to turn his house over, either. Ben and Ashok nipped down there late this afternoon, and while they couldn't get in, when they peered through the windows it all seemed tidy. One next-door neighbour reckons the other one has a key to Bircher's house in case of emergencies. Unfortunately, she was out today. They left a note through her door, so hopefully we won't need to break in when we get a team to Tumulus Gardens tomorrow. The car wasn't there, either." Robin pushed his plate away, then picked up his beer. "Why nick a car and leave the rest? Unless the killer was interrupted when they were rooting out his pockets, although that doesn't ring true to me."

"They may have wanted access to his house but didn't actually know where he lived." Adam grimaced. "That's lame, isn't it? How many car parks are there at the woods?"

"Two main ones, but if you wanted a decent hike, you could park elsewhere, like in the village, and walk in. Are you wondering how the killer knew where the car was?"

"Sort of." Light bulb moment time. "I was asking myself whether the car could have been the target. Or its contents. Alice, at work, was telling us that during lockdown, an Amazon delivery driver dropped a parcel into a house three doors down from hers and in the thirty seconds or so that he was out of his car, it got nicked. He'd left the keys in because these people are always in a tearing hurry. Great speculation locally about whether the thief was someone who happened to be walking down the street who saw their chance or whether the driver had been targeted."

Robin, nodding slowly, said, "I'd be inclined to go with the first option, especially if the road gets a lot of footfall. Increases the chances of the wrong person walking past and thinking, 'Look at all those parcels I can help myself to!' If it was pre-planned, how would they know where the driver was delivering, unless he was being tailed on the day by another car? Interesting idea, though. A red Yaris doesn't sound top of the nick-to-order list, so it might have been what was inside it."

"Say this Bircher bloke had something in his car or his house or both—drugs or whatever—that the killer wanted. He'd only take the keys because they were the things he needed."

"That does make sense, especially if there were other important keys on that ring, as well. Ones for a lock up somewhere from which Bircher ran his empire in counterfeit Rolexes. Joke," Robin added, although it might only have been half a one. "There could be an innocent explanation, I suppose."

"Like he lent his car to a mate and got to Kings Ride in an Uber? Or said mate dropped him off and has been oblivious to all calls for information and is happily driving around in a car he's legitimately borrowed? That could explain the lack of a car key although not the rest. He'd need to get in and out of his own house."

"Indeed, Mr. Headteacher. A question I don't have an answer for yet, unless the silly sod simply left them in the house and didn't realise he'd done so, in which case they'll be waiting there tomorrow for the forensic mob to find. Let's clear the table, get comfy, and I can tell you the other thing about this case which is a stonking great coincidence."

Once they'd done all their domestic jobs and were settled again, with Hamish choosing to curl up at Adam's feet this time, Robin continued. "So, coincidence two. Mark Bircher got into researching his family history after his wife died. I don't know if he was doing it generally or pursuing the answer to a specific question, but he enlisted the help of a chap called Ryan French. Ryan came in today to say he knew Mark through this freelance work he does, helping folk who can't do the ancestry sleuthing on their own. It's highly unlikely *he's* our killer, unless he's managed to fake the perfect alibi, so I wondered if he'd be able to help Mum."

Adam nodded. "That's a great idea. He'd be much more of a practical help than either of us could be. Do you know how much he charges?"

"Not as much as some. Ben had a quick flick around the internet and he found people quoting nearly a hundred quid an hour."

"A hundred quid? I'm in the wrong job."

"Ryan's quoting much less than that because he does it as a paying hobby. Linking up with him might have to be my only contribution on the *Dad's birth family* front for a while, though." Robin pulled an apologetic face. "Not only due to the fact I'm busy, because I'm aware you've always got plenty on your plate as well, but I don't want to blur boundaries."

"Won't they be blurred enough if your mum engages him to work for her, and anyway, aren't there other people offering their services that she could employ? Albeit at a steeper price." Adam noted the sheepish expression flitting over his husband's face. "Are you up to something? Do you actually want a subtle eye kept on him?"

"I hope I'm not that obvious when I'm in an interview room, trying to get some villain to tell me the truth." Robin knocked back the last draught of beer. "On the face of it, Ryan's a good citizen doing his duty by reporting to us with information. I'm pretty certain that first impression's right and Ben agrees with me. However, I also reckon Ryan might know more than he thinks he does, because he does come across as a details man and it'll be a matter of homing in on the right detail. You see, he's also the world's most *boring* man. I literally felt myself at risk of nodding off when we talked to him, despite the fact he had plenty of valuable stuff to tell us. Trouble is, it was all wrapped up in dozens of words and digressions from the point where one or two would have answered the question."

"You want to inflict that on your mum? Although I guess she'd be prepared, having developed the patience of Job, putting up with you for so long." Adam swayed to avoid the cushion which had been chucked in his direction. "Are you hoping he'll let something slip to her that she can report back?"

Robin, who'd woken the dog with his cushion throwing, now had a bleary-eyed Hamish scrambling onto his lap. "Your other dad's not daft, is he? Him and Mum have ears like bats, as well, so if Ryan were to make a significant aside about Bircher, they'd spot it. Even if it was hidden amongst his aunt Josephine's medical history and what cruise ports they went into."

Adam considered the idea for a moment. "It would be easy enough to ask him to meet up for coffee, no obligation on either side about making it a paid arrangement. He's bound to spot the connection because of your mum's name, but there's no need to hide it."

"If he's as good at the details when it comes to genealogy, then he could be a real help to her. Win-win." Robin stifled a yawn. "I could do with half an hour of something mindless on the telly and then a good night's sleep. Anything on the box?"

"Probably some footie, although I've got some new episodes of *Air Crash Investigation* recorded."

"Go with the footie. I don't want the boy being scared by images of planes going down in flames, badly CGI'd or not."

Which was no doubt a good idea. Watching that sort of programme so close to bedtime wasn't likely to lead to pleasant dreams. Adam would be unsettled enough at the thought of some poor sod lying undiscovered in the woods because two lads made wrong choice after wrong choice.

As Robin drove to the dentist to get his permanent crown put on, he hoped Thursday would bring as much news as Wednesday had, although it would be good if it also brought answers, rather than further questions. By the time he got into the station and gathered his team for a slightly later than normal briefing, it became clear that he was going to get both the things he'd wished for.

News had just come in that Bircher's car had been found in a Kinechester multistorey car park. It hadn't been burned or damaged, nor had anything obvious been stripped out of it, as though somebody had merely parked the thing up and gone off to stay in a city-centre hotel for a few days. The Yaris might have not been noticed at all had the parking payment not run out. Did that suggest forethought, given that a vehicle would be less likely to be noticed if legitimately parked rather than abandoned at the roadside? Time gained for whoever had taken it.

"A twenty-four-hour ticket was bought late on Tuesday—after the news broke about the body being found—but parking there's free overnight," Pru said, "so the multistorey wasn't patrolled again until this morning. Which is when the warden spotted it. She was aware of the appeal we put out yesterday for a red Yaris and contacted us. The local officers have taped off the scene, and we've got our CSIs going down there once they've finished at the house."

Robin nodded. "Hopefully they'll find the neighbour at Tumulus Gardens waiting with the house key and the spare car key tucked away in a drawer, so they won't need to break in to either. I don't need to tell you to check the CCTV from the car park, because I'm sure you're on it."

"Like a car bonnet, sir." Pru chuckled.

Robin, groaning at the joke, turned to study an incident board which was becoming satisfyingly populated with information. "Adam and I were discussing the car last night. He's always useful to bounce ideas off, not having a horse in the race, and we wondered if the keys to the Yaris, or the keys in general, were the particular thing the killer was after. What if Bircher had something dodgy going on, like dealing drugs out of his car or a lock-up?"

"Could be, sir, although if he's been doing that, he was never caught," Ben said. "I've checked his record, and he's got nothing listed apart from a speeding fine four years ago. I've also been going over his social media, and what little he's got is pretty sparse. Not a lot from his wife, either. She apparently made a point of not posting much, especially pictures, when she became seriously ill."

"Did you access that from his phone?" Robin asked.

Ben shook his head. "That's gone to the tech specialists, since none of the obvious passwords worked to get in. I got the Facebook stuff off the usual internet trawl."

"Okay. You and I can get down to his house when we've finished here, before we head off to see Suzy's family. Pru, I'd like you and Ashok to keep following up the Yaris, so co-ordinate with the CSIs to meet them at the Kinechester multistorey. Danielle, that leaves you here to field anything coming in. Think of it as being in charge." Robin grinned. "Pru, I'm assuming that you found nothing significant when you were at Kings Ride Woods or you'd have texted me."

"You assume correctly, sir. We do have a couple of pieces of information, though. Someone who heard shouting around noon on Saturday and an update on the car parks. We'll get that out of the way first. Danielle and I interviewed a woman who says she goes to those woods pretty much every day unless she's on holiday, although normally earlier than we saw her. She was late getting there yesterday because she had a flat tyre that needed changing. Anyway, she runs one of those day-care services for dogs, where you get them walked while you're at work. Happy Hounds, it's called. I don't think you use one for Cam—sorry, Hamish." Pru pulled an embarrassed face.

"We still call him by the wrong name too," Robin reassured her. "You're right. We're in the lucky position of having someone who comes and 'does' for us as well as him. The snakes don't put this woman off taking her 'happy hounds' there?"

"They don't appear to. Regarding Bircher, she said she doesn't think she's ever seen him there, and she definitely hasn't spotted a red Yaris in the car park recently. She could swear to that because her first motor was that make and colour, so apparently she always notices any cars the same. That said, there are two car parks between which she alternates, so Bircher might have been located in the other one at any point and she'd be none the wiser." Pru turned to Danielle, who had her notes to hand. "She was in the west one on Saturday?"

Danielle nodded. "Yeah. It's what the locals call the top car park, and she was parked there from eleven to two. No dogs with her this time, only her kids and their pals, to have a picnic and let off steam before term started."

"Was she the person who heard the shouting?" Robin asked.

"No. That was a Mr. Rashid. He's a twitcher who's been there on and off recently, to look for spring migrants. Don't." Pru raised a finger to ward off any daft jokes. Why was it that people seemed to find twitchers a source of amusement? "Mr. Rashid was very helpful, not least because he told us that the east car park—the locals call it the bottom one—had a notice of closure displayed on Saturday morning. It said the area was going to be shut from 1300 that day until Monday at 0700 for exclusive Forestry Commission access."

"Did he spot Mark's car?" Robin resisted making a pun on bird-spotting.

"He couldn't say one way or the other if there was a red Yaris there when he tried to park at half ten in the morning, because his mind was on the risk of getting locked in. He had to go back to the road and use a lay-by, and he found it all rather stressful. He did say there weren't as many cyclists as usual, although there were some milling about." Pru moved towards the incident board. "This is the best bit. He remembers hearing two people shouting around twelve noon because they were loud enough to scare off the bird he was watching. However, he didn't hear their precise words and he says the lesser-spotted-hoojit was pretty nervous, anyway. So, anything might have spooked it."

"We're getting some real characters for witnesses this time," Ben observed, with a roll of the eyes.

"I really liked Mr. Rashid," Pru said. "He was an absolute sweetie. Anyway, he guessed he was overhearing part of an argument, although it didn't last very long and he couldn't be absolutely sure if it was between two men or between a man and a woman with a deepish voice. When we asked him to point out on the map where he'd been bird-watching at the time, it was the other side of the copse from where our victim was found. He might have been as close as a hundred yards."

"That's consistent with the time of death, isn't it?" Danielle said.

"It is, although it could be coincidental. Good work, though." Robin pointed at the board. "Get the times and location from Mr. Rashid up on there. Then you can contact the Forestry Commission, because the people they had on site might have seen or heard something. There was time for the Yaris to be moved between Mark's death and the car park being shut. Any other news?"

Ashok raised a hand. "There were no fingerprints on the wallet or phone other than the lads', Mrs. Hill's and the dead man's. So, either Bircher took them out of his pockets himself or the person who did so wore gloves. The vomit is consistent with being Archie Hill's, given his stomach contents."

"I've got nothing much on Suzy's parents," Danielle said. "Justin Packer—the father—has been done for possession of weed, but not recently. Mrs. Packer, Izzy, got herself arrested in 2020, at a protest against a 5G mast. Bound over to keep the peace and seems to have been behaving herself since."

Robin, who'd already built up quite a mental image of the Packers, reminded himself not to fall for stereotypes, no matter how tempting. Depending on the timings, and assuming Mrs. Packer had only been in trouble once, she might have temporarily gone off the rails when she'd heard about Suzy's illness. He'd also have to take into account that they might be defensive if they were still feeling the loss of their daughter and bearing a burden of guilt for her death. Many tragedies were played out to an accompaniment of *if onlys*.

The forensic team were still going through the house at Tumulus Gardens when Robin arrived, although they weren't hopeful that they'd come up with much of use. A spare key to Bircher's car still hadn't appeared. There was no indication he'd been killed at the property or that anything else untoward had happened here. The house resembled a typical home that had been left while the owners went out. Apparently, the alarm had been set, although the helpful neighbour had given the CSIs the code to unlock it. She'd also confirmed that it hadn't sounded over the last few days, nor had she seen anyone hanging around the property.

Half a dozen pictures of Mark with Suzy or Suzy alone—clearly taken at different times, including one of them on bikes together when she seemed a picture of health—were on the walls and sideboard. He had to be the man they'd found. His wife had been a striking woman, who wore a broad smile even in what appeared to be a relatively recent picture, while Mark couldn't hide his besotted smile from the camera.

"Should I get one of these for the incident board, sir?" Ben asked.

"If you can't find any copies lurking about. It doesn't feel right to move the originals without permission." Although, who could they ask?

"Will do. Do you want to talk to the neighbours, while we're here?"

"I'd like a word with the one who had Mark's spare key," Robin said. "Maybe the ones on the other side too. You and Ashok spoke to them—why hadn't *they* linked him to the bloke whose picture was all over the local media?"

"Mr. Armstrong's blind, so he'd not seen what was on the news or in the papers. Mark wasn't the sort to play loud music or otherwise make his presence felt so the Armstrongs didn't particularly register a lack of noise from the house. And then it turned out Mrs. Armstrong thought Mark was away on holiday, so wasn't surprised at not seeing him. She admitted that she may have got the dates wrong."

"Sounds like she did. There's a note on the fridge calendar about a holiday," one of the CSIs chirped up. "Reminding Mark to cancel some regular food delivery for when he wasn't going to be here, but that's not until May."

"The Armstrongs told us that Suzy and Mark used to go away a lot, both when they lived here and when they were at Kings Ride," Ben said. "City breaks on the continent or off to somewhere in this country with their bikes. As a combination of the pandemic and Suzy's condition deteriorating, they tailed off travelling. Once the restrictions started to ease, they were going to try a last hurrah to the south of France but they left it too late."

Robin remembered the out-of-date European medical treatment card, which seemed rather poignant now. "You didn't report any of that back."

"We didn't think it relevant, sir. Sorry."

"Remember, you never know what's relevant at this point in a case, Benjamin." The constable should have known that fact by now, but everyone had off days. "Let's go and ask the person with the key whether she could have mistaken the dates too. What's her name?"

"Mrs. Crouch, like the footballer. She's not as tall, though." The CSI grinned and got back to the job in hand.

When Mrs. Crouch opened the door, she barely came up to Robin's shoulder. She was probably in her early sixties, and immediately invited them to come in and have coffee, the latter of which they declined, on the grounds that Robin and his constable were on a tight schedule. Once they were settled in her lounge, Mrs. Crouch expressed her shock at Mark's sudden death and how the local community had been horrified, especially following on from Suzy's death. Apparently, they'd been a nice, professional couple, who'd generally kept themselves to themselves but had always been ready to help in an emergency. Mark had replaced her fence panels when they'd taken a pounding from the wind during the winter.

"Suzy hadn't been long dead at that point, but I think he was happy to have something to occupy him. My Freddie had put his back out playing golf so was no help, apart from passing Mark anything he needed." She rolled her eyes at her husband's indisposition. "When Mark said he was going to start taking his weekends away again, I was so pleased, because he clearly needed a break. While Suzy was still well enough, the pair sometimes just upped and went on an adventure if they could get last-minute cheap flights and a bargain hotel booking. Especially if it was to some exciting part of Europe and there was a rugby match on."

"Is that what you think he did this weekend?" Ben asked. It wasn't like him to be quite so leading and almost put words into the mouth of a witness. Not on his best form at all at present.

"Along those lines. To be accurate—and the police on the telly always like accuracy, don't they?—I knew he'd be away. One of those weekends he mentioned to me a fortnight ago."

"It was definitely *this* weekend?" Robin asked.

Mrs. Crouch shot him a withering glance. "Of course. I'm not losing my marbles, you know. I can still read a date in a diary."

"I'm sure you can, and I didn't mean to imply anything. Perhaps *we* got confused." Robin tried his most winning smile. "You see, Mark's got a note on his calendar about going away in May." Now he'd met Mrs. Crouch, he saw how unlikely it was that both sets of neighbours could have made a mistake about dates.

"He may have, but *I've* got a note on mine to put his bin out on Tuesday, which I did." The scowl had been replaced with a triumphant twinkle in her eye. One over on these whippersnappers of policemen. "I saw him drive off about eleven o'clock on Saturday morning. That's why we didn't report him missing and why it never occurred to us that he was the chap you found in the woods. We thought he was in Woodhall Spa, doing something connected with this family history business he was looking into. I think he might have had another trip planned for the same thing."

"I'm probably going to come across as rather dim compared to your TV cops," Robin said with his best self-deprecating grin, "but I need to get this absolutely straight in my mind, given that we've had no indication so far that Mark was going away for the weekend. Which days did he say he'd be away from and to and did he take his car with him?"

"Last Saturday until Tuesday night and yes. There's no train station at Woodhall Spa anymore." She spoke slowly, evidently thinking that Robin wasn't living up to his surname. "I don't know exactly where he was staying—hotel or guest house or whatever—only that he'd be visiting Woodhall."

Where he'd evidently never arrived. "One last question and it's a long shot. You clearly knew the Birchers well. Can you think of anyone who might have wanted to hurt him?"

"Nobody. I know he didn't get on well with his in-laws but that's not uncommon, is it? I mean, Freddie hated my mother when she was alive, but we didn't end up all murdering each other."

On this sobering note—and with Robin remembering, yet again, that he was damned lucky to have a partner who actually liked his mother—they expressed their thanks and went back next door.

"I'm going to check Mark's fridge calendar," he said as he entered the house. "If Mrs. Crouch said she thought he'd be away last weekend, I'm inclined to believe her."

The reminder on the fridge about the delivery—a bright yellow Post-it note—couldn't be easily missed. Nor could the large month-to-view calendar, which had an intended short break marked on the page for May. Not to Woodhall Spa but to East Kirkby. Wherever either of those places were.

"Where's April disappeared to?" Ben asked.

"It might have fallen off and gone under the fridge. You're younger than me, so you can get down there."

Ben did so, wincing in the process. He came up shaking his head. "Can't see anything, sir."

"Are you all right?"

"Not really. We had a takeaway the night before last, and I've regretted it ever since. I think I might have food poisoning."

That would explain a lot. "You should go home. You're not on your usual form."

"I'm aware of that, sir, but I'm not really ill enough to take time off sick. It's pretty well all out of my system now—TMI, I know—although I'm still getting stomach cramps."

"Well, don't be a martyr." Robin could sympathise, though. Unless he was flat out with an illness, which was thankfully rare, he wanted to be active. "You have a shufti down here and I'll take a look around upstairs. Keep an eye out for the usuals—old-fashioned address books or the like and especially that April page from the calendar."

It was Robin who found the missing sheet, however, in one of the spare bedrooms that had been made into an office, as lots of folk had done during lockdown and from which many still worked for part of their week. It had doubled as a place for exploring family history, with various files, notes, and a sapling family tree on display. Pinned on a noticeboard was April, with Saturday to Tuesday marked, *Woodhall Spa*.

"I've found the sheet from the calendar," he shouted down the stairs. "Mark was due to be away now, exactly as Mrs. Crouch said he would be. The only other thing on there is an entry marked *Beer with Ryan*."

"I bet that was going to be the highlight of his month." Ben snorted.

Robin went back to studying the other material in the office, starting with the—mainly torn up—contents of the wastepaper bin, which he tipped into a bag for one of the admin support team to reassemble. A small Post-it caught his eye, bearing the words: *Honesty. No. Discipline. No.* What did that refer to and would he find a clue on Mark's desk?

As he read the paperwork there, a chill down his spine developed that was nothing to do with the room temperature. Mark Bircher had kept a neat, objective timeline, added to as he'd uncovered information concerning his family. It began with him discovering his mother had been adopted, a fact he hadn't found out about until 2021, when she was dying.

"Ben? Can you come up here for a moment?" Robin called down the stairs.

"On my way. Got something?" The constable came up at a more leisurely pace than his usual, bounding two-stairs-at-a-time.

"There's a desktop computer for you to take away and play with, but that wasn't what I wanted you to see. Look at this." Robin handed over of the most relevant of the notes he'd found. "Can you believe that somebody in their thirties wouldn't know their mother was adopted until she made a deathbed confession?"

Ben scrutinised the papers. "Yes, if she decided she'd never tell him until that point. How old would she have been if she was still alive? Fifties, sixties?"

Robin checked one of the family trees. "He was born in 1986 and she—Eleanor—was 1948. Bit late for her to be having a first child, if Mark *was* her first."

"It does happen though, especially if she married late."

"True." One couldn't judge a life story on raw dates. "Eleanor was a post-war baby. Plenty of hang-ups in that era about illegitimacy, so the birth mother may have had no choice but to give her away. That stigma could have stayed with Eleanor, so she was too ashamed to speak about it, let alone tell Mark himself, until she was at the point the shame wouldn't matter any longer."

Ben cast a glance around the room. "Poor bloke. Lost his mother, lost his wife, discovers that his granny isn't really his granny, not biologically, anyway. No wonder he wanted to dig deeper."

Robin bit back on saying that not every adopted child wanted to probe their background. Maybe the time would come for the team to know how closely Mark's situation mirrored his—and how different it was at the same time—but that could wait. "This could have nothing to do with his death, but when things don't make sense, my rozzer's nose twitches. Add that to him not getting wherever he was supposed to be going and it's twitching like anything."

Ben's brow crinkled as he stared at a family tree. "Let's say Eleanor's mum was sixteen when she had her. That would make her ninety now. It doesn't seem likely that Mark arranged to meet her in the woods to confront her and she got so angry she belted him one."

"No, but I wouldn't rule out the same scenario with a half uncle who didn't want his mum's shame exposed."

"It certainly fits with your favourite theory about victims being most at risk from friends and family, sir."

Robin nodded. A family Mark Bircher didn't realise he had until it was too late. In all senses of the term?

Chapter Five

As Ben drove them through the estate, on the way from Bircher's house to where Suzy's parents lived, they passed a tall, elegantly dressed woman striding along the opposite pavement. Robin immediately glanced back over his shoulder at her. "Can you turn the car around at the mini roundabout, Ben, and then pull up next to that lady?"

"I didn't think you were the type to be stopping for a woman in a mini skirt, sir. I mean, not because you're gay, it's . . . Sorry." He stopped, clearly embarrassed.

Robin snorted. Ben's stomach issues must have been affecting him badly for such a stupid remark to emerge. Still, everyone had their off moments, officers as good as this one included. "I'd stop digging that hole if I were you. This isn't the seventies."

Red as a beetroot, Ben concentrated on manoeuvring the car, doing a complete turn and gliding to a stop as requested.

"Christine?" Robin said, as he got out.

"Yes? Oh, is that Mr. Bright?" Christine Probert broke into a wide, charming smile.

"I think you can call me Robin by now. How's life?"

"Very good." The brightness of her smile certainly gave that impression. "How's Adam settling in at Wickley?"

"He's happy as Larry." They spent a few minutes swopping news, including the fact that the murders at Lindenshaw hadn't put her off being a school governor and that Adam and Robin's marriage had been the talk of the village a few years back.

"I bet you're here about Mark Bircher. That's all over the local gossip network too." Christine pouted disapprovingly. "Some people do talk tripe."

"Tell me about it. It's our job to sort the tripe out from the fillet steak, isn't it, Ben?" Robin nodded at the constable, who'd joined them and was evidently trying to unblot his copybook by keeping quiet. Although the joke about tripe was probably doing nothing for his food poisoning. "This is Mrs. Probert, who was a valuable witness in the first murder case I had charge of. Christine, if you hear anything that might be relevant this time round, I'd be grateful if you could let us know. I can trust you to sift fact from opinion."

"I can do that right now. I didn't know Mark except to say hello to, but I used to see his wife, Suzy, at art classes in the village hall. I guess you know she died young—too young—and that may have been because her family stopped her getting proper treatment for cancer?"

"We'd heard something similar. Good to have it verified. Was it the cancer that killed her?"

"No, it was Covid. I mean, the cancer didn't help because it lowered her resistance, obviously, and although she'd had all her jabs, the virus was too much for her to take in her state, even with hospital intervention. I think she developed septic shock." Christine, who'd been sounding increasingly choked, fished out a tissue and blew her nose.

"It's a cruel disease." Which might have been a cliché but it was true. "What kind of cancer was it?"

"Leukaemia. I don't know what type because Suzy didn't like to talk about the details and I didn't want to pry."

Robin nodded. Christine had always been a good sort. "What was Suzy like?"

"Sweet. Funny. You know how teenagers rebel against their parents by taking drugs or whatever? She told me her act of rebellion was wearing Marks and Spencer clothes and taking golf lessons. She loved her mum and dad but couldn't stand all that new-age stuff they're into."

Ben at last found his tongue. "Were there tensions between the Packers—Suzy's parents—and Mark? It can't have been easy if he felt they'd been partly responsible for her death."

"Partly? Suzy said he blamed them completely for the state she'd got into. Now, don't get me wrong, because I'm not linking this to his death. I can't imagine her parents getting into an argument with Mark that turned violent. According to Suzy, they're all peace and love." Christine's moue of disapproval hinted that she didn't entirely believe that and she was probably right. The most virulent advocates of nonviolence could have a breaking point.

"Did *Suzy* blame them for persuading her not to get proper treatment?" Robin asked.

"A bit, but not as much as she blamed herself. She told me she'd had the feeling something was wrong years ago and had gone into denial. You know how that kind of thing happens." Christine's eyes welled.

"I do." Robin paused while Christine collected herself. "We heard Mark and Suzy used to live in Kings Ride. Any idea why they left?"

"The official story was that they wanted a brand-new house— and the ones on this estate *are* lovely, with larger gardens than you usually get on a modern estate—but Suzy told me that they both wanted to move farther from her parents."

"It sounds like she felt she could confide in you." Robin thanked his lucky stars that he and Ben had been driving down this road, at this time. Useful information to have before meeting the Packers.

"Only with a glass or three inside her." Christine grinned. "We weren't close friends, but it was just the way things worked out. You see, the art club planned a do, back when the pandemic was raging, so what was supposed to be taking place at Christmas ended up postponed to the spring of 2021. I drove Suzy to the pub and back, and because she'd had a touch too much wine, the floodgates opened on the way home. I knew about her illness by then—she'd never hidden that from us, although she made sure she was looking as well as possible—but this time I heard great chunks of her life story. How her parents were always dropping into her old house in Kings Ride. Usually to give their opinion, subtly, about all the wrong choices they reckoned Suzy had made.

They hadn't been able to do so that easily once she and Mark were at Lindenshaw, because the Packers refuse to own a car, so it's cycle or bus everywhere for them apart from when they have no choice."

This was valuable background and from a proven reliable witness. "Were the wrong choices about her middle-class lifestyle or was there more? Like her choice of husband?"

"The first, I'd say. She thinks they quite liked Mark, but she did add that was probably because he always took the line of least resistance. Agreed with them, buttered them up, anything for an easy life and to get them out of the house. You know the sort of thing." Christine rolled her eyes. "It was all a bit of a soap opera with Suzy, but some people's lives are like that."

"True. Thanks, Christine, that's really helpful." Could Mark's placid agreement have led to family stress if he had—for example—agreed to do something and then hadn't? Surely Mr. and Mrs. Packer would at some point have realised they were being humoured and that could have rankled, especially if the promise not kept involved the issue of Suzy's medical treatment. Such family grudges could fester for years. "I'm so pleased we stopped for a chat. Ben and I are heading off to see the Packers right now, and every bit of background helps us to be prepared."

"Glad to be of help." She flashed them both her delightful smile. "Give my love to Adam. Tell him if he's thinking of moving school, Lindenshaw would have him like a shot."

"I will. If you promise you won't go killing the incumbent to make it happen." Robin returned the smile, with a frisson of guilt at making jokes about murder.

As they got back on the road, Ben said, "Mrs. Probert seems really nice. How reliable a witness is she?"

"As good as we're likely to get. It's not as good as Suzy telling us her side of things, but I don't think Christine would have any axe to grind, so I hope she'd give us the truth. As she understands it," Robin added. Didn't all information come to them through filters of one sort or another, and didn't every step removed from a source introduce another tweak to what they were told?

"There's a mismatch, though, sir. If Suzy hated new-age stuff and went mainstream to rebel against her parents, how come she's still influenced so much by them that she doesn't get the proper treatment early enough? Doesn't make sense."

"It might if you remember the axe-grinding part. If Suzy was in denial about being ill until it was too late, she might have told her husband that the Packers had influenced her choices. He'd be ready to blame them—most likely behind their backs—and so that's the story he told Ryan. Maybe with embellishments or perhaps missing out bits that didn't suit his agenda."

"It'll be interesting to see what their take is on things." Ben paused as they pulled onto the bypass. "Do you think the Packers knew about his family mystery? Bircher must have told his wife, surely, even if he left the digging until after she died."

"I bet he did, but she might not have wanted them to know. *He* probably didn't." Robin gazed out of the passenger-side window, watching a film of water forming from the drizzle which had started as they left Lindenshaw. "We're making too many assumptions, you know. Saying what someone we've never met would think about a situation."

"As long as we remember they're assumptions and not fact, we're okay." Ben's tone changed, a note of concern creeping in. "Can I ask if *you're* okay, sir? Tell me to shut it if I've overstepped the mark."

"Yeah." Time to come clean, at least in part. Ben knew him well enough to spot his distraction and deserved an honest answer. "This case has raised a strange coincidence, that's all, and it's one I'd rather you kept to yourself until I'm ready to tell the rest of the team. My dad was adopted, although he never hid the fact from me. He had no interest in finding out who his biological parents were because he said they meant nothing to him. I had no reason to doubt that. Still don't." Was that over-egging the pudding, and was it an admission that he *did* have doubts lurking in his mind? "Mum's become keen to find the truth, though, and she wants Adam and me to help her get on the trail. I thought I might put her in touch with Ryan if we've eliminated him as a suspect."

"Ryan?" Ben grinned. "Would that count as a help or a punishment, sir?"

The rest of the journey passed in a discussion of witnesses they'd come across and who'd been the most boring, the most annoying, or the like. A nice, safe conversation that allowed Robin to regather his thoughts and put the lurking doubts back where they'd been, until he had the proper chance to deal with them.

The smallholding was a good forty minutes' drive from Tumulus Gardens, a journey that would probably be longer during the rush hour and not one you'd necessarily attempt on a bike. It would take much longer on two wheels and add on miles if you wanted to keep safe by avoiding the main road. Ben drew the car up outside, not because of lack of space on the gravel-covered hardstanding the other side of the gate. No vehicles were parked there, but there was a large goat in occupation, and they'd have to brave the beast when they went in through the pedestrian access.

Just as Robin was planning how to defend himself if attacked, a woman emerged from the house. She said, "Sorry! I'll get her tethered," and then took the nanny goat round the back. Hard on her heels was a man who introduced himself as Justin Packer before opening the gate and ushering them into the house and through to the kitchen.

If Robin had been making a TV murder mystery, he couldn't have chosen a better property in which to shoot any "Police interview new-age couple" scenes. Homemade items—cushions, paintings, wine, and what might be medicines—were in evidence throughout, as was an apparent lack of much that could smack of modern consumerism.

Suzy's mother and father could themselves have come straight from a TV casting agency—and wardrobe department— who wanted to present a stereotypical hippie couple in their early sixties. Justin Packer had long greying hair, bore a distinct resemblance to Robert Plant, and sported a faded T-shirt clearly bought at a concert in the 1980s. Izzy had dreadlocks, was adorned with multiple necklaces, and wore a cheesecloth skirt and sandals.

A bigger contrast to their daughter's dress style, as evidenced in the photographs at the Bircher's house, couldn't be imagined.

Both Robin and Ben declined the offer of "own brew" tea and coffee, asking for water instead, although a freshly made batch of biscuits smelled too delicious to resist. The array of baking equipment on display, and the same old-fashioned style of solid chairs and table, reminded Robin pleasantly of his grandmother's kitchen.

"We were so sorry to hear about Mark. Shocked, too, naturally." Izzy was well-spoken, with a pleasant, husky voice, and held herself with a natural grace that seemed rather at odds with her image.

"When did you see him last?" Robin asked.

"Ages ago. A fortnight after Suzy's funeral, which was late January." She crinkled her forehead. "Not the start to the new year anyone could have wanted."

Presumably she meant Suzy's death, rather than meeting Bircher. "And you've not seen him since?"

"We've had no reason to. The last time we met was at their house, to pick up some keepsakes of Suzy that she'd wanted us to have. This necklace included." Izzy fingered a delicate pendant which was almost lost among the others round her neck.

"That's right." Justin sipped his odd-looking coffee. "I wouldn't say that we had a lot in common with Mark, but we tried to get on with him, for Suzy's sake."

Robin put on his most insouciant voice. "Did you have a lot in common with your daughter?"

The couple both smiled ruefully, shaking their heads.

"At first, yes," Izzy said. "She seemed such a chip off the old block as a child. A free spirit, same as us, although like so many children, she changed as she grew up. Suddenly, you find that your own child is like a stranger to you."

The hurt was palpable; Robin couldn't help but feel compassion for a couple who had, in effect, lost their child twice over. Still, he would have to raise the matter of Suzy's illness. He kept his tone sympathetic. "That must have been difficult for you, especially when she moved from Kings Ride and then became ill. We've been told that you weren't too keen on her receiving traditional treatment."

"Who said that?" The fury on Justin's face appeared to reflect genuine outrage and upset. "It's a complete and utter lie. How could we be so heartless to our little girl?"

"It's all right." Izzy patted her husband's arm.

"We've heard a similar story from two people, though. Are you saying they're both mistaken?" Robin asked, puzzled.

"Yes. Folk take one look at us and come up with the most ridiculous rubbish." Izzy gestured wildly. "I know we probably come across to you and everybody else as rabid anti-vaxxers or whatever, just because we've adopted an alternative lifestyle, but we're not so stupid as to think we know better than health professionals. With us, it's more a case of living like Tom and Barbara from *The Good Life*, if you've ever seen that programme, rather than being on the hippie-trail. People jump to stupid conclusions."

"Don't get upset, Izzy." Justin, who seemed to have calmed down a bit, now comforted his wife. "Mr. Bright, let me assure you that we never brought up Suzy to reject everything modern, especially where health was concerned. She had all her jabs when she was little, because it was the right thing to do. Living on a smallholding, we all had to be up-to-date with tetanus, for a start. We weren't risking our daughter scratching herself on a rusty nail and getting lockjaw. Want me to show you my Covid-vaccination card as proof we're not conspiracy theorists?"

"No. I'll believe you." Robin had heard many witnesses lie to him over the years, but this sounded like the truth. "You tell us your side of what happened with Suzy when she was ill."

"Okay. She and Mark used to live a pleasant cycle ride from here. Thirty-two Cranmer Drive. We could call in there after U3A meetings in Kings Ride Community Centre. That's the University of the Third Age, for us old crumblies who don't want to stop learning." Justin paused, as that was jotted down. "They moved—Suzy and Mark, not U3A—when the new estate was built in Lindenshaw, but I guess you know all that?"

"We do, although for the moment assume we know nothing. Isn't that right, Ben?"

The constable, who'd been taking notes, had become suspiciously quiet and had turned a bit green around the gills. "Yes, sir. Sorry, I felt queasy again. I think I've got a touch of food poisoning," he explained to the Packers. "Comes on and off in waves."

Izzy rose from the table. "I'll make you a tea that'll help. Very good for my IBS, so it should do the trick. If it doesn't, you can find the loo by the front door, and Mr. Bright will have to make his own notes."

If Robin hadn't already known about Ben's illness, he might have wondered if it was the kind of ruse seen in cop shows on telly—an excuse for the constable to leave the room and have a poke around the house—but that would be out of character. At least the Packers were unlikely to harbour similar suspicions, because the constable couldn't be faking the colour on his cheeks. "Give me the notepad, Ben, and you concentrate on feeling better. Carry on, Mr. Packer."

"We used to like having Suzy living close by, although maybe the temptation to drop in was too great, back then. I don't know if you have children, Mr. Bright, but it's not easy to let them fly the coop. They'll always be your little girl or boy. You never want to lose them."

Robin nodded and carried on without remark, although he could sympathise with the sentiment. Hadn't he been in a terrible state on the occasions Campbell had hurt himself? "Was that why they moved to Lindenshaw?"

Justin blew out his cheeks. "We suspected so. In part, anyway. Admittedly, Suzy had always wanted a brand-new house on a brand-new estate, so when the Barrow Farm estate started to be built, she was all over it like the proverbial rash. Would you agree, Izzy?"

"Yes," Izzy said over her shoulder as she prepared Ben's drink. "It's a bigger house, as well, which was what Mark wanted. Came in handy during lockdown, so they could both work from home without being under each other's feet. Not that they would have been thinking about that in early 2019. Nobody was really."

Robin nodded. "What jobs did they do?"

"They both worked for that big drug company with the manufacturing site on the Kinechester industrial park. Haveland and Sons. That's how they met. Mark got a post there on the IT side and Suzy was in HR. She'd been with the company for years and had got herself very highly thought of. She used to do a lot of travelling to their different sites pre-Covid, which I think is one of the reasons she was so slow to get herself checked out properly. Always too busy with work." Izzy presented Ben with a mug of minty-smelling liquid before sitting down and bursting into tears.

"I'm sorry," Robin said. "I know this must be painful, but we have to ask these questions."

Justin, one arm around his wife, raised his other hand. "We know you have a job to do. We'd like to help." He took a deep breath, clearly fighting his own emotions. "As we understand it, Suzy hadn't been right for most of 2019, but she put it down to the stress of the house move and juggling that with work. Then 2020 came, and she decided it was too tricky trying to get any medical help at all because of the pandemic and everyone being in a bit of a lather. She didn't like her own GP, either, which didn't help. When she eventually told us she wasn't feeling well, she said she'd decided to wait until things evened themselves out as she didn't want to go into a clinic and come out with Covid, given the risks. I don't know if that was simply her putting off getting a diagnosis, burying her head in the sand. Well, by the time she did get proper help, they couldn't do anything much for her because the cancer had spread everywhere. The doctor at her work had got the ball rolling, but it was all too late. He was very upset and apparently gave her quite a rollicking for being slow off her marks. Anyway, she did well to survive as long as she did, because it had likely been lurking for years. If we'd known early enough, I'd have dragged her to a specialist as soon as I could, going private if need be. We could have found the money. We'd have sold some of our land here if need be."

That wasn't the story Mark and Suzy seemed to have been putting about. Robin quickly checked on Ben, who was sipping his drink and gradually getting a better colour on him, although he apparently hadn't registered the mismatch. "When *did* she tell you she was ill?"

"Spring of 2021. That was a great birthday present for me. Sorry." Justin raised his hand again. "It hurt. It still hurts. Then, early this year, Suzy got Covid—which is what she died from— and that was that. You feel so helpless. She'd have been wired up in the hospital and hardly able to breathe, and we couldn't even visit her because the hospital was awash with cases and had banned all visitors. If only she'd got an ambulance sooner."

"Hush, it's all right." Izzy stroked her husband's hand.

Robin didn't doubt the Packers' anguish. Not quite the same situation as when Campbell had died, but he could identify with that heart-wrenching sense of helplessness. "And Mark blamed you for the delay in cancer treatment?"

Justin nodded. "Clearly he did, Mr. Bright, although he never said so to our faces. I wish now we'd had the chance to talk it out and put things straight, but I'm afraid we've barely spoken to him these last couple of years. Eh, Izzy? Izzy?"

"Sorry. I was thinking about a conversation I had with Mark the back end of last year. I was at the farm shop the other side of Kings Ride, saw him, and asked how Suzy was. I'm afraid the news was worse than expected, and I got terribly upset. To my surprise, he was sweet as pie about everything and seemed really sympathetic."

Playing the *anything for an easy life* card that Christine had spoken about? Or had Mark been one of those unpredictable characters whose personality turned almost on the flick of a switch? Ryan might have some input about that: Robin suppressed a smile at how another interview with the bloke might be exactly the thing Ben needed to take his thoughts off his dicky tummy and maybe act as a relaxant. *Thoughts back to the interview in progress.* "When was this?"

"October time? I'm pretty sure I was there to buy a pumpkin because we never have any luck growing them. Funny how you remember strange things like that. Anyway, when I got upset, Mark said he understood entirely. That when someone was ill, all the focus went on them, rather than the people around them, who'd also be feeling the strain. Suzy had told me he'd said something similar when she miscarried early in their marriage, that he'd found it depressing that everyone asked how *she* was and ignored the fact he'd also lost a child." Izzy inhaled loudly, clearly steadying herself. "I felt rather shamefaced when Suzy told me that because I'd been guilty of focussing on her when they lost the baby. I'm digressing. Back to the farm shop. What I really wanted to say was that Mark told me his brother had 'been on his case' about some family business."

"We didn't realise he had a brother," Ben said, facial colour much improved. "He's not been in touch with us, and there was nothing obvious at the house. Not even on the makeshift family tree."

Justin sighed. "I don't think they were that close, and from the little we heard via Suzy, Kevin—the brother—wasn't the sort to make any effort to keep in touch. It wouldn't surprise me if he's sat at home waiting for *you* to make contact, rather than getting off his backside and doing it for himself."

They'd picked up an address book at the house, which Robin had intended getting one of the civilian staff to go through, although now he'd be going straight to the B or the K page himself. He turned to his constable again. "You're definitely looking better, Ben."

"Yep." He gave Izzy a sheepish grin. "This is good stuff."

"Excellent for hangovers too, with a couple of paracetamol. I'll give you some to take home, although if you have a repeat episode, I have to say that the best thing, to be horribly frank, is to let nature take its course, unpleasant as that it. Get it all out of the system."

Robin thought they'd better press on before matters intestinal took over, one way or another. "This family business. Was it to do with Mark's mother being adopted?"

"I couldn't tell you." The adoption part clearly didn't come as news to the Packers, though.

"And did you know that he was supposed to be in Woodhall Spa this weekend just gone?" Ben asked.

Izzy shrugged and Justin said, "Nope. But he wouldn't have got in touch to tell us if he was. Woodhall?" His face wrinkled in thought, aging him. "617 squadron territory. I used to make Airfix kits when I was younger, and the Lancaster was my favourite."

"He still would. I've had to ban them. Dust accumulators." Izzy chuckled. "I wonder what Mark was doing up there? Or supposed to be doing, I should say. I guess he didn't get nearer his destination than Kings Ride."

Robin nodded. "Indeed. He didn't share your enthusiasm for aircraft, Mr. Packer?"

"Not as far as I'm aware. It was a topic of conversation I tried but failed with. The only point we had in common—apart from Suzy—was a love of rugby. No Premiership teams near Woodhall, though. Not sure about the lower leagues."

"I'll get Ben here to check the fixture lists." Robin smiled, then put his serious face on again. "I'd be remiss if I didn't discuss your police record."

"Oh, you're not thinking that had anything to do with Mark's death?" Justin seemed amused rather than outraged at the suggestion. "I haven't touched weed since we had Suzy. An indiscretion of youth, like many people will have committed."

Robin turned to Izzy. "And what about the 5G protest?"

"I was a bloody idiot to get involved." Sighing, she put her fingers to her mouth. "A friend was completely wound up about the things and wanted me to go along. To keep her company. I was feeling pretty low, because it was around the time Suzy was getting worse, so I let myself be persuaded. The daft tart got carried away and started to cause damage. Next minute I'm in the back of a Black Maria. Are they still called that?"

"Sometimes. Police van does for me." Robin didn't feel the need to probe deeper at present. "I've got a couple of further questions and an unpleasant request. I don't know if the brother's local, but if he isn't, will you come in and do the formal identification? I'll get a car sent out for you."

"That would be very much appreciated, as we don't have one." Izzy's brow crinkled. "I've a feeling Kevin lives the other side of London, so maybe it would be easiest if we identified the body. It's the least we can do for Mark."

"Thanks. Now, we talked about Kevin not coming forward, but why didn't *you* contact us when Mark's body was found?" Robin had assumed before he'd met the Packers that would be because they weren't the type to watch the telly or surf the internet, but there was a radio in the kitchen and a phone on the side, so they couldn't be totally disconnected from the world. How many more assumptions about this pair would prove false?

"We did hear the news about the dead man on the radio, but we never thought of connecting the body to Mark. We don't buy newspapers, so didn't see any pictures and anyway, as far as we were concerned, he'd shaken the dust of Kings Ride off his shoes when he and Suzy moved to Lindenshaw. That's what he told us the last time we saw him, earlier this year. Said he wouldn't come back here if you paid him."

But he did. "He must have had a pressing need to return, then. Could he have been visiting friends here despite his vow not to return?"

Justin shrugged. "That promise could have been merely bluster, although he could be very stubborn if he wanted to, so if he'd said it offhand, he may have felt he had to stick to it. Suzy could be stubborn too, which must have made matters interesting at times."

"I'm sure they still did have friends at Kings Ride," Izzy cut in, "because there were some at her funeral, although, like Justin said, it wouldn't surprise me if he deliberately met up with them elsewhere."

Perhaps stubbornness ran in the Bircher family, which could explain Kevin's attitude. "One last question. It's purely routine and we're asking everyone, so you can guess what it is. For elimination purposes, where were you on Saturday?"

"Here," Justin said, to which his wife nodded. "As we usually are, milking the goat and doing stuff on the plot. This time it was getting the soil ready for the next lot of planting."

"Can anyone verify that?" Robin asked.

"Not during the day. We had pals around in the evening for dinner and drinks, but earlier on, I'm afraid not. There's always traffic up and down this road, so somebody might have seen us, although we rarely get pedestrians, so not much passing footfall, either."

At last, two people close to the victim who didn't have an alibi for his time of death. Although what motive could either Justin or Izzy have had for killing him? Robin would have put a tenner on neither of them being the sort to use violence in an argument. What about Kevin, though? Was he "on Mark's case" because of family business related to their mysterious maternal descent? And where did Woodhall Spa come in?

Chapter Six

Thursday evening, Adam arrived home at a decent time, although he'd brought work with him to complete for Monday. He wanted to keep Friday after school entirely free for entertaining Mrs. Bright, who'd earlier dropped them both a message to say she'd bring all the ingredients with her for cooking dinner so they needn't worry about shopping, and would Hamish need feeding? With the domestic arrangements for Friday settled, he concentrated on the day at hand. Individual pizzas and a bowl of salad was a perfect combination for the present busy circumstances.

He'd just got his dinner on to cook when Robin arrived home, more chipper than he'd been the last few days.

"Making progress? And shall I put your pizza on as well?" Adam gave his husband a hug before returning to cooking duties.

"I think so and yes, please. We're at the 'lots of information and a few semi-suspects' stage."

"Sounds intriguing. Although, if you want to discuss it, it'll have to be over dinner as I've got homework I need to complete tonight. Sorry."

"I guessed you might. Hello." Robin bent to pick up the dog. "No, not a good idea. You're getting too heavy for this." He put Hamish back on the floor, then got on his haunches to fuss over the Newfoundland. "I'd appreciate talking it over with the pair of you. Spectator gets a better view of the game than the players and all that, so you might do your usual and spot something we've missed."

"I'll try not to disappoint. Although *he's* only going to be able to contribute any wisdom if it concerns food."

"Nothing dog biscuit-related at all in this case, I'm afraid. All I have are in-laws who don't have an alibi for the time the victim was killed, which we've been able to narrow down a bit because we've a witness who heard a loud argument when he was bird-watching near the crime scene. We've found Mark Bircher's car too, *and* I saw Christine Probert, who both sends her best to you and proved a mine of information."

"You *have* been a busy boy. I wish I'd brought some stickers home from school to reward you with."

"Up yours." Robin rolled his eyes. "I'm about to be busier still. I've got to go and see Mark's brother, who lives in Bedford. He says he's got his lower leg in plaster from a football injury, meaning he isn't that mobile. He's got a hospital appointment in the morning, so we won't see him until early afternoon. M25 on a Friday. Bliss."

"Further bliss driving home on the same road early evening. Ah." Light dawned. "You're standing me up for our date with your mum?"

"It's a possibility. I'll pack a case but I don't want to stay over, so I'll only do that if anything turns up that wants investigating at the Bedford end or farther north. Otherwise, chances are I could be back late. I'll keep you both updated. No, I'll keep all three of you updated," Robin added, giving the dog another scritch. "I'll ring Mum in a minute and let her know what's what. Unless you want to rearrange entirely?"

"Nah. I'm happy to do some son-in-law bonding, especially when we can discuss your faults ad nauseam behind your back. As long as you give me a heads-up on anything your mate Henry in fraud has reported on this inheritance lark." Adam was pretty well prepared on that front, already having scoured Ryan's website, which displayed some glowing—assuming they were genuine—reviews of his services. He would happily discuss the strategy of using a professional with his mother-in-law because, irrespective of whether the inheritance turned out to be a swindle, she might still want to delve into Bright history. Ryan would definitely have a wider range of experience in that area than either Adam or Robin could offer.

"Henry thinks it's above board, unless it's a totally new and extremely well worked-out variety of scam. It certainly doesn't match any pattern he knows of. He's quite a little tinker, is Henry. He rang Mum's solicitor to discuss it and managed to wheedle enough information from him to satisfy his natural scepticism. Possibly more than Mum did."

"Why is that mischievous? Isn't it a case of doing his job?"

"Well, the fraud part is, but I'm not sure it was his job to emphasise the income and inheritance tax angle, although I suppose that's always a good card to play."

Adam chortled. "That's how they caught Al Capone. Very useful weapon if all else fails."

Robin slapped his forehead, overdramatically. "Hey, maybe that's what's going on. My mum's secretly a gangster and this is a cunning plan on behalf of the authorities to entrap her. That's why there's all the secrecy."

"Twit. Come on, ring your mum and give her the bad news, then we can get this eaten and you can tell me the rest."

Once the call had been made and they were settled at the dining table with their food, Robin said, "Right. Not sure where to begin briefing you."

Adam snorted. "'Briefing'? I'm not the local gutter press. Start with anything related to your mum, because that's the bit I need to remember."

"I've thought of that already, so it's already in writing. I left it in the bedroom in case *himself* got tempted to eat it. There's some stuff about tax treaties to share with her because Henry thinks that might narrow down where the money's coming from. He's not hopeful about finding some legal loophole that will force any other parties involved to reveal the identity of the mysterious benefactor to Mum's solicitor."

"Hm." Adam chewed at a pizza crust. "I keep thinking this sounds like something out of Dickens. Money put into trust to be handed over at some unspecified point in the future when the donor is gone. So whoever could be harmed by whatever was being covered up getting uncovered can no longer be hurt."

"Could be. I hope this murder case turns out to be less tangled, but you know how often they aren't." Robin tucked in again. "I met the dead man's in-laws today, and I had to reassess all my stereotypes. Never pre-judge people." He waggled his knife in the direction of Hamish, who appeared as uninterested in the life advice as Campbell would have been. "They came across as a nice couple. Didn't set my rozzer's nose twitching, which is actually a shame, given they have no alibi for when we think he died, but they've no obvious motive for a bust up with him. Not from their side, anyway."

Adam picked up the hint. "From his, though?"

"Could be. Turning out to be a bit of a mystery man, Mark Bircher, or at least somebody I can't get a handle on. We've been told by two different people that the Packers—the in-laws I met today—had stopped her getting traditional treatment for her leukaemia until it was too late. They insist that's a load of cobblers and they'd have paid for her to have private treatment if they'd known early enough."

"I realise you never met the dead bloke, so it's a one-sided analysis, but who do you believe?"

"That's one of the problems. In each case I believed what I was told, although I don't have Mark's point of view from the horse's mouth. The Packers came across as truthful, and while I don't know Ryan the genealogist from Adam—excuse the pun—he'd have to be an incredibly accomplished actor to have been lying through his teeth." Robin picked up the final piece of crust on his plate with evident relish: leaving it for last was a ritual he always went through when they had pizza.

"Perhaps he bored you so much you believed him as a line of least resistance?"

Robin grinned. "Maybe. But Christine Probert confirmed much of what he'd said. She gave a slightly different slant on things because she said Suzy had admitted that some of the blame, if that's the right word, was her own denial of the problem. The

Packers told us the same thing, although Christine also reckoned that Mark blamed the parents *completely* for what happened."

"Perhaps he did. Perhaps he told Ryan what he thought was the truth, because that's what his wife, Suzy, had told him and it fitted with his point of view." Easy to put the blame on other people in such a harrowing situation. "Did he see her parents often?"

"I don't believe so. Why?"

"That would reduce the risk of the inconsistency coming out. If she'd told the two parties slightly different stories." Adam finished the last of his salad, watching as Robin thought through his suggestion.

"Okay, that's possible, although why would she lie to him or to her parents? Because she enjoyed playing both sides against the middle?"

"What about if she was lying to herself too? It's always easier to blame someone else than blame yourself. Actually—" Adam drummed the table "—it may not be what Suzy *said* so much as what *he* wanted to hear, if that makes sense. What if he felt guilty that he hadn't spotted something amiss with her and could only cope with that guilt by deflecting it elsewhere?"

Robin nodded slowly. "Or there could be another person entirely, one perhaps we haven't come across yet, who's been stirring the shite and playing one side off against the other. Maybe Mark discovered he'd been misled and gets into a row with *them*."

"His death does sound increasingly like an argument that went wrong. Not that I'm an expert." Although Adam was gaining so much experience discussing cases, he'd put money on being able to hold his own in an incident room. "Any idea of who this mystery person could be?"

"A cousin he didn't realise he had until recently? Yeah, I know"—Robin waved his hand—"it's similar to Mum's enigmatic inheritance, but that's not the Bright family history informing my thinking. Mark Bircher's mother was adopted, and he had no idea until she told him in the days before she died."

"Blimey, that's a spooky coincidence. Although if that programme they're always going on about in the staffroom is anything to go by—the one we keep seeing advertised about reuniting family members—it's more common than you might imagine." That show wasn't the kind of thing he and Robin would watch, but during lockdown they'd found a great Judy Dench film, based on a true story about forced adoptions, that would have moved them both to tears irrespective of the family connection.

"What's more common? Adoption or not telling people their true family history? I can't imagine Dad hiding the truth from us, if he knew it, or why anyone would want to." Robin's face clouded. "I'm starting to really feel for this victim, despite whatever flaws he had. Maybe it was finding that out about the adoption so late in the game that made him want to blame parents generically for everything."

"I wonder why his mother didn't tell him when he was planning to get married. He and Suzy might have been cousins."

"Either Mrs. Bircher senior knew enough about her family history to be able to eliminate that for herself, or she was too scared to speak up. From what little I've gleaned, I don't think she passed anything she knew down to her son. Hence him calling on Ryan to help out." Robin blanched. "Unintended incest."

"Eh?" Adam felt like he'd missed a step in the conversation.

"Sorry, I was remembering aloud. I came across a case of it when I was a sergeant. Tragic, really. This couple turned out to be half siblings via a shared father and either their mothers hadn't known or deliberately hadn't told them until it was too late. The woman had been adopted."

"That's terrible." Adam had seen that kind of plot in a couple of TV shows but never come across it in real life, although it was always possible that it had occurred among the various school communities he'd worked in and he'd never realised. Families played their cards close to their chests. "Any chance something similar went on with your dead man?"

"I don't think so—it was his mum who was adopted, not him. I don't know why Mark and Suzy didn't have any children, or why she'd miscarried one, but we can't rule out consanguinity. However, there are all sorts of reasons, including a matter of choice, why people don't." Robin shrugged. "Anyway, I'll see what the brother has to say about the family background and why Mark was heading to Woodhall Spa. Which is somewhere in Lincolnshire and where Mark was supposed to have been visiting last Saturday through to Tuesday. If I end up there tomorrow night, don't say you weren't warned."

Lincolnshire. That rang a bell. "Was he into war history as well as family stuff?"

"Not that I'm aware of. Why?"

"I'm sure it was Woodhall that one of the teachers at school was raving about visiting. It's got some connection to the Dambusters." Adam tried to recall the conversation. "They had their mess there, I think."

"If the Dambusters were 617 squadron, then you're probably right. His father-in-law mentioned the connection. Your teacher's keen on Lancaster bombers, is he?"

Adam rapped the table. "Robin Bright, you can go and sit on the contemplation step and think awhile about stereotypes. *She's* keen on Lancasters. Dragged her husband to some airfield up there so she could have a ride on one. Went to see the memorial flight too, because everything was in a relatively small area."

Despite the admonishment he'd received, Robin's face brightened. "Does East Kirkby have an air force connection as well?"

"No idea. Why?"

"Because Mark was due to be going there in May. I can see I've either got a Google session coming up, or we'll need to get Ryan in a second time, because if that area still had service personnel based there after the war, Mark's biological grandfather might have been one of them. His mother was born in 1948, so she could have been a slightly delayed war baby. That couldn't apply to my dad, of course."

Back there again. Robin obviously wasn't ready to leave that topic alone.

"This is hitting really close to home, isn't it?" Adam said.

Robin flashed him a sheepish grin. "Just a bit. I mentioned the family adoption coincidence to Ben, although I've asked him to keep quiet for the moment. He's a good lad, he'll do what he's told, but it's not fair to make him hold on to secrets for too long. What do you think—should I tell the rest of the team?"

"If you're happy to. It'll look more suspicious than it should if you don't, especially if it turns out the adoption angle is relevant to the murder. They'd know something was up, anyway, every time you mentioned it." Adam leaned over to stroke his husband's hand. "You'd be great to play strip poker against because you do tend to wear your feelings on your face."

"Remind me not to get into a game of it, then. Unless it's with you." Despite the lighter note, Robin's voice still bore a hint of constraint.

"Is that all that's bothering you? Might as well take the chance to get everything off your chest to everyone's favourite agony uncle, Adam."

"You really can read me like a book, can't you?" Robin glanced at the dog. "Hamish, you won't be able to get away with anything when Adam's on the case. Remember that." He turned back. "I've had a few unsettling thoughts, and I don't know if they're new or if seeing the family history stuff in Mark's home has stirred up some uneasiness I've tried to bury. Dad always told us he didn't want to know who his real parents were, but what if he was only saying that?"

Adam squeezed Robin's hand. "*Would* he have lied to you about it? Even if it was only a white lie?"

Robin clearly needed to consider that for a moment, then shook his head. "That wouldn't have been in character. He never told us fibs, apart from the usual stuff—like pretending that Santa had called on Christmas Eve and his reindeers had left the half-eaten carrot under the tree. I was wondering whether he might have been lying to himself. Saying that he was happy not knowing who his parents were, because that was an easier choice, a less painful option than maybe uncovering something better left covered up."

"Do you want me to ask your mum tomorrow? I could text her and suggest she bring an overnight bag, given that you might be home late. I'll make up the spare bed, get a couple of glasses of white in her, and ask a few son-in-law-type questions. Always a chance she'd open up to me in a way she might not to her best boy."

"I'd appreciate that." Robin, hunched shoulders relaxing, was clearly happier now he'd aired his doubts. "Let me clear the table while you get on with your homework. I could do with something mindless to fiddle about with. I might take Hamish for a once round the block and get us both some fresh air."

Adam got up and gave him a kiss. "Do whatever you need to do. I've got a date with some school improvement plans."

"Enjoy." Robin snorted. "I think I'd rather have this murder to solve."

"Sez you."

It was a relief to see his husband's humour restored.

Chapter Seven

The Friday morning briefing took longer than it typically would. It was the first occasion the entire team had been able to get together since the equivalent meeting twenty-four hours previously and all present—Robin included—needed to be brought up to speed on everyone else's news.

"If anyone's wondering about the new name on the incident board, Kevin Bircher is Mark's brother. Ashok and I are off to see him later today, and where we go next will depend on what we find out. That should make better sense by the end of the briefing." Robin took a breath. "I suggest we start with matters car-related, given that I'm increasingly convinced it or its contents were the target of the key theft. His neighbour, Mrs. Crouch, saw Mark drive away in the Yaris on Saturday morning, around eleven. She's not the sort whose word you want to doubt. Not to her face, anyway. He was supposed to be going to Woodhall Spa for a few days, possibly to do with his family history research. More about that later." He nodded towards Pru and Ashok. "He must have had a suitcase or bag with him. No chance it was in the car?"

"I'm afraid not, sir. We *have* got the bunch of keys, though," Ashok said. "Well, technically we haven't, because they're with forensics at the moment, although nobody's very hopeful of them turning up anything. Not a lot else on the ring—house and car keys, something that probably opens a luggage lock, and that's about it. Nothing appears to be for a shed or a garage or whatever."

"Where was the bunch found?" Robin asked.

"About three feet away, under a pile of crud." Ashok pulled a face. "Pru thought of kicking through it, and there they were."

"Lucky I had my old boots on." The sergeant grinned. "The keys had been tucked in there, rather than dropped, I'd have said. We did wonder if that had been deliberate so the culprit could return to pick them and the car up. They wouldn't have had to worry about being tracked via a fine for overstaying their allotted parking time, because that would have gone to Mark's address."

"They couldn't be traced through Ringo or whatever app the car park uses?" Trust Ben to assume whoever had been driving must have used their phone.

Pru shook her head. "They paid with coins when they parked up. If they have tried to return, us being there in force might have made them do a U-turn."

"Why leave the keys at all, though?" Danielle said. "If they wanted to return to the car, why not take the bunch away rather than risk someone else nicking them *and* the Yaris?"

"Maybe the culprit didn't want to have to explain to anyone else why they had them in their possession," Ashok suggested, a touch sheepishly. "It could imply local knowledge, like the phone signal business did. If they knew the car park wouldn't be routinely cleaned, they might have assumed the keys would be safe. It's not the kind of place you get rough sleepers. Wrong end of Kinechester, for a start."

That was worth consideration, not least because the car park didn't have the reputation of having vehicles broken into. "Okay, that's another mystery to add to the mix. What about the car itself?"

"Nothing obvious, sir," Pru said. "It's got a bike rack on the back, which seems a bit odd for that size of car."

"The neighbour said they used to do a lot of cycling before Suzy got ill," Ben chipped in. "Mark probably never got round to taking it off. Or maybe he kept it for sentimental reasons."

Pru nodded. "The CSIs were going to dust it for prints. They were also going to test the car for drug residues or whatever, but I wouldn't count on them finding anything. Ashok and I bounced some ideas around, like what if he'd habitually carried something that the other person wanted. When I was first a constable, we came across a bloke who used to keep his stash of porn among his work stuff in his car boot. Didn't want his wife to know about it. I'm not saying Mark had a collection of smut, but it's an idea to consider."

"Although we didn't know then that he was supposed to be having a weekend away." Ashok was clearly a touch aggrieved that fate hadn't provided this information before they'd gone to Kinechester. "It could be as simple as them wanting from the weekend case."

"I like simplicity," Robin said. "So at present I'm inclined to think that the most likely explanation."

Ben raised his hand. "If we're talking simple, is there something we've overlooked? What if the killer and his victim went to the woods together in the Yaris? The killer then took the car not only to get their hands on the suitcase but to get themselves home. Didn't want to stand out by dragging a suitcase along the path or lugging it onto a bus. They then abandoned the car in what's—let's admit it—a pretty clever way. You don't torch the thing or otherwise bring attention to yourself. Park it legally and wait for it to be found."

"I think that's got a lot going for it. It would explain their leaving the keys, too, because they get distanced from the killer." Robin glanced at the incident board again, focussing on the map. "Although it still begs the question of why Mark and our culprit needed to go to Kings Ride Woods in the first place, unless they were meeting a third party there before he set off up the M1. Pru, CCTV for the car park?"

The sergeant rolled her eyes. "Joy of joys, most of the cameras are out of action, including the floor we're interested in. Some joker's smashed them."

"That was on the local news, a couple of weeks back," Danielle said. "Maybe whoever took the car there knew about it."

Pru nodded. "Ashok's going to get what little footage there is and work through to see if we can spot matey exiting on foot—we have the time stamp from the ticket to narrow things down—but, again, we're not hopeful. I don't suppose we have enough details about his travelling bag to put out an alert?"

Robin shook his head. "Can you put out a general one for any abandoned cases that turn up in the local area, please, especially in the corridor between Kings Ride and Kinechester? Although my gut feeling is that it's either been flung in a skip and long gone or hidden in someone's attic until people have forgotten about it. Anything else, people?"

"I have an idea about why Mark was in Kings Ride Woods," Danielle chirped up. "I've got the map on my phone and if you were heading from Lindenshaw to the dual carriageway and then towards the motorway, a diversion to Kings Ride Woods wouldn't be too far off your trail. If the person he was meeting with was also local, they may have agreed on that as a convenient place."

"That would argue against them needing the car to get away," Ben said. "Although if they really wanted whatever he was taking to Woodhall Spa in his case, that theory could still hang together. Dump the car in and take the case back to Kings Ride or wherever on the bus. You get a fair few tourists in Kinechester, so you'd seem less out of place pulling along a suitcase there. All of this assumes he *was* parked at the woods."

"He was," Danielle confirmed. "I spoke to the Forestry Commission people, and they gave me contact details for the guys who were doing work at the woods last weekend. One of them saw a small red car—he couldn't tell me the make because apparently they all look the same to him nowadays—but he particularly noticed this one because he almost hit it. He said it was badly parked, although that could be an excuse for the guy being a bad driver. It had gone by the time they closed the car park."

"Any other vehicles catch his eye?" Robin asked.

Danielle consulted her notes. "He said they were the usual mix of big and small, including a couple of camper vans. They keep an eye out for those because people aren't supposed to park up overnight, though they do. He hadn't heard or seen anything out of the ordinary, not even the flasher or the usual courting couples. He reckoned that car park can be a bit of a place at nights for folk to hang out. Literally," she added, with a snort of laughter.

"Maybe that's an explanation for what Mark was up to there," Ashok said. "Some people get a thrill about doing it in the open air. Maybe he was feeling lonely after the loss of his wife and thought he'd found a willing partner for some alfresco sex. He could have been getting in a session before he set off on his jolly. Only the partner got cold feet."

"Cold other bits too," one of the admin staff muttered.

Robin felt like Adam must when he was addressing errant seven-year-olds. "Can we please discuss this sensibly? Irrespective of the sex angle, it *is* possible Mark had a new girlfriend, either locally or in Lincolnshire. Or a boyfriend. If the new partner was local, they might have been going for a romantic stroll together before he headed up north."

"If so, it's highly suspicious that this partner hasn't been in touch with us," Pru said. "I'd struggle to believe that they're yet another person who has a legitimate reason for not having seen his pictures in the paper or worried where he was. Let's say this romantic stroll took place, during which Mark tried it on and she didn't like it. Or vice versa. She wants more from the relationship and he's not ready. They had an argument—the one Mr. Rashid heard—and it turned into a fight."

"What about the blunt instrument he got hit with?" Ben asked. "We know he didn't fall and hit his head on a rock or whatever, so this wasn't a case of argument that ended in a tragic accident. There had to have been a weapon, and the killer had to have brought it, unless Mark was the one who came armed for some reason and his strategy backfired. Not many people walk around carrying something that could have made that dent in his skull unless they're looking for trouble."

Pru patted the constable on the shoulder. "You probably don't want to hear this, but it's an eye-opener. A mate of mine at uni used to carry a huge backpack wherever she went. She told everyone it was so she didn't have to take two bags for when she was doing sport or going shopping after lectures. This one was big enough for everything she needed. Anyway, one girls' night in and a couple of bottles of wine later, she confessed the main reason she had her large bag was because she could carry an old-fashioned police truncheon in it. One of those large, polished wood jobs. For self-defence."

"Was your uni that rough, then?" Ashok asked.

"Not particularly. She just had an overprotective family. Her granny had kept that truncheon hanging in her hallway for years, in case she needed to protect herself when the grandad was away at sea on his merchant navy runs."

Ashok, eyes narrowed, clearly couldn't decide if they were being conned. He should have known that Pru wouldn't joke about something so serious. "Where did she get this truncheon, then? Coppers in the family?"

Pru snorted. "It was a case of *don't ask*. Don't tell, either. My mate never had to use it, as far as I know."

"My grandad used to say if any burglars came in our house, they'd soon regret it," Ben said. "Gran would have them with her rolling pin or the carving knife."

Robin raised his hand. "Before we get into whether *she* ever used that—I don't want to know if the answer's yes—can we scroll back to our killer?"

"I think we'd better," Pru said. "I was wondering if he or she may have routinely carried something around with them for protection, rather than specifically taking it on Saturday to biff our victim. A smaller baseball bat, for example, as per the postmortem indications."

"That description could match a truncheon, actually," Robin pointed out. "Not that we've had a hint of any suspects with police officers in the family. Right, moving on swiftly but still talking of families, we now have a better idea of what Mark wanted to know about his. His mum was adopted, although she didn't tell him until she was dying and that could well be all she did tell him. At present, we don't know if his dad wouldn't or couldn't answer his questions on the subject, but we might get a clue on that when we see the brother."

"It could be relevant to the case, couldn't it, sir?" Pru said. "The long-lost relative who didn't want to be found or who wanted to preserve the family reputation."

"Agreed, despite the fact we've no evidence of that yet." Precious little evidence of anything much, but it *was* still early days. "And so you all know, my dad was adopted, so we'll have no making assumptions or stereotyping about what went on with Mark's mum, please. Now, I hope you'll notice I'm resisting using another clichéd link here because we're still on the subject of family. Ben, do you want to take us through what we learned at the Packers' place?"

"Yep." He moved towards the incident board. "When the boss spoke about stereotyping, it could equally apply to the assumptions we made about them. They seem like typical new-age hippies, goat and all, but they kept surprising us. For a start, they're adamant they'd never have persuaded Suzy not to have mainstream medicine when she was ill." Ben went on to give an efficient summary of the interview and the things it had turned up. The constable then outlined what they'd learned from Christine prior to the interview. He was on better form today, so either nature had fully taken its course or the herbal drink Izzy had given him had solved the problem.

"So, we've got several mismatches," Ben concluded, "and not just about why Suzy didn't get the medical help she needed. Mark wasn't supposed to get on with them, but Mrs. Packer said she'd seen him last year and he'd been lovely to her, pouring his heart out."

"He does seem to have been the sort who liked an easy life. Which could mean he was two-faced, slagging them off but only behind their backs," Robin added. "He also told the Packers he'd never come back to Kings Ride once he'd moved away, and they reckoned he was keeping that promise, but we know he did return."

Pru said, "Maybe he changed his mind about returning and didn't want them to know, especially if he'd got a new person in his life who lived there. They might think it was too soon after his wife had died."

Robin nodded. "That wouldn't surprise me. What about the two different accounts of what went on when Suzy was ill?"

"How reliable is Christine Probert?" Pru asked.

"Both Adam and I would swear that if she says something, you listen. Unless we've misjudged her for years." Robin didn't want to entertain that thought. "Don't forget, what she said was in line with what Ryan told us. Chances are they couldn't both have got the wrong end of the stick, so either they've been lied to or had the truth stretched."

"Could Suzy have been stretching the truth, sir?" Danielle said. "Playing both ends against the middle for sympathy?"

"That would be no surprise, either. It might have made her feel less bad, given that she seems to have been in denial and didn't get help soon enough." Robin pointed at the picture of the couple which Ben had put on display. "We're seeing her solely as a victim here, but people with an illness can be as manipulative as healthy ones. Occasionally worse." He puffed out his cheeks. "There was an odd little Post-it among the waste bin things. 'Honesty. No. Discipline. No.' It looked like Mark's writing, although I don't know what it referred to. The brother? His wife or in-laws?"

Danielle raised a hand. "It could be to do with his rugby team. I know it sounds daft, but there are four values plastered round the Saracens stadium: Honesty, Humility, Discipline. Can't remember the fourth."

"Work rate," chirped Ashok, who'd obviously just googled it. "Impressive that you knew them."

"My dad's a Tigers fan and I was remembering all that stick he gave Sarries when the financial irregularities were uncovered. About how their values were a joke, especially the honesty one. He might have been making notes about that?"

"Or using them to refer to his biological grandparents?" Pru suggested. "Lack of honesty in their dealings."

"Could be. Although it might only refer to a word puzzle he was working out." Robin shrugged. "Total change of tack alert. Has anybody come across a mention of Woodhall Spa or anywhere else in Lincolnshire? Or Mark liking RAF history, despite Justin Packer saying he didn't reckon the bloke had any interest in the subject?"

"Not that I know of." Pru's puzzled expression was matched all round the room.

"Well, let me know if you do. Especially if it comes up today when we're halfway there. His brother might shed some light on what Mark was supposed to be doing this weekend, although sods law says he won't and it'll only be when we're back in the car park here that the Lincolnshire connection will turn up. Anything else to share?"

Danielle raised her hand. "I've spoken to Mark's boss at Haveland and Sons. He was a highly valued employee, as was Suzy. She'd been a real high flyer. He confirmed that Mark had booked Monday and Tuesday as annual leave—which is why they'd not been alarmed at the lack of contact from him—and was supposed to be working from home the rest of the week, although that isn't unusual for the company. The boss then put me in touch with the guy he thinks was Mark's closest colleague, although I didn't get a lot from him. He said that Mark and Suzy had been a pretty self-contained couple and apart from her night classes and his rugby, their social life revolved around each other." She shrugged. "Nothing to follow up there, yet."

"Okay." Robin viewed the board again. "Let's be clear on what we do next. Ben, have you got anything from his phone or PC?"

The constable pulled a disappointed face. "There's nothing much on the phone, I'm afraid. The tech people got into it, but it looks like he was either a habitual deleter or he didn't have many incoming messages or calls. I'll get onto his phone company to access his records. The PC will be my job for today, so I'll keep an eye out for any references to a hotel booking and messages from a new girlfriend or boyfriend. I'd hate to have to ring round all the hotels and guest houses in the Woodhall or East Kirkby area to see if we can locate him and find out whether he'd made a joint booking."

"There was no mailbox on his phone?" Ashok asked.

Ben shook his head. "Nope. He accessed his mail through Safari. Actually, the lack of apps in general seems a bit odd if he was in IT, so he shouldn't have been a technophobe."

"It's not necessarily odd," Danielle said. "I've got a mate, Rod, who refuses to have anything on his phone that's got an automatic login. He says it's a matter of security. Even fingerprint or facial recognition doesn't work a hundred percent of the time in terms of stopping unauthorised access. His brother could activate Rod's banking app, and they're not that similar in appearance."

Robin brought the discussion back to Mark's phone, as opposed to Rod's, interesting as the digression was. "Did they get into his mail via his browser, then?"

"Yes, although he had very little in his inbox and what he didn't chuck he labelled and filed. I'll be going through any stuff he's got squirreled away."

"If he was supposed to be staying with someone—or meeting them—then why didn't they realise something was up and try to call him? Habitual deleter or not, he couldn't erase his call records if he was already dead," Pru pointed out.

"Agreed," Ben said, "although they might have called him after his battery ran out, couldn't get through, and didn't want to leave a message. Nothing suspicious in that, because lots of people hate using answerphones. Anyway, they may have thought he'd stood them up and gone, 'Sod him, then.'"

All of which was true. It was far too easy to assume someone's actions were dodgy when there was a perfectly reasonable explanation. "Well, that'll keep you busy, Ben. Ashok, before we head off into the wilds of Bedfordshire, could you see if any service personnel were still based in the general Woodhall Spa area as late as 1947 or early 1948? Don't overwork it, I'd simply—and personally—like an idea of whether Mark's mum could have been a war baby. Of course, we may be able to get that information from our mate Ryan. Who wants to volunteer for that?"

"Talk to Ryan again?" Ben pulled a horrified face, as though Robin had asked for a volunteer to go and clean the men's toilets. "Can I be excused, sir? I know there's no harm in him and he's really well-meaning, but he's so boring. He rambled on last time and I zoned out. He could drop in some vital piece of evidence and I'd miss it among all the details of who he met and every word they said and what Ryan thought when they were saying it. Can't someone else have a go?"

"*I'll* talk to him," Pru said. "He can't be that bad. Maybe he'll respond better to a different person or to a woman."

"Good luck with that, then." Robin grinned. "Maybe you could play the 'think of me as your mother' card and scare him into giving concise answers. We need everything we can on what Mark had found out and how it might relate to the weekend away he'd booked."

Sliding off the desk he'd been perched on, Robin headed for his office to clear some decks before they hit the road. He was five minutes in when Ben knocked on the door.

"Contents of that waste bin have been put back together, sir." He proffered Robin a pile of taped papers. "I've had a look through and they seem like they're the results of a sort-out. Torn-up bills from a couple of years ago, that kind of thing. Exception is this one on the top. Seems his printer cartridge ran out."

Robin nodded. The faded text on the page faded completely after a couple of lines, as though Mark had been printing off a wodge of material and not keeping an eye on it.

You can do this. You're strong.

It doesn't feel right.

The last line faded, barely legible. *It may not but you've got it. Remember . . .*

"What do you make of it?" Robin asked.

"Not sure. Could be a copy of a conversation. Could be the draft of a novel." Ben grinned. "I wondered if it dated from the same time as the bills and had somehow got among them."

"Ryan told us Mark had got some stuff off Suzy's phone that backed up a theory he had." That little nugget had got lost among Aunty Josephine and the cruise and the adopted baby. "Could be this and he's taken it to mean they were talking her out of traditional therapy."

"While it wasn't?"

"Who knows? I don't remember seeing anything else like this, though."

"Me neither. Want me to go back and search again?"

Robin considered for a moment. "Put it on hold until we've spoken to the brother and followed up what he has to say. We need to know what we're looking for."

"Will do, sir. I'll go through these again, though." The constable scooped up the papers and exited, leaving Robin speculating about whether the answers they needed lay here or in Lincolnshire. He had the awful feeling he and Ashok would be completing the journey Mark hadn't been able to.

Kevin Bircher might have had his lower leg in plaster for a broken metatarsal, but he was a damn sight more mobile than he'd suggested over the phone. While he couldn't have driven himself from Bedford down to Abbotston, he could have *been* driven, and there appeared to be no reason he couldn't have got into the local police station. Still, bearding the lion in his den was always useful, and the impression Kevin's house gave reinforced the view that he wouldn't get off his backside unless he had no choice. The exterior paintwork was badly in need of attention, as was the side gate, which was rotten in places.

Kevin greeted them at the door before they rang, saying that his wife was on night shift at the moment so was presently in bed asleep. "She's a nurse at the local hospital," he explained, as he ushered them into the sitting room. No offer of refreshments was forthcoming, so it was as well that they'd got to Bedford early and had been able to stop off for a cuppa beforehand. Please God the M25 would be as kind on the return journey.

Once he and Ashok were settled, with a view of the back garden, Robin suspected there might be an old-fashioned delineation of domestic duties operating in the Bircher household. The interior of the house was clean and tidy, the windows spotless and the flower beds well-tended, whereas the lawn was a straggly, weed-strewn mess that spoke of recent neglect. Kevin's domain whereas the rest was his wife's?

"Do you need us to come and identify Mark?" Bircher asked, as he sat down with what seemed to be an over-theatrical wince as he manoeuvred his leg into place. The question seemed to be begging for the answer no.

"Not unless you want to come and see him. Suzy's parents have already done that duty, this morning. As soon as they could get in," Robin added, not able to resist a dig at a witness he'd taken an instant dislike to.

"That's good." The implied criticism was either being ignored or was water off this duck's back. "I'll pass on the offer of viewing the body because I don't want to see him like that."

"Didn't you see his picture in the papers or on the news?" The constable was remarkably chipper, having shared the driving duties with Robin and having been spared the usually fraught M25 stretch past Heathrow airport. It would be interesting to see how he coped with it on the way home, as it was unlikely to be flowing as freely as had been the case earlier.

"We don't get a paper. Can't stand the tripe they print." Kevin broke into a sneer. "So, it was a hell of a shock when we saw the story on the BBC website. That was after he'd been named, and I was getting people messaging me to ask if we were related."

"When was that?" Ashok pressed him.

The question seemed to catch Kevin on the hop. "What's today? Friday. It must have been Wednesday evening. All the days run together when you're stuck here. I'm a delivery driver, you see, so I can't work at present. On sick leave." Kevin didn't appear too upset at the fact.

"Why didn't you contact *us* at that point?" Robin asked. Surely being bone idle couldn't entirely explain his behaviour?

Kevin spread his hands. "I assumed you'd be ringing *me* if you needed to talk."

"Not being telepathic, we didn't know you existed at that point." Robin took a deep breath. Acting snarky wasn't going to help. "Did you have a reason why you didn't want us to talk to you?"

"Should I have?"

Ashok, from whose ears the metaphorical steam was clearly rising, said, "Please don't answer a question with a question. It isn't going to help track down your brother's killer."

When Kevin didn't respond apart from staring at his cast, the constable ploughed on. "Were you close to him?"

"Not really. He was younger and always used to tag along with me and my mates when we were kids. Typical annoying little brother." Kevin paused, face for the first time showing any emotion at his loss. Perhaps the reality was only hitting home now. "We didn't have much contact these days, but I am going to miss him. Nobody to buy me a stupid Christmas present, for one thing." He paused, voice catching.

Robin motioned to Ashok: they needed to give the witness a bit of time to compose himself.

After a few moments, Kevin said, "Okay, you can get on with the grilling. I've pulled myself together."

"We'll try to make it as little like a grilling as possible." Robin nodded. "Had your brother fallen foul of anyone who might have wanted to hurt him?"

"I don't know. There's a bit of a back story with the parents, but I can't believe it went that far."

"Go on."

"Well, I assume you know his wife, Suzy, had cancer, so there was needle between Mark and her interfering parents, and he wasn't best pleased with the health professionals who treated her. Or failed to treat her."

Robin raised his hand. "Hold on. We've been told she didn't actually die of cancer but of complications from Covid."

"Same difference. Mark reckoned if she hadn't been so ill to start with, she'd probably have shaken the virus off." Kevin waved the interruption away. "Anyhow, you asked about my brother falling foul of people. It's just struck me that if he'd been killed at another place and time, then it could make sense. For example, if he'd gone to the local hospital and got into a fight with one of the consultants in the clinic, especially if that had happened just after she'd told him her prognosis, because he was livid at the time. Livid enough to ring me up for a chat. But getting killed in the woods sounds like a random mugging rather than anything personal."

"Except that he appears only to have had his keys taken at the time of death. Not his wallet and not his phone," Ashok said. "Any idea why somebody would have wanted his car?"

Kevin shook his head. "It wasn't a flash model, like a Merc. I'd have thought it likelier they'd have taken the keys to get into his house."

"Why? Did he have stuff there that was worth nicking?"

"Only what the average person would, apart from the Jack Russell."

Ashok shot Robin a puzzled glance. "Did he have a dog, sir?"

"There was no evidence of one when we visited his house. What's so funny?" Robin bridled as Kevin startled to chortle.

"Not a *dog*. A different Jack Russell. He kept wicket for England—I thought you'd have known that, Constable—and now he does painting. Dad bought two of them, so Mark and I got one each."

Robin wondered if Ashok had noticed the jibe about cricket and how he'd react. While not necessarily racist, it was stereotyping at its worst: not every Brit of sub-continental family origin was into the leather on willow game.

"Never heard of him," the constable said, with a snarky edge to his voice that confirmed he'd logged the remark.

"This is one of his," Kevin said, clearly oblivious to any offence caused. He pointed to a small oil painting, one that was pleasing despite employing what might be seen as unrealistic colours. Robin had seen a similar one to it, in what appeared to be an identical frame, in the study at Tumulus Gardens. "It's worth about a grand, I'd say."

"Well, it's still there at Mark's house, so the killer couldn't have been targeting that," Robin said. "Anyway, we don't think his house has been entered. His car has turned up in a car park at Kinechester, though, with the parking fee paid after he was dead."

"Free of any fingerprints on the high touch areas, except for Mark's, and many of those were smudged, so whoever drove it wore gloves," Ashok added.

Robin returned to what Kevin had implied when he'd said the two sons had got one painting each. "Did your father leave you the paintings when he died?"

"No, he's still alive. In body, anyway. We got them when we cleared the house last year, when Dad had to go into a home. That was hard on the heels of Mum dying—I think he'd been on the wane for a while and either he was hiding it for her sake or her death was the last straw. That and the pandemic, which threw everyone, didn't it? Dad's in a place a couple of miles outside Cambridge, so I get to see him as often as I can, although I'm not sure if those visits are to benefit him or me."

The affection with which Kevin had referred to his parents was in marked contrast to the way he'd spoken about his brother. Another assumption gone astray. Robin would have guessed that Mark would have been the one to want his father close at hand, despite having nothing concrete to base that opinion on.

"Did Mark come up and visit him?" Robin asked.

"Not often, although that's maybe understandable what with all the stuff about Suzy and not only the calls on his time. When you're losing one person, you don't want to be confronted with another one." That was a valid—and empathetic—point. "He might have been meaning to call in at the home on the way to or from Woodhall. It wouldn't be far off his route."

Ashok looked up sharply from making notes. "You knew Mark was supposed to be going to Woodhall this past weekend?"

"Yes. We exchanged texts when I hurt my leg, and he told me he was going to be getting a few days away for the first time in ages. I didn't make a note of exactly when he was going to be travelling because he wasn't due to be calling on us."

"Was he travelling on his own?" Ashok asked.

"With a friend? I doubt it. Very solitary, our Mark." That was stated as fact, without any judgement.

"Surely not entirely solitary, given that he'd been married," Robin pointed out. "Could he have been in a new relationship?"

Kevin evidently had to think about that one. "He didn't say, although it's quite possible. I know he was in a total state about Suzy's death, but a man has to move on sometime. It may have been too soon, only a few months after her death, although who knows what could have happened if he'd met somebody with the right shoulder to cry on. I guess he'd been mourning Suzy even before she died. Perhaps it was as well that Covid got her when it did. Rather than a drawn-out, horribly painful death."

Robin turned the discussion to Woodhall. "Was Mark into military history? He had another visit lined up to the area. East Kirkby, which is an old airfield that's now a museum."

"I don't think he was into going to poke around aircraft, although it might have been another new passion. Like family history was. I'm probably telling you what you already know, so stop me if you need to, but when Mum was at the end of her life, a couple of years back, she told us both that she'd been adopted. It didn't bother me a jot because I've no interest in whether my granny was my granny in terms of her DNA, although it began to get into Mark's head big time. Especially when he was dealing with Suzy's illness and her being in denial about it for so long. He had the feeling that life was being unfair to him on all counts, you know? A real sense of injustice." Kevin, again with a touch of theatricality, adjusted the position of his leg. Perhaps he'd become so engrossed in the conversation he'd forgotten it was supposed to be giving him a lot of trouble.

"Your father couldn't furnish any information about the adoption?"

"Nope. He was as surprised as we were. She'd apparently been too ashamed to tell him, which did strike me as odd, and apparently the only birth certificate he'd seen had the people he knew as his in-laws listed on it and came from the registry office in Peterborough. I know about that, because when I saw Mark at Suzy's funeral he was moaning about how we'd likely never know the truth. I suggested that maybe Mum hadn't been adopted, that she'd got increasingly confused as she was ailing. He went ballistic." Kevin rolled his eyes. "He started banging on about her being as sane as anyone and how that certificate could have been manipulated. You know, a dodgy clinic or an obliging midwife—baby gets scooted off when newly born and the new parents register the child under their own names rather than that of the actual mother and father. Who'd check?"

Who indeed. Hadn't there been plenty of stories emerging over the years about dubious practices around unmarried mothers in the delivery room? Clearly Kevin had given the topic more thought than he'd let on, unless Mark had given him a full briefing. And if the latter had become as obsessed with the matter as it appeared, perhaps he had. "Can we talk to your father?"

"You can try but I think it would be a waste of your time. Our parents had us quite late in life and time's taken its toll. And his dementia has probably been made worse by his heading big leather footballs for years. He was a professional, before he ran a sports shop." Pride swelled in Kevin's voice. "Never at the highest level, although he turned out for Cambridge United and the Posh."

"Peterborough," Ashok said, with an appreciative nod.

"That's right. Anyway, if you do go to see him, I'd take what he says with a whole cellar of salt, let alone a pinch." Kevin wagged his finger. "I wouldn't be surprised if he'd forgotten what he knew about Mum or deliberately didn't want to remember. If that makes sense."

"It does. How did Mark feel about that?"

"How do you think? It added to his paranoia—if that's not too strong a word. He kept banging on about how people wouldn't be straight with him. Not the highest level of emotional intelligence, our Mark." Kevin sighed.

"If you could give me the contact details for the home, we'll give them a ring. Might as well try to see him while we're up here. We won't lose much by doing it." Apart from a couple of hours when they could have been on the road. "Before you get us the phone number, and now that you've had time to think, can we just check again that there's nobody who might have resented Mark?"

"Apart from the average Exeter or Harlequins supporter who's still annoyed at Saracens and that salary cap business? That's a joke, by the way. No. Nobody."

Robin believed him. "And we have to ask this. What were you doing on Saturday?"

"What do you think?" Kevin tapped his leg. "Resting this and watching the sport on the telly. Mags—my wife—can vouch for that because she had the day off before she started her run of nights."

Which seemed entirely plausible too.

They rang the nursing home as soon as they were back in the car, but any thought of going there that afternoon was soon discarded. The sister on duty told them that Mr. Bircher had the flu and was quite poorly with it, so not only was the man in no fit state to receive visitors, he was particularly confused at the moment. It would be unlikely that he could give a lucid answer to any questions they put.

Robin was about to hit the road for home when a call came through from Pru.

"I wish you could see us, sir," the sergeant said. "I've been raising my arms in surrender and Ben's got the smuggest grin I've ever seen plastered all over his gob. Because I've got to admit it, I was wrong and he was every shade of right. I rang Ryan for what I thought would take five or ten minutes."

"It's an hour of your life you won't get back," Ben shouted in the background.

"An hour?" Robin asked.

"Not quite." Pru snorted. "Ben's offered to take him next time. If there *is* a next time."

"That's noble but we should share the pain. It'll do Ashok here the world of good to have to deal with Ryan. He's just winced at the suggestion." Robin grinned at the constable's discomfort. "Think of it as an important part of your career development. You can use him as an example in job interviews of when you've had to deal with a tricky witness."

"We'd risk channelling him and boring the panel to death, sir. Anyway, in amongst his aunt's medical history and a beginner's guide to cruising, he confirmed that Mark was looking into his mother's family and that they'd made some progress. Ryan was ninety percent certain they'd found Mark's mother and that she was born in or near Kirkby on Bain, which isn't far from RAF Coningsby, where the memorial flight is. While they hadn't tracked down who Mark's grandfather was, they both suspected he might have been stationed there. Based on nothing but intuition, which Ryan told me about ad nauseam."

Mark didn't appear to have shared that with his brother, though. "Did Ryan happen to say—in amongst all the other stuff—whether that was why Mark was supposed to be up in Lincolnshire this weekend? Searching parish records or whatever it is these people do to make the ninety percent certainty into a hundred?"

"That was part of it. He was apparently going to see a bloke on Sunday who might be his great-uncle. I'll email you all the details in a minute, because while Ryan only provided the name, Danielle's been like mustard getting an address and a landline number. The chap's called Thomas McKay and he's younger than his sister would have been."

"She's dead, then?" If Miss McKay had given birth to Mark's mother at sixteen, as a ballpark estimate, that would make her ninety now.

"Ryan doesn't know one way or the other. That's one of the reasons Mark was meeting Thomas. To see if they'd identified the right woman as his gran and whether there was any chance of seeing her."

"Did you get a sense of why Mark was so obsessed about his biological family? Not as if *he* was adopted."

"I didn't. People *do* get bees in their bonnet, though. I had a friend who was a serial obsessive. Every year a new 'thing.' Maybe Mark was like that." Pru sighed. "Does any of that help?"

"I'm certain it will in the long run." Given time and more information, Mark's fixation might make perfect sense. "Ashok and I are probably heading north, then. I only hope that—given Thomas's surname—we don't end up having to drive all the way to Inverness."

"What's that about Inverness, sir?" Ashok asked, when the call had ended.

Robin summarised what Pru had told him, concluding with, "I was joking about driving to Scotland, purely based on the McKay bit. I don't remember seeing that or any other surnames on the maternal family tree in Mark's study, though."

"Maybe he didn't want to fill the names in until he was entirely sure," the constable said. "Tempting fate, if you know what I mean."

"I do indeed. Ryan seems to be on the ball if he's already turned all that up." Hopefully he could do the same for Robin's mother, who might be upset at not seeing her best boy any time soon. He'd need to make a couple of phone calls home as soon as he knew whether McKay could see them. "When Pru's sent the stuff, we'll give Thomas McKay a call. It won't be that far to travel, although we might want to make it an overnight job."

"Do you think he can tell us much, sir?"

"I have no idea. What I do know is that if we don't chat to him, I'll be left wondering if we've missed a trick. Mark didn't seem to be that close to his brother or his father-in-law and he didn't have his father to confide in, so it's possible he grabbed at another male relative to develop a relationship with." Rather like Robin, he might have been grabbing at straws.

Torn between satisfaction at what they'd learned and gloom that he likely wouldn't be home this evening, he forced a smile.

"Want me to find us a hotel, sir?"

"Get some options lined up while I try to get hold of Mr. McKay. We could be walking in the steps of the Dambusters soon."

Chapter Eight

Friday late afternoon brought Adam news that Robin was going to be using the overnight bag he'd packed. He and Ashok were off to the Woodhall Spa area and had stopped for a comfort break, so Robin was taking the chance to get in touch while Ashok was off somewhere ringing his girlfriend whom he'd be standing up that evening.

"Thanks to some neat work by Ryan French, we're in search of the guy who might be Mark's great-uncle. Plan is to interview him on Saturday morning about his sister Moira. I'm hopeful that Ryan could definitely help Mum if he's tracked down a birth family so quickly. Maybe at some point I'll be thinking of meeting *my* biological great-uncle." Robin sounded surprisingly wistful at the prospect.

"He might have been the one who left all this money. I say *all*—" Adam snorted "—because we don't know if it'll turn out to be seventy-three pounds and eighty-two pence."

"That would be enough for a pub lunch. I have had one unsettling thought, though. If abortions had been acceptable back when my dad was conceived, then there'd have been no *me* now."

"Don't go having an existential crisis. Your mum would still have been around, so it would only have been a slightly different you."

"That makes sense. It worries me less than if there'd been no murder at Lindenshaw school, because that might have meant there was no *us*."

The conversation ended with some endearments, one bonus of Ashok not being within earshot.

When Adam got home, Mrs. Bright was already ensconced in the kitchen. She didn't seem too disappointed about her son not being there, possibly because Robin had explained the night before that Adam would have plenty to update her on, including the details of someone who could help her.

"I suppose you've grown used to his unusual hours, like I did," she said, once Adam had cast the dust of the working day from himself and a bottle of white had been opened. "It's not quite the same as when he was still living at home, because in those days he was merely a constable so he didn't have the responsibility, but there could still be long days to work. When he was part of a team working on a big case, I'd make sure we lived on things that could be reheated quickly. I always wanted him to eat with his dad and me, if we could manage it."

"I bet. It's good to have some comforting routine amongst the uncertainty." Adam settled on a kitchen stool, enjoying the aromas from the stove and a heap of affection from Hamish. "I was half-prepared for this kind of life, anyway. In theory teachers might keep regular hours and get all the school holidays off, but in reality we don't. A bit more predictable work-wise than coppers, though. This little lad will have to get used to the unpredictability too."

"He'll not know anything different. He didn't start with only one of you to care for him like Campbell did." Mrs. Bright put her hand to her mouth. "Should I have mentioned him? I didn't want to upset you."

"You're okay, Alison. He was a good age for the breed, and I think I'm getting to the point I can believe he went in the way he'd have liked to go. Quick, relatively painless—or so the vet says—and in a blaze of glory."

"You'll have to make sure Hamish doesn't attempt any such heroics." The dog had come to investigate what she was up to and got a tickle behind the ear as a reward.

"We've thought of bringing him up believing he's a cat so he doesn't have any thoughts of doing water rescues, but Robin reckons it's in his nature and there's no point fighting it."

"Well, don't you forget that losing a dog hits you like any kind of grief. It'll take longer than you think to get completely back on an even keel, and there'll be steps backwards on the way." Mrs. Bright sipped some wine. "Don't tell Robin I told you this, but he was in buckets of tears when he came round and broke the news. Started talking about your wedding and Campbell carrying the rings." She blinked back a tear. "Right, Alison, you're getting unnecessary. Change the subject and get dinner on the plate."

Adam helped her serve up, then they took the food and wine to the already laid-up dining table. Once they were a few mouthfuls in—and after a stern word to Hamish about remembering his manners—they turned to the inheritance.

"I don't know how much Robin's told you about what's happened the last few days," Adam said. "Probably not a lot, given the other things he has on his mind. I suspect he would have quite welcomed the distraction tonight would have brought. He's also frustrated he can't do more for you."

"I'm grateful he's managed anything at all. He said something about the fraud department."

"Yes. His mate Henry works there and seems pretty confident this inheritance is above board, unless it's a scam they've not encountered yet. *New times, new crimes.*" Adam laughed.

"I like that. Is it from when you do Staying Safe Online with your pupils?"

"No. I made it up, spur of the moment, but I'll have to use it in the future. Anyway, Henry managed to prize a bit of gen from your solicitor, some of which I can update you on."

"Ah." Mrs. Bright gestured with her knife. "I did wonder, because Mr. Caswell rang me to say he'd had police contact. I had to explain."

"I hope that didn't cause difficulties?"

"Not at all. I think he was quite impressed I was taking— What did he call it?—due diligence. He knows about Robin's job anyway, so he'd have guessed who'd put Henry on the trail." She scooped up some gnocchi. "One of my better efforts, this. I've put a couple of portions aside to freeze for both of you."

"You're a star." The meal was certainly proving a gastronomic treat: simple yet good-quality food, well prepared. Maybe it was a sign of age that Adam preferred this kind of meal to something experimental and exotic. "Did your Mr. Caswell mention tax treaties?"

"Yes. He said he couldn't say much but I should research them, which I did on Google, although I'm not sure I'm much the wiser. Was Henry behind that?"

"I believe so. He was hoping the stratagem could help narrow down where the money's coming from, geographically. The solicitor was playing his confidentiality card on that, so Henry leaned on him a bit to clarify the position tax-wise. It must have worked, because Mr. Caswell told Henry that the money hadn't had inheritance tax paid on it in the country of origin because that country didn't have such a tax in place."

"How nice. Or is it? What do you think, Hamish?" Mrs. Bright must have worried that the dog was feeling left out of the human conversation. "I guess you have to raise money somehow or other, unless you want to cut back on public services. I wouldn't want to be a politician and make those decisions."

"We won't let Hamish go into politics, either." Adam grinned at the dog's puzzled expression. "Henry's sure that New Zealand has no tax on legacies, but before you assume he's hit bull's-eye with his first dart, Australia doesn't, either. There could be a whole raft of Commonwealth countries in that category, although the information could be useful alongside the family history stuff."

Mrs. Bright nodded. "I'll be like Robin with one of his investigations. Putting various clues together to build up a picture. I hope his case is moving on."

"He's certainly getting plenty of information." He didn't seem that optimistic it was getting him closer to the killer, however. "He'll probably be grumpy that I said this, but the case is a bit near to home. The dead bloke's mother was adopted, although he didn't know until she was at the end of her life. He was on the trail of his biological grandparents, which is why Robin's gone off to Lincolnshire, to talk to the guy's great-uncle. He's told his team about the similarity to his dad."

"Very sensible. Otherwise, some bright spark's bound to make a thoughtless comment." They finished eating and topped up their glasses before she continued. "I wish you'd known David. He'd have liked you. And the dogs."

"That's what Robin always says. That the pair of us would have gone off to the pub, leaving you two to wonder what we would be talking about together."

Mrs. Bright giggled, the wine clearly having an effect. "That sounds right. I think—Robin doesn't know any of this, so don't go telling tales out of school—the one reservation David did have about Robin being gay was that he'd have come home with somebody like Larry Grayson on his arm. You probably don't remember him, but he was as camp as a scout's outing. I mean, David would have been charming and not said anything, because parents shouldn't have a view on their child's choice of partner, as long as they don't go knocking them about."

"I'm with you on that." Adam had seen too much parental interference among his friends, gay or otherwise.

"But he'd have definitely preferred a bloke's bloke. Like you are."

Adam would take that in the spirit it was offered. He'd come across plenty of camp gay men—plenty of camp straight guys too—and more power to their elbows if that was the way they were. As the pupils at Wickley were encouraged to think, people were all different, on the outside and the inside and they were all of the same worth. But it would be stupid to ignore the fact that some of the stereotyping on the TV and radio through the years hadn't helped the cause of equality. If every fictional gay man people encountered was a screaming queen, it would naturally lead to people thinking all gay blokes were like that.

"If we're talking about not telling tales out of school, then I'm going to hold you to the same promise," Adam said. "Robin's having a few doubts about what his dad really felt about being adopted. I know your David made it plain to his son that he had no interest in who gave birth to him, but was that a white lie? Not least to himself?"

"Oh, bless him. This case has given Robin a right shake, hasn't it?" If the white wine was making Mrs. Bright a touch giggly and rather flushed on the cheeks, it wasn't affecting her perceptiveness. "I could have a word with him, offer a bit of reassurance, although seeing as we're not supposed to be having this part of the conversation, I can't offer it out of the blue."

"We'll have to be subtle. You *can* reassure him, then?"

"To an extent. David did have the odd wobble." She paused, no doubt collecting herself. "I'll tell you all about it over a bowl of crumble, and then you can decide how much you want to share. You can say I got maudlin over the wine, then let it all come out, and I'll pretend I can't remember much about what I said or why."

"You're a treasure, Alison." Adam kissed her cheek, and they set about clearing the table.

The crumble smelled wonderful—so wonderful that Hamish had to be threatened with locking in the kitchen if he didn't leave off trying to cadge bits at the dining table.

"So, when Robin was small, one of David's cousins was very ill and needed a bone marrow transplant. He's fine now, thank God and modern medicine, but it was touch and go back then and they were testing family members to find a match. Poor David felt really bad that he couldn't make the offer. Nobody in the family blamed him for not putting his name forward, because they all knew what the situation was, but it got to him. Not only that he couldn't help Aaron—the cousin—but that somebody in his birth family might be in the same position and David wouldn't be able to help them, either."

Adam nodded. Robin would probably have had a similar wobble in the same circumstances: he was definitely his father's son. "Robin would have been too young to remember that, I guess, although it could have registered at some level and be the cause of his disquiet."

"That's possible. I managed to come up with a good solution, though. I got David to sign up with a bone marrow register, so if one of his biological relatives *did* need help, they'd be able to match him. It doesn't mean he wanted to be found, though."

Mrs. Bright seemed sure of that. "*I'm* the one on the trail and this mysterious inheritance has given me a great excuse to do it."

"Did you need an excuse?"

Mrs. Bright turned her gaze onto her glass, which she was slowly twirling. "It does feel a night for confessions, so I'll add another. It's going to sound totally daft, but Clare lent me one of those crime books she likes. It was better than the usual twaddle she reads—don't tell *her* I said that, either—and the story concerned a murder that resulted from people keeping family secrets to themselves rather than making everything plain. I know that's not what's happened with David, although it left me feeling upset. I wanted to get to the bottom of whatever had gone on with his parents. I'm guessing it's nothing other than the usual story of an unmarried girl finding herself up the duff and having no alternative than do what people were telling her was the best for her baby. I'd like to know, though." She faced Adam again. "Does that make sense?"

"Perfect sense, as far as it goes. I'd appreciate it if you'd tell me the whole truth." Adam briefly squeezed his mother-in-law's hand.

"Am I that obvious?"

"Only to someone who cares for you and doesn't want you or your best boy hurt."

Mrs. Bright paused, then forced a smile. "This money, Adam. What if it's from Robin's biological grandparent and turns out to be the proceeds of crime, which is why they're being so secretive?"

Adam stifled a laugh; she was serious. "Maybe Henry from the fraud department could hold your solicitor's hand to make sure he covers all the angles in checking it's legit. He'd do it for Robin's sake."

"I'll suggest that. I don't want it plastered all over *The Sun* that Robin's benefitted from laundered money. Which is also part of why I want to find out about David's parents. I know me poking around in his family might dig up all sorts of unsavoury things, but Robin would want to know one way or the other, surely? Before someone else discovered the dirt and made trouble."

Adam thought of the tabloids at their worst, then remembered the conversation in the car heading home from Mrs. Bright's. "He's aware of the risks and he knows he can cope with whatever emerges. As long as he's got us to help him."

"You're a star." Mrs. Bright blew her nose, clearly pulling herself together.

"Thanks. This star agrees to support your point of view but you two need to pick your way through the revelations together, as well." Adam pushed his plate away. "Now, if and when this money turns out to be squeaky clean, do you have any secret plans for what you'll do with it?"

The conversation moved on to the many choices Mrs. Bright had before her, a round-the-world cruise with Clare apparently being number one if the total ran to that, although her conscience was pricking her to make a big donation to the RSPCA. The discussion lasted until they'd stacked the dishwasher, let Hamish have a run around the garden, and got themselves comfy in the lounge, with glasses topped up and the dog snoozing on the carpet.

"Before I forget," Adam said, "there's a witness in Robin's case who was working with the dead bloke to find his mother's birth family, and we think he's been successful. This guy's not a suspect because he's got a solid alibi, unless he's somehow faked being on a cruise with his aunt. We thought he could be useful to you. I gave his website the once-over and his charges aren't unreasonable, compared to what some similar services are quoting."

With an air of nonchalance that would fool nobody, Mrs. Bright said, "What's his name?"

"Ryan French."

Mrs. Bright licked her forefinger and made a stroke in the air. "One up to Alison. I've already contacted him. Actually, we're meeting tomorrow for a pubby lunch and a chat. I don't think he knows I'm connected to Robin."

That was a blessed coincidence. "Great minds think alike. Why him?"

"He's local, and one of the testimonials on his website appeared to be from somebody I knew. I contacted her and she said he's the business." Mrs. Bright giggled again. "As far as families are concerned, I mean. He's supposed to be a bit on the boring side, bless him."

"We were going to warn you about that. You'll need to keep him to the point or else you'll be hearing all about his aunt and his cruise and everything he's ever done."

"Perhaps you and Hamish could come along and keep him under control? Given that Robin won't be back until late afternoon at the earliest."

"Sounds great. Hamish can practice his pub etiquette. He hasn't lost his L-plates yet."

On cue, the dog raised his head, gave them both a withering look, and went back to sleep.

Saturday morning dawned dreary. Robin had managed a good night's sleep: the hotel bed proved comfortable and his exhaustion meant he'd gone out like a light. Perhaps they'd take a leisurely breakfast, as they wouldn't be seeing Thomas McKay until ten o'clock, although any thoughts of making the most of the opportunity to explore a bit of the local area beforehand had been put paid to by the weather. He and Ashok would have to make do with coffee, checking emails and reading the complimentary newspapers in the hotel until it was time to hit the road. First, he rang Adam.

"Morning, gorgeous," Robin said, pleased at the fact his husband answered quickly and wasn't still lying in a hungover haze. "How did it go with Mum?"

"Great. Good food, good chat, a bit of a heart-to-heart that I'll tell you all about when you're home. I've just heard her get up so she can't have too much of a headache." Adam certainly sounded chipper.

"How many bottles of wine did you two get through?"

"Only one and a half. We were both yawning by then."

"And you haven't even got an interview with Ryan to blame for that."

Adam laughed. "True. We're meeting him for a pub lunch today, so if anything turns up that we should know about, drop me a text. We could subtly quiz him on it."

"Will do. Can you do the same?"

"Yeah, although I suspect you'll have greater success than us."

"Let's not tempt fate. That was quick work about getting in contact with Ryan, by the way."

"It was all done and dusted before your mum arrived." Adam chuckled. "She'd already emailed him, independent of us, because of a recommendation from a friend. Anything I should be particularly listening out for?"

"I have no idea. I assume that you're experienced enough by now to know what's worth reporting back. Better than some of the constables I've worked with."

"Smooth talker." Adam lowered his voice. "Just to keep you in the loop, a couple of things came out last night about your dad. I think he was telling you the truth about not wanting to know the details surrounding his biological parents, but he did have what your mum called a couple of wobbles." Adam related a story about a crisis of conscience and a much-needed bone-marrow donation. "Your mum seems to have played a blinder on dealing with that—I'll tell you everything when you're home—because you'd probably have been too young to remember it happening. Doubt they'd have told you what was going on, at that age."

Robin nodded, then grinned at himself for doing that when Adam couldn't see him. "I might have picked up something in the air, though."

"That's what I thought. Something that's lurked at the back of your mind and maybe gave you doubts about what he really felt."

"Yeah." Robin would need to process that but, as a theory, it seemed both plausible and reassuring. "We'll have a lot to discuss later."

"Don't we always? Never a dull moment round here."

And Robin was eternally grateful for that state of affairs.

Chapter Nine

I t was only a ten-minute walk through Woodhall Spa to McKay's house, although the risk of being soaked through by the thin yet persistent drizzle made driving there the better option. They parked up on a road that seemed entirely to consist of bungalows that might have been built any time from the sixties onwards. All well-kept, with neat front gardens and little in the way of litter in the gutters, so maybe the locals made a determined effort to preserve their environs.

Mr. McKay was waiting for them at the door and seemed genuinely pleased to meet them, an attitude Robin and his team didn't encounter that often. He shook their hands warmly before ushering them into the little living room where he sat them down on a firm yet comfortable settee. Robin had scanned the man's face—and some photographs on the mantelpiece of what must have been him in his younger days—for any resemblance to Mark Bircher, but all he could spot was a distinctive line to the shaggy eyebrows. A family trait or a case of seeing what he was seeking?

"You'll have to take me as you find me," McKay said, with a grin and a Scottish edge to his voice. "I try to keep things tidy, but since my wife, Dorothy, died, I'm not keeping up with the housework as I should."

"No need to worry, Mr. McKay," Robin said. "You can imagine some of the places we have to visit." He wouldn't judge any man of that generation in the same position and, anyway, there was no real evidence of slovenliness on view.

"Now, we'll have no calling me Mr. McKay. That sounds too much like the chap out of *Porridge*. I'm Tom. You'll be wanting a cup of coffee, I guess?"

"I'm going to decline the offer, if that's okay, because I've had so much coffee already today I might be flying back to Abbotston," Robin said.

"Hmphm." Tom nodded. "You'll not want to get the jitters. How about you, Constable? Dorothy would turn in her grave if I didn't look after my guests."

"A glass of water, please." Ashok's constrained expression suggested he felt he had to ask for something in order to be polite. "Would you like a hand?"

Tom waved the offer away. "Thanks, but I'm fine." He headed off in what must have been the direction of the kitchen.

"Do you think he was offended?" Ashok asked, voice low. "You never know with that generation."

There wasn't an opportunity to answer, because Tom reappeared with a glass of water and a steaming mug among other things on a heavily laden tray. In pride of place was a plate of shortbread; undoubtedly homemade, so either he was more efficient in the kitchen than he'd let on or he had a good supplier in the form of a WI market or similar. Given that Tom wasn't a bad-looking chap for his age—and going by those photographs he'd been a stunner when he was young—some local dab hand at cooking may have set their cap at him and was attempting to plight their troth with baked goods. Ashok clearly found the refreshments welcome, but he was still at the age of hollow legs. For good manners' sake, Robin took the smallest piece of shortbread to nibble at.

Tom, seated again and sipping from his enormous mug, said, "I was shocked to hear about Mark. I'd not met him in person, although we'd spoken over the phone. He seemed a nice lad, and it's such a shame about his wife dying so young. And then him being killed not knowing one way or the other about his granny. Such a shame all round."

"Do you think his gran *was* your sister Moira?" Robin asked. Interesting that their host had shown the most regret at

Mark's murder of anyone they'd yet interviewed. Sorrow at an opportunity missed?

"I do. Based on the dates and what I've pieced together. I'd got all this planned to say to Mark, so I'll tell it to you, save it going to waste. That's the sort of thing a canny Scotsman would do." With a twinkle in his eye, Tom took another sip of coffee, maybe to fortify himself for the tale ahead. "Our family hails from Dundee. I know Mark liked his rugby, so it would have come as a shock to discover he had Scottish blood in him."

"It would give a different outlook on the Calcutta Cup." They should press on, before they were forced to discuss recent results in the fixture. "How did you end up here?"

"We came down because my father got relocated during the war—he was an air mechanic and a handy one with it, they say—so he was drafted into the team at what was a new airfield. He decided he wanted to settle in the area afterwards, because he preferred it to home, so we moved down, in instalments, as it were. My mother came in 1944 and found lodgings nearby. At Dogdyke."

That was another local place, one whose name had struck Robin when he'd been perusing a map. His grandfather had been fond of a song about disappearing train stations and Dogdyke had been one of those, so it had stuck in his mind. With a glance at Ashok to make sure he was getting everything noted, in amongst filling his face, Robin said, "You say you came down in instalments—I assume you and your sister stayed in Dundee when your mother moved?"

"Aye. We were with my grandparents. I was only a wain, born in 1940: a bit of an afterthought, you might say, as Moira was ten years older. If I tell you she was a six-month baby, I'll leave you to figure out the rest. Still, my parents were happy until death did them part, so they must have married for love."

"Six-month baby?" Ashok asked, clearly puzzled.

"I'll explain that to you later." Robin chuckled. "So that we've got all the details straight, when did you and your sister come down here?"

"Moira arrived in early 1945, because our mother had found her a good job, waitressing at a hotel, which was better than she could get at home. I followed her down south on around VJ Day so I could start school. We were a very content family." Tom took another drink of coffee and a piece of shortbread. "Now all the next bit is what I've pieced together, because nobody was going to let a wee lad know that his unmarried sister had gone away to have a baby. I was told Moira had gone off to get further experience by working at a big hotel in London—she'd always had ambitions to do well in her career—and because we'd grown used to being apart for stretches of time, I thought no more of it."

"This was 1948 and she'd gone off to have a baby and give it away for adoption?" Ashok asked.

"Aye. I don't know who the father was or where the baby was born because we only discussed the matter once, when I was a young man myself and her best friend Isabel decided I should know the truth. Moira admitted what had happened, said that it was a mistake any girl could make, especially if she found herself being taken advantage of. She said she never wanted to talk about it again because the little girl she'd had wasn't *her* little girl anymore. I think she was trying to keep herself from being hurt."

Robin nodded. So many echoes of, and possibilities for, his own history. Had his biological grandmother been in the same position, got pregnant by a man who wouldn't stand by her and had she felt the same about her son? "It's an intrusive question—you might call it bloody rude—but given that Moira was conceived out of wedlock, wouldn't your family have been sympathetic?"

"I'm sure they would. In fact, Isabel's pretty certain my mother offered to raise the child as her own. Not unknown in those days, families in which the youngest brother or sister was actually your niece or nephew. But Moira refused to take up that solution. She had a plan for her life, and while she could have left the baby in the care of my parents and got on with her career, I don't think she wanted that emotional draw. Or the feelings her child would have stirred in her every time she visited home. She'd got the chance of a place as a stewardess on the cruise ships, you see, and very successful she was at it. Isabel reckoned Moira could have had her choice of men from among the passengers—with offers of fur coats and all the rest—yet she turned them down. Didn't want to be beholden to a man if she didn't have to be, and that might have included raising his child. I hope Eleanor—that was what Mark said his mother was called—never knew any of this." Tom paused, sniffing back a tear. "I didn't even know the baby's name until he told me."

"Take your time," Robin said. "It can't be easy."

"It's thinking about what my sister was like in the prime of her life," Tom said at last. "You know, we're speaking about her as if she's dead, but she isn't. Although she might as well be. The Moira I knew is long gone."

"Dementia?" Ashok asked, just ahead of Robin. "It's a cruel disease."

"It is that. She went downhill quite rapidly, after a fall, which is often the way. She's well cared for, in a local home, but I rarely visit her nowadays. She doesn't know me and I can't connect with her, so I doubt it would be worthwhile either of you visiting. I think Alex still goes when he can, though."

"Alex?" Had Robin missed a name somewhere?

"Oh, I'd forget my head if it wasn't screwed on." Tom tapped his scalp. "Her son. Alex Hanley. In her midthirties, Moira met a chap called Douglas on the ships. He was a lovely man. Isabel—who always had a view on everything—said he was the only man who could tame Moira, although I suspect she was jealous that she'd not met him first. Douglas and Moira married and had Alex the year that England won the cup. We didn't have any children, me and Dorothy. Well, we had one, but he didn't survive and it's not quite the same with a nephew, is it?"

"I guess not." Robin had detected a hint that Tom and Alex didn't really get on that well. Douglas had been described as *lovely*, but not his son. Perhaps that was why Tom had been so keen to meet Mark—a younger member of the family with whom he could connect? "Can I take a moment to get the names straight? Moira's your sister, Eleanor was her daughter and Isabel's a family friend."

"Aye. Eleanor was Mark's mother and we're assuming she was my niece. Isabel . . ." McKay snorted. "She's a busybody but her heart's in the right place."

Robin nodded. "Just as well Moira had a son afterwards, not another female name for me to juggle with. Can you give us a number for Alex, please? Mark might have been in contact with him."

"I can, although I don't think he could have been. As far as I know, Mark only had my details, and as you're aware, he wasn't yet certain we were related. He wanted us both to do a DNA comparison test, which he'd have paid for. I told him it wouldn't be necessary because I was pretty convinced he was my great-nephew by matching what I knew to what little *he* knew. He sent me a photo too, and he had quite an air of Moira about him. I'd have done the comparison for him, like a flash. Too late now, though, I suppose." Tom wiped his eye.

"You could do a comparison with Kevin if he's interested," Robin suggested.

Tom frowned. "Kevin?"

"Mark's brother." Hadn't he got a mention?

"Ah, I see. Mark said he had a brother, although *he's* apparently not that interested in the family history. If Mark told me what the chap was called, I've forgotten it. It's not only you who struggles with lots of new names." Tom rose. "I'll away and fetch my phone. Alex's number is on there."

A half uncle? Ashok mouthed at Robin, with what appeared to be an attempt at a meaningful look.

"In his fifties, from the year of birth. An ever-expanding family."

As Tom returned with a number for him to jot down, the constable asked, "Is Alex local?"

"He lives in Lincoln, so it's not too far for him to visit here, although I usually get his news when I chat to his wife on the phone. She calls every week." More evidence that Tom and his nephew weren't on the best of terms? "Only you won't catch either of them today because they've been off in their camper van this last fortnight and aren't due back for another week. The perks of working for yourself."

"Any idea where they've been touring?" Robin said nonchalantly, although he knew it would be a long shot to expect Tom not to recognise his growing interest in Moira's son and his whereabouts.

"There's a postcard on the mantelpiece." Tom pointed in its direction.

"I'll get it." Ashok leaped up to fetch the card. He held the thing writing downwards, clearly not wanting to intrude on private messages until offered the chance. "I think I recognise the place, although I can't put a name to it."

"Broadlands. Alex's wife Lucy is a huge fan of the royal family, so they've been ticking off some places on the Prince Philip trail. Isle of Wight for his grandparents' grave, then Broadlands for Mountbatten."

"He and the queen spent part of their honeymoon there too," Ashok said. "My mum has the same fascination with royalty, so she must have shown me pictures."

Tom nodded. "Lucy's dad was one of those who did protection duty for the royals, so it's a personal thing for her."

"I'll tell my mum and she'll be dead jealous." Ashok passed the postcard to Robin.

"May I read this, Tom?" he asked.

"Of course. Nothing to hide. They don't mention meeting Mark, though, if that's what you're seeking," Tom said with a shrug.

"You've seen right through me." The text of the card proved to be the usual stuff about the weather and places visited on the way south. Maybe Lucy had been the one to write it. "When did this arrive?"

"Yesterday morning."

Robin nodded. Most likely it had been sent earlier in the week, although knowing the postal service, that might have extended to the week previously. Of greater significance was the fact that Broadlands wasn't too far a drive from Kinechester and the surrounding towns. For all the jokes about murderous half brothers turning up on doorsteps trying to protect their mother's reputation, here was a half uncle almost on the doorstep at the time Mark Bircher had been killed.

Next step had to be to talk to Alex and his wife. Please God they were still in the local area and hadn't headed off to Cornwall.

Chapter Ten

Late Saturday morning, Adam was giving Hamish a spruce up—how did one young dog manage to accumulate so much muck on his ears?—when his phone notified him of a call from Robin.

"Hiya! You've caught us before we hit the road to the pub. How's life?"

"Interesting. Met a couple of people who've helped fill in some of the details around Mark's life, one of whom gave us some of the best shortbread I've ever tasted. I was given a piece to have later, but there's none for you chaps-who-lunch." Robin chuckled.

"Mean."

"Actually, one of the things that turned up has made me think about *our* family mystery. Mark was rugby mad and it seems his grandmother was Scottish, so I keep thinking how that would mess with a supporter's mind. Mine too, if it turned out my ancestry had an element of one of the other six nations in it. Daft, isn't it?"

"Not a bit daft. I've always thought of myself as a fully paid-up Englishman, shouting for the three lions or the red rose, so if I ever found out I might have a drop of Scottish blood in my veins, I'm not sure how I'd feel about the fact. But whatever the outcome of your mum's enquiries, you're still you and always will be."

"No wonder I love you so much."

"The feeling's mutual." And hopefully it always would be. "What are your plans for the rest of the day?"

"Heading home, in stages. Ashok and I have to go and follow up a new lead this afternoon, but it's only at Oxford, so we can swing round via the A34. Should be home in time for dinner, unless we find out something that sets us off on our travels again. I hope it won't, or else I'll run out of boxer shorts."

"We'll see you when we see you, then." Maybe it was as well that Adam would get a decent lunch and could make do with a roll at dinnertime given the uncertainty. "You can have your portion of yesterday's dinner, reheated. That's a treat, not a punishment. There's crumble for pud too."

"Excellent. I'll have earned it."

"Is Ashok's driving that bad?"

"No, he's coming on. We'll see what he makes of the dual carriageway stretch down from the M40."

"Yeah. That's always trickier than it should be." Adam's mum had vowed she'd never drive on it again and that the intersection with the M4 was a nightmare. "What's up, then?" Because clearly something *was* bothering him.

"I'm having the usual doubts about whether we're on the right track, despite it being my favourite track. Friends and family. When you see Ryan, could you casually mention that I've been to Lincolnshire to see Mark's great-uncle, and that we've been put on the trail of his mum's half brother, then see where that leads?"

"Will do. Although I'll have to drop the bombshell that we're married, for a start, because I don't think your mum let on and he may not connect the surname. If Ryan's a rampant homophobe, he might storm out on us. Potential clients or not."

Robin grunted. "I've met him. If I had to place a bet, I'd say he rides on our bus."

"I'll see if I'd put *my* money on that." Not that either of their gaydars were terribly reliable. "I'll tell him about your travels. Anything in particular you want to know?"

"If Ryan knew about this half uncle, for a start. If Mark had mentioned him at any point over the last few weeks, especially if he spoke about meeting up with the bloke. Said uncle has been travelling around down our way over the last week or so. It may be nothing other than a big coincidence he was there, although something important must have drawn Mark to Kings Ride Woods."

"Okey-dokes. Should I fess up about you at start or end of lunch, by the way?" At the start would make it less likely to catch Ryan off his guard and so reduce the chance of an offhand remark. At the end didn't feel like fair play, although Adam wasn't bound by the Police and Criminal Evidence Act.

"Do it at the start. I don't want a defence barrister screaming, 'Entrapment!'"

"Will do. I'll brief your mum in advance too. She may not want us using her meet-up to do some subtle detecting."

"Knowing Mum, she'll relish being involved."

"I can see me being her wingman. Don't forget the milk, by the way."

"I won't. Don't you forget it, either."

"It's code," Adam explained to Hamish, as he ended the call and went back to tending the dog's ears.

Mrs. Bright had chosen to meet Ryan at The Lamb and Flag, a pub about five miles from where Adam lived and one that was fast building up a reputation as a gastropub. They settled at their allotted table in the conservatory, Hamish evidently delighted to be given a bowl of water and a handful of dog biscuits.

"Get a load of that face," Adam said. "He thinks he's the king of the bar."

"He *is*." Mrs. Bright patted the Newfoundland. "A prince, anyway. Ooh, is that Ryan coming in? He said he'd wear a vivid red tie so that I'd recognise him."

"Mrs. Bright?" A chap in his thirties—not bad looking, well dressed and bearing a briefcase—came over to their table. "Lovely to meet you. Is this your son?"

"No. This is Adam, my son-in-law. Robin's husband." Mrs. Bright played her part well. In the car on the way, Adam had explained about the need to be upfront, and she'd suggested it would be less awkward if *she* broached the subject. "The same

Robin Bright you met when you were so helpful about the murder case."

"Oh!" Ryan's surprised expression soon turned to one of delight. "How terribly exciting. I would never have guessed the Chief Inspector would have been . . . you know . . . or that the police force would be so enlightened. Is that why you contacted me, Mrs. Bright, because your son had run across me already? It's not a problem if so."

"Call me Alison, please." She flashed him a smile. "And it's a total coincidence. The lads had no idea I was after professional help, nor that I'd found someone local. When I saw a friend's name—Natalie Dow—among the people giving testimonials on your website, I asked her about you, and she was full of praise."

"That's wonderful." Ryan sat down, laid his briefcase on the spare seat, and gave Hamish—who had clearly put himself on scrutiny duty—a friendly pat. "Obviously I hope this will be the start of a productive working relationship between us, but as I said over the telephone, it's important that we feel we can get on with each other before I start to do any research. All sorts of personal things can come out that people subsequently decide might have been better hidden." He turned to Adam. "Since I met your husband and that other charming young constable, I've been stewing over whether something I discovered about Mark's family—or something he found out for himself—led to his death."

The frustratingly ill-timed arrival of a waiter to take their orders meant that Adam had lost the natural opportunity to probe, assuming he'd been able to get a word in edgewise.

Again, Mrs. Bright played her part. As soon as the waiter had gone, she said, "Robin would never forgive me if I didn't ask you what you'd concluded with your stewing."

Ryan sat up straighter, almost preening himself at being asked his opinion. "I'm afraid I haven't a lot to tell. Has Robin mentioned what I'd found out for Mark?"

"That his mother was born up in Lincolnshire and that she had an uncle whom Mark was supposed to be visiting the weekend he was killed." Which was only the previous one, although it now seemed a lifetime ago to Adam.

"That's right. What Mark may not have known—because I hadn't seen him since I turned it up and I didn't want to drop the bombshell via a text—is that *he* also had an uncle. *Half* uncle, to be precise. The grandmother married relatively late and had another child."

Adam grinned. "I'm afraid I know that too. Robin's meeting him today, so I'm sorry to steal your thunder."

Ryan returned the smile, evidently unbothered. "I should have known he'd keep you in the loop. Let's see if he told you this, though. The half uncle, Alex Hanley, has a conviction for assault, which was reported all over the Lincolnshire Live local news website. He'd got drunk as a skunk in Skeg-Vegas and belted some bloke who insulted his family. Not a specifically personal insult, as I understand it, just the random kind of slur about female relatives that I won't repeat here. It must have cut too close to the bone, and Alex said he wanted to stick up for his own. He got a suspended sentence."

Adam couldn't recollect any hint that Robin was meeting someone with a criminal past.

"He didn't tell me about an assault, although that means nothing. He meets people with criminal records all the time."

"How do you find all this stuff out?" Mrs. Bright asked, evidently impressed. "I mean, I can see how you'd find the local news stories once you have a name to put into Google, but how do you get the name in the first place? Or is that a trade secret?"

Ryan chuckled, plainly enjoying the banter. "I could be doing myself out of a job now, couldn't I? Mainly it's a matter of knowing where to search, and that comes from years of experience, because it isn't always in the obvious places. Once you have one name—from a register of births or a list of ship's passengers or wherever—then you're away. Often some of the work has already been done for you because somebody else is interested in part of the same family tree, so you find they've laid it out on one of the online sites. You always have to check their work, naturally, because people do make false assumptions that the Freddie Finch they've found is *their* Freddie Finch when it isn't. That first step is the big one, though, and it can be a stroke of luck which helps, like the name on a wedding telegram or a newspaper clipping that somebody kept. Which is what helped in Mark Bircher's case."

Adam, about to excuse himself so he could contact Robin, held his fire, in case there was anything else he needed to report. "A newspaper clipping?"

Ryan nodded. "Mark had found them among his mother's things. There was a whole box of stuff, some of which appeared completely random—to an untrained eye, that is. We were lucky someone hadn't chucked it all, because as I started to go through it, I began to see patterns. The newspaper clippings were all from 1969 or later, although other material, for example cruise liner brochures and postcards from holidays to Scotland, was dated much earlier. Some of those went back to when Eleanor—that was Mark's mother—was only a little girl, so I doubt she'd collected it. I concluded, rightly or wrongly, that her parents might have told her she was adopted when she turned twenty-one and she began to assemble information that she might have felt relevant. I also assumed that her parents had some details about Eleanor's birth mother, and what I subsequently discovered supports that idea."

For once, Ryan paused—to take a drink—at the point things were becoming interesting. What if this was something else that Robin needed to know about before talking to Bircher's uncle?

"You can't leave it at that," Mrs. Bright said, flicking her hand at Ryan's wrist although not actually slapping it. "What was it that helped you up that first big step?"

"The name of a book. In that box there was a list of old titles and their authors. Most were to do with particular Scottish families. You know those kind of glorified pamphlet things you can get in souvenir stores that give a brief insight into some aspect of local history. A couple of the listed titles had notes by them, saying they'd been read. Mark wasn't sure whose handwriting those notes were in but he guessed it could have been his mother's from when she was younger. There was also a note of some novels, which I subsequently discovered have a common theme of abandoned or adopted children. Bunched with *those* was a title that turned out to be nonfiction. Another one of these local little books, although this was about a woman who had a reputation as a bit of a white witch, who lived at Kirkby on Bain. To cut a long story short, I discovered she'd helped local young women who'd found themselves in a difficult situation. Not by the usual herbs and potions which would make the situation go away, if you get my drift, but by delivering the baby safely and finding it a new home. That bit happened via an unnamed vicar she knew who helped childless couples in the Peterborough, Kings Lynn, and Cambridge triangle. Eleanor was registered in Peterborough by the people who adopted her. That was the big clue."

"Why didn't Mark follow any of this through himself?" Adam asked, itching to get on the phone to Robin but still afraid that some gem might be lurking.

Ryan spread his hands. "Like many people, he didn't know where or how to start. Lacked the hands-on experience, for a start. Anyway, I promised I'd cut this story short, so I should. I started poking around the Kirkby on Bain area for a family with a Scottish surname and a daughter of the right age to have a child in 1948, a daughter who might subsequently have worked on cruise ships. About three weeks ago, I hit gold dust on a forum where someone from another branch of the McKay family was following the story from her side. Rumours of an illegitimate child which she was asking about. So, a mixture of knowledge, luck and an ability to follow through family tittle-tattle, which is what I have to offer all my clients. I'm afraid I can't work magic; I'm not Gandalf."

An interesting insight, although it didn't feel relevant to report back to Robin at this moment.

"I need to make a phone call," Adam said, rising from the table. "I won't be long."

"Give Robin my love," Mrs. Bright replied, with a grin. Adam waved away the remark.

Once in the car park, Adam crossed his fingers that he wouldn't be greeted with either the answerphone or Ashok: for a start, would the constable know about this meeting with a witness? Luckily, Adam got straight through to his husband.

"That's good timing," Robin said, against a background of noise. "We're taking a comfort break. A minute later and I'd have been in the gents'."

"Don't pee yourself, then. I'll be quick. Mark's uncle Alex has a conviction for assault."

"What? Hold on, I'll find somewhere less like a scrum." After a few moments, Robin resumed. "That's better. Say it again, please."

"Mark's uncle got drunk and lumped someone in Skegness. Apparently because they'd insulted his family. I wasn't sure if you'd checked his record already, and Ryan could have got his facts mixed up."

"I bet he hasn't. I've been waiting for the team to get back to me with anything about him, but you've beat them to it. What else turned up over your lunch?"

"Not much else important, so far. Details about how he made progress on the Bircher family history but they can wait. They're a bit convoluted."

"You've not died of boredom yet?"

"No, although it's tricky trying to get a word in." Adam snorted. "Right, I'm off. See you later."

He returned to the table at the same time as their food was arriving. Mrs. Bright—who'd evidently decided to commission Ryan's services—had clearly begun the process of giving him details of her husband's family history as far as they knew it, many of which she'd typed up and printed off. They'd reached the matter of the mysterious inheritance and tax treaties, Ryan making further notes for himself on an A4 pad, notes that appeared to be as verbose as he was. Still, the guy obviously loved what he did and appeared to be good at it.

"Shall we concentrate on eating for the moment?" Mrs. Bright suggested. "My sandwich looks too good to spoil with me trying to explain things and you jotting them down."

A flicker of disappointment on Ryan's face was soon covered over. "Good idea. Would it be rude to ask if you've had any thoughts about your inheritance, because what with those cruise brochures I mentioned and having just come off one myself, I wondered if you'd considered something like that?"

The rest of the meal passed in a discussion of the pros and cons of cruising, especially for passengers who were singletons. Adam tried to contribute but soon found himself zoning out and thinking about the upcoming difficult conversation he was going to be having with Jane, the Wickley learning assistant whose performance, never great, had gone downhill and who was refusing to acknowledge anything was wrong. That wasn't an unusual situation in a primary school, especially where the staff members were older and weren't used to being held to account for what they did in the classroom. Matters weren't helped by Jane starting to depict herself as a victim to anyone who'd give her an ear in the staffroom.

Planning that interview felt a more profitable use of time than listening to whatever Ryan was banging on about. Even Hamish had begun to gently snore, either the talk or the excitement of a new place having tired him out.

The arrival of a waiter to take their emptied plates brought Adam's attention back to the present, and Ryan soon returned to business. "I guess it's too much to hope that your husband left a similar treasure trove to the one Eleanor Bircher did?"

Mrs. Bright shook her head. "I'm afraid not. As I said, David didn't want to know anything about his biological parents. I can't think of a single clue to give you, apart from what I've already said or written down."

Ryan flashed her a smile. "No problem. Now, this next question is quite intrusive so feel free not to answer, although it could help if you did. Are there any little medical things you could tell me about? I know it's a long shot, but something genetic, maybe, that David could have inherited?"

"He was born with two webbed fingers. Can that be passed on through the family?"

That got Adam's attention. If the condition was an inherited trait, Robin didn't show any sign of it.

"Syndactyly? Yes, I believe it can sometimes be passed down. There are various versions, I think, although I'd have to check if there's a genetic link to one of them. While it's not something in and of itself that would give me a start, it could be corroborative, rather like the information about Scotland that Eleanor's parents kept, because she had Scottish blood."

To prevent Ryan launching into a diatribe on the topic, Adam asked, "Which of David's fingers were webbed?"

"These." Mrs. Bright indicated the middle and ring fingers on her left hand. "Not that the webbing was there when he and I met, because he'd had it operated on when he was younger, so there was simply an old scar to show. He used to tell people who noticed it that he'd fallen on some glass when he was a toddler, because it was easier than going into the taradiddle about the fingers being joined. Children can be very cruel and take the mickey something wicked."

Adam, nodding, couldn't recall Robin having any blemishes like those on his hands, either. Maybe it was as well, given how he'd been bullied at school anyway, irrespective of scars.

"His parents were clearly upfront about David being adopted, so did they mention if the syndactyly was familial?" Ryan asked.

Mrs. Bright nodded. "They'd explained about the webbing once he was old enough to ask why he had marks on his hand that other children didn't have. Later they told him that any children he fathered might have syndactyly, so almost the first thing he did when Robin was born was check his fingers and toes. Here's a confession." She gave Adam a sheepish grin. "David and I wrestled with whether we should tell Robin about that risk, given that he came out to us quite early and we doubted he'd have any offspring. But in this modern world you never know what will turn up, so we *did* tell him, although David didn't know for certain which of his parents he'd inherited it from. None of which helps, I suppose."

"It could, if I discover somebody who had the condition, who's recently died in Australia and has left peculiar bequests in his will." Ryan appeared excited at the prospect.

"Can you find out that kind of detail?" Mrs. Bright asked.

"You'd be amazed what you can turn up on the internet or by poking around old parish records. I could bore for England on the topic if I wanted to." Ryan waved his hand, clearly oblivious to his tendency to bore at the best of times. He outlined some of the remarkable—to him at least—things he'd stumbled across, Mrs. Bright giving every impression of finding the topic fascinating and chipping in comments and questions. Perhaps she did find it interesting, but most of it left Adam cold.

He returned to contemplating his upcoming staff interview and how it was likely to progress to a full-blown competency procedure. As Adam drifted back into the moment, he found that Ryan had swung round to the fact Mrs. Bright had contacted him independent of her son and how coincidences cropped up with scary regularity. Apparently, he'd got involved with Mark's enquiry because he'd known a friend of a friend of Mark's wife, Suzy.

"And the things I could tell you, Alison, about her when she was younger. As I said, she reminded me of a character from a story." Ryan took a breath, clearly about to launch into another of his tales. It seemed an appropriate moment to wind things up.

"Sorry to interrupt, but shall we get the bill?" Adam asked. "I need to get this boy out to cock his leg."

"Take him out to the car park while I settle up," Mrs. Bright said. "No arguing, boys. My treat. I'll see you out there in a moment."

Adam shook Ryan's hand, said that he was keen to see what he discovered, then led Hamish from the pub—not a moment too soon, as it turned out.

"Who's a good boy for holding on so long?" he asked, once the dog had relieved himself. "You're a very good dog. Yes, you are."

Hamish looked adoringly into Adam's face, clearly pleased as punch.

"I'll tell your other dad all about how well you've behaved yourself today. A credit to the Matthews-Bright household." He tickled the Newfoundland behind his ear. "He'll probably need something to brighten his day. Unless he can wrap up the case because this uncle bloke suddenly confesses and we can get back to a normal life."

There were two chances of that, though. Fat and slim.

Chapter Eleven

As they left Lincolnshire, en route to Oxford, with Ashok taking the first stint of driving, Robin had tried to line up his thoughts. Were they any further forward with the case? In terms of understanding the victim and some of his relationships, yes. In being any closer to knowing who killed him? There was the rub.

"You're quiet, sir," Ashok said.

"Mulling stuff over. When I was talking to Adam earlier, I told him we're going down the line I like—you're most at risk from family or friends—but I still don't think we have a motive for any of the family wanting to kill Mark. Or an obvious person to put in the frame. Not Kevin, who seems too bone idle to murder anybody, nor Tom, who seems too nice. Before you remind me, I know looks can be deceptive and killers can be cunning beasts."

"I wouldn't dare remind you of that, sir." Ashok chuckled. "Harold Shipman was a well-respected GP, wasn't he?"

"Yep. Many of his patients thought the world of him. The ones he hadn't murdered, of course, and maybe they'd still have liked him up until that final moment. Trusted him implicitly, as well." Didn't the revered and popular teacher or vicar or whoever often turn out to be not only an abuser but someone who'd groomed people to think they were wonderful?

"I'd agree that Kevin doesn't appear to have any reason to kill his brother, though," Ashok said. "As for the McKay side, what about preserving Moira's reputation? For all we know, she's been a pillar of the church and community and all of a sudden her chequered past has come back to haunt her."

"Maybe. Although it sounds like Moira's so far gone that she'd not be any the wiser whether she was being gossiped about, and Tom doesn't appear fussed about acknowledging this side of the family. Whose reputation would he be guarding? It might be different if Tom was illegitimate himself and say belonged to some strict sect where he'd get kicked out for the sins of his fathers. Same for Alex. It doesn't seem like that applies."

"Alex who drives a camper van. Didn't somebody say they'd seen one of those parked at the woods?"

"I think you're right. Pru's Mr. Rashid maybe or the Forestry Commission bloke. There's a lot of them about, camper vans, so let's not get ahead of ourselves. Easy to get our hopes up in a case like this where you find yourself grasping at anything. I'll make a call to base and get some balls rolling, though. Including following up on who inherits whatever Mark's left." That had been Pru's baby, and she'd be the best person to talk to anyway, because she could divvy up what jobs needed doing.

It hadn't taken long for the sergeant to eliminate Mark's worldly goods as a motive for murder, unless Kevin had been motivated to do the deed to get five grand. All the rest of the money—which was unlikely to be a lot once the mortgage was settled—was divided between the Matt Hampson Foundation and My Name'5 Doddie, both of them charities with a strong rugby connection.

"So apparently that's the 'killed for the legacy' option out," Robin said, after he'd filled Ashok in on what he'd learned. "I never really expected it to apply."

"No." Ashok performed a tricky overtake of three lorries which were tailgating before resuming. "No cancer charities, though. I'd have expected them, given what happened to his wife."

Robin shrugged. "Maybe that would have been a bit too painful?"

"Maybe. Anyway, that six-month baby thing Tom mentioned. Am I being thick? I didn't think babies that small could survive back in those days."

"They probably couldn't. But an awful lot of children were born fit and healthy and about six months after their parents' wedding."

His constable's expression turned from bewilderment to exasperation with himself. "Doh. Shotgun wedding. I *was* being thick."

"You're forgiven. I think it's always been pretty common, whether the bride and groom were forced or went willingly to the altar, even in what were supposed to be respectable families. Get married quick enough when you get the news that a baby's on its way and when that baby comes, hope that people don't count back. Or if they do, they're too polite to mention it in the new parents' hearing. But that doesn't apply to Mark's mother. His gran was the one whose imminent arrival prompted the wedding."

All these generations and connections. Would it be as complex as this when they got to the bottom of Robin's family history? The story of Moira wanting nothing to do with her child, so not taking the option of her mother caring for the baby, stuck in Robin's craw. Had his father been similarly abandoned or did his biological grandmother have no choice but to give the baby up because her family couldn't have their reputation sullied? That scenario would be a damn sight easier to swallow. They carried on the journey discussing uncontroversial topics like sport, Robin determined to drag his thoughts away from matters Bright.

By the time they'd completed their stop for what Ashok called output and input, Robin felt better and not only for using the gents'. Adam's phone call and the news it contained had come at precisely the right moment.

"I'll take the next driving stint," he told Ashok as the bloke emerged from the shop with a bottle of fizzy drink. "Alex Hanley is said to have a conviction for an assault in Skegness, and I want you to check up on it. See if there's anything else lurking in his record."

"Will do, sir," Ashok said. "I once went to Skegness, and I can't say I was that impressed with it. Mind you, I was on a stag do, so most of what I can remember is around playing endless crazy golf and drinking lots of beer. They had plenty of pubs and miniature courses. Maybe Alex was on a stag as well, in which case there'd be no surprise he got into a fight."

None of that sounded a great advert for any seaside resort. Stag and hen do's were becoming a blight on many holiday towns, profitable as they might be for local hotels and clubs. "You could be right. If you can get the team back at base to check the details while we're on the road—matter of urgency—we'll be better placed for tackling Alex. It'll be interesting to see if anything else crawls out of the woodwork."

Unfortunately, it didn't. Apart from the assault, Alex and Lucy Hanley didn't have as much as a speeding ticket on record. The incident at Skegness had happened two years previously, just before Covid changed everyone's plans, so was hardly a youthful indiscretion on Alex's part. Although a stag do *was* involved: his son's. The younger Hanley had been left highly embarrassed by his father's antics, according to various stories which Ashok had found on the local news sites. He'd dragged his father from the victim and acted as peacekeeper. The guy who'd been on the end of Alex's fists had apparently made the sort of off-the-cuff offensive remark about the man's mother that anyone could make, especially if they were drunk. No indication that he was aware his insult would have a personal significance. Interesting that the son hadn't stuck up for his dad, which was what usually happened in these types of incidents, irrespective of who was in the wrong.

"All sounds a bit like what happened to Mark," Ashok said, after he'd read aloud the key parts of the news story. "An argument ends in violence, although in Mark's case there's nobody there to pull the assailant away. He could have said something about Alex's mother that he took as an insult or a threat."

Robin nodded. This gave them a potential name in the frame and a possible motive to boot. A thin motive, admittedly, but the best they'd got so far.

They'd arranged to meet Alex and Lucy Hanley at three o'clock in a park and ride facility near Oxford, a couple of hundred metres off the A34. Ashok had joked on the way about being relieved they wouldn't be going into the city itself, given the high crime rate as shown on the telly or in books. As Robin himself often pointed out, if you believed everything you saw on the box, then you not only wouldn't want to live in Oxford, you'd avoid any leafy village in the heart of England. You'd also think the police relied entirely on forensics, that they still played "good cop, bad cop", that they could draw on unlimited budgets and employed the most bizarre disciplinary procedure of any large organisation.

When they'd arrived at the destination and parked up, Robin and Ashok made their way to the main bus stop, where they'd arranged to meet up. A couple in their fifties were standing there already, and they'd let the bus go without getting on it, so Robin approached them, fingers crossed. "Mr. and Mrs. Hanley?"

"Yes. You must be Chief Inspector Bright."

Introductions all round were followed by the Hanleys suggesting they all make their way to the hotel which was located on the edge of the site. They thought there was bound to be somewhere to sit in the entrance area, where the four of them could not only talk without being overheard but could also get a pot of tea to wet their whistles.

"We've stopped here before," Alex said, as they walked across the car park, "when we were up to our armpits in snow. Thought we'd be marooned for days." The bloke seemed pretty relaxed at meeting them, but he'd had time to get his game face on. And it wasn't like he hadn't had practice in dealing with the police.

"Do you travel this way often?" Robin asked.

"Not particularly, but that journey stuck in our minds," Lucy said, in a deep, throaty voice, the kind which would be perfect for voice-overs. "As you can imagine."

She would stick in anyone's mind too. If you didn't remember her voice or charming smile, you surely couldn't forget her purple hair, which was like a blue rinse on steroids.

A discussion of trips taken in bad weather and the advisability of making sure you had food, water, and blankets in the boot, carried them through to being settled in the hotel with their refreshments ordered.

"Thanks for seeing us. Ashok's going to make some notes, although this isn't a formal interview. Yet," Robin added, to let them know he meant business. "We're investigating the death of Mark Bircher, who was, we believe, the grandson of your mother Moira."

"So you said when you rang," Alex replied, with a hint of asperity.

"I did." Robin ignored the jibe. "Were you aware of Mark's existence?"

Alex shared a glance with his wife. "Partly. We knew a little about his mother. As you may or may not know, *my* mother is in the advanced stages of dementia. What she says doesn't always make sense, so when she started talking about having given birth to a baby at the end of the war, we thought at first that she was raving."

"When was this?" Robin asked. "I mean, when did she tell you?"

"Not long after Christmas, two years ago," Lucy cut in. "A bit before that first lockdown and a couple of months after we began noticing she was going downhill, memory-wise. She'd had a bout of flu, and at the point she was really poorly with it, she started rambling. It may sound daft, but I was quite convinced she'd got caught up in all the stories about baby Jesus and somehow thought she was Mary. It was only when we mentioned it to Uncle Tom—and that was really in the way of a joke, you know, 'You'll never guess what she's been saying when she had her fever!'—that we learned she'd been telling the truth. Quite a shock for Alex to discover he had relatives he never knew existed."

Two years previously—early 2020—would have been around the time of the assault case, which could explain why Alex had been so touchy in Skegness.

"Nobody had ever hinted at your family having a secret? Not even Isabel?" Ashok asked.

Lucy raised an eyebrow. "Oh. Have you met her?"

"Not met, although Tom mentioned her as being a source of information." That was probably Ashok finding a nice way of saying Isabel was a gossip. "We didn't know she was still alive."

"She's clinging on. Physically frail although sharp as a pin, which is the opposite of how Mum is." Alex sighed. "I'd call Isabel a source of tittle-tattle rather than information. Anyway, Tom told us that he knew nothing about my half sister apart from the blunt fact of when Mum had given birth to her. *He* doesn't know where she was born or what happened to her afterwards, as Mum had decided not to have any connection with the child."

"I know things were very different back then, but that does seem a bit harsh," Ashok said. "To cut yourself off so entirely."

Lucy shook her head. "It may seem harsh to our eyes, but I think it was a case of self-preservation. Not having to grieve for what you've lost or worry about what's happening to your child as she grows up, like fretting over whether the adoptive family were treating her well. What you don't know can't hurt you, can it? I can tell you how much we still fret about our son, and he's grown up."

"Did you wish Tom had told you years ago what little he knew?" Robin asked.

Alex shrugged. "He did what he thought was right by his own flesh and blood. Any of us would, so I don't hold it against *him* that he kept the secret—her secret—for so long."

"Do you hold it against your mother?"

A flicker of pain registered in Alex's eyes. "If I said no, I'd be a liar. It would have been nice to know the truth earlier, when I could have asked her the full story and got an answer I could rely on as being accurate. But I've tried to understand why she kept shtum."

"What Alex means is that hers was a different generation," Lucy chipped in, although that wasn't quite what her husband had said. "Morality had to be seen to be observed, though what went on then wasn't a lot different to nowadays. Sex wasn't invented in the 1960s, was it?"

Robin, amused at the brief expression of embarrassment on Ashok's face, noted how it was Lucy who kept producing the defence of her mother-in-law. Something about this story was making Alex profoundly uncomfortable, and Robin wasn't sure it was the obvious *"My mother never told me I had a half sister."* How did that discomfort link with Alex's reaction to what the other bloke had said at Skegness? It would also be interesting to know if he'd assumed Robin didn't know about his criminal record because the police would have had no reason as yet to look into it?

Robin risked a personal remark about McKay family history, to gauge the reaction. "Extra marital sex was alive and well around 1930, Tom tells us. I believe your grandmother was pregnant with Moira when she married your grandfather."

"What do you mean by that?" The reaction had been generated: Alex was only being kept in his seat by his wife's restraining hand on his arm.

"That's surely not relevant to Mark's death, Chief Inspector." Lucy kept her voice impressively calming.

"Only in that it might have mattered a lot to our victim," Robin said. "I'm trying to build up a picture of him and his absolute determination to get to the truth and part of that process is to get my head around what happened back in 1948 when his mother was born. If Moira herself had been conceived out of wedlock, then I struggle to believe her family would have forced her to get rid of her child. Was it entirely her decision?"

Lucy answered for both of them. "We believe so."

Robin, determined to get Alex talking again, asked him, "Would you have liked to have had the opportunity of meeting your half sister Eleanor?"

The reply came, although Alex kept his gaze fixed on his shoes. "I don't know. I'd obviously have liked the chance to make an informed choice, though, rather than discovering when she was already dead and it was too late."

"What about meeting your nephew, Mark? Had you made an informed choice about that?"

The question evidently stung Alex, given his wince. Was it guilt or the fact that any reference to his mother, however oblique, got under his skin? "I'd have thought it's obvious the same applies in his case. Too late now to have the chance."

"You may not have known for certain that Mark existed, but you could have made an educated guess that Eleanor would have produced a family, so you've had two years to find out whether that was so, the way Mark found out about his family. And," Robin pointed out, "he was obviously still alive when he got in contact with Tom. You could have arranged to meet him then, especially if you were going to be travelling down his way."

"What are you implying?" Alex, hands tightly clamped together, was clearly fighting another bout of anger.

"Simply that he'd still have been alive before you set off on your road trip. If you'd been off doing the royal family trail, it would have been easy enough to find a couple of hours to nip over to Lindenshaw." Or indeed Kings Ride Woods.

Lucy forestalled any answer her husband might have given with another grip of his arm. "You're quite right that we could, although we didn't do that. We were waiting to see what transpired with Uncle Tom and whether they organised a DNA test between them. After that we could have been certain because, for all we knew, the whole thing might have been a mistake and Mark wasn't actually Moira's grandson."

It was a reasonable point, although something about the statement didn't ring true. Maybe it was worth drilling down now. "There was a camper van seen in the Kings Ride Woods car park on Saturday, around the time Mark was murdered. Was it yours?"

The Hanleys shared a glance before both saying, "No."

"On Saturday we went to see Timsworth Abbey," Lucy stated. "I'm afraid we can't prove that because we didn't keep the parking ticket and we paid cash so there's no card receipt to show you. They might have caught us on CCTV, but I don't remember seeing any cameras. And it wasn't one of those car parks with a barrier, so there won't be a record of our registration."

That all seemed to have come out too pat and with a suggestion of pre-preparation. An apparently solid alibi although with nothing concrete to support it. Perhaps there was an innocent explanation: the couple must have known they'd be asked for their whereabouts that day so could have prepared the answer in order not to seem suspicious because they were flustered.

"You don't have a receipt for the abbey? I'm sure you have to pay for entry." Robin admittedly might have been getting confused with the cathedral, where you definitely had to get past a ticket booth, although the question would keep the pressure up and show he felt he was being strung along.

"No. At the abbey they ask for a suggested donation, rather than having a ticketing system, which is something I really can't stand. We didn't pay anything, on a point of principle," Alex said, chest swelling pompously. "It's scandalous that churches charge anything at all for entry, voluntary or not, so we said we were there for prayer and got in free."

If any prayer actually took place. Admittedly, he couldn't judge anybody's spirituality on appearances or a relatively brief conversation, but this pair didn't strike Robin as the sort who'd be spending time in contemplation. Perhaps he was doing them a disservice: maybe his rozzer's nose was starting to let him down because it continually expected to be lied to. Only time would tell.

"You couldn't have contacted Eleanor and maybe you didn't meet up with Mark but what about Kevin?" Ashok asked. "Have you made your mind up whether you want to get to know him?"

"Kevin?" Alex's face was an exaggerated blank. Robin was pretty certain he'd been about to play ignorant about the brother when Lucy chipped in again.

"The brother? The same applies as with Mark. Once we know for certain that he's Moira's grandson, that'll be the time for making plans. Perhaps he'd like to come and visit our local area, the air bases and the like."

If he can be bothered to get out of his chair. Although Robin noted Lucy had talked about Kevin visiting the area rather than specifically visiting his relatives. Time to mention Skegness. "Mr. Hanley, we've obviously checked your police record, as a matter of routine, and you have a conviction for assault."

"I'm not denying it." Alex's body language—arms crossed, shoulders hunched—suggested he'd have liked to try.

"And you'd also agree that the fight you got into was prompted by the other man having made a remark about your family?"

"Yes. How would you like it if some stranger called your mother a whore?"

"I wouldn't have appreciated it at all." Robin had experienced a lot worse insults hurled at him and had become almost immune, so it was sometimes difficult to imagine another person's reactions. Given the circumstances, he could understand how Alex had been touchy. "I wouldn't have belted the bloke, though."

Alex didn't respond, arms still tightly crossed, maybe afraid that he'd be tempted to lash out again or say something he'd regret.

"If this guy you hit was a total stranger, why did you take things so personally?" Ashok asked. "Your son called it a throwaway comment, so I guess it wasn't dissimilar to the abuse that gets hurled at football referees every weekend."

It was a good point. The police weren't alone in being the target of insults, because rightly or wrongly, people threw around abuse on social media or in person without any regard for other people's feelings. Not all of them ended up being physically attacked, though. Why had the "whore" remark cut so close to home for Alex if he didn't know much about his mother's history? If Moira *had* been selling her favours—with Eleanor being a result of that—he couldn't have been aware of the fact.

Lucy, inevitably, answered for her husband. "Blame the whole incident on too much beer and a natural desire to stick up for your family. I'd have thought you would understand, because you must see these kind of fights all the time."

"We don't see everybody sticking up for their family by lashing out with their fists," Ashok pointed out. "Even your son was embarrassed by the episode."

"Alfie, our son, didn't know the full story behind why I did it. He still doesn't." At last Alex unlocked his arms. "All right, I'll come clean. I found out about my half sister's existence— although not her name or other details—literally a fortnight before Alfie's stag do. And Mum didn't bother to tell *me*, first off. Lucy went round to take her a cake, and the whole story came out, like she said earlier." It no doubt still hurt that Moira hadn't told her son first. "I confronted Mum the next day over the phone, but she denied everything, even that she'd told Lucy about a child. I made the mistake of pressing her and she became very distressed. I said we'd discuss it face-to-face after the Skegness weekend although we never got the chance. When I went round to see her that week, I have to say I was dreading it.

Not only to do with this adopted-child business but in case she'd discovered anything about the scuffle I'd got into on the stag do. Anyway, in the end none of that applied because I couldn't get a reply when I rang her bell. I do have a spare key, although I don't like to let myself in uninvited, as that feels rude. I wish now I'd done that first off, because you never know if that minute I spent dithering on the doorstep could have made a difference. She'd been taken ill, you see."

"I know this can't be easy, but please go on." Robin nodded sympathetically. "The more complete a picture we can build up, the better."

"Well, I let myself in and that's when I found her, in the lounge. I reckoned she'd had a bad fall and it looked like she'd suffered a stroke on top of that, although we never found out whether the stroke caused the fall or the other way round. That was the start of her going downhill in terms of her mental health. I'd never realised the deterioration could happen so rapidly." Alex sounded like a different person now, his voice quieter and lacking the earlier aggressive note.

Robin glanced at Lucy, who was hanging on her husband's every word, clearly concerned. At the fact he was upset or in case he deviated off some script? How likely was it they'd come prepared for questions about Moira's fall?

Alex continued. "I keep thinking about that day. All the things I wanted to know and then couldn't, because the chance had gone in those few minutes. Since her stroke, even when she's had her lucid moments, she's continued refusing to discuss anything else about the matter and Tom, while he's been keen to help, doesn't know much, either."

Lucy seemed to know about the potential family connection to air bases, though, given what she'd said about Kevin visiting the area. Had that been a reference to Tom and Moira's father, meaning their great-grandson would possibly be interested in seeing where the man had worked, or was there something else? "You mentioned air bases, earlier," Robin said. "Did Moira's lover work at one of them?"

"We think so," Lucy said, then immediately put her hand to her mouth, too late.

Robin smiled. "How would you know that unless Moira told you?"

"We might as well tell them, Lucy," Alex said, with an air of resignation. "We heard from Isabel, of course. She of the big mouth and bigger ears. Ears that picked up every bit of gossip she could."

"In her defence, she *has* kept your mother's secret pretty well intact outside of the family, which isn't her usual track record." Lucy pulled a disapproving face. "Some of the tittle-tattle she's spread locally doesn't bear thinking about, but she never spoke to Alex concerning Eleanor until Moira had already broached the subject, and I don't think she's discussed it with anyone else apart from Tom. She used to be Moira's best friend when they were younger, and they've kept that up all through their lives. She's Alex's godmother."

"How much did she tell you?" Robin asked. "And when?"

"When? After Mum had her stroke. I think that was the point when Isabel decided it couldn't do much harm for me to know some of the story."

"Which was . . .?" Robin prompted.

"Not very much, as it happened." Alex shrugged. "When Mum got pregnant, she obviously confided in Isabel, who's always been her closest friend. She never told her who the father of the child was, though, just that he'd been a mistake she'd been stupid to make. Married man, although Mum didn't know that until it was too late, apparently. Explains why there was no shotgun wedding and, I suppose, may have influenced the adoption decision."

"If Isabel wasn't told who Eleanor's father was, how did she know about air bases?" Ashok asked.

"She guessed from a couple of hints Mum dropped that he was associated with one of the local air bases, maybe someone Mum met when she was waitressing at the hotel because they had a lot of the remaining air crew dropping in there. I knew all about her hospitality work and her life on the cruise ships, which is where she met my dad. I never realised there was a gap in the narrative." Which patently still rankled with him. "The rest of what Isabel said surrounded the official story my grandparents put out. They told folk a great opportunity had come up for Moira to go and work in London, although she never actually travelled far from home. My grandmother wouldn't have let her go all that way to give birth, for one thing. The family wanted her near at hand at such a difficult time. At least, according to Isabel."

"She may be a gob mouth, but she does tend to tell the truth," Lucy said. "Which probably makes it worse, because you can't discount what she says."

Robin suppressed a smile. Yes, he could imagine what a loose cannon Isabel would have been, if it was known she was a reliable source of gossip. "Did Isabel say *where* Moira gave birth? I know it may not seem pertinent to Mark's death, but if he was due to visit someone in the area, it might form an important link in the chain of events."

Both Alex and Lucy shook their heads, this time without any obvious consultation between them.

"That I don't know," Alex said. "Somewhere local, because of my grandmother not wanting Mum to go into confinement unless she had someone close to hand. Maybe *holding* her hand, for all I know. As you can guess, *she* didn't speak about it, either. I grew up quite oblivious." He sighed. "I've gone through all my mother's documentation—I need to, because I have power of attorney for her and I've had to fish stuff out—and there's nothing related to Eleanor there. Or any indication of a place that could be significant."

"Eleanor's birth certificate says she was registered in Peterborough by her adoptive parents," Ashok said. "That doesn't mean anything to you?"

Alex evidently didn't feel any need to consult his wife on this, either. "It's not far away from the area we're talking about, although Mum's never mentioned it. I don't think she's ever been there, but that could be another secret."

"Okay. Swinging round to Mark again; you've told us that you didn't meet up with your nephew." Robin put a slight emphasis on the word *told*. "So that I can cross all the t's about interaction between the McKay family and him, has your son Alfie been in touch with him?"

"As I said, Alfie doesn't know everything, including the fact Mark exists," Alex stated. "Existed."

That lack of knowledge could go towards explaining why he'd not stuck up for his father in Skegness.

"What about other cousins? Do you have any full siblings?"

Lucy gave the reply. "Alex is an only child. Moira had a really rough time giving birth to him, so she didn't want to go through the process again."

Alex narrowed his eyes. "I don't think the police need to know every detail of my mother's affairs, Lucy. Irrespective of what the chief inspector has been saying about getting a full picture, I'm sure what happened in the delivery room when I was born can't be relevant to their investigations."

"You'd be amazed what turns out to be relevant, although in this case, I think we don't need the obstetric details." Robin noted that Lucy's remark had elicited a strong response from her husband, confirming the impression that matters concerning his mother still galled him. "One last question, then, to make sure that I'm totally clear. Have you had *any* form of contact with either Mark or his brother? Even if that's a text or an email which you deleted without reading or replying."

"No," Lucy said, looking Robin squarely in the eye.

"Mr. Hanley?"

"No." Alex's answer didn't seem as assured. Maybe his wife didn't know what he'd been up to or perhaps she was the better liar.

"Thank you," Robin said. "I think, given the circumstances, we need you both to provide us with a formal statement. In complicated cases like this one, we need to cover all our bases, especially when the victim was due to visit your home area last weekend."

"Which means he couldn't have been meeting us," Lucy pointed out smugly. "We were still on our travels."

"Not unless you changed your plans," Ashok replied, with an equally smug smile.

Robin ignored both comments. "I'm happy to take statements here or you can report to your local station as soon as you're home. Unless that's going to be weeks away."

"We're heading homewards today. Nose back to the grindstone on Monday." Alex rolled his eyes at the prospect. "I'd rather hit the road now, if we can, while the traffic isn't too bad."

That suited Robin, as well. "Then maybe you can get it done tomorrow. The sooner that chore's completed, the sooner we can get down to eliminating you from our enquiries. If you give us your full contact details, we'll get in touch with your local station and make sure they're ready to do the necessary."

The Hanleys, with evident relief at the prospect of an imminent departure, gave Ashok all the contact details he needed.

As they watched the Hanleys walk back to their camper van at a spritely pace, as though the pair couldn't wait to shake the dust of the park and ride from their feet, the constable scratched his head. "What was all that about? The details about the visit to Timsworth aside, something's going on that they didn't quite get their stories settled about in advance, although I can't work out what."

"I'd agree. It'll be interesting to see how far their official statements vary from what they told us. Always different when you have to put your name to an account. That was good timing with the Kevin question, by the way. I could have sworn Alex was going to deny all knowledge of him before Lucy leaped in. I'd like to get that bloke on his own for a chat, but without any proper evidence of their involvement in the crime, we're going to have to tread warily."

"His assault conviction and them having been in roughly the right area isn't enough?"

"I'd need more. I don't want to be accused of harassment." Although they'd seen for themselves that Hanley was the type to lose his temper when he felt his family reputation had been threatened. "Get me some hard evidence and it'll be a different ball game."

Ashok nodded. "Evidence like them having been in touch with Mark or not having been in Timsworth at all? I'll ask Ben to check his phone records for their mobile and landline. Want me to find out about the car park CCTV too?"

"If there is any. I've not been to Timsworth in a while, but from what I remember, I doubt the car parks are those places where they record registration numbers, either. Although if the van *was* there, it's no proof both the occupants were. It wouldn't have been hard for one of them to drop the other off and head for the car park, to begin setting up their nice alibi. *Oh*, right." Robin wagged his finger. "That could fit in with Mark's car being nicked. It gets used to transport the culprit away from the scene to somewhere—in this case the Kinechester car park—where they can be picked up. Taking the Yaris to Timsworth and leaving it *there* would have made too much of an obvious connection." Although where the missing suitcase fitted into that scheme wasn't clear. Unless it contained something damning about Moira that needed to be destroyed. A criminal record for soliciting, or was that stretching theorising to breaking point?

"I like that idea about the Yaris, sir. If we can't fix the Hanleys' position via the car park, there's a chance someone at the abbey might remember them if they kicked up a stink about not paying."

"They might remember her hair too. I could be doing them a disservice, but I bet they don't see many tints quite that powerful."

"Want me to chase that too? Or get one of the team on it?"

They'd arrived at the car, but at the last minute, Robin swung himself round to the passenger side door. "Actually, I think I'll take that chore off your shoulders, if you'll do driving duty again now. At least get us down the road a way, because I need to make some calls, and not merely to warn the Lincolnshire police about the Hanleys turning up on their doorstep." Robin had quite a list of chores to get through, which he'd have to jot down before starting, or risk losing some in the process of juggling remembering with doing. "I'll get Danielle onto both the CCTV and the abbey stuff, as a matter of priority. If both Alex and Lucy have an unshakeable alibi, then there's no point in working the Bircher connection too hard, and the other aspect that I'd like you to get onto won't be so relevant."

"What bit's that, sir?" Ashok, settling into the driver's seat again, was clearly interested. Admittedly, anything would be preferable to ploughing through car park footage, although that short straw had to be drawn sometimes.

"I want you to get onto Skegness or whichever station in Lincolnshire dealt with the assault. Find out everything you can about the case from the investigating officers and say you don't simply want what's in the official statements. Hopefully you'll jog their memories, because anything they can tell you could be useful. Like what was said by the other bloke and whether Alex gave any indication why he was abnormally touchy about comments concerning his mother. Any impression they got that he might do the same thing again—or worse—to someone who threatened her reputation or managed to say the wrong thing at the wrong time. While you're at it, see if you can find out anything about the fall and stroke that his mother had. The nursing home she's in may be able to help."

"I can get the name of it from Tom. He might know who her doctor was, as well." Ashok skilfully negotiated his way around a group of coach passengers, all of whom seemed determined to walk exactly where they wanted, irrespective of whether that was in front of moving vehicles.

"Good. The staff at the home might be able to tell you if there's any tension between mother and son. The next job needs careful handling, because I want to know if anyone—including Tom himself if you can ask him subtly—harboured any suspicions about Alex's version of what happened to his mother when he went round there and found she'd fallen. I got the impression he and his nephew don't hit it off that well, which might be a long-term thing, although if it's recent, I'd love to know when it dates back to."

Ashok didn't give a full reply until they were safely back on the dual carriageway. "You think Alex lied about what happened to his mother? The circumstances of the fall?"

"Possibly. He was obviously an angry man back then and he's still angry now, isn't he? The slightest adverse mention of his mother seems to get his hackles raised, even if Lucy makes it, and

I can't help feeling he's got a lot of conflicting emotions going on about the situation he's found himself in. Feels like it's a mixture of annoyance at having secrets kept from him—ones that he only discovered because Isabel was too loose with her tongue—and annoyance because his mother wouldn't tell him anything further about his sibling. Plus a touch of shame at having a mother who bore a bastard child, because some people still feel that sort of thing strongly."

"He's certainly het up about something, and it wouldn't surprise me if you're right about all of those and maybe another factor we've not identified yet. Although I don't see what's it got to do with her having a stroke."

"Maybe nothing, but I've conjured up a mental image of Alex going round to his mother's house to confront her again about his half sibling in an effort to get to the truth. He's admitted he was worked up about the run in with the police and the worry that she'd find out about it. The story about knocking and having to wait for a reply didn't take place. Not on this visit, anyway. He's too wound up to wait, so lets himself in. Maybe that makes her *cross* and they soon get into an argument."

"And he's angry enough to give her a push that sends her flying?"

"Something like that. Then the fall itself or the shock it causes precipitates a stroke. I don't know if that's possible, so clarifying the medical stuff could be a job for you too. Or get one of the admin team onto it." Maybe the stroke hadn't been the immediate result of a fall, but it may have triggered a delayed response. How long had that visit to Moira been and had anyone noticed a discrepancy? "I'd love to know if they took an official statement from Alex at the time."

"I doubt it. If he'd called for an ambulance, they'd have taken her to hospital and unless somebody had cause to follow it up—like she said he'd knocked her over—then she'd probably be another old woman who took a tumble."

Sad but true. "If anything turns up that gives you cause for doubt about Alex's version of events, then feel free to dig a bit deeper. Unless we get a better lead on somebody else."

"Will do, sir." Ashok visibly glowed at the prospect of tackling the job. "That's worth driving *all* the way back to Abbotston for."

Robin hoped that wonderful buoyancy would carry them through both the journey home and the task ahead. It felt like they'd made a step forward, but would Sod's Law apply and that progress end up with them going two steps backwards?

Chapter Twelve

Adam expected his husband to be tired when he got home but was pleased to see it turn out to be tiredness tempered with a bit of optimism. He cracked open a couple of bottles of beer, got Robin settled on the settee with his drink and an adoring Hamish—who was acting as though his constabulary dad had been away for years, rather than overnight—then got on with heating up dinner.

"Are you in work tomorrow?" Adam asked, hovering in the lounge doorway with one ear on matters in the kitchen.

"I hope not. I've told all the team they need to get a break on the principle that we all could do with recharging our batteries. If anything notable turns up, we might have to reverse that strategy, but the Hanleys won't be making their official statements until tomorrow afternoon at the earliest, and everything else is in a holding pattern while we wait to hear back from people or work through stuff." Robin grinned. "Boring police work, the kind they don't tell you about on the box because it would turn off the viewers in droves."

"Now you've met this Alex bloke, do you think there's a chance he's the killer?"

"He's done something. I'm sure of that." Robin scratched his head, earning a dirty look from the dog, who evidently thought that hand should be employed stroking him. "Daft baggage. Hamish, not you."

"Glad to hear it. If you want to talk it through tonight, that's cool—I've got a bit of stuff from Ryan I'd like to share which may or may not mean something. Happy to leave it for the morning, if that works better."

"Let's do that. No work talk tonight will let me clear my brain. You can tell me about Mum and Ryan, though. Did she doze off?"

"Actually, I was the one who kept zoning out, while she seemed to get on with him really well. Hold on. Cooking duties."

A cry of, "She probably reminds him of his aunt Josephine," followed Adam as he headed towards the kitchen.

Once he was back, with some snacks for himself and something more substantial on a tray for Robin, Adam said, "I guess all the family tree stuff on the Mark Bircher side helped give your mum an insight into how they might move forward on *her* mystery. She's going to engage Ryan's services on your dad's history and the inheritance front while *he's* going to help her pick her way through the cruise minefield. I don't have a lot to add apart from that." Adam paused. "No, that's a big lie. Something did come up of interest. Don't get over-excited, though, because it isn't anything you won't know."

"I'm still intrigued."

"It's about your dad being born with skin between two of his fingers." Adam indicated which two, which he then realised was stupid because Robin would know where the webbing had been, but it had been a long day and he wasn't thinking that clearly. "Ryan seemed to think that might be helpful corroboration for anything he turns up, given that the condition can be familial."

"Yep, Dad showed me his scar, and they warned me it could be inherited. Not that there's any risk of me passing it on down the line." Robin ruffled Hamish's ears to the dog's evident delight. "No webbed paws for your pups, sunshine."

"Are we breeding him, then?" Adam asked, which led into a conversation about how much Hamish's stud fees—or whatever they called them in the dog world—would be. Any discussion about any human offspring was superfluous because they'd already thrashed out the whole *adopt, foster, have their own using a donor* topic and decided it wasn't right for them. Not at the moment, anyway. They'd stick to the canine variety of dependant for the time being and revisit children further down the line, maybe when one or other of them was retired.

"Talking about things genetic," Robin said, when they'd exhausted the topic of the Newfoundland's DNA, "you said you'd tell me the bone-marrow story."

"Oh yes." Adam related, pretty well verbatim, what he and Mrs. Bright had discussed. "She's a canny woman, your mum."

"She is. I'd always wondered why Dad insisted I went on the bone-marrow register, like him, when I was old enough. It never occurred to me it was linked to his adoption rather than civic duty. I think that puts *that* worry to bed. Or at least gets it into the bedroom." Robin snorted. "What did Ryan think about you being my husband, by the way?"

"Totally nonplussed. In fact, I'd say he was delighted, so you're no doubt right about where his own preferences lie. He'd be a nice bloke if he'd shut up once in a while. Is he single?"

"I have no idea. Why?"

"I was wondering whether his constant chatter puts blokes off, because he's reasonably handsome."

Robin snorted. "You could be his agony uncle. *Adam's advice on your love life. All treated in confidence.*"

"Don't. Your mum dropped a similar hint on the way back from the pub and I don't think she was joking. I told her it would risk Ryan thinking I fancied him, so that shut the idea down." Adam stretched limbs, which were getting wearier by the minute. "Perhaps we could get her to give him advice. They've clearly clicked, and I bet if she said, 'Ryan do try and cut down what you say by seventy percent and then you'll find true love,' he might take it to heart."

"It would be generic advice, though, because I don't think she knows about Grindr or gay bars. Although nothing would surprise me about what her and Aunt Clare discuss." Robin, laden with dog, shifted himself into a comfier position. "As long as he doesn't expect us to fix him up with a partner. Not sure I know any available gay men at present, and we're both too busy to act as matchmaker."

The ensuing discussion about gay friends, some of whom they'd lost touch with, led Robin and Adam into poking around on social media trying to find what they were up to. The mostly successful exercise took them through to bedtime. A bedtime that wouldn't see much if anything in the way of romance, but that didn't matter. Having the love of your life next to you when you went to sleep and again when you rose was plenty to be thankful for.

The next morning dawned very differently, weather-wise, to the previous Sunday. Wet, dank, the conditions which made Adam and Robin want to hunker down and have a leisurely morning, with copious mugs of tea and plenty of biscuits. The forecast was an optimistic "brighter later," which could allow them to get some fresh air and stretch Hamish's growing legs.

Over breakfast, Robin asked Adam to outline what else he could remember from lunch the previous day. "If you didn't lose concentration entirely."

"I did listen to some of it, I'll have you know. There were a few quite interesting bits, especially when he talked about how he'd pinned down where Mark's mother had been born." Adam described the box with the brochures, the clippings and list of books. "Shame your grandparents didn't leave something similar to start him on the trail."

"Yeah. Nothing like that which I'm aware of and Mum would know if there was because Dad would have either told her or left it in an obvious place to find. They had no secrets. Like us." Robin squeezed his husband's hand. "That story of the local witch fits with what we heard yesterday, which is good."

Adam nodded, knowing how much Robin liked to gather the loose ends and have all the parts of a story link up, whether they were important ones or not. "I'm not sure anything else of great importance appeared. I've a feeling Ryan said he knew Suzy before she married Mark. Or did he just know *of* her? Sorry to be so useless, but I found it hard to keep track of everything he said with the whole 'use a hundred words where ten would have done' thing."

"No need to apologise. Pru, Ben, and I all felt the same, and we're trained to hang on every word that a witness says. And in theory we're supposed to be able to pick the ten important ones from the ninety fillers."

"Well, he definitely mentioned a mutual friend and that Suzy was like someone out of a book. If that makes any sense or helps at all."

"It helps in that it confirms something Christine Probert said. She told us Suzy's life was like a soap opera."

Adam nodded. "I've seen a few of those in every school I've worked at. Jim Rashford used to say that he suspected some of the Culdover parents used *EastEnders* as a guide on how to live your life. Screaming and swearing included."

"Will I sound terribly old if I say the media has a lot to answer for? Oh, hello." Robin smiled down at the furry canine head which had arrived to snuggle against him. "You've had your breakfast, so don't angle to get any of mine."

"Trouble is, he's sussed out which one of us is the soft parent."

"Nice cop to your nasty?" Robin chuckled. It was great to see his normal good humour being restored, which was further evidence that the case must be making progress. "I guess it could be worth us talking to Ryan again as he's clearly been doing research over and above the family tree stuff. Like the news article about the Skegness punch-up. So pleased we knew about that before we met the Hanleys, by the way."

"My pleasure to help, Oh Great Detective."

Robin snorted in derision. "He didn't mention he'd uncovered something equally juicy?"

"Nope, or I'd have said." Adam sipped his coffee. "Who draws the short straw this time? Maybe you should let Ashok or what's the other one . . . the new constable?"

"Danielle."

"I need to get that into my brain. Danielle." Adam nodded. "Let one of that pair talk to him. It'll be good experience."

"Sharing out the pain you mean? I guess he has good intentions. Trying to be helpful," Robin informed the dog, who seemed completely oblivious to the words but enjoyed the attention.

"That's damning with faint praise. You don't know of any nice, gay cops you could introduce him to? Save your mother a job?"

"Oi! I'm not playing matchmaker, either. Anyway, we don't approve of interactions between officers and witnesses." Robin had the grace to grin.

"Hamish, tell your father not to be a hypocrite." Adam sighed happily. A bit of banter, the three of them being a proper family. He'd have to hope that such a good start to a Sunday might presage an excellent week ahead.

Monday morning, the atmosphere had subtly changed in the incident room. Irrespective of whether it was at last having someone—Alex Hanley—who might just have the magic combination of means, motive and opportunity, or a day's rest working its trick, the team seemed revitalised. A flurry of activity was taking place, which allowed Robin a bit of time to catch up on emails and paperwork before getting everyone together to discuss what they'd turned up in their investigations.

He'd briefed Cowdrey on the events of the weekend and promised he'd let the boss know immediately if anything came from the discussion with Ryan, which Robin had decided not to delegate. It wasn't only a matter of sparing his team the potential boredom: if Robin's mother got mentioned, while he had nothing to hide about her meeting Ryan, it could lead to awkwardness and having to make long explanations. It was far easier to handle things himself.

He'd texted the bloke to arrange a telephone chat midmorning, getting an immediate and apologetic reply saying that the present moment would be good, or else it would have to be tomorrow. Robin rang him right back, not wanting to wait—with any luck, not being face-to-face might cut down on Ryan's prattling. As it turned out, the bloke appeared to be a different character when on the telephone to Robin than he must have been with Pru. Respect for the rank or recognising the slightly changed relationship? Whatever the reason, Ryan proved to be very professional-sounding, making a brief reference to meeting both Robin's mother and husband before saying that time in the pub was separate to police business and he'd make sure he kept it so.

"That's very much appreciated. I'm happy for my team to know she's taken up your services—they already know my dad was adopted—but I don't want them distracted from the business in hand. Right, thanks to the information you gave Pru, I've been meeting various members of Mark's family over the weekend, although only one of them, his brother, Kevin, gave me the kind of details we need about Mark's life." If Kevin's statement could honestly be said to have done that. "We do have a much clearer picture of his family relations, but Mark remains a puzzle, especially as we've been getting conflicting accounts from different people. For example, he didn't get on with his in-laws according to some folk and then according to others, he got along with them fine or at least pretended to."

"Hmm. It's possible everything you've said has an element of truth, because in my estimation Mark was a complex person. Then I suppose plenty of people aren't straightforward and *they* wouldn't have the challenges that life threw Mark's way over the last few years. I always think of Lance Armstrong, doing all that good work with his charity and then it turned out he was a drugs cheat. The cheating and the charity were two sides of the same man. Not that Mark was up to anything dodgy."

That reminded Robin of his conversation with Ashok about Harold Shipman. Was the aura these people built up around themselves merely part of a conscious grooming process or were they genuinely, as Ryan said, people with two greatly contrasting sides?

"What about Suzy? I know you didn't know her, but did you get the impression, from what Mark said, that there were two sides to *her*?"

"I don't know about two sides, but she was quite a character. I'd met her a few times—years ago, before she was married—through a mutual friend. The one who recommended my research work to Mark. This pal also worked at Haveland and Sons, in the research and development department, which is on the site where Mark and Suzy were based, so it's rather incestuous, if that's the right word to describe interrelations within a company. I suppose it's natural that people have flings with each other." That sounded rather wistful: perhaps a wish that *he'd* had the opportunity for such a work-based relationship.

"Can I clarify something?" Robin was getting quite efficient at knowing how to cut in when Ryan paused, no matter how briefly. "Is this friend the person you spoke about at the pub?"

"Yes, that's the chap. Name of Nick Archibald. He'd got himself a bit stuck following up one branch of his family line, because his great-grandmother had the surname Cox and there's a lot of them about. I should have mentioned him to you or one of your officers when we spoke previously, but there seemed so much else to discuss. I really don't know how you and your sergeant pick through it all."

"You probably didn't realise he'd be of interest." Robin wasn't sure he was, either.

"Oh, I should have done, because they were going out for a while. Another one of her Haveland boyfriends."

"In that case, I'm definitely interested."

"Hence my apology." Ryan chuckled. "Anyway, I met her at Nick's birthday party. They were still going out at the time, so this was pre-Mark. Her ex was there too, and he worked for the company as well—something on the drug approval side, I think—so everything was potentially hashtag awkward, although not to her. Water off the proverbial, as far as she seemed to be concerned. Not long after that, Mark must have come to the company, which is when my mate got chucked over. I think it was all very amicable, the split, or else why would Mark have asked *me* to help with the family history stuff on Nick's recommendation, like your mother's friend suggested me to her?"

Was it unchristian to think that Nick's recommendation had happened as a form of mild revenge on the bloke who'd taken Suzy? Inflicting Ryan and his endless chatter on the man who'd stolen his girlfriend? More importantly, stealing Suzy might have provided a motive for Nick to want to take a stronger revenge, if the resentment had festered over the years.

"I'm surprised this pal of yours, Nick, would have wanted to do Mark any favours, if he was the reason Suzy had ditched him."

"Oh, he didn't mind that much, to be honest. If she hadn't gone off, he'd probably have been doing the ditching." Ryan snorted. "He's married now, with a lovely wife and rather cute twins, so he reckons Mark was welcome to Suzy. That sounds very cruel, doesn't it, given how she must have suffered when she was ill, and the whole thing about not speaking anything nasty concerning the dead, but I know you want the truth rather than a story that's sugar-coated. Both about what happened and how people feel. Or felt."

"We certainly do," Robin leaped in. That might spike any theory about Nick having a motive to kill Mark, although it would be easy enough to pretend you were pleased with your new set up while harbouring resentment about your old one. Especially if Nick still felt any affection for Suzy and held the belief that somehow Mark had been the one responsible for her not getting the medical help she needed in time. "What you say about Suzy and her relationships can't harm her now, especially as it'll only get mentioned in court if it's relevant to the case. When and if we ever get someone in the dock, of course."

"Well, if you're encouraging me to be absolutely honest, I have a feeling Nick didn't entirely trust her. When he first went out with Suzy, I'm not sure she and her previous chap had completely broken up—at least, that's what Nick told me, so I appreciate it's only what you call hearsay. It wouldn't surprise me if she was two-timing Nick with Mark in their early days, or maybe with another person. Something along those lines, anyway. One of those complicated situations that you always get in soap operas. Well, I assume you get them in soap operas, because I never watch the dreadful things, but my mother and grandmother were obsessed by *Neighbours* and were always trying to encourage me to give the thing a try. I resisted."

As Ryan carried on about the box-watching habits of his female relatives, Robin wondered if "playing away from home" was part of what Christine Probert had been referring to with her comment about Suzy's life. She'd also used the words *soap opera*. Robin could imagine those revelations coming out as part of Suzy's wine-fuelled heart-to-heart.

"Hello? Chief Inspector?"

"Sorry." Not a good idea for Robin to admit he'd been miles away and hadn't heard the last few sentences. "I was having to deal with something, case-wise."

"No worries. I was asking if you wanted a contact number for Nick."

"Yes, please." Robin really needed to concentrate or he'd miss something of importance. Despite what he'd said to Adam about training in interviewing techniques, he was struggling to apply them to Ryan. "Is he still in the area?"

"Yes. Not working at Haveland's these days, which is perhaps just as well. I have a feeling he might have gone to Suzy's funeral, but you'd need to check that with him."

Robin would. While that invitation to attend might indicate Mark had no beef with the bloke, the reverse didn't apply. Was it too large a leap of deduction to think that words had been exchanged at the funeral, words which had riled Mark? He'd certainly appeared to be worked up, according to Kevin. Maybe his "going ballistic" at the family history stuff had been him letting off steam at something else.

"While I have you on the line, Ryan, can I ask if you turned up anything unusual about Mark's grandmother, Moira? Something that could have been in any way embarrassing if it became public knowledge and not only just post-World War II."

"More embarrassing than having a child out of wedlock? Or getting into a fight in Skeg-Vegas?" Ryan chuckled.

"Yes. Some really personal stain on her character, like being caught soliciting or working in a brothel." That felt a fitting term for the era, rather than being a sex worker, which was not what it would have been called back then.

"Funnily enough, I did. Not quite the same as being caught standing on street corners, because it didn't apply to her sexual behaviour so much as a friend's, but it's exactly the kind of thing that might have caused a rumpus back in the forties or fifties. Even now it's the type of business that some people—unenlightened people if you're being kind and bigots if you're not—still feel uncomfortable about now. This friend of Moira's got caught cottaging in Lincoln. He was one of the waiters from the hotel where she worked, and she appeared in court as a character witness for him. I found that in an old newspaper too, but only a couple of days ago, so Mark wouldn't have known about it. Although I located it in a digitalised archive rather than amongst those newspaper clippings in the box Mark's mother had kept. Did *your* mother mention those?"

"Adam did. He knew I'd be interested in what methods you employed and it's possibly relevant to this case, not just my family history. Was this court appearance all you've discovered that could have blackened Moira's name?"

"So far, yes, apart from a letter to the newspaper damning her by association as well. This all happened not long after she'd had Mark's mother, so it may have been an added incentive for her to go off working on the ships until all the fuss died down."

"Quite possibly." Robin thanked Ryan, said that they'd no doubt be in touch again about the Bright family mystery, if not about the murder, and cut off the call.

If Alex had known about the indecency trial and his mother's name being splashed all over the papers in a defamatory manner, he might have resented that fact as another shameful secret which had both been kept from him and affected his family's reputation. Although who would have told him about it? Would Isabel have seen it as appropriate fodder for feeding to the family? Robin shook his head and shrugged, despite nobody being in his office to see him. He'd better ring Nick to arrange a chat, after which he'd need to go and talk to the team, before he fell down the rabbit hole of speculative thoughts.

Call made, Robin emerged from his office and scanned the incident room, which was still a hive of activity. Pru had not long been back from Mark's house, where she'd been looking for anything that might link the Hanleys to him and asking the neighbours if they'd seen a camper van around. As the other constables were also present, it seemed the ideal time to take stock.

Robin rapped a table to get everyone's attention. "I've been talking to Ryan, and I'm pleased to say he's not that bad when you've worked out how to handle him. He's given me another avenue to explore, one of Suzy's exes called Nick, but before I get onto talking about him, is everyone up to speed with what Ashok and I learned on our travels north of the Watford Gap?"

"Ashok talked us through it, sir, and filled in some of the gaps—excuse the pun." Ben grinned.

"I've put the key information up on the board too." Ashok jerked his thumb, superfluously, towards his annotations and newly pinned photos.

"Great. Let's follow up all the Hanley stuff before we branch off into boyfriends." Robin gave the team a summary of what he'd learned about Moira during the telephone call. "It's all of a piece with the 'shame and scandal in the family' business that seems to get Alex Hanley so het up."

Danielle raised her hand. "Sir, given the timings, is there any chance that this waiter Moira spoke up for in court was also her child's father?"

"Doubt it." Ashok snorted. "He was caught in a compromising position in a men's loo, remember."

Robin resisted leaping in to correct his constable, allowing Danielle the chance to respond. Always interesting to see an officer's wider view on life.

"That means nothing," she said, fulfilling Robin's hopes. "He might have been bisexual. Or deeply in the closet and putting it about on occasions to reduce the chance of being found out."

"But Isabel told Alex that his half sister's father was a married man, which Moira didn't realise until too late," Ashok pointed out. "Although I grant you that might have been a lie. Better in those days, I guess, to admit to adultery than to sleeping with a gay bloke."

"Or he could easily have been married and still be either bi or gay," Danielle said. "It happened back then. It *still* happens."

Pru, who'd quietly been taking everything in, no doubt to process it in her usual efficient manner, said, "If he *was* the father, irrespective of his marital status, his sexual proclivities could have added to Moira's self-imposed pressure not to keep the child. She might have wanted to avoid imposing potential scandal on them. By the way, there were no obvious links to Alex or Lucy Hanley amongst Mark's stuff, and neither of the neighbours had seen a camper van around. I doubt they'd forget it, because the sheer mention of such a vehicle got their noses turned up. Not the sort of thing the Tumulus Gardens mafia would approve of."

"I bet." Robin nodded. "Where are we with phone calls and emails, Ben?"

"As expected, plenty of contact between Ryan and Mark, via both of those methods. I've also found Tom, although no match for either the Packers or Alex on the mobile phone unless it's from a long time ago. We're still waiting to hear about the landline records."

"I can tell you the last number to call him on that. I rang 1471." Pru beamed.

"One up to you. We forgot to," Robin admitted. "I'd say it was because we assumed so few folk use their landlines these days but that would be a lie. Simple oversight."

"It only occurred to me to do it because Mrs. Crouch's phone went when I was talking to her but she didn't answer it. She said people who rang were generally trying to con her, so she tended to let the thing ring out and then check who'd called, via 1471. If she recognised the number, she rang back and apologised for being in the garden when the original call came. I'll remember that for when I'm retired. If I ever get there, given the way they keep putting the retirement age up. I'll fetch the number." As Pru went to find it, she said, "It'll probably only be one of these hard to trace 'you've got a virus on your computer' things. Does this mean anything to you, Ben?"

"I can tell you for certain it's not a scam, unless Alex Hanley's taken to doing them. It's his number, all right." Ben waved the slip of paper triumphantly. "We're lucky that people don't use their landlines much, or this would have been replaced by a more recent call. When did it come in?"

"The Wednesday evening before Mark died. Alex did say he hadn't been in contact at all?" Pru asked.

"He did, the liar." Ashok scowled.

"Being devil's advocate, it's possible that he didn't get a reply on the Wednesday evening when he rang so didn't feel that counted as actually being in touch, but I suspect that's taking an overgenerous view. Why not confess to the fact?" Robin glanced at the incident board: how many other lies had the people named there told? "1471 still records calls which were answered, doesn't it? Not only the ones you missed. Ben, can you put pressure on the landline company to get the duration of the call and whether there were any others from that number? Ashok, anything from your Lincolnshire enquiries yet?"

"A few bits. The sister at the care home was working there when Moira was first admitted and remembers Alex going on and on about how terrible his mother's fall had been and how he wished he'd broken with custom and walked into the house. She said he clearly felt a great burden of guilt over what happened."

"I'm sure he did, although maybe not for the reason given." Robin needed to ensure the rest of the team were clear about his thoughts. "I know you're not mind readers, so I should explain where I'm heading with this. Ashok and I both felt the Hanleys were hiding something. It may have been this phone call Pru's tracked down, but it's probably more and that *more* isn't necessarily all to do with Mark. Alex is a very angry man, especially concerning his mother, so I'm wondering if he lashed out at her like he lashed out at the guy in Skegness."

"Causing her to fall?" Pru, bottom lip stuck out in thought, tipped her head from side to side, clearly weighing up the options. "Did anyone suspect that at the time?"

"Not as far as I can tell," Ashok said. "The officer who dealt with the assault saw Alex after Moira's fall, because the case clearly rumbled on a bit until it was heard in court, and says the bloke was mortified at what had happened to her. He read the situation as a dutiful son feeling helpless about an aging parent, like so many people do. I got her old address and did some digging on Google Maps, though, and discovered she lived in a bungalow that was probably not overlooked by anyone. So, Alex could have said what he liked about how long he spent on the doorstep before letting himself into the house and nobody would have dobbed him in about it."

"My rozzer's nose—which is often right—tells me that something's off-kilter about the story of what went on the day Moira had her stroke. Ashok, when Alex was telling his version of events—all the business about ringing the bell rather than just barging in—Lucy had her eye on him, didn't she? As though she was afraid he'd let something slip. Wasn't the first time during that interview that she seemed to be on tenterhooks. In fact, the pair of them had edgy moments. I'd really like to know what they were scared of."

"Sir, I was thinking about this yesterday. Kept going back over the interview with the Hanleys in my mind and I had a thought. It's only an idea to consider and I don't know if it helps or complicates things." Ashok bit his lip.

"Given that we don't yet have any firm line about exactly what went on when Mark was killed or his grandmother took her fall, let's have all the ideas going, as far as I'm concerned." Fresh insight certainly couldn't hurt at this stage.

"I wondered if we might have got things the wrong way round. I know I'm not explaining myself very well but it's more a feeling than logic. Like when your rozzer's nose twitches." The constable took a deep breath. "We know Lucy's protective of her husband, and throughout that interview she seemed concerned he might say something he shouldn't, not solely about standing on that doorstep."

Robin nodded. "And for the benefit of the others, the couple did appear to have a pre-planned story that either wasn't pre-planned well enough or which they couldn't, for whatever reason, stick to. What do you think we read wrongly, Ashok?"

"What she was worried about—apart from the mother's fall and Alex's contact with Mark. What if we're mistaken thinking that Lucy's covering for her husband being the killer and worrying he might let slip something that incriminates him. What if *she* did the killing and she's anxious about him saying something to incriminate *her*?"

"Did she seem like a potential killer?" Ben asked.

Ashok shrugged. "Don't lots of people have the potential to kill if they find themselves faced with a situation where their loved ones are in danger?"

"There's nothing I saw on Saturday to argue against her being a suspect. Haven't we seen plenty of women who've murdered to protect themselves or their families?" Robin paused. "Ashok. We were told something about Lucy, I think by Tom."

Ashok frowned. "That's she's mad on the royal family?"

"That's it!" Robin gave the team a grin. "No, we've not gone potty. Lucy likes the royals because her dad was once part of the official protection team. That's made me think of Pru's mate. Ashok, can you bend Tom's ear about it? See if by any wonderful chance Lucy acquired her dad's truncheon—or anything else you could use for self-defence—like the girl with the holdall did."

"I'll get onto it as soon as." Ashok seemed delighted to be allowed to follow the trail of something that might support his new theory.

"I hate to be a party pooper, but we don't know for certain that the blunt instrument that killed Mark was a truncheon," Ben pointed out, "and even if Lucy had one, her husband could have borrowed it."

"Which are totally valid arguments, the second of which would argue in favour of them planning the attack. Or for the possibility of one," Robin replied. "What I had in mind was that Lucy might have routinely carried it round to protect herself, especially when on holiday. Irrespective of the legalities, a blunt instrument would help protect both when they're in that camper van parked up in the back of beyond."

"That could work, sir," Ashok said with renewed confidence. "Let's say they arrange to meet Mark in the woods but Lucy goes instead of Alex, as part of shielding her husband from having to face the half nephew he'd like to disown. Mark's not happy about the swap, and the pair get into an argument. She feels she's being threatened and lashes out. Doesn't realise how hard a blow she's struck until it's too late. Realises he's dead, panics, and legs it."

"What about the car?" Pru asked. "How does that fit into a fight gone wrong rather than a planned attack?"

"A stroke of luck on her part." Ashok jabbed his thumb towards the photo of the car. "She takes the Yaris to make it easier to get away and meet Alex, rather than him having to come and get her."

"What about Mark's missing suitcase? What reason would she have for getting rid of that?" Trust Pru to pick up on the very element that continued to flummox Robin.

"She knew the car was going to be found at some point and dumped the case to try to confuse the trail?" Ashok clearly didn't feel confident about his suggestion.

"Maybe Mark had also, independently of Ryan, turned up the story about his grandmother's appearance in the witness box and had printed it off to discuss with Tom," Danielle suggested. "He mentions all of that in the argument, and she sees a chance to get rid of it."

Pru slapped the desk, making them all jump. "We're being blind. Forget about a trial seventy years ago and look for a louder ticking time bomb than that. Think about what happened to Moira in 2020. If Mark had somehow turned up information that cast doubts on Alex's story about his mother's fall, that would be a damn sight more dangerous to him and Lucy than an old story about sticking up for a mate in court. Mark might have been taking *that* to discuss with Tom. He'd want to know what happened to his granny."

A rumble of agreement ran round the team, one in which Robin joined. "You could be onto something, Pru. In that scenario, I'd guess the Hanleys could have known about that information when they agreed to the meeting and went in with a plan in case something went wrong. Otherwise, why set up the Timsworth alibi unless they thought they'd need it?"

"How could Mark have found out about the fall, though?" Danielle asked. "I'm not doubting the idea, just getting it clear in my head."

Pru shrugged. "Maybe he talked to the people at the care home. I assume he'd have asked Tom whether Moira was still alive and got the story you did."

"Mark could have spoken to the chief gossip," Ashok said, then had to explain whom he was referring to. "Perhaps we should do the same. I bet Isabel's got a view on what happened the day Moira had her stroke."

"If she's as sharp as she's supposed to be, I bet Isabel's got a view on Mark's murder too. Assuming she knows about him." Robin pinched his top lip, trying to work out the next step. Legging it all the way back to Lincolnshire felt premature, so a telephone call might be best. "Ashok, I know it's your idea, but I'm going to ask Pru to ring Isabel once we've got a number for her, which Tom can probably provide. It'll be a tricky interview, because we want information *from* the woman, not to provide her with gossip fodder. That's the reason I won't ring, because a call from a chief inspector would surely raise her suspicions."

"I agree, sir." Pru gave Ashok an apologetic smile and got a resigned nod in response.

"Okay. Last bit about the Hanleys for the moment. Where are we on their alibis, Danielle?"

The constable pulled a frustrated face. "There's no functioning CCTV in the car park they're said to have used, I'm afraid. I could check traffic cameras for the area, sir."

"Leave that for the time being. It would be a pointless exercise if we discover they were both at the abbey at the time they said." Plenty of opportunity to go through traffic footage, or examine mobile-phone location history, if the investigation ended up no further forward from more traditional methods.

"I've got something else on the abbey angle." Danielle nodded. "I've been in touch with the parish office. They reckoned the stewards are a pretty laid-back crew and apparently don't pounce on visitors and force them to pay as soon as they enter the place. But the very helpful office lady I spoke to did let on that they'd had a new volunteer on duty that Saturday. There'd been a few complaints about this newbie being rather officious. You know, trying to get everyone to consider donating as much as they could afford. The office lady went through the emails they'd received to kick up a stink and none of them were from the Hanleys, so perhaps this volunteer cowed them into coughing up, despite what they told you and Ashok. I'm going to ring her later and see if she remembers them."

"Good. She might recall them, even if they meekly paid and didn't want to admit the fact to us. While Alex is like every slightly grumpy bloke of his age, I'd say Lucy could stick in people's minds. Purple hair for a start and I don't mean a blue rinse. Deep voice, too." Robin stopped. *Deep voice.* "Pru, that argument Mr. Rashid said he heard. Remind me about it."

"While he couldn't say for certain, it was between a guy we think was Mark and either a bloke or a woman with a deepish voice. Could have been your Lucy. Do we have any other women we've spoken to who could fit the bill, vocally?" Pru asked. "What about Izzy Packer?"

Robin shrugged. "Maybe. More husky than deep, I'd have said, but maybe she sounds different when she shouts. The only other female witness I've spoken to is Christine Probert, and she's a soprano rather than a tenor, if you get me."

"We also spoke to Mark's neighbours, sir," Ben said. "Although I can't see either Mrs. Crouch or Mrs. Armstrong doing the deed."

"Okay, so let's leave that aspect and get back to Suzy's ex-boyfriend. He's called Nick Archibald, and I'd like to interview him as soon as possible." Robin strolled over to the board, writing the man's name on it. "He seems to have been pally with Mark, despite any love rivalry, so I'm not saying he's automatically a suspect."

"Seems like we've got your favourite pairing of friends and family to put in the frame, though," Pru said.

"I didn't want to mention that." Robin chuckled. As his sergeant would, with any luck, be dealing with Isabel, he'd need to find another partner for what might prove a crucial interview. Time to involve the new recruit. "Nick's working from home today so he's happy to see us whenever we can drop in. He lives on one of the new estates at the top of Abbotston, so I'm proposing heading up there now. I'd normally have Pru in tow but another one of you will have to draw the short straw this time. Ashok and Ben have had an outing, so it has to be Danielle's turn."

The constable beamed. This would be the first occasion upon which they'd worked together interviewing a witness, and she'd no doubt see it as another step in her integration into the rest of a fairly established crew. "I'll be right there, sir. Let me grab my bag and visit the ladies'."

"I'll visit the gents' and see you in the car park."

Robin—as he always did with a new officer—let Danielle drive him and was pleased to quickly discover that she was a highly sensible motorist. Memories of Anderson, another one of his protégés and a bit of a demon behind the wheel at times, could still make Robin shudder.

"How are you settling in?" he asked, once they were on their way. They'd have a relatively short trip miles-wise but the journey time would be longer than usual, impacted by the rash of local roadworks which had sprouted up over the last few weeks.

"I'm really happy, sir. Everyone's been so helpful, especially Pru. You don't mind putting in every ounce of effort if you feel it's appreciated."

Robin shot her a glance, although the constable's face proved impassive. "That sounds like your efforts haven't always been appreciated in the past."

Danielle shrugged. "I don't want to dob anyone in, sir, so can I just say that you're right and leave it at that?"

"We can, as long as what you've experienced is only lack of appreciation, because if it's anything worse, I'd like to know. It's not dobbing in if the behaviour you're reporting on is unacceptable." All kinds of things were crawling out of the woodwork all over the country, to show that misogyny, racism, and homophobia in the police force weren't things of the past. Robin wouldn't stand for any of it on his teams—people could have plenty of banter and laughs without resorting to cheap and nasty shots.

"It was only that, sir, honest. I'd have been confident telling you if it was anything bad." Danielle smiled gratefully. "You've a reputation for being straight up. Didn't you sort out the previous crowd at Abbotston?"

"I was part of the cleanup, yes. Mr. Cowdrey's another who's got as little time for this stuff as I have. I think he'd like all the crud chucked out of the service before he retires, but that's a vain hope." Robin feared it would be long after *he* retired that all the bad eggs were got rid of, because new ones kept hatching.

"All that makes me extra pleased to be here rather than at Kinechester." Uncertainty flickered across Danielle's face. "I have to confess I was a bit worried, because the bloke who was supposed to be at Abbotston and then got the place *there* told a mate of mine that *he'd* got the plum job. Bigger station and more serious cases at Kinechester, rather than the humdrum stuff we usually deal with. I bet he's spitting nails because I'm getting the experience of working on a murder."

"I bet he is too." Robin could state that with added confidence as he'd heard via the Cowdrey grapevine that the constable concerned had been assigned a spate of petty thefts to investigate and had taken the task with ill-disguised resentment. "Nobody would pretend that these serious cases are pleasant—the only thing worse is anything involving children being hurt—but you'll learn plenty if you watch what everyone's doing, because there are a lot of different skills in the team. Don't watch them to the detriment of your own work, though."

Danielle grinned. "Don't worry, I've no intention of blotting my copybook, sir. Not that we blot anything these days, because I don't know anyone who uses a fountain pen, but these old sayings do hang on."

"Yep. My partner's got a book about the origins of common sayings and it's a fascinating read. A lot of them seem to go back to the days all ships had sails. *The devil to pay. By and large.*" The ensuing discussion on the topic of adages that people used without knowing the original meaning was only cut short when they arrived at the estate where Nick lived. At which point they had to focus completely on locating his home—and somewhere convenient to park—among the rabbit warren of streets.

Eventually, they found the house tucked away up a cul-de-sac off the main part of the road.

When Nick answered the door and warrant cards had been flashed, he asked, "Where are you parked? I never thought to warn you about how tricky it can be to find us."

"We found a space marked for visitors," Robin assured him, with a grin. "Once we'd been round the block a few times."

Nick rolled his eyes. "It's the only complaint I have about the estate. I bet the planners wanted to discourage car usage, but that strategy won't work when public transport is so rubbishy round here." He ushered Robin and Danielle into the house, steering them towards the dining room and apologising for any toys they might find lying around. "Luckily the twins are at the nursery, so it's less chaotic than it usually is. Can I get you tea? Coffee?"

"Tea, please," Robin replied.

"Same. Thanks." Danielle perched on one of the wooden chairs as their host went to get the drinks. "Lack of parking aside, I really like this style of property. There are loads of similar places around Abbotston, although the prices shot up over the last few years. Not sure I could ever afford one."

"I think we've all felt the same at some point. The first step onto the housing ladder's the hardest." Especially in some parts of the local area, such as Kinechester, where it was easy to commute to London. "These kinds of houses were all built at a similar time. I won't say I can remember when it was all fields round here because it'll make me sound very old but I've seen a lot of change."

"You're a spring chicken, sir."

As the constable got herself ready to take notes and then checked her phone, Robin thought back to his own days as a lowly officer. He'd been lucky to find a relatively cheap flat, one that his dad had helped him do up, and later on there'd been his old boyfriend Patrick to help pay the bills. He and Adam had driven past Patrick not six months previously and—like Ben with Christine Probert—Robin had suggested they go back round to check whether it really was him. They'd not stopped for a chat on that occasion, though, partly because of the potential awkwardness and partly because time had clearly not been kind to the bloke. Robin had felt a bit guilty at encouraging Adam to keep driving, but life had moved on, and he hadn't been sure he and Patrick had anything to say to each other any longer. Certainly not with a husband on his arm.

The kettle must have been quick to boil because Nick was soon back with tea and biscuits. "I was sorry to read about Mark," he said, while pouring out the brew for all three of them. "Any idea when the funeral will be or is there an inquest first?"

"Yes to the inquest and no idea to the funeral. After the coroner adjourns matters and releases the body, but more than that I can't say." Robin hadn't previously given a thought to who would be organising the function. Kevin? Kevin's wife? The Packers? "Danielle, could you make a note to let Mr. Archibald know if and when we get any news on that?"

"Will do, sir." She jotted down the required reminder.

"I think you're the first person who's asked us that question," Robin said. "I have to confess I'm surprised."

Nick raised an eyebrow. "Because the other people you've spoken to didn't? They may have thought you were the wrong person to ask."

"Less that than because, while I know you recommended Ryan's services to Mark, so you must have been on speaking terms, I'm used to love rivals not being exactly the best of buddies."

Mark chuckled. "Love rivals? Did Ryan call us that when you spoke to him?"

"Not quite, although he did say that Suzy had chucked you when she took up with Mark. He also said that you weren't too upset about the fact, which doesn't match our usual experience of these situations, either." Robin blew on his tea before taking a sip. The brew was strong, tasty, and very welcome. And while he'd usually be delighted to meet a witness so welcoming and clearly ready to cooperate, he couldn't help feeling a touch of regret that Nick—at least on first impressions—seemed too open and genuine to be Mark's killer. *Don't forget the earlier conversations about Lance Armstrong and Harold Shipman.* "Tell us what really happened."

"To be honest, I *was* angry with Mark at one point, because he did in effect steal Suzy from me, although on sober reflection—that's literally sober reflection—I soon concluded that I didn't think anyone could ever steal Suzy. Not completely." Nick paused, no doubt having registered the bewildered expression Danielle was wearing. "I'm not making any sense, am I? Afraid I'm not good at talking about the touchy-feely stuff at the best of times and I've never had to talk to the police about a murder."

"Say things as they come," Robin suggested. "We can ask for clarification if we're not sure what you mean."

"Okay. What I was trying to say was that Suzy was a free spirit, probably because of her hippie upbringing. Did what she wanted, even if that meant keeping two blokes on the go at the same time or ditching one because she'd found a better prospect." Nick blew out his cheeks. "She may not have resembled her parents on the outside, but the apple didn't fall far from the tree."

Robin took another drink of tea, buying time to frame his thoughts. "We were told that she'd rebelled against the things her parents stood for."

Nick shrugged. "Maybe, in terms of how she dressed and her rejecting the whole 'grow-your-own and don't have a car because it'll kill the planet' thing, but the essence of the sixties was ingrained in her somewhere. Women free to do what they want and all that, irrespective of what other folk thought."

Danielle glanced at Robin. "Can I ask something?"

"Go ahead." He nodded encouragingly.

"Was Suzy cheating on Mark? Either before or after they were married?"

"I have no idea. It wouldn't surprise me if she was, given her track record, but I'd be a liar if I said I knew for certain or that I could hazard a guess who with, unless it was one of her exes. It wasn't me, for a fact." Nick sounded a touch flustered; maybe he was getting his defence in before he was confronted with the question.

"Did she two-time *you?*" Danielle asked.

"Yes and no." Nick ran his hands through his hair, leaving it spiked up like a small boy's. "She was supposedly still with her previous guy—Harry—when we first went out. I think she was monogamous with me for most of our relationship, although that might have been wishful thinking on my part. I'm pretty sure Mark and I overlapped, but you never could get a straight story from Suzy at the best of times. She wasn't a straightforward type."

Robin nodded. Ryan had spoken about Mark being a complex bloke. Clearly, like had called to like in his choice of partner. That double-whammy of two convoluted characters in a relationship could go towards explaining a lot of the contradictions in the accounts Robin had heard of who got on with whom and who was being blamed for what. "Would you say Suzy was the kind who might play both sides against the middle? Maybe slag off her parents to her husband and vice versa?"

Nick didn't appear surprised at the question. "Yeah, I would. She certainly liked people to be on her side and was happy to bend the truth a bit to maintain that."

Robin recalled the earlier conversation with Ryan, when he'd been musing about conscious grooming. Certainly Suzy's behaviour could have been said to be on the greater grooming spectrum. For instance, had her wine-soaked discussion with Christine been a calculated thing, at least in part, to garner sympathy and make sure Suzy's version of what had happened was believed?

"Did Suzy's death come as a shock to you?" Danielle asked, jogging Robin back into the moment.

"Yes. Partly because I'd lost touch with her, so didn't know for a long time that she had become ill. To be frank, we all had other matters on our mind when Covid struck and keeping up with old flames wasn't top of my priorities." Nick's point was valid. It had been a different world back then, on many fronts. A world that now seemed ancient history. "Then one day I ran into Suzy— not in any deliberate way—about six months before she died. By then I'd heard the rumours from ex-colleagues who were still at Havelands that she wasn't well."

Danielle glanced up from her notetaking. "You didn't immediately get in touch when you were told she was ill?"

Nick shook his head. "I consciously decided not to contact her. It was on the one hand feeling that it would be intrusive to pop up out of the blue and say something like, 'Sorry you're dying' and on the other hand sheer bloody cowardice. She might have wanted to cry on my shoulder, and I didn't want that to happen. I'm not good with the touchy-feely, as I said. Anyway, I happened to see her at Burton's Garden Centre, the other side of Abbotston. It's got a play area so it's a place I take the twins to give Rosie—my wife—a break. I was there one weekend and saw Suzy going to the coffee shop, apparently to have a catch-up with a mate. We didn't have time to chat much, especially with those two tugging on my arm." Nick pointed with evident pride and affection at a large portrait of the youngsters. "Suzy didn't look as bad as I feared she might, but cancer's an awful disease, isn't it? Doesn't always show that much outwardly until right at the end, and anyway people can make an effort to hide it. Suzy would have done."

Robin remembered the photograph in Mark's house and how happy Suzy had appeared in it. Putting on a show for the benefit of the camera? If so, who could blame her. "Could any of Suzy's ex-boyfriends have posed a threat to Mark? Somebody who didn't feel as happy as you did at their splitting up?"

"Nobody springs to mind straight away." Nick peered into his mug, face wrinkled in thought, before looking up blankly. "Nope. To be honest, if somebody had a target on their back, it would have been Suzy herself. Not only about splitting up with people—plenty of blokes hate being two-timed."

They did. But it was Mark who'd been murdered, not his wife. "So my team can get everything linked up properly, time- and relationship-wise, can I take you back to a party you threw, years ago? Ryan said that *he* was there, as was Suzy and one of her previous boyfriends, even though she was going out with you at the time. Was the ex at the party the Harry you referred to?"

"If it's the party I think you mean, then yes. I can tell you categorically that you can eliminate Ryan from being a love interest for Suzy, because he's on the other bus." Nick's remark came across as purely factual, with no snide edge. "I've got some pictures of that evening, if you're interested in seeing them."

"If you wouldn't mind fetching them, we'd be very interested. Thanks." Robin waited until Nick had left the room, presumably in search of an old photo album, before saying, "How are you enjoying—if that's the right word—your first proper interview for a murder case?"

"It's very instructive, sir. In fact, the whole investigation so far has been." Danielle grinned sheepishly. "See, I grew up thinking police work would be like it is on the telly, and since I joined the force, not a week goes by that I don't revise my ideas. They don't get a lot right on TV, do they?"

"Nope. I guess the reality wouldn't make good viewing." Robin snorted. *He* wouldn't make very good fodder for the small screen. Not a maverick or a rule breaker and with a stable home life, to boot. Like the first Barnaby on *Midsomer Murders*, maybe, but with a better regard for wearing the proper equipment around a crime scene. "They get the false leads and red herrings right, though. It's what we're seeing here. The Hanley family history on the one hand and Suzy's love life on the other. Either could be the trail to the killer. Or neither."

Danielle nodded thoughtfully. "And what generally gives you the big breakthrough in a case, sir? The clue that tells you you're on the right track? Forensics?"

"Sometimes. Other times it's as lucky as a chance remark a suspect lets slip or as mundane as scrolling through traffic camera footage, hard work though that is." Then there were occasions arising out of discussions at home, over a meal or a beer, when something Adam said had provided such a fresh insight it led to a major leap of deduction. All coppers would benefit from having such an effective sounding board available.

The sound of descending footsteps on the stairs put paid to the discussion.

Instead of an old-fashioned photo album, Nick had a tub of memory sticks, one of which he had in his other hand. "Took me ages to find these. Another thing we had to hide when the twins came along. Anyway, I think I've got the right one, but in case I don't, I brought the lot. Hang on while I bung it in the laptop."

Nick soon found the folder he wanted and was able to display a selection of typical party photos, people either posing for the camera or caught off guard and distinctly worse for wear.

"Is that Ryan?" Robin asked, pointing to a man with a moustache among several people with facial hair, some of it unsuccessful.

"Yes. A few of us did Mo-vember that year, which didn't suit everyone, as you can see. I've never attempted it since." Nick snickered. "I think Ryan was one of the few who could pull off a tache, although Harry wasn't bad, either. This is him." Nick indicated a tall, wiry individual standing to Suzy's left, while *he* stood to her right. "Harry Foakes, who was another of the Haveland mafia, you might say. Although it's a pretty big company so I guess it's difficult locally to get away from people with a connection to it."

"He worked there?" Robin confirmed.

"He was the company doctor and the person who first spotted something was wrong with Suzy. Well, after *she* did and had left it too long to get help, if that's the right story."

"That's broadly what we've been told, although the account varies depending on who's telling it. A bit of debate about whether her parents prevented her getting proper treatment. They insist that's untrue." Robin paused to let Nick respond.

"I only met them a couple of times so can't vouch for their character, but if they deny it, I'd be tempted to believe them. I can't imagine anyone forcing Suzy to do what she didn't want or to stop her doing what she *did* want. If treatment was delayed or she received the wrong sort, she'd be the driving force. I *can* imagine her being in denial about her illness because she could be very stubborn at times. As for the story varying—"Nick shrugged. "People believe what fits their agenda, don't they?"

Robin nodded. Mark would perhaps have been open to anything that put his in-laws in a bad light, while Suzy might have opted for whatever got folk on her side. It was the same with the McKay family: Alex finding the slightest remark insulting to his mother and Tom McKay maybe eager to find a young male relative he could get on with. It could also apply to police officers, concentrating on the clues that fitted their theories.

"Was it Harry Foakes who referred her to a specialist?" Robin asked.

"I have no idea. I don't know how these things work, in terms of his relationship with the NHS, so I'm not sure he would have had the capacity to do so. Not formally, anyway. He might have been able to point her at one of his mates who did private work to get an initial diagnosis, but I don't think Suzy had private cover. Maybe he wrote to her own GP and started the ball rolling or forced her to go." Nick paused. "Suzy's problem may have shown up in a works medical, because Harry performed those routinely, although his main role at Havelands was on the medical advisory side. He's in a similar position with a multinational, now. If this is important, I could try to find out for you."

Robin raised his hand. "No, you're okay. We'll follow it up ourselves if we think it's relevant. At the moment, we're trying to make sure we have the fullest possible picture and haven't missed any details. Was Harry at Suzy's funeral, by the way, or would that have been too awkward all round? Given the possibility that she might have resumed the relationship with him at some point, maybe during her marriage."

"Are you really asking me if her having an affair, if she did have one, might be relevant to the way the diagnosis came about?"

An odd question, one that Robin couldn't quite make out. "How do you mean?"

"Sorry, I should have made myself plainer. I've just remembered seeing something on telly, years ago—on *Casualty* or whatever the spin-off from that was—where this doctor found a lump in his lover's breast while they were having nookie. It did cross my mind that something of the kind might have happened with Suzy." Nick sighed. "You know, Harry spotting that something was wrong when he and Suzy were at it. He could have forced her hand to take the issue seriously, because she wouldn't have been able to stay in denial then."

Danielle paused her note-taking. "That might also explain why the story around her illness and treatment is inconsistent. You can't exactly admit to your hubby how your diagnosis came about if it happened in those circumstances."

"Exactly my point." Nick gave her a smile. "Anyway, getting back to your original question: whatever Harry and Suzy were or weren't up to, he wasn't at her funeral."

"Would you have a contact number for him?" Robin asked. Irrespective of whether Harry was another potential suspect, they needed to hear what *he* knew about life chez Bircher.

"I don't, but I know where you can track him down. The fact he'd moved jobs to one of Haveland's bigger rivals is itself reason enough for him not to have attended Suzy's funeral, because there'd have been plenty of his old workmates present. There was a bit of bad feeling when Harry left the company, although I'm in no position to criticise anyone for taking up the opportunity of a better job. It's what I did myself."

"Okay. Well, thanks for taking time to consider the question. You'll probably guess what I'm going to ask next, and I have to say we've asked everyone we've talked to the same thing, which is to tell us what they were doing on the day Mark died. We think that's the Saturday before last." Robin deliberately left the time vague: it would be interesting if Nick homed in on a specific part of the day.

"If you're asking about the morning, I was with the twins at yet another playpark, and this time it was the one near the entrance to this estate. I chatted to Mel, who's another one of the local mums. I don't have her number, although Rosie might. She knows Mel through the nursery the twins go to, so *they* were the ones she recognised at the park, rather than me. Comes to something when your children have a better social life than you and are the reason people introduce themselves." Nick snorted. "Then I came home for lunch, after which we got the kids down for a nap and put our feet up. The rest of the day was spent prepping for Rosie's parents coming over for dinner that evening. They arrived about six so they could put the twins to bed while we finished cooking. Need anything either side of that?"

"Not at the moment." A nice wide range of time accounted for, although his alibi for around the time they thought Mark had been killed was the one easiest to fake, relying only on his wife's say so. "If you could get Rosie to text us Mel's number that would be useful, although I don't think we need to bother your in-laws at the moment. It's all so that my team can tick off another box on their lists and make sure we don't leave anything undone. I have nightmares about some future case in which I decide not to check a person's alibi because I don't think they have anything to do with a case and then it turns out they're the culprit." That was a slight exaggeration, but Robin did value doing for himself—or getting one of the team to do—all the boring bits of work that it was easy to pass over as unimportant and which turned out to be vital.

"I wouldn't have your job for the world," Nick said. "I'd rather be on permanent nappy duty."

Danielle made an appropriately disgusted face at the word *nappy*, then asked, "We've discussed Suzy's exes, but can you think of anyone else who'd have had cause to hurt Mark? Or even a reason to get in an argument with him?"

Nick shrugged. "When I read about his death on the local news site, I assumed he was the victim of a random mugging that went too far, but that's not what the media are saying now. Unless they're making things up, as they like to."

Robin noted what might be a deliberate, yet neat, sidestepping of the question. "In this case they're right. If Mark was mugged, the assailant took nothing of apparent value, apart from his set of keys. Presumably to access his car, which turned up parked legally in a multistorey in Kinechester."

"I read about that too. There was an appeal for anyone who'd seen it." Nick scratched his head. "It's all a bit bizarre. Mark drove a small car, didn't he? Not like he ran a big Jag or some other make it would be worth nicking to order. Any idea why it was taken?"

Robin shrugged. He had plenty of ideas but wasn't going to discuss them with the witness, not least because some were quite feeble. "Could have been nothing other than to get out of the

Kings Ride area—with all the questions that raises about how the killer got there in the first place—but that theory's probably too simplistic, and I'm not sure anything about this case is simple. Back to my constable's question: Who might have had a grudge against Mark?"

"Couldn't tell you, or I would have told you. I don't think he got on with his in-laws, but if everyone that applied to ended up murdered, the world would be quickly depopulated, wouldn't it?"

Which was absolutely true and—for the purposes of investigation—horribly depressing.

As they drove back to the station, Danielle asked, "What do you make of an ex-lover being in the frame, sir? Whether it's Nick or Harry or somebody we've not run across yet."

"You tell me what *you* think," Robin countered. Always useful to see the workings of a junior officer's mind.

"I think an old boyfriend of Suzy's as her husband's killer has got a lot going for it, especially as we find out more about her. Explains one of the oddities we've come across, for a start."

"Which oddity in particular? We've got a few in this case."

"The meeting with Mark taking place in Kings Ride Woods. Why do that? Unless the killer arranged it there because they're married or in a relationship and didn't want to risk being spotted and then have to explain to their partner what they were up to. I'm getting the impression that in some of these local villages you can't sneeze without somebody noticing and reporting it back."

Robin chuckled. That described Lindenshaw to a T. "I've certainly been coming round to thinking it was the other person rather than Mark who arranged the meeting place. Assuming it was an old flame of Suzy's, what was their motive for the meeting or the murder or both?"

"Revenge. Maybe Suzy spun said ex a tale about her illness, saying Mark was the one reluctant for her to have treatment. That could be consistent with what we're learning about her character. Old flame wants to meet Mark so he can confront him about it.

Says the air needs to be cleared or . . . Hold on, sir. Let me think." Danielle paused. "Perhaps he says he'll tell Suzy's parents what went on and how he thinks Mark's attitude contributed to her death. Maybe threatens to spill the beans to Havelands or to us. In any case, to somebody Mark wouldn't want told what Suzy had said, even if what she alleged wasn't actually true. We all know how people believe there's no smoke without fire and they then let rumours breed."

"Okay. I agree it must have been an important meeting for Mark to go out to the woods when he still had to drive up to Lincolnshire that day and blackmail's important enough business. Where in your theory does the Yaris come in?"

Danielle broke into a self-satisfied grin. "Well, it had a bike rack, didn't it?"

"Yep. One that was free of fingerprints apart from the victim's." The CSI report had proved another frustration for the team. The car had yielded very little. Not the merest sniff of weed, let alone any hard drugs or anything else that might have made the vehicle a tempting target.

"Cycling gloves that covered the fingers," Danielle said, "would be very handy for hiding prints and wouldn't be as out of place as winter gloves would at this time of year. Mr. X, our killer, having arranged to see Mark, tells his partner he's off on one of his usual bike rides. He cycles to the woods, meets Mark, and gets into an argument with him. As a result of this dispute, Mark ends up dead, either from a blow struck in anger and with no malice aforethought or as part of a planned attack. Afterwards, Mr. X—again, either in a panic or with a degree of planning— takes Mark's keys, cycles to the car park, loads his bike on the Yaris, drives to Kinechester and then cycles home. All of which, journey-wise, acts as a blind. For both his partner and for us."

That hypothesis held together. Just. Mr. Rashid had mentioned cyclists being around, although that was slender evidence. "And where does the suitcase that we can't find come into things?"

Danielle frowned, clearly not having fitted that into her theory yet. "Well, perhaps it held something in it that Harry or Nick needed to get their hands on. Like proof of his affair with

Suzy. Or maybe he ditched it on the way, in order to muddy the waters. Killers do try to be over clever at times."

"They do." Robin could think of several high-profile examples and, in his own experience, a random turnip in a dustbin that had the team puzzled and which turned out to be left solely to baffle them. "That suitcase still hasn't turned up, though. If it was slung away somewhere, it was done very effectively and the same applies if it's been hidden. How would Mr. X get it home and past the partner?"

"He couldn't have taken it home on his bike, sir, so that doesn't apply." Danielle cast him a sidelong glance before evidently realising it wasn't that serious a suggestion. "Although if it had been slung in a garden somewhere, it would have been reported. Same thing applies if it had been left in one of the back alleys in Kinechester—somebody would have called out the bomb squad."

Robin nodded. The story of a missing suitcase or overnight bag had been given to the media without bearing fruit. Various ideas had been bandied around the team and the best they'd come up with was that the suitcase had been taken home by the killer to be disposed of piecemeal or maybe tucked into a convenient skip full of household junk.

"Anyway, it's only an idea about the bicycle," Danielle said.

"It's not a bad one. Theories don't have to explain everything. Not at this point, anyway. That fun begins when we get someone in front of a jury."

If they ever got that far with this exasperating case.

They'd not long been back at the station when Danielle knocked on Robin's office door.

"I've got that contact number for Harry Foakes, sir." She placed a slip of paper on his desk. "I also found out where he lives. Do you know a village called Bishop's Manor?"

"I've heard of it but I'd need a map to see where it was." Robin noted the barely hidden excitement on the constable's face. "It's clearly significant."

"It is in terms of our conversation in the car. It's halfway between Kinechester and Kings Ride." And with a beaming, self-satisfied grin, the constable backed out through the door.

Chapter Thirteen

Monday felt like it had lasted forever, despite Adam getting away from work by half past five. He'd had the much-dreaded delicate conversation with Jane, the Wickley staff member, which went better than anticipated because she'd expected it. With a flurry of tears that might have been genuine, Jane said she'd been on the verge of resigning anyway because she wasn't sure that Wickley school was the place it used to be, which might have been code for her no longer finding enough sympathetic ears in the staffroom. She'd also admitted that she couldn't imagine how she could improve her performance, which she said had always been good enough in the past, a lack of self-awareness which for Adam summed up the problem.

On the way home, he reflected that her departure would mean having to recruit, although that was probably going to be the best outcome for the school and its pupils. A square peg in a hole that had gradually become rounder didn't help anyone, least of all the peg itself. With a smile, he thought of Robin and his boss easing the unwanted constable into the Kinechester team, and wondered if he could steal some tips about how to give a reference that was factually accurate but didn't read like a hatchet job.

He got home in a good mood, if tired, to find Robin already there and on kitchen duties.

"That smells great," Adam said, as he kissed his husband.

"I'd say it was all my own work but you know it's not. One of Kate's specials." Robin stirred the casserole that was re-heating on the stove. "She left a note saying she'd made it for a family lunch do yesterday and ensured she had plenty left over for us, given how busy we are."

"What a legend. We should get her some flowers when your case is done and dusted. For going above and beyond the call of duty." Adam stretched, feeling better by the moment, not least because he'd deliberately not brought any work home with him. "Had a good day?"

"A productive one, yes. I'll tell you and Cam— Damn, I thought I'd cured myself of that."

"You're getting better. Give it another year and you'll have *Hamish* off to a T."

"I hope so. I was thinking about the old lad today. Somebody mentioned the Abbotston Slasher case and Campbell came to mind."

"Another batch of his heroics." Adam gave him a hug. "Anyway, you were saying you'd tell me something."

"Yep. An update on the case, over dinner. Talking of which, I'm expecting a call, so apologies in advance if it comes at an inconvenient time. Which Sod's Law says it's bound to." Robin rolled his eyes. "I'm trying to get hold of one of Suzy Bircher's old flames, but he's away at a conference in Birmingham, according to his answerphone, so I've left a message asking him to call back."

"No worries. If it's confidential, Hamish and I can amuse each other." Adam glanced across to where the dog was happily chewing one of his toys. "An old flame of hers. That's the way the case is heading?"

"I couldn't tell you where it's going, at the moment." Robin snorted. "We've got three people at least whom we know that Suzy was involved with, two totally separate strands to the investigation and at least one bloke we're sure is lying, but he's on the non-flame side of our enquiries."

"And a partridge in a pear tree?" Adam cut in, while the joke could still work. "Sorry, couldn't resist."

"Pillock." Robin took Adam's hand. "Don't ever change from being *my* pillock, though. You're exactly what a hard-working policeman needs to come home to at the end of the day. You keep me sane."

"I try my best." Adam pulled his husband tighter. "You keep on keeping me sane, as well. When I hear the sort of crap you're dealing with, it puts all the school stuff into perspective. I—"

Robin's phone sounded, so they broke the clinch to allow him to take the call. It turned out only to be some scammer insisting Robin had been involved in an accident that wasn't his fault. A quick mention of his rank put an abrupt end to the call. "I wish these people would find a proper job and not occupy my line."

"I usually ask them if their mothers know that they spend the day conning people. I'm not confident it'll prick their consciences, but it makes me feel better."

"I should have guessed it was dodgy when I didn't recognise the number, because the bloke I'm expecting has one that ends in triple seven. Can't not answer it, in case it was from Woodhall Spa, though." Robin's expression turned pensive. "One of the few witnesses I've really taken to in this case got rushed to hospital, and it might have been his neighbour ringing me with an update."

"Nothing serious, I hope. Or suspicious, given you're in the middle of a case," Adam added, remembering occasions when there'd been a second victim or the violence had spread.

"Not suspicious and nothing too serious, other than the march of time. It's Tom, the bloke Ashok and I went to see up there. Pru tried to ring him today to get contact details for somebody else and said the neighbour had answered his landline." Robin sighed loudly. "Tom had suffered a fall and was taken in for observation, which is why the neighbour was there, packing him an overnight bag. He should be home tomorrow, God and all the tests willing."

"Poor bloke." The perils of getting old: it came to everyone, if you lived that long. Adam quickly shrugged off the memory of Campbell's demise, determined to live in the moment and count his current blessings. Including Hamish, who'd come across to give him a proper welcome. "I hope you don't have to head back up to Woodhall Spa anytime soon."

"So do I, although I expect I'll have to visit the area. My liar lives in Lincoln." Robin chuckled. "I don't fancy saying that after a double scotch."

"Then keep sober until the food's on the table, and then you can tell me all about your long-legged liar from Lincolnshire who lives in a lorry."

"It's a camper van, actually, and he only lives in it when he's on his travels. Although I suppose his wife might boot him out there on occasions when she's fed up with him being around the house. That wouldn't surprise me."

"I suppose that'll all make sense at some point. I'm off for a spruce up." Adam pulled Robin close for another hug, one whose tender nature soon got spoiled by a growing canine inserting himself between the pair. "Oh, you want in, do you? Not enough for you being spoiled by Kate today?"

Adam made a suitable fuss of the dog before escaping to the bathroom, where he could lock the door against interruptions by creatures without opposable thumbs. Or indeed with them.

Over dinner, Robin updated him about where the case now stood. Adam listened, only chipping in with encouragement regarding the progress made or to ask a clarifying question about what seemed an increasingly complex investigation. One which was touching on unexpected areas, such as blokes caught cottaging, as well as the commonplace ones like possible adultery.

"Suzy reminds me of Jane, the learning assistant I had to have a serious talk with today," Adam said. "I'd been dreading it, but the result was good, because she's taken umbrage and is going to resign, which is no doubt the best outcome. I'll be picking your brains about references at some point, because I've never had to complete one for somebody who adds so little value."

"You'll have to hope it's a matrix which you can fill in honestly and leave the personal stuff to, 'her attendance was good.' Assuming it was."

"If the rest of her performance matched attendance and punctuality, I'd have had nothing to complain about. Anyway, Jane's been trying to create an image of herself as somebody who's been hard done by, although I don't think anyone at Wickley's been taken in by the act. They'd seen the truth behind the image before I arrived, Alice told me."

Robin nodded. "Yeah. It does sound like Suzy, because the image of her is starting to tarnish. It's still sad about the medical side of things, I'm not disputing that, but she wasn't the innocent victim of fate that people had been making her out to be."

"The living-in-a-soap-opera thing again?"

Robin's phone sounding cut off the conversation. It soon became clear it was the call he'd been expecting, because he took himself off into the hallway to talk. Adam had cleared the table, loaded the dishwasher, and let Hamish out for a wee before Robin reappeared.

"Sorry about that. That was the ex, Harry Foakes. He couldn't chat much now, as he's off to the conference dinner, and I suspect he'd already got one or two drinks inside him. Typical medics, always living it up." Robin rolled his eyes. "I'm going to interview him late on Thursday, when he's back down here. He owns a bike, by the way, which supports Danielle's theory, although he was surprised when I asked him about it. Or pretended to be surprised—I can never really judge unless the witness is in the room with me. Long story short, he says he hadn't run across Mark for years and only saw Suzy occasionally when she was ill. States that was more on the medical side than the social."

"Do you believe him?"

"I'm not sure. As I said, I like to be able to see someone's face when I'm questioning them so I can read the body language. He did say something odd, though, right at the end of the call. About looking forward to seeing me and how it would be the first time he'd ever had to go through the whole, 'What were you doing at twelve fifteen on Saturday?' routine. Before I could ask him why he was being so specific about the time, he rang off. It may have been nothing more than an off-the-cuff remark, but that's suspiciously close to when we think Mark was killed."

"And as far as I can remember, you've not been that specific in the media reports." Adam called the dog back in from his post-wee frolicking.

"Exactly. It could be purely coincidental."

"Or Foakes might know the bloke who overheard the argument, they've discussed it, and he's guessed that's the time you're focussing on. Stranger things have happened."

"I guess so." Robin's phone—still in his hand—rang again. "It's Mum. I wonder what she wants? Hello? I'm putting you on the speaker, so make sure you don't say anything rude about Adam."

Mrs. Bright snorted, in exactly the same way her son would have done at such a quip. "How he puts up with you, I don't know. I have news. Perhaps."

Robin pulled a puzzled face. "Hold on. Hamish can hear you and he's getting overexcited. Speak to him for a moment, while we relocate to somewhere comfy." He edged backwards, phone at waist level, while his mother told the Newfoundland that he was a good dog, *yes he was*, and that she'd be round to see him soon. The three of them processed into the lounge, where they all snuggled onto the same sofa. "Let's hear this maybe-news, then."

"It's from Ryan. He rang just now to say he'd been working on our mystery for most of what was left of the weekend, and he thinks there's a chance he's struck gold already. A chap in Australia."

"That's quick work," Adam said. "How did he manage it?"

"He said he came at it backwards. Started with the money somebody wants to give us and the name of the solicitor who contacted Mr. Caswell. Mr. Brown. He focussed on obituaries from possible countries—your tax treaty stuff helped there—and a time window of when the death was likely to have happened, what with probate and so on. He said he simply had to keep plugging different combinations of key words into various search engines and wherever else he goes hunting for his information. He says I'm not to get too excited, because he's had false dawns before and the chances of him hitting a bull's-eye straight away are pretty remote."

How remote? To the point, it begged the question of why Ryan had felt the need to share the tale so soon. Adam asked, "Why didn't he wait until he was certain before saying anything?"

"Because—and this is only what I'm thinking, not what he said—he's actually surer than he's letting on. Ryan's built up a lot of information about this man from various obituaries, because he'd made a lot of money in banking after emigrating from the UK and was heavily involved in supporting local charities, so his death got a fair amount of coverage. The rough date he left England fits with David's birth too. A bit beforehand." The injunction on Mrs. Bright not to get too excited was clearly being ignored and her voice was full of relief that the money seemed to be totally legitimate. "Anyway, when Ryan's a bit more certain, he's going to send the stuff over, because he thinks the human interest in the story's enough to intrigue me, anyway, even if it doesn't turn out to be David's dad. He's going to look for further information about this chap and the will he made. Do you know where Lutterworth is, by the way?"

Robin and Adam shared a baffled glance. "Couldn't tell you. Is that where this possible relative came from? And does he have a name?"

"Yes, he does have a name, but Ryan says he's not going to share it until he's done more work. He joked that I might terminate his contract prematurely. Lutterworth's where this chap came from originally so I shall be off googling it in a moment but wanted to share the location in case it meant anything. I don't recall your grandparents mentioning the place."

"Neither do I. Hold on. Adam's already got it up on his phone."

"It's a few miles off the M1 on the way to Leicester."

Robin took Adam's phone, scrolling the map out so they could see the detail. "I must have driven past it on the way from Woodhall Spa to Oxford. How bizarre."

"Perhaps it was somehow meant to be, that you'd be so close, especially when your case has got such a similar strand. Or it's a huge coincidence on both counts," Mrs. Bright added with another snort. "Anyway, when I know the fuller picture, you two will be the first to hear. Robin, give Hamish a big kiss from me and give Adam a hug."

"Will do. Take care."

"Well, what do you make of that?" Adam asked, when the call had ended and he'd had his hug, which was evidently second in Mrs. Bright's priorities to Hamish's kiss.

"Like Ryan ordered Mum, I'm not getting my hopes up. Especially as this Lutterworth bloke—Lutterworth Len, I'll call him—sounds like the kind of person anyone would want to have on their family tree. Successful, charitable." Robin gave him a smile. "It'll be difficult to prove, of course, whether or not the inheritance does come from him, because his solicitors might insist on keeping the waters muddied and say he was administering it on behalf of someone else. Whoever set up this inheritance for Mum clearly wanted their privacy respected, and if this guy he's tracked down had a reputation to keep up, he might not have wanted people to know he'd got some woman up the duff and either abandoned her or got sent away in disgrace. Maybe Ryan can trace things back to something concrete that'll prove he was Dad's father, but I'm not holding my breath. It's not like the solicitor would want the family bothered by a request for a DNA sample from a half great-nephew."

"Would you want to ask to do the test, anyway?" Adam asked.

"Probably not." Robin blew out his cheeks. "I think Mum and I will have to be satisfied with the level of proof demanded in a civil case. Preponderance of evidence—clear and convincing evidence if we're lucky—rather than proof beyond a reasonable doubt. That would be enough for me, and we'd have to persuade her to be satisfied with it too."

Adam rubbed his husband's arm. "I think she'll be relieved enough knowing that Lutterworth Len isn't Parkhurst Paul or Pentonville Pete. That night on the white wine, she was worried sick you'd be benefitting from the proceeds of crime."

"Oh, bless the old girl." Robin wrinkled his nose. "And bless Ryan if he can put her mind at rest."

"It's actually a bit of a pain that he's discovered something so quickly. I was hoping you'd have your case all put to bed before Ryan had anything to offer you. So you could clear your mind of one thing before tackling what you'd want to do if you did have a name—beyond reasonable doubt."

"Actually, I think it might be beneficial having work to focus on. I've spent thirty odd years not knowing who my biological grandfather was and I'd have carried on blithely if it hadn't been for this windfall. I'm not saying the news hasn't made me think again, but I need to consider it cooly." Robin produced what seemed an unforced grin. "Maybe when we're both retired we could take a plane down under or a car up the M1 and pay some quiet respects of our own. What this case has taught me is that stirring up the waters of family history mightn't be the safest thing to do."

"Very wise." Adam pecked Robin on the cheek, then offered to go and make them a hot drink, which would give his husband some time alone in which to process what they'd heard. He'd just got the kettle on for a cuppa when the doorbell sounded.

Robin called, "I'll get it. It's like Paddy's Market around here this evening."

Adam could hear muffled voices, then the sound of the front door closing, before Robin popped his head into the kitchen and said, "It's Pru."

"Pru? That sounds ominous." They'd lived in this house for a while now, and the sergeant had never dropped in on the off chance, despite it not being too far off her route home.

"She's full of apologies but says it's important. Can you make that tea for three?"

"If it's her, I'll break out the good biscuits rather than the own brand."

"Thanks, Adam!" came from the hallway, where it sounded like the sergeant and Hamish were getting acquainted, given the outbreak of, "Who's a handsome boy, then?"

"That would be me!" Adam quipped, as Pru and the dog came to the kitchen door.

"He gets worse," Robin said.

Pru snickered. "As banter goes, it may be predictable but it's not offensive. Anyhow, I hope you two don't mind me calling in on my way home. I was going to wait until tomorrow, but by the time I decided I should ring tonight I was only a couple of miles away and in a blackspot. I promise I won't make a habit of this."

"I know you won't." Robin smiled.

Adam nodded. If Pru had important news to share, he hoped he'd be allowed to hear it as well. If not, he and Hamish might be banished to the kitchen.

"*I* think it's important," Pru said, leaning against the door jam and fussing over the dog again. "I've spoken to Isabel, sir."

"Call me Robin while we're on home turf. I can't be doing the 'sir' stuff while you're eating my best biscuits." Robin must have been making sure that Adam would get the update as well, or he'd have surely already whisked his sergeant off to somewhere they could speak confidentially. "That was quick work with Isabel."

"Thank Tom and his neighbour for that. I'd left work this evening to meet up in town with a mate who's having a birthday meal. I said I'd only stop in for a drink beforehand, because I don't like her boyfriend, although she doesn't know that. Good job I wasn't committed to the meal, because Tom's neighbour rang me ten minutes after me and my mate sat down, to say she'd been in to see him at the hospital. He'd insisted she go and get Isabel's number for me, rather than us having to wait." Pru smiled appreciatively. "Good timing, because it meant I could legitimately say to my pal I had to go back to the station, before the boyfriend arrived."

Robin snorted. "Winner winner."

Adam, who'd got the tray of refreshments all laid out, began swirling the teapot, ready to pour. "If I'm permitted to listen in, we should go where it's comfy. If not, I'll have a cuppa out here with Hamish."

"As far as I'm concerned, you're an unofficial member of the team," Robin said. "Unless what Pru has to say is strictly confidential."

The sergeant shook her head. "There's nothing Adam and Hamish can't hear, s— Robin."

Once they were settled on the sofas, steaming mugs in hands, Pru continued. "So, I nipped back to the station and spoke to Isabel. Well, she spoke to me. A lot. She's not quite as bad as Ryan, but if it turned out she was his granny, I'd believe it. Genetically."

"Adam's met him, so he'll get the idea." Robin cradled his mug. "There has to be useful stuff in amongst the gossip, though, or you wouldn't be here."

"Yep. It's possible you might have to go on your travels again, so I wanted you to know as soon as I could. I'll start with some other stuff first, though. The bloke in the dock for cottaging, Graham, wasn't the father of Moira's baby. Isabel was big pals with him as well, and reckoned if Eleanor had been Graham's child, he'd have insisted on marrying Moira or at the very least having the baby brought up by a member of his family. Actually, Graham *did* offer to marry her, so she could have the baby made legitimate. Offer not taken up, possibly because it would have been a celibate affair. Graham apparently couldn't face doing it with a woman."

Robin's eyebrows leaped up almost into his hairline. "Sounds like you had a very full and frank conversation. How did Isabel know all this detail?"

"She and Moira were Graham's confidantes, which shows you it wasn't all benighted attitudes back then. I guess he was what you'd nowadays call the typical gay best friend and the women—well, if it's not offensive, what did they call fag hags in the forties?"

"I dread to think. I bet the setup's as old as the hills, though. Go on." Robin, clearly morphing into work mode, showed an alertness of expression and posture never normally displayed when he was chilling out on the sofa.

"Isabel said *she'd* have gone into the witness box if Graham had needed her to act as character witness. She's certain he was entrapped by a handsome police officer who'd gone into those loos to act as bait, which was apparently pretty common back then. She and Moira were furious about their mate being set up and wanted to try everything they could to get him off the charge. As Moira already had another job ready and waiting that would take her out of the country, she'd said she'd avoid any flak for having stood up for him, so took on the character-witness role. And yes, some people were horrified that she'd done so. It caused quite a scandal, although it didn't lose her the job, which it might have done."

"Scandal enough that Alex Hanley didn't like any reference to it? I wonder exactly what that bloke said at Skegness to rile him so much. May not have been about his mother's supposed promiscuity." Robin sipped his tea.

"Hold that thought about Hanley. Actually, could you also hold my tea while I get out my notes? I don't want to put it on the table and then Hamish knocks into it and scalds himself."

Adam leaped up to take her mug. "Let me, Pru."

"Thanks." The sergeant passed over the drink, then consulted her notebook. "So, this next bit is specifically about Mark. Isabel saw Tom about a fortnight ago when he dropped in, which he does every couple of months. He said how excited he was at the prospect of meeting a new family member, and he got Isabel to do some googling for him about DNA tests and how they worked. Isabel suggested he should invite Mark to come and visit her, if and when they knew for certain he was Moira's grandchild. As inducement, she promised to tell him as much as she could about his grandmother."

"This is Isabel's principle of keeping the gossip in the family rearing its head. If she knew he was a McKay by heritage, he'd be allowed into the inner sanctum." Robin paused. "Although Tom wasn't allowed in, was he? If what he told us was correct, he'd only been given the bare details, although he might have been holding something back for whatever reason. Maybe to protect his sister, especially as he felt she was no longer in a position to protect herself."

"Could be. Anyway, Isabel's quite the silver surfer, and since Tom told her about Mark, she's been finding out about him on social media and the like. With a renewed emphasis when she heard about his death. She says she rarely gets out so has to live via her laptop, and apparently being active on there is the single thing that helps her keep her marbles."

"If that's what she believes, it probably does," Adam chipped in. "Power of the mind."

"I'd say you're right. As a result of her surfing, Isabel was certain she didn't need a DNA test to confirm that Mark was Moira's grandson, because of his eyebrows, which were identical to how hers had been at the same age. Isabel says it's that thing about distinctive traits skipping a generation." Pru made a *go figure* face. "Maybe Isabel saw what she wanted to see in Mark's face, but it wasn't only the eyebrows that she said reminded her of Moira. She made this weird remark about how her old pal had been a bit of a pushover for a sob story. Moira wasn't always a great judge of character, which was why she'd got taken in by Mark's grandfather. Isabel didn't quite state it categorically, but she gave the impression that it was the old tale of this bloke saying, 'My wife doesn't understand me' until he'd got his leg over enough to satisfy him. At which point he decides that his wife understands him perfectly well and he's going back to her."

"I think I might need to cover Hamish's ears." Adam chuckled. "So why did she think Mark was a pushover like his gran was?"

Robin pointed at Adam. "I said you were an unofficial copper—I was going to ask that very thing. Was it something about Suzy's illness or her love life?"

"Initially the illness, which Tom had told Isabel about, although she'd done her own poking around on the net. There was a page for Suzy at one of these memorial sites, as well as an announcement on her Facebook wall, so Isabel read all the comments there and used them to fill in some of the story blanks. I'd already had a look at those, and while Suzy naturally generated a lot of sympathy, there are clear inconsistencies in terms of who she told what about why treatment was delayed. A pal of Izzy Packer's weighed in at one point to try to tell the family's side of the story." Pru raised an eyebrow. "That didn't escape Isabel's notice, nor did a barbed comment about Suzy being no angel. Isabel said it wouldn't surprise her if Mark had been duped in some way."

"The dying woman having a last fling? That would fit with Danielle's theory." Robin, lips pursed, thought for a moment. "It's a long shot, but can you remember any comments on those sites from Nick Archibald or Harry Foakes or anyone else who might have been an old boyfriend?"

"Not that jumped out at me but that was before we had those two names, so I wondered if Danielle might like to go through it all again. She might see something I've missed. Mind you, this Suzy angle might be irrelevant, because the main reason I dropped in tonight—apart from your best biscuits—is Alex Hanley. As you might have guessed by now, Isabel likes to read all the local news sites, and she saw the story about Alex's fight in Skeg-Vegas. She was pretty mobile a few years back when the assault happened, so when she saw the story, she called up a cab and went as quick as she could round to Moira's to discuss it."

"I bet she'd have beaten Usain Bolt getting there. Quicker than Hamish with his Bonios." Robin flashed Adam a grin that didn't simply appear to be linked to having made the quip. He was clearly getting excited about what Pru had to share.

"I think you'd win your bet quite safely." Pru rose to fetch the remains of her tea from where Adam had been cradling it. "This is where things get interesting. According to Isabel, Alex hadn't told his mother anything about the fight, just texted to say that his son's stag do had gone off well, despite it turning a bit rowdy. The grandson hadn't mentioned it either, although he'd not seen her since then. Moira didn't appear shocked when she heard about the assault, merely disappointed, and that seemed to be because Alex hadn't told her about it himself."

"I'm going to play devil's advocate," Adam said. "He may not have primarily been trying to cover up his misdemeanour. People don't like upsetting or worrying elderly parents, do they?"

Pru shrugged. "I'd agree with you in general but in this case Moira was already worried because of the business about the child she'd given up for adoption and the way Alex had reacted. He was due to visit her the next day because when he'd found out about Eleanor he wanted to discuss the matter in full, whereas Moira wanted to forget about it. She told Isabel that she could maybe wrong-foot Alex by asking him about the fight because then he'd be less likely to throw her own misdemeanours back in her face."

"Knowing how arguments usually go, I'd have thought that was a vain hope." Robin, onto whose lap Hamish had been slowly wriggling himself, gave the dog a scritch. It was evidently well received, because if Newfoundlands could have purred, Hamish would have done so. "It sounds like Moira didn't automatically make excuses for his behaviour. Same as Alex's son didn't."

"Exactly." Pru turned towards Adam. "You must see that a lot, when you've had to call parents in about their little darlings."

Adam nodded. "Plenty of times. It's a pretty common parental reaction to trot out the 'he's not a bully, he was provoked' excuse or offer a dozen reasons why their child couldn't possibly have done what I've seen with my own two eyes. Was Isabel surprised that the family's reaction was far from the usual?"

"Not at all. Nor was she surprised at the assault charge because she knows Alex has got a bit of a temper on him. Isabel told Moira to call her the day after she'd visited, once she'd seen her son, in case she needed some moral support, but clearly the call never happened. She got a bit tearful with me and said that was the last lucid conversation she and her best friend ever had." Pru drained her tea, then laid down the mug. "I felt really sorry for Isabel. She has no children of her own—she got hitched in the early fifties but hubby died in a motorcycle crash at the Isle of Man TT and she never remarried. Lived her life vicariously through her friends' families and still does."

Like Adam with his husband's cases, a spectator who sometimes had a clearer and wider view of the game? Robin, given the glance in Adam's direction, might well have been entertaining a similar thought.

"Did Isabel have any suspicions that Moira's fall wasn't an accident?" Robin asked.

"Actually, she did. I didn't want to nudge her into saying that, obviously, but I needn't have worried about leading a witness on. She volunteered the theory as soon as we got onto Alex and his temper. She said her feeling that he'd pushed or hit his mother wasn't strong enough for her to contact anyone about it at the time." Pru smiled ruefully. "Whatever else she is, Isabel's still fiercely loyal to her friend and she knew that Moira wouldn't have wanted allegations flying about."

"What if the allegations were founded on fact?" Adam said.

"Isabel's streetwise enough to know that there are facts and facts. If Moira had been compos mentis, then an allegation might have been worth pursuing, but her mental state went downhill so quickly that if she'd alleged her son pushed her, the police or social services may not have believed her. After all, there was no other witness to what happened."

"Did Moira actually tell Isabel she'd been pushed?" Robin stroked his chin, every idea evidently being given due consideration. "Even in a non-lucid conversation between the pair of them?"

"Not in so many words." Pru blew out her cheeks, clearly frustrated at only being given tantalising glimpses of what might have gone on. "Isabel visited Moira in hospital after her fall, and there was some remark made about Alex being rough with her, but when Isabel pressed for further information, Moira denied she'd said anything at all about his visit. Whether that was dementia speaking or she realised she'd said too much and was playing forgetful, Isabel couldn't say. What I do know is that Isabel had seen mother and son get into arguments before, and while she'd never personally witnessed any physical aggression from Alex since he'd grown up, it wouldn't have surprised her if he'd got violent with his mother. And I don't think Isabel was just being wise after the event, like people too often are when they say they saw something coming."

Adam raised his arm, then pulled it sharply down, grinning sheepishly. "Sorry. I was so intent on the conversation I thought I was back in class. You said Isabel hadn't seen any aggression from Alex 'since he'd grown up.' Does that mean he was violent when he was younger?"

"Apparently, he used to be fond of using his fists when he was a boy. Moira thought he'd grown out of it, but when Isabel told her about the Skegness incident, she'd got very upset and said he clearly hadn't."

Robin heaved a sigh, disturbing Hamish in the process and getting an aggrieved look. "Sorry, sunshine, but if you will sit on me don't expect I'll act like a mattress. Chances are your dad's heading up to Lincoln, and he'll be taking Aunty Pru with him."

"Me?" Pru sounded surprised, although not unhappy, at the suggestion. "I thought you'd have Ashok with you, as he's done all the Hanley side of things."

"Normally I would, for continuity, but Alex Hanley's lied to us already, he's got form for assault and a dodgy alibi, all of which adds up to me wanting to rack the pressure up on him a notch or two. Ashok will be disappointed, but things have become more serious and this is a job for a higher ranking officer. It might mean I'll have to postpone seeing Harry Foakes until later than planned, but we need to get the family side of things clarified."

"Right. Then I'll get onto Alex first thing tomorrow, and if he can see us Wednesday, shall I book us a hotel for that night? On the principle that there may be extra work to do up there if it turns out we think he's our man?"

"Sounds good. Do you think it'll be worth going to see Isabel, or do you think we've got everything we can from her?"

Pru shrugged. "I'd say she's told me all she knows that's relevant, for the moment."

"I've got another question, and maybe I shouldn't be asking it, but I do feel like an honorary copper at the moment." Adam paused.

"Ask away. I know you won't spread anything we've discussed, and I'm sure Pru's got used to me putting ideas past you and reporting back to the team with, 'Adam wondered . . .'" Robin gave him one of his special smiles. "If it's bad practice, then it's still productive and Cowdrey knows about it and turns a blind eye. Your question?"

"This Isabel sounds very switched on, and she's clearly not only following the case via the news but doing her own armchair research, like poking about on social media sites. I'm assuming that's harmless, so long as she isn't on these sites commenting and muddying the waters." Armchair detectives were all very well, but when they got it into their heads to get out of their chairs and go to the scene, poking around and potentially destroying evidence, it was no longer an innocent game. "Does she have a theory about who killed Mark?"

"She does, although I wasn't going to mention it, because it's a bit fanciful. Which she knows, because she has the sense to admit she didn't really know enough to make an informed judgement. Thing is, she watches a lot of crime shows on the telly and she

said she approached the subject by thinking along those lines."
Both Pru and Robin rolled their eyes at the same time, bursting
into laughter as soon as they realised what they'd done. "Yeah,
that's what I thought. I was dreading what she'd say. Actually,
Isabel had several ideas, one of which she knows is a bit bizarre,
but I'll share it because it made me laugh. She said that if this
case *had* been televised, Moira would have been played by Judi
Dench, *she'd* have been played by Penelope Wilton, and I'd have
been 'the nice one off the film about the racehorse,' whoever she
meant by that."

"Shame she hasn't met Robin," Adam said. "I'd love to know
who she'd cast for his character."

"Away from that fascinating topic and back to this bizarre
theory," Robin said.

"Well, if it *was* a TV show, Isabel's sure we'd have three main
suspects, Alex and Suzy's parents, all of whom would be acting
suspiciously. Then, right at the end, it would turn out that the
murderer was Suzy herself, who was never dead in the first place
but had secretly gone off to get a radical new treatment. She'd
then returned to take revenge on her husband."

Adam chuckled. "That sounds exactly like a plot twist they'd
come up with."

"Yep. As Isabel said, TV cop shows were having increasingly
ludicrous endings that she's sure bear no resemblance to the real
world, although she did add that everything she's read online
gives her the impression that Suzy was a nasty piece of work.
One who probably didn't worry about whether she was telling the
truth or a lie and got away with it because people felt sorry for
her." Pru spread her hands. "People don't like to speak ill of the
dead, especially when the circumstances of the person concerned
are so tragic, but that doesn't help us get to the truth."

"And I'd say there's definitely a grain of truth in Isabel's
character judgement of Suzy," Robin said, "even if the rest of her
thinking is far-fetched. If Isabel picked all that up from what she
read online, maybe we should second her onto the team, because
we're only getting there ourselves. Mind you, I think I'll keep a
resurrected Suzy only for when we run out of all other hypotheses,

because I'm not sure I can justify digging up a grave to see if it's empty on the say so of an old woman, no matter how techno-savvy or streetwise she is."

Pru giggled. "Mr. Cowdrey would think you'd lost your marbles."

"I'd lose my badge. Interesting that she seems to see Alex as a credible suspect for the murder, though."

"Yeah. She said that was because he'd 'got previous' and I can imagine her grinning when she said it. You know, we must have made her day, getting in touch, because she's clearly an intelligent woman with perhaps not a lot of outlets for using her brain. Oh, hello." Pru's lap was being invaded by Hamish, who was obviously relishing all the strokes he was getting. "Interesting that she also fancied the Packers for Mark's murder."

Robin brushed some dog hairs off his trousers. "Another example of Isabel being astute, I'd say. Given that she's picked out the one person we know lied to us and the couple who have no alibi."

"Neither of which I mentioned to her, so yes, astute. Unless she had inside information, which I doubt, because I'm pretty sure she'd have told me in that case. The last thing she said was that she wanted us to get to the truth."

Adam sighed. "What if the truth is her best friend's son got so angry with her he put her in hospital and later went on to murder her grandson in a similar fit of rage?"

"I think so. 'We need the truth, whatever it turns out to be,' she said, and I believed her."

"Then she's a brave woman. Too often the truth is the last thing people want." On which sombre note, Adam began mentally preparing for his husband having another few days away.

Chapter Fourteen

Another day, another drive cross country, up the M1 and all points northeast. Robin subtly manipulated who drove when so that he did the stint past Lutterworth, as he didn't relish having to explain to his sergeant why he was wistfully eyeing the sign for it. Or scanning the local countryside to see what the area was like. There were a dozen valid reasons—including the case in hand—why he shouldn't be considering whether he had roots stretching back to the town via Lutterworth Len, although he'd concluded overnight that one of those wasn't his indifference. The hours since his mother had rung had made it plain to Robin that he wanted to know who his grandfather was, even if he'd never get to meet the man and genuinely had no interest whatsoever in connecting with any living relatives. Maybe it was simply the detective in him that didn't want to leave a question unanswered.

Robin had confessed this to Adam over breakfast—slightly shamefaced as he'd insisted for so long that he didn't give a toss about his ancestry—but his husband had, as ever, been a rock.

"Whatever's best for you works for me. No right or wrong answer to this one. It's not a SATs paper."

Just as well it wasn't a test, because Robin's answer would have been rubbed out, rewritten, and rubbed out again no end of times. Still, they had other family mysteries to deal with first before the issue of the Brights could be settled.

Robin and Pru had arranged to interview Hanley formally, at his nearest nick, with his wife coming in afterwards to make an updated statement. First, there'd be a briefing with Inspector Ericson, to expand on what had been communicated between her team and the one at Abbotston. Robin had made it plain in a phone call to her, before they'd set off, that there were two separate cases here, of which the murder clearly took precedence.

When he'd been planning the phone call, Robin had anticipated facing some insistence that a local officer be present at Hanley's interview, given that if the roles had been reversed Robin would have wanted an ear on what was said. But in his morning briefing with Cowdrey, the boss had dropped him the word that was unlikely to happen. The Lincolnshire team were dealing with an unsolved series of sexual assaults, so a bloke getting into a violent argument with his mother a couple of years previously, with little chance of making any charge stick, wouldn't be the top of their priorities. Especially if there was a chance that the Abbotston team could hand a confession to them on a plate.

"How likely is it that Hanley's the man for this murder?" Cowdrey had asked.

Robin had started his reply with a shrug. "Fifty-fifty. He was in the general area, with no clear alibi for the time, he's got 'previous' for assault"—Robin had suppressed a grin at recalling Isabel's use of the word—"and we've identified lies in what he told us. I'd put twenty quid on him hiding something, but whether that's attacking Mark, I couldn't say. If it turns out to be *only* hitting his mother—although there's no *only* to be applied to a case like that, is there—then at least we won't come away empty-handed."

Cowdrey had snorted. "Run the race, get the consolation prize, and that then goes to the Lincolnshire force. A rozzer's lot, eh?"

Robin replayed the conversation in his mind as he drove. Lurking deep in his psyche, partly as the result of the bullying he'd endured at primary school, was a fear of failure. That one day he'd be confronted with a case he couldn't solve, one that his name would always be associated with. And while interviewing Alex Hanley was only a small part of a bigger investigation, if they came away with nothing at all, that would hurt like hell.

"Too often the truth is the last thing people want." Adam's words again, this time from the evening before, reminding Robin that

his job didn't involve finding things that were convenient or comfortable for him. Frustrating though it might feel, every time they eliminated a hypothesis, perhaps because of an unbreakable alibi, then they surely got nearer to the correct solution.

The sign for the A46 junction, where they'd need to turn off, alerted Robin to the fact he was letting his attention drift. They'd have no chance of getting at the truth if they ended up under the wheels of a lorry.

On arriving at Nettleham, where they'd be conducting the interviews, Robin and Pru completed their—extremely brief—briefing, aware that the last thing they should do was get in the way, especially as a report of yet another sexual assault had come in that morning. The anxiety to get that case solved was palpable throughout the station and much of that pressure was apparently, and naturally, coming from local media and women's groups. Pru and Robin had nothing but sympathy for their colleagues and promised not to get under their feet.

The pair grabbed a quick coffee and cleared their minds before getting to grips with Hanley. As they walked down the corridor to the interview room, Robin noticed that Pru was fighting a smile. "What's amusing you?"

"I just remembered Isabel and her cop shows. If we were on the telly, we'd do the interview and it would turn out that Alex Hanley didn't kill Mark *or* hit his mother. Instead, he'd be the one who's been carrying out these assaults. You'd spot the clue and leave Ericson torn between delight at solving the case and fury at the soft lot from down south having solved it."

Robin snorted. "Then I'm eternally grateful that we're not on the TV, because that would take the biscuit."

They'd reached the door of the interview room where Hanley and his solicitor would be waiting. Time for a deep breath and a real effort from Robin at getting his game face on.

They began the interview as they always did, making introductions, explaining what would happen in terms of the procedural legalities and the recording equipment, all the time being as professional as possible. No point in creating a tense atmosphere in order to pressurise the witness—most people were nervous enough at the thought of a formal interview and Hanley's pale, drawn face suggested he was already feeling the strain.

"I owe you an apology," he said, sitting forward and with a glance at his solicitor, Natalie Rednall, before Robin or Pru had been able to ask a question.

"What for?" Robin asked.

"For saying I hadn't tried to ring Mark, when I had. Stupid to lie, I know, but think of it from my point of view. He was murdered and the way it happened was similar to what happened at Skegness." The statement came over as carefully prepared, evidently with input from the solicitor, who'd nodded encouragingly. "I thought I'd look the obvious suspect."

"You looked still more obvious a suspect when we discovered the lie," Robin said. "Why have you decided to come clean now?"

"Lucy's been on my case. We've been talking about this ever since we got back from our travels, and she said I was bound to be caught out because you'd investigate his phone records."

"So, when did you ring him and how often?" Robin was pretty certain he'd get an honest answer, given Lucy's stating the obvious to her husband.

"A couple of times, a few days before he died. It was after he'd spoken to Tom but before they'd had the chance to meet in person."

That certainly accorded with what the team had discovered from the phone records. "In which case, how did you get a contact number to ring Mark? Tom said he hadn't passed on to you the one he had."

"I'm rather ashamed about that." Alex fixed his eyes on the table. "I was round at Tom's, after he'd rung me about this new family member we were supposed to have. He was pleased as punch at making contact with his great-nephew, but I wanted to find out all I could about the bloke, because you never know these days if people are who they say they are. Tom always insists on making a cup of tea or providing a slice of cake for any of his visitors, so when he was out of the room doing host duty, I had a shufti in his address book. I know that's where he's always kept any contact details, because he doesn't trust having them solely on his phone, so I only had to turn to the B section and there Mark's number was, for me to make a note of. Tom's going to be cross with me when he finds out."

"So, when we met outside Oxford, your wife insisted you hadn't had any contact with Mark. Why?" Robin asked.

Alex put his head in his hands. "She was protecting me, as usual. Lucy didn't know about the first time I'd spoken to him until I fessed up. She went flipping mental that I'd been keeping something so important secret from her. Especially given all the fuss I've made about Mum not telling me about Eleanor. Like mother like son, Lucy said. Actually, she said a lot else besides but that's the only repeatable bit if it's going on the tape." He raised his head and grinned sheepishly.

"Seems like a lot of anger breaking out," Pru said, in a matter-of-fact tone. "You wanted to know about Eleanor. That's understandable. But were you ashamed of having an illegitimate half sibling?"

Alex, sitting back, shrugged. "I was torn in two. On the one hand I wanted to know all about her and on the other I wanted nothing to do with that side of things. One of the reasons I told Mark to leave the family alone was to buy me some thinking time. I tried taking the angle that Tom was old-fashioned, that he'd only been being polite when Mark made contact but that the rest of the family didn't want interference."

"Interference?" Pru's tones were less objective now. "He had as much right to be told the truth as you did."

"That's what *he* said." Alex leaned forward again, elbows on the table. "And, you know, that's what really bugged me. That Mark turns up out of the blue and Tom's overjoyed—like it's *his* long-lost son—and he's ready to spill the beans. It felt like everyone was suddenly bending over backwards to tell him what they hadn't been prepared to tell me over all those years. Yes, I know that's probably an exaggeration because Tom's maybe not told Mark anything other than he's told me, but the timings hurt."

Robin cut in. "Hurt enough to get into an argument with Mark?"

"No. Not face-to-face. That's one of the reasons I extended our holiday—easy to do that when you're self-employed—to make sure I wasn't around when Mark came up to visit. It never occurred to me that his trip might not happen. Tom's still upset about the whole business, and I wouldn't be surprised if he's worked out I tried to put Mark off. He's not stupid, although he's too much of a gentleman to mention it. Not inherited the fiery genes."

Maybe Mark had, though, which had got him into a fatal argument.

"He might have figured it out, or Mark could have rung him after your phone call and told him." Robin recalled forming the impression that Tom and Alex didn't get on that well. Was that entirely due to the business with Mark or the latest manifestation of something longer standing? Maybe tension had arisen between uncle and nephew if Tom suspected Alex had played a role in Moira's fall and her subsequent deterioration. It might have been logical for Isabel to have aired her suspicions to her old friend's brother.

Alex shrugged again. "I wouldn't have put it past him."

Robin was struck with an idea. "When did you last see Tom?"

"Not since before we went on holiday, that time when he went for cake and I got Mark's number. I've been keeping my head down with him, especially after the murder." Alex frowned. "Lucy's seen him, because she went to visit him in hospital the day before yesterday. Did you know he'd had a fall?"

"Yes." Robin studied Alex carefully. "Although not as serious as your mum's by the sound of it. I hope he doesn't go downhill as rapidly."

Alex, who'd winced at the mention of his mother, nodded. "Please God."

Pru, who'd shot Robin a quizzical glance at his question about Tom and would no doubt grill him about it later, asked, "You've said how angry you've been at your family keeping secrets from you. Was Eleanor and all the mystery around her the only reason you got angry with your mum, or was it also the fact she'd been standing up for this gay bloke and might have brought shame on the family because of that as well?"

"What gay bloke?" Alex glanced at Ms. Rednall, getting a shrug and a shake of the head in response. It appeared to be genuine surprise on his part, but he'd had enough time in advance of this interview to prepare and practice his answers. Although given that he'd clearly come today with his strategy planned—evidently with his solicitor's endorsement of it, given how little she was reacting—then this part of the tale had either been omitted from that planning or really did come as a shock.

"The bloke she stood up as character witness for in court, when he'd been caught cottaging," Pru said. "Graham. We don't have his surname. He was a big pal of Isabel and your mum, around the time she fell pregnant with Eleanor. He stepped up and offered to marry Moira, so the baby would be legitimate, but she refused."

"I had no idea about any of this." Alex looked from Pru to Robin to Ms. Rednall and back again. His start at the word *cottaging* appeared to be one of surprise rather than disgust. "So, she could have saved face with a sham marriage, although I suppose in that case I might not have happened. Nobody's ever told me this story."

"Not even Isabel?" Pru asked, with deceptive sweetness. She'd caught many a witness out with her softly-softly approach. "She knows all about it, obviously, as she also offered to be a character witness."

"She knows all about a lot of things which she hasn't seen fit to tell me." Alex's cheeks suddenly burned; they'd clearly hit the sore point again. "Anyway, what's any of this to do with Mark?"

Pru smiled. "I'd have thought it's all relevant to Mark, given that your mother's the point of connection between the two of you. She knew about your altercation at Skegness, didn't she, when you went to visit her that time she had her stroke?"

"I . . ." Alex paused, no doubt weighing up whether to reply.

Pru pressed on. "I'm sure you did, although you forgot to reckon with Isabel going round and telling her old friend everything she'd discovered."

Alex turned to his solicitor, eyebrow raised. She nodded, then mouthed what seemed to be, *If you're sure.*

If Robin had been like some of his older colleagues and inclined to bet at the drop of a hat, he'd have had a tenner on another confession coming, although only a couple of quid on what Alex would put his hands up for.

Alex said, "This is going to look bad for me again. I've been worried that you'd ask about Mum's fall, and I've decided I should be open about what happened. Ms. Rednall agrees. You don't need to caution me, because I know what I'm doing."

Robin glanced at the solicitor, then back at the suspect. "I'm going to caution you, anyway, for your own protection."

After the official words had been said, Alex took a deep breath. "Fact is, this has been preying on my mind for too long. I'd managed to put it on the back burner, but this business with Mark had made it flare up again. I've barely slept a wink since we met in Oxford."

Robin had already noted the bags under the suspect's eyes. "We're listening."

"That last time I visited Mum at her house, she was furious with me. About the fact I'd got into a fight and that she'd had to hear about it from Isabel, not directly from me. Mum could easily have rung me as soon as she'd heard from Blabbermouth but, no, she didn't. So by the time I arrived at her house, she'd got herself totally wound up."

Robin raised his hand. "Can we get the exact chain of events clear, because previously you told us that you went round to your mum's to discuss Eleanor, rather than the assault, and you didn't actually talk to her because she didn't answer the door. You went in and found her on the floor, in need of medical help, so how could she have been angry with you face-to-face?"

"Isn't it obvious? Because I got there earlier than I said. I rang the bell, Mum answered the door, and I was still on the step when she started to give me a mouthful about Skegness. How I'd brought the family into disgrace, which was a bit rich, given her history and what I'd come to talk to her about. Especially with what I've learned today about standing up for this bloke in court.

I mean, don't get me wrong, one of my best friends is gay—live and let live, I say—but back then it would have caused a scandal."

Robin let the remark go, even if his experience had taught him that variations on *Some of my best friends are . . .* never boded well. He asked, "Did you throw that bit about family disgrace back in her face?"

"Yes. At which point she went ballistic. Said *she'd* had the decency to make sure she'd preserved the McKay reputation, which I didn't really believe. I think she didn't want to be stuck with a baby." Alex's head was back in his hands again. "The argument grew and grew, because I was angry about a lot of things by then and not just her failing to tell me about my sister. For Mum not being interested in what had happened to Eleanor, for a start. Anyway, it developed into a slanging match because she didn't hold back, either. Two hot-headed people in a room is a recipe for disaster."

Two hot-headed people in Kings Ride Woods as well? If, as it appeared, Alex had inherited his angry nature from his mother, had it also passed down from her to Mark?

Robin kept his voice calm. "A recipe for disaster? What happened?"

Alex lifted his head. "I really don't know for sure, because I was so angry I almost blanked out of things. As far as I can remember, she came at me and started pummelling me with her fists, so I pushed her away. She fell, hit her head on the edge of a table, and was knocked out cold. If she'd fallen a foot to the left or right, she'd have been fine. I swear the rest is exactly as I already told you—I tried to give her first aid and then rang for an ambulance when I realised how serious things were." His voice carried genuine notes of affection and regret. "I never meant to hurt her. Not physically, anyway—I only meant my words to sting. But all the time she was punching me I kept thinking how a mother shouldn't do that to her son."

Robin could envisage the scene, hurt piled on hurt, Alex's sense of being rejected. Not that he condoned violence, but he saw how such a situation could escalate and actions be taken that would never happen otherwise.

"Did your mother tell anyone you'd pushed her?" Pru asked.

"No. She's never mentioned it to me, afterwards, and I assumed she'd forgotten all about it, because the stroke or the dementia had taken away that part of her memory. Maybe she'd shut it out of her brain because she was embarrassed at hitting me. Knowing her character so well, I could perhaps see her taking the incident as some kind of punishment, either for not telling me all the facts or for abandoning her child in the first place. Despite all the stuff Mum's said to Tom about not wanting to get in contact with her other child and it being better that my half sister was adopted, I think she carries a deep-down remorse about Eleanor."

"She's told you that?"

Alex shrugged. "Only since she started to lose her faculties. It's as though the barriers she's kept up have now fallen, so when I visit her she sometimes mentions Eleanor, although I have no idea whether what's she's telling me about her feelings is truth or more lies. Which doesn't help *my* emotions."

That could certainly explain why Lucy had been trying to deflect and defuse the discussion at Oxford. It would be understandable for anyone to want to protect their loved one. Maybe it was time for Robin to calm the situation, given how the witness was flushing again.

"Mr. Hanley. Alex," Robin said. "Take a moment to compose yourself, because we do need to discuss Mark's murder, and it won't help either of us if you get into a state."

Alex flashed him a grateful smile. "Thanks, but I'll be okay. That's the worst over and done with as far as I'm concerned."

Robin had the disappointing feeling that could be true, but Alex had misled them before and might do again. He turned to Pru. "Sergeant Davis, you wanted to talk to Mr. Hanley about Timsworth."

With a nod, Pru said, "We've checked your alibi and can't turn up any evidence to support what you and your wife told us. No CCTV at the car park, I'm afraid, and the volunteers at the abbey don't remember anyone kicking up a fuss that day about not paying a voluntary contribution. In fact, they're very laid-back about it."

"Oh hell, this is another backtracking, isn't it?" Alex's expression was more embarrassed than belligerent. "Lucy and I *did* make a donation—the woman we met doing the welcoming was bloody scary and I wouldn't have dared not to."

Pru snorted. "So why on earth did you tell Mr. Bright that you hadn't?"

"This is where I'll come over as a total twat. You see, I recently made a post on social media about how wrong it was to have to pay to go into certain places that should be free to enter. I was sure you'd find that and spot a discrepancy if I told what had really happened. I overthought it and you caught us out, anyway."

"You do get yourself mixed up about what's truth and what's a lie, don't you?" Pru asked, with a hint of amusement. "A good prosecuting brief would tie you in knots."

"Yeah, well, I'm an idiot, as Miss—sorry, Ms. Rednall knows. But I swear to God I didn't meet up with Mark on that Saturday or any other day. First time we talked on the phone I was only after information, but I didn't get it because he didn't have much to say. He started grilling me about my son and other family stuff, just so he could fill out his family tree. I refused to tell him anything and he rang off in a huff. I was going to leave it at that until he'd seen Tom and they'd done whatever tests they wanted to do, but things festered. To the point that a couple of days later I rang him to tell him to keep away from my side of the family. I was going to be calm and only tell him he was making us uncomfortable by being so persistent when we didn't really know if he was family. A few weeks or whatever it takes to do a test wouldn't have made a scrap of difference."

Except that delay had made all the difference in the world to Mark. As the suspect paused to take a sip of water, Pru filled in the obvious blanks. "But the phone conversation between you got heated?"

"Yes. I told him to back off entirely, not just from me but from Tom as well. Only I didn't put it so politely. He said I was lying about Tom, that talking to his great-uncle had been the best thing that had happened to him in ages. How Tom was so welcoming, how it was great to have a proper family again, and how he wasn't going to let me get in the way of that."

Pru pounced on the admission. "Did that happen over the phone or was it part of the conversation between you and Mark in Kings Ride Woods?"

Alex flinched. "Sorry?"

"If Mark was so determined to connect with his newly discovered family and had heard you were in the area, I bet he asked to meet up with you before he headed off to see Tom. Perhaps he said it was to ensure he'd be prepared for that interview." The point hadn't arisen before—trust Pru to make such a sensible leap of logic. An accurate one, to boot, if Alex's uncomfortable expression was anything to go by.

"He did ask to meet, and I told him where to get off."

"Really? You didn't decide it would be easier to give in and have that meeting so he'd stop pestering you?" Pru in action, trying to get to the truth, was an impressive sight. "A meeting at which you yet again got into an argument. Maybe he hurled some insults at your mother, perhaps because of abandoning *his* mother. Things got heated between you, like they did between you and your mum."

"I told you, I was never in those woods." Alex was sitting forward again, hands drumming the table. "Okay, you're right when you said he wanted to meet up. That was part of what we quarrelled about on the phone, because he was like a dog with a bone and wouldn't let go. I refused to connect in person, and you must have guessed why I didn't want to. After Skegness and then Mum, I've been dealing with my anger issues and I'm not losing it as much as I used to, but I'm still what Lucy calls a work in progress. I couldn't have trusted myself to be in the same room as Mark. Not until I knew what was what."

The subtle changes in Hanley's body language that Robin had been noting throughout the interview—the man leaning forward every time he was making a confession—suggested that this was the truth continuing to emerge. A man who recognised his own capacity for violence trying to avoid another incident. "Would Mark settle for that answer? Did Lucy go to meet him instead?"

"Lucy?" Alex raised an eyebrow. "No. She was with me in Timsworth."

"Which we still can't verify," Robin reminded him. "Can I clarify something? Her father was a policeman, wasn't he?"

"Yes. As she told that young constable of yours when he rang to bother her about the fact. Neither of us could work out why it was so important. Neither can Ms. Rednall."

Robin addressed his reply to both suspect and solicitor. "We simply wanted to know because Mark was killed by a blow from a blunt instrument, similar to a truncheon, and they're not that common."

"It wasn't Lucy's dad's. She hasn't seen it since he retired from the force." Alex took a deep breath and blew out his cheeks. "I've been upfront with you today. I swear every word I've spoken in here has been the truth. I may have been losing sleep over what happened with Mum, but I've nothing to regret where Mark was concerned. I didn't hurt him and neither did Lucy."

Ms. Rednall cut in. "Timsworth. Tell them about the twenty-pound note."

"Oh, yeah. Good job I've got you here or I would have forgotten. Again. Lucy reminded me that we'd picked up two takeaway coffees in Timsworth, after we got out of the abbey. It was at a little place, on the way back to the car park near Waitrose, name of Teapots or something. We paid cash, as we usually do, and by mistake nearly tried to use an old note. Lucy must have had it lurking in her purse since lock down. The young lad taking the order made a joke about how we weren't the first people to get mixed up, so he might remember us."

Robin suppressed a growl. "Why on earth didn't you tell us this before?"

"We thought you'd done with us, after we made our statements. You didn't get back in touch, so . . ." Alex spread his hands.

"I sincerely hope we *have* done with you." Robin got his papers—such as they were—together.

"I'm going to stay while you talk to Mrs. Hanley," the solicitor said, "even though I've been told she's not under caution."

Robin smiled sweetly. "That's fine by us. Mr. Hanley, we'll give the local officers your confession about pushing your mother. They can deal with it as they see fit." It wouldn't hurt to let the bloke sweat a bit, despite the fact that Robin couldn't see the case proceeding. "I'm going to take a comfort break and we'll see Lucy in ten minutes."

Robin met Pru as they emerged from their respective toilets.

"What do you think?" she asked.

"I have an awful feeling he's come clean at last. The solicitor must have worked on him, and I don't suppose that was merely an overnight thing."

"That's the impression I got too. Perhaps she represented him for the Skegness business and he might have had her lined up if the locals came knocking about his mum." Pru rummaged in her bag for some hand cream. "I notice you asked about when he last saw Tom. Any particular reason?"

Robin sniffed. "Have a guess."

"Okay. I should know how your mind works by now. Another older relative, one who's at odds with Alex, has a fall. Was Tom pushed by his nephew?"

"Yep. I didn't think it was likely, because I bet Tom would have reported him, at least to his neighbour if not to us. I couldn't have gone home with the question unasked, though. And in a strange way—while I don't think Alex is guilty of anything other than hitting his mum and being generally an idiot—it would have been good if Alex had pushed Tom, because we'd have had a chance of pinning it on him."

"You really don't like Alex Hanley, do you, sir?"

"He rankles with me. I don't think he deliberately hurt his mother, and I've no doubt he regrets it, but . . ." The man had an air of the bullies who'd blighted Robin's schooldays, although that could have applied to a number of the suspects Robin met. "Right. Lucy. There's no longer a need to press her about Alex and his mother or the phone calls to Mark. Just cross the t's on those bits."

"Agreed, sir. I'd still like to cover whether she met Mark in her husband's stead. As you say, can't go home with the question unasked."

"Then let's go and ask it."

As Ms. Rednall emerged, they scooped her up to go to the other interview room. Robin hoped she wouldn't insist on having some time alone with her client, so that he could ensure Lucy didn't know her husband had confessed to the fight with his mother. His hopes were realised.

The interview with Lucy proved fairly perfunctory, compared to her husband's. She trotted out much the same as Alex had about contact with Mark, but with enough of a difference to suggest she wasn't reading a pre-learned script. She confirmed the donation at the abbey, the story of the dodgy note, and the fact that her husband was an idiot at times.

"An idiot with a temper?"

Lucy nodded. "He got that off his mother, because his dad was as meek as a lamb. He's doing anger management and it helps, but you can't change overnight, especially when things come back to rile you again. That's why we were both so edgy when you interviewed us before. Nothing to do with Mark and everything to do with Moira's stroke. If it hadn't been for that, we'd have remembered the café and paying for the coffees, but I was so stressed my mind blanked."

"Moira's stroke?" Robin asked, insouciantly.

"I assume Alex has told you?" Lucy studied him and Pru, then nodded. "He has. The silly sod's tormented himself long enough about it and he's been tossing and turning in bed so much the last few nights I said he should put on his big boy's pants and come clean. Because I'd rather deal with the consequences than see him make himself ill with remorse."

That was plausible, helping to explain why Alex had confessed so readily. Robin asked, "One last thing, then. Back to Mark. Alex says he refused to meet him. Did *you* speak to him, instead?"

"Not in person." Lucy fingered her bottom lip. "The second time Alex rang him, I could hear him getting agitated, so I grabbed the phone and tried to calm things down, because Mark was angry too. Asked him for a bit of consideration because the news about Eleanor had come as a shock."

"What did Mark say to that?"

Lucy winced. "Less said than shouted. Told me that if anybody was due consideration it was *him* because he was sick of finding out he'd not been told the truth. People were lying to him on all sides. He said a lot of swear words in amongst it, so I won't quote him. Anyway, after he'd vented, he rang off and we didn't speak again."

Robin and Pru shared a glance. *"Not been told the truth"*? Was that a reference to Suzy's affairs and did the solution to this mystery lie with one of her ex—and maybe not so ex—boyfriends?

Chapter Fifteen

On Tuesday, Adam made sure he arrived home at a decent time, despite Robin not being there. He'd brought a ton of stuff with him. Nothing important, just the routine, time-consuming bits that kept falling to the bottom of the "to do" pile. Better to clear them while snuggled up on the settee with Hamish, rather than staying late in his office. The one good thing about Robin going away overnight with work was Adam not having to feel guilty about crashing through a pile of paperwork or emails during an evening spent together.

Hamish was clearly delighted to see him, in a typically doggy *you've been away for weeks and I've been inconsolable* way, which produced a different pang of guilt about the situation. Adam would be with a loved one tonight, irrespective of it not being *the* loved one, but Robin wouldn't have anybody—not even a slobbery Newfoundland—to give him a goodnight hug.

Adam had his dinner and had made a huge dent in the work he'd brought home when the landline rang. Immediately assuming it would be a scammer because hardly anyone else used that number, Adam considered not answering. But Robin's aunt Clare sometimes used the house phone, as did an ex-neighbour who liked to keep in touch and swore that she didn't trust mobiles, so he shifted a protesting dog and went to the hallway.

"Adam?" A vaguely familiar voice sounded down the line.

"Ye-es?"

"It's Ryan. I'm sorry for ringing on the landline, but I know Robin's away with work, because Mrs. Bright told me so, and I didn't want to ring his mobile. She gave me this number so I can leave a message."

"Hold on while I get a pen and paper." The phone was used so rarely they no longer kept such things to hand in the hallway. As he fetched them, Adam remembered his grandmother being very proud of a black leather mat which her phone sat on, one with a notepad and pen holder built in. It had been very professional looking and for the young Adam the height of swish and sophistication.

"Right, I'm ready to make notes. Although if you're going to tell Robin you've located a bloke from Lutterworth who died in Australia who might be his grandfather, then Mrs. Bright told us all about it last evening."

"Yes, she said that to me. A very sensible woman, your mother-in-law. If only everyone I had to deal with was so shrewd."

Time for a pre-emptive anti-droning strike, or else Ryan might go on for half an hour about his clients, canny or dim. "Ryan, sorry to butt in and be a pain, but I've got a pile of school stuff to do and I'm taking advantage of himself being away to do it. I'd love to chat; however, not right now."

"Oh, okay. I've only got a couple of things to say and I'll make them brief, because I do know I go on a bit at times." Ryan snorted. "This chap in Australia, whom I'm still trying to verify as *our* chap, I've run across him on a couple of these family tree sites and one was of particular interest because they were discussing occurrences of syndactyly in the family. *He* had it."

"That is encouraging." And put in an admirably succinct way—the bloke could do it when he tried. Adam felt some praise was needed. "Robin's really grateful for your work, by the way, and he's happy not to be given this guy's name until you're as sure as you can be that he's the one we're after."

"I guessed that would be the case. He of all people would know how dangerous it is to jump to conclusions. People looking at family histories can end up like newspapers reporting on the same story—they all put their own interpretations on what they see. Take a basic set of facts and twist them to suit the narrative they want to expound, ignoring the ones that don't fit."

"That's what we try to teach our year-six pupils to avoid doing." Adam smiled. Ryan wasn't hard to talk to if you kept him on topic. Or near topic. "You said there was something else you wanted me to pass on to Robin. Is it family-tree business?"

"No, although it stemmed from that. I saw some 'own narratives' stuff when I was browsing these family history forums, and it made Mark come to mind."

Adam's ears pricked, like Hamish's now did when the dog biscuits got opened. "Do you mean he had his own narrative?"

"Where Suzy was concerned, yes. He'd clearly worshipped his wife—possibly to the point it was unhealthy—and if she said something was so, he'd never have doubted it. I think, from the questions he asked me, Robin's got it in mind she'd been playing away, which is highly likely from the bits of gossip I heard about her. However, I think there's more."

"Like what?" Adam remembered the previous evening and Pru recounting the strange theory about a resurrected Suzy. Would this "more" turn out to be something equally odd?

"Remember I said she reminded me of a character in a book?"

"Yes." Although for the life of him, Adam couldn't recall if a specific one had been mentioned. "Sorry, but my brain's in school mode at present, rather than pubby lunch mode, so remind me who you meant."

"Walter Mitty. Short story version, not from either of the dreadful films."

"I've read it." A charming tale, and Adam would agree with Ryan's assessment. It had been blown out of all proportion and ruined when adapted for the big screen. "An old friend of ours also knew her and told Robin that Suzy's life resembled a soap opera, so you're not alone in thinking that. Although do you mean she overdramatised things or that she lived in some imaginary world, inside her head?"

"A bit of both. It may have nothing to do with his murder case, but can you tell Robin that when Mark was talking about her, he let the odd thing drop that implied . . . Well, implied she was portraying things as worse than the reality had been. He'd already suspected that she was stirring up the conflict between him and her parents and maybe not telling either side the truth, so he'd become suspicious."

Which would accord with what Robin had said about the disparities in people's accounts of what had happened or what they'd been told had happened. "So, was she telling other people there was a conflict, say between her parents and Mark, when there wasn't that much of a one?"

"Something like that. Thing is, I'm used to picking my way between conflicting stories—it goes with the job—and sometimes I pick up an idea of what's really going on." Ryan took a deep breath. "You may not be able to answer this or you may not want to, but do the police have any reservations about Suzy's medical situation?"

"I genuinely couldn't say one way or the other." Although, hadn't Robin mentioned something about Suzy telling everyone that it had been her parents who hadn't wanted her to have mainstream cancer treatment and them saying that was a load of nonsense? "Why?"

"This afternoon I spoke to a U3A group about researching family history. I mentioned Mark's case—not by name—to show that you can end up doing unexpected things as a result of being involved in research. It turns out Suzy's parents were in the audience. They nabbed me afterwards and asked if I'd been talking about Mark and how they'd appreciated me not divulging personal details. I told them all I could about what I discovered, family-wise. Mrs. Packer got very upset when I talked about his birth grandmother apparently giving up her baby—she said she couldn't understand how anyone could do something like that."

"That's understandable." Adam felt distinctly disappointed that nothing new seemed to be forthcoming.

"That's what I said. Anyway, she had to go off to the ladies' to compose herself and Mr. Packer apologised. Said his wife had been getting into a state ever since she found out that people were saying *they'd* been responsible for delaying Suzy's treatment, especially now it appeared that their daughter herself may have been the origin of that tale. So, long story short as I promised, I had a terrible thought as I was driving home. What if Suzy hadn't been as ill as she'd made out? We know it wasn't the cancer that killed her in the end, it was coronavirus, so she might well have been in a less advanced stage of the disease than she'd told people she was. That in itself might explain some of the mystery around her treatment or lack of same. It's only an idea . . ." Ryan trailed off, awkwardly.

"Ryan, it's a good enough idea for me to pass straight on to Robin when he rings me. He'd want me to say thank you."

"It's a pleasure. I think. Anyhow, I'll let you get back to your school stuff. Hope to speak again soon. Bye." Ryan put the phone down, leaving Adam with the sense that the bloke might have hit on something important. And if only *he* hadn't rushed out from their pub lunch, he might have registered the Walter Mitty comparison then and already passed it on.

Twenty minutes later, Robin called.

"Sorry to be ringing later than intended. Pru and I got dragged out for drinks with some of the local team because they think they've cracked their assault case. Got a tip off this afternoon from a woman who thinks her husband's been acting suspiciously and at last she's summoned up the courage to dob him in."

"That's good news. Are they certain?" It would surely be too early for anything like DNA tests to have been completed. This wasn't the telly with its almost instant results.

"Ninety-five percent sure, based on his lack of an alibi and the stuff they've already recovered from his house, apparently. Still got all the forensic to do, but they wanted to buy us a pint as they believed we brought them luck. It *was* only the one pint, by the way, because I said we had to be on the road early."

"Everything finished in Lincoln? Were you successful?"

"Yes and partly. The Hanleys appear to have found themselves an alibi and while Mister has put his hands up both to pushing his mother over and contacting Mark, I don't think he's the killer." Robin's disappointment was audible. "But rather than wait for Harry Foakes to get home from his conference, we've arranged to swing round to Birmingham and interview him there, tomorrow morning."

A frisson shot up Adam's spine. "He's the company doctor? If so, that's a big coincidence because I've had Ryan on the phone earlier—he had a bit of news on the webbed fingers front but that can wait. He said he'd met the Packers when he was presenting at a U3A event today and what they said got him thinking. Remember when I was telling you about lunch with him and your mum? How I missed some of what he said?"

"Ryan does have that effect on people. I think he's lonely, although he knows his stuff, and when he emails me it's always very businesslike and to the point."

"He's okay when he's chatting too, if you lay down the ground rules. He was relatively succinct today. Anyhow, he said that Suzy reminded him of Walter Mitty and since his chat with the Packers he's been wondering if she wasn't as ill with leukaemia as she'd told people. Hello? You still there?"

"I am. Having a think. That's not a bad shout, especially as I'm not aware of any photos that show her really ill. It would also explain some of the inconsistencies, like why she'd apparently delayed treatment. Maybe she hadn't needed serious medical intervention." Robin paused again. "Maybe she hadn't needed it at all until she got Covid."

"Are you saying she might have made up everything about having cancer? Is that even possible?"

"If the doctor who makes the diagnosis is your lover—or your ex-lover—and he's willing to lie for you, or blackmailed into doing so, then it could happen. I don't think leukaemia manifests in really obvious symptoms like a growing lump, and Christine did say that Suzy hadn't wanted to talk about exactly which type of leukaemia she had."

"Hmm."

"Yeah. Makes you feel a bit sick, doesn't it? Isn't there a name for pretending you're ill?"

"Munchausen syndrome. I've never come across it personally but I've heard of a genuine case of Munchausen syndrome by proxy, only it's not called that nowadays and I can't remember the proper name." Adam would have to look that up, later. "A few years back one of the local schools had one of the mothers pretending her daughter was very ill, in an effort at getting her own back on hubby, who'd ditched her. The headteacher told us about it at one of our cluster meetings, in case we had anything similar. Nasty business."

"I bet it was. You can tell me all about it when I get home because, much as I regret it, I think I'll have to love you and leave you. I'd better bring Pru up to speed and then ring the team with a list of jobs for them to get onto first thing. Might be a bit much to expect any results by the time we see Foakes tomorrow but a man can dream."

"He can. I hope if I dream, I have sweet ones of you and not nightmares about Isabel and Ryan teaming up to list their latest daft theories. Although if it was Ryan droning on, it would send me to sleep within my sleep."

"He could start a business on the side, making insomnia podcasts. Love you, Mr. Headteacher, and give himself a pat from me."

"Will do and love you too, Mr. Policeman."

Adam ended the call to find Hamish, who'd been lying quietly, staring up at him expectantly. "Your other dad says hello and sends you this pat on the head. He should be home tomorrow, all these villains notwithstanding."

The Newfoundland, face serious, bounced up to give Adam a lick on his nose.

"Thank you so much. Now sit quietly while I finish off my work, and then we'll have ten minutes' fresh air before bedtime. I'll need to clear my head of people who lie and cheat."

Especially where the lying and cheating led to the innocent being hurt. And maybe, ultimately, to Mark Bircher being murdered.

Chapter Sixteen

Robin woke early on Wednesday, experiencing a sensation he'd have called butterflies in his tummy when he was small. While not all the odds and ends were explicable by this new hypothesis that he, Adam, and Ryan had come up with—and it didn't necessarily identify Mark's killer—either Robin's nose or his experience was telling him they'd taken a significant step forward.

The previous evening, as soon as he'd finished talking to Adam, he'd rung Pru to put the new idea to her, because if it was totally silly she'd have told him. However, she'd thought it well worth following up. They'd subsequently met in the hotel lounge, put together a plan of action, and had rung the rest of the team to dole out jobs. If the stars aligned, they might have some initial answers before they met Foakes.

Over breakfast, Pru said that having slept on the idea, she increasingly liked it. "It could get us over the motive hurdle, if Mark had confronted whoever he thought had helped his wife con him. Assuming she did con him."

"I'm trying to keep an open mind on that, but it's not easy. I keep thinking of that Post-it. 'Honesty. No.' could apply to Suzy if she'd deceived her husband. Maybe we'll have some proof after we've spoken to Harry Foakes."

"Maybe we'll have our killer."

Once they'd hit the road, Pru taking her turn at the wheel, Robin wasn't optimistic about hearing anything from his team until they'd got back to Abbotston, but as they reached the outskirts of Birmingham, Ben called. He was at Mark's house, where he'd gone searching for anything related to Suzy's illness. He said he'd already been on the phone to both the surgery and the hospital requesting access to her medical records, although he didn't think that would happen anytime soon and nobody was to talk to him about NHS admin or he'd pull his hair out. What he *had* discovered was a file labelled *Suzy's medical stuff* in Mark's office, tucked right at the back of a cabinet, although said file was empty apart from what appeared to be a copy of an application.

"This form says he applied after Suzy's death to get her GP and hospital records," Ben said. "If he succeeded, they're not filed with the rest, so they've either been taken or he's hidden them so well I haven't found them yet. I'll keep on the hunt. There's another folder of certificates, including the death one for Suzy. That was signed by the hospital staff and seems pretty straightforward."

"Maybe he put what he found in his case, to confront someone with, which is why it was taken," Pru suggested.

"I was thinking along those lines," Ben said, "although I wondered whether he took the stuff out of the car and carried it with him to the meeting in Kings Ride Woods. Then whoever killed him scooped it up and used the suitcase as a convenient way to dump it. Remember that first interview with Ryan, sir?"

Robin snorted. "I'm never likely to forget it. Why?"

"I'm sure he said something about Mark wishing Suzy had got help when she needed it. We assumed that meant treatment for her cancer, but what if he'd meant support for a mental health issue?"

"Could be." Another example of where they might have got here faster if Ryan hadn't droned on so much. It would be a lesson for them all.

"You're not letting on much, sir." Ben chuckled. "The rest of the team are itching to know what new lead you're following, by the way. All this Suzy medical stuff seems to have come out of the blue."

"They'll have to wait until we brief them later today. You're on right lines but it feels too much like tempting fate if I explain our thinking now, not least because it's a bit unusual. Just tell the troops that the interview with Harry Foakes could be crucial." Robin left it at that.

No sooner had they parked up at the hotel where the conference was happening than Ashok rang to say he'd confirmed the Hanleys' alibi. Robin automatically put him on speakerphone. The constable said that the chap at the café *did* remember the business with the old note and had said it had been awkward because they *did* have older people coming in who were a bit forgetful, trying to pay with out-of-date notes or not knowing their pin numbers for their cards. He'd particularly remembered Lucy's purple hair because it was so striking he'd discussed it with his mum who worked there as well, telling her not to try anything as alarming next time she was at the hairdresser. Between them, they pinned down the date and a rough time, meaning the Hanleys were at last eliminated from the enquiry.

"I've spoken to Kevin too," Ashok added. "Asked him if he could tell me anything else about how Suzy and Mark got on and whether he had any gossip on the medical front."

This was showing initiative: neither Pru nor Robin had asked the constable to do that. "What did he say?"

"That she was one of the reasons why he became more distant from his brother. Kevin didn't like Suzy and she didn't like him. She said he was bone idle, to which he admitted she probably had a point, although he'd wondered if it was really because he saw through her."

"Saw through her in what way?" Pru asked.

"All her flirting with other men, for a start. Mark knew about the string of blokes she'd had previously, although she apparently swore she'd settled down when she married him. If Mark suspected her of lying about that, then he never mentioned it to his brother or parents, but Kevin has a feeling she could have been playing away from home. He also said it struck him that she always wanted to be the centre of attention. Overdramatized things, like when she had the miscarriage. His exact words were—" the sound of paper rustling "—'I'm not saying she exaggerated her illnesses but she milked them for all they were worth.' She liked being the victim: the unfortunate child of weird parents, that type of thing. Does any of that help?"

"Yeah. If only to confirm what other people have said. Keep up the good work." Robin ended the call, then raised an eyebrow in Pru's direction. "Might have been useful if he'd said that when we met him last week."

Pru shrugged. "You might have ignored it, putting it down to bad blood between them. Although what Kevin said is suggestive when taken with Mark wanting access to his wife's medical history. The more I think about it, the more I wonder if he suspected she was exaggerating things. I've come up with some ideas of how she could have carried out a con, illness-wise. If she could persuade Foakes to back her up in person, it could have been relatively easy to fake letters from the hospital or medical reports. I've heard of it being done."

"Ditto. Easy to mock up documents these days given all the software available."

"Thing is, sir, I don't yet see how it connects to Mark's death. It might have been different if he'd murdered *her*, in a rage at discovering he'd been conned, but he didn't."

"Been there, thought of that, came to the same conclusion that if she'd died at home, it might have worked as a theory." Robin blew out his cheeks. "She catches Covid, he rubs his hands at a chance of getting rid of her, and everyone will assume it's the virus."

"Exactly. She's deep asleep, maybe doped up on cough syrup, and he sticks a pillow over her mouth, knowing it's unlikely they'll look for fibres, especially if her doctor knows she's tested positive and has maybe visited her already. I wondered all the way through the pandemic whether there weren't a few deliberate deaths hidden among all the natural ones, and people were too run off their feet to notice. Although in Suzy's case that's blown out of the water because she died in hospital and the Packers said she wasn't allowed visitors." Pru frowned. "Have we checked that? I can't imagine they'd have lied about it but even so."

"We haven't. Can you get Danielle on the case? I'm not hopeful, but we'd seem right prunes if it turned out Mark had been the one to tell them they couldn't visit while he was going in and . . ." Robin still couldn't come up with a workable hypothesis, "somehow finishing her off. Once you've done that, it'll be time to grasp the nettle with Foakes and see if we're constructing a house built on stone or sand."

They met Harry Foakes in a secluded corner of the hotel lounge. Robin estimated the doctor was a little older than him and he was well-dressed, handsome, and blessed with a charming smile. If one that seemed to be a little nervous. They did the introductions, ordered coffee, and then got straight down to business.

"Can we start with you telling us what your role at Haveland and Sons involved?"

Foakes noticeably relaxed at Robin's question, evidently having anticipated a harder first question.

"Yep. If I say it was all the medical bits for the drugs they make, I don't necessarily mean the research stuff. I had a variety of responsibilities, like signing off that the packaging and inserts were accurate and the marketing material didn't claim what it shouldn't. I did works medicals and the like and also ran a surgery for staff—which was very helpful for them, especially during lockdown when it was so difficult to see a GP, and I was happy to do consultations over Zoom. I know that's unusual for companies these days, despite it being fairly standard in the past. The company my dad worked for had a permanent dentist on site, if you can believe it. Still, Haveland and Sons is quite an old-fashioned organisation when it comes to its employees." Foakes paused, maybe wondering if he'd said too much or too little.

"Thank you for clarifying that." Pru flashed him a smile. "You knew Suzy Bircher through work. Can you tell me the nature of your relationship with her?"

"We used to be an item, pre-Mark, when she was Suzy Packer. Pre-Nick as well, if you know about him."

Robin nodded. "I've met him. It was Nick who suggested we talk to you. Did that relationship with Suzy continue after her marriage?" He paused, noting the first hesitation in Foakes providing a response. "Remember we're dealing with a murder here, so we need to get to the truth. None of it will come out if it isn't relevant to Mark's death."

"Okay, we had the odd relighting of the old flame, if you get me, because Suzy wasn't really a one-man woman. Mark didn't know about it and neither does my wife. It didn't hurt anyone; probably helped both marriages by keeping things fresh." Foakes sounded like a man trying to convince himself, let alone anyone else.

"Doesn't having a patient as your lover get you in trouble with the General Medical Council?" Pru asked. "That would be a useful thing to blackmail a doctor with."

Foakes waved a hand. "We were an item before I worked at Haveland and Sons, so it's not an issue."

Robin would need to check if that were the case, but at present he'd let it ride, not wanting Foakes to go too defensive on them. "Yet, despite all the time you were in a relationship, you didn't attend her funeral?"

"No. That could have been rather awkward, couldn't it? Mark did send me an invitation, rather out of the blue, because he said he wanted the church full for her."

And maybe he'd also wanted to engineer a confrontation. Kevin had said how Mark had gone ballistic at the funeral, ostensibly about the family history business, but had there been more to his anger?

A waiter arrived with their coffees, an eyebrow raised at the sight of Pru's notebook. Once he was well clear of them, Foakes continued. "I had to have a dental implant put in that day, thank the lord. I know I could have cancelled the appointment, but I'd already had to reschedule the procedure once and didn't want to do so again. It gave me a convenient excuse, so it wouldn't look like I was snubbing anyone by not being there. I did send flowers."

"What did Mark make of your floral tribute?" Robin asked.

Foakes shrugged. "I have no idea. I didn't get any acknowledgement of it, although there were general thanks from both him and her parents on Suzy's remembrance page so maybe nobody got a personal thank-you."

Pru took up the questioning, while Robin grabbed a swig of coffee. "Did Mark get in touch with you at all after Suzy's death?"

Foakes paused mid-drink. "Why should he? We were never anything other than acquaintances."

"So, you didn't go to meet him in Kings Ride Woods two Saturdays ago?"

"Of course not, Sergeant. What would we have had to say to each other? If he'd discovered that Suzy was being unfaithful, he'd made no effort to confront me about it."

"Sergeant Davis isn't referring to that." Robin leaned forward, cup in hand. "We're talking about him discovering that Suzy was never as ill as she'd made out she was." Robin had rarely seen a witness crumple in quite the way Foakes did. Ashen, lips pressed hard together, he'd laid down his coffee with trembling hands, spilling some into the saucer. "Can you respond to that, Dr. Foakes, or should we take your silence as agreement?"

"How did you find out?" Foakes managed to force out the words.

"By putting lots of bits of information together, like we always do." Robin wasn't going to admit that the question had been a bow drawn at a venture. "Things like discrepancies in accounts regarding her treatment and Mark having applied for her medical records. We concluded that he might have suspected that he was being duped and wanted verification, although the key question is when he began to suspect."

"I honestly can't answer that. The week before her death, Suzy rang me to say she was worried that he'd guessed, although he hadn't said anything to her directly."

The germ of an idea started to grow in Robin's mind. "Did she have cancer at all?"

Foakes heaved a sigh. "This is the ironic bit. She did, although when she first told people that she'd been diagnosed, she was actually all clear. She *had* been unwell, with a range of nebulous symptoms, and she'd consulted me about it. We did the usual array of blood tests—you couldn't criticise Havelands for the support they gave employees on that front—but those came up negative apart from her lacking some of the essential

B vitamins. That was easily remedied with injections and tablets, but she pretended she was being treated for something very serious. Nobody's going to be the centre of attention for an easily avoided vitamin deficiency, are they?" Foakes snorted. "Anyway, about six months before she died, she asked me to examine one of her moles she was concerned about. I thought it was dodgy so I got her to see her own GP for a referral. One thing I would criticise Haveland for is that they don't have a company private-health insurance scheme, not like my present employers. Anyway, the GP got a dermatologist to give it the once-over, which was a good call because it turned out to be an early-stage melanoma. Nothing threatening if whipped off quickly, which it was, but rather than giving her the reality check she needed, it added to the story she'd been fabricating. Nobody could accuse her of lying, once she'd got a real diagnosis."

"They could, though," Pru pointed out. "If anybody discovered the truth, they weren't likely to have forgotten about all that time she'd been duping them. Or that *you'd* been duping them."

"Me?" Foakes flinched.

"You must have known what she was saying about her illness, because it would have been all over the work gossip network, surely?" Pru said. "I suspect that didn't shut down with lockdown."

Foakes gave no response, so she continued. "You could have put people right or at the very least given us the heads-up. Can doctor-patient confidentiality still apply if the patient's lying and those lies are hurting other people?"

Still no reply. While Robin hated stepping in, sometimes it needed another voice to jolt the witness into responding: Pru would know he wasn't playing the *Answer me because I'm a man* card, because she'd been the one stepping in on past occasions. "We really do need an answer, and I'm happy to sit here until we get one. Did you or did you not support Suzy's story?"

Foakes raised his hands. "All right, I did, but mainly by keeping shtum and not contradicting the tale she was putting around. That patient confidentiality you mentioned was a great excuse."

"But why would you do such a thing?" Robin asked.

"Because she threatened me. If I didn't help her, she'd tell my wife that I'd been unfaithful and she'd also stir up shit with the GMC. Although I should have known that once I'd initially agreed not to dob her in, Suzy's hold over me would increase." He ran his hands through his hair. "She was very persuasive, saying that Mark was losing interest in her and she wanted some means to get his attention back. Like an idiot, I fell for it."

"You don't think that was true?" Pru asked, not unkindly.

"I don't know. You'll have realised how much she liked weaving stories around herself, but she wasn't only living in a dream world. I think she had a hard-nosed, vindictive streak, one I wasn't aware of until it was too late. She liked manipulating people."

The puzzle pieces were slipping into place. "Did that hard-nosed streak include forging documents to support her story?

"Yes, although I refused to be involved in any of that. She didn't need me anyway, because she kept gloating about how easy it had been." Foakes paused, thoughts having clearly run ahead. "She definitely died from sepsis, probably caused by Covid, though. I know one of the doctors on the ward where she was admitted, and she told me that Suzy was proper poorly and they'd known from the start she might not make it."

"It couldn't have been cancer weakening her ability to fight it off though, could it?" Pru pointed out. "Unless the melanoma was more advanced than you're telling us."

"It wasn't. But the stupid bint refused to have the vaccine, so she had no protection. Damned lucky not to have contracted Covid before, to be honest, and I kept telling her that being young was no guarantee of getting over the thing quickly. I've known seventy-year-olds who caught it and had barely a snivel while younger patients were flat on their backs."

Robin barely registered the last bit, still reeling from the information about Suzy's lack of vaccination. "Why on earth didn't she get the jab?"

"Apparently her parents persuaded her not to. Said there were too many risks involved." Foakes rolled his eyes. "If you'd met them, you'd understand."

"I have," Robin said. "And they told me they believed in vaccinations—tetanus, coronavirus, the lot. Are you sure it was them behind it?"

"Not from the horses' mouths." Foakes paused, light evidently dawning. "It sounds like I was Suzy's dupe, as well."

"That wouldn't be a surprise." Robin smiled sympathetically. "Tell us all you know about her death. We think it's relevant to our enquiries."

"I can't say much, really. I got a text from her the day she came down with it and tested positive, saying she felt like crap and how long would it go on for? I gave her the same advice as I've given anyone with the virus about when to get extra help. She replied straight away, saying she was worried that Mark would ring the hospital about why she wasn't getting specialist care immediately, given her supposed medical condition. If he did so, the game would be up. I don't know if he did so."

"Perhaps he already had a good idea that she was lying so didn't waste his breath?" Pru suggested.

"You could be right. I've always wondered if he cottoned on when she had her melanoma diagnosis. He wasn't daft, so if he'd done some reading around and there was a mismatch between the genuine treatment she was getting and what she should have been having if she was as ill with leukaemia as she said . . ." Foakes shrugged. "Getting back to your question, I had another, rather garbled, message from her the next day, saying her cough was getting worse and she felt like shite but Mark had gone all quiet on her. I told her he might be full of worry but to get him to ring for an ambulance if she didn't feel better soon, and he must have done so because she was admitted that night. I didn't hear from her again, I'm afraid."

There was no mistaking that the man was truly upset at Suzy's death. Upset enough to take revenge if he believed Mark had been neglectful?

Foakes drank the rest of his coffee, although it must have been cold. "If I tell you something weird, I'm not deflecting attention from me, honest."

"Go ahead," Robin said, knowing it was likely he was doing just that.

"Ever since Suzy died, I've wondered whether her catching Covid and then developing sepsis on top was nice and convenient for Mark. Given that he might have been right royally hacked off with her because of the cancer nonsense, if she'd died at home, I might have had a quiet word with someone about doing a postmortem. You know the sort of things to look for—marks on the face or fibres up the nose from a pillow over the mouth, and the rest. But it can't apply, though, because she died in hospital, and I can't fathom how he could have killed her there without raising suspicion."

"Can you give somebody sepsis? Sorry if that's a stupid question," Pru said.

"Not stupid at all. Theoretically, I suppose it's possible, although I doubt Mark could have done it. People can develop septic shock off the back of a nasty lung infection—although it's not common, thank God—and nobody was suspicious about her death." Foakes shrugged. "Anyway, I know that Mark couldn't have been on the ward because the friend I mentioned earlier told me it was sad that desperately ill people couldn't have their loved ones visiting. Hospital management had decided they couldn't risk people bringing the virus in afresh. There'd been an outbreak among staff, and the place was on its knees. So, Mark had no opportunity, even if he had motive. Unless he'd been very clever and spectacularly lucky. Mark's dead though, so even if he hastened Suzy's end, he's beyond facing justice."

Robin suddenly saw a possible scenario, as clear as if it were currently being acted on a stage in front of him. What if Mark hadn't murdered his wife directly but had stopped her getting medical help when she needed it? She'd said he'd "gone quiet" on her, which might have indicated suppressed anger. Robin could imagine Mark delaying calling an ambulance despite the terrible state Suzy was in, maybe taunting her that she was getting a taste of her own medicine. She'd been spreading a story about treatment being delayed until it was too late—well, now she'd know how it felt in reality.

He'd need to discuss this with Pru, to see if it fitted together, but that could wait until later. For now, Robin kept to, "Perhaps you're not the only one who's been speculating about what went on between Mark and Suzy. Irrespective of what happened concerning her death, which might give someone a motive to harm *him*, the fact she'd told lies gave *Mark* a motive to get into a row with anybody he'd felt had helped her keep up the deception. You, for example."

"I know." Foakes, wincing, stared at his hands. "I guess it's going to be worse for me if I don't come entirely clean. You're bound to check back through phone records and things. Mark must have wanted to talk, because somehow he'd got hold of my number—maybe off Suzy's phone or from wherever he got my address—and rang me. That was ages ago."

"What do you mean by 'ages'?" Pru asked.

"A few weeks after Suzy's funeral. I told him exactly what I told you, that I had nothing to say to him. He pestered me about letters and reports she'd shown him, and I could say in all conscience that if such things existed, I'd never seen them and had nothing to do with them. I also told him that my involvement with Suzy's health was around her Vitamin B deficiency and the melanoma diagnosis." Foakes looked up at last. "I was hoping he'd leave it there. He wouldn't. He asked the same sorts of questions as you had. Was Suzy really as ill as she'd made out? What part had I played if she wasn't? I ended the call and blocked his number."

Pru stuck out her lip, clearly not believing him. "And he didn't try to get in contact again? From a different number?"

Foakes raised his right hand. "I swear he didn't. Like I'd swear the same thing if I had a Bible in my hand."

Perhaps he'd need to do exactly that if they ever got this case into court. Robin pressed on. "The fact remains of Suzy's proven duplicity—both in terms of romance and medical history. That would provide motive enough for Mark not only to ask questions but to scatter accusations around, concerning anyone he felt had helped her." Robin leaned forwards, hands together between his knees. "So, you can guess exactly what question we're going to ask next, although let me clarify something first. When we spoke on the phone on Monday evening, you made a quip about us asking about your movements on the day Mark died."

"Did I? I'm afraid I'd already been on the sauce so the exact details escape me."

"Let me refresh your memory. I remember every word, because the time you mentioned when you joked about me asking for your alibi—twelve fifteen—was pretty specific. It's also remarkably close to Mark's time of death, as best we can narrow it down."

"Is it?" Foakes ran his hands through his hair again: the neat coiffure had become quite a mess. "That was a lucky stab in the dark. Or maybe an *unlucky* one for me if I got so close. I genuinely just plucked a time out of the air because I was being a bit of a smart alec. Anyway, it wouldn't matter what time you're interested in if we're talking the middle of that Saturday, because I couldn't have been there killing him. From about half eleven in the morning to around half past six I was at my in-laws' house for their wedding anniversary do."

"Isn't that an abnormally long lunch?" Pru asked, evidently thinking they weren't getting the truth.

"It wasn't all taken up with lunch. Sal—that's my wife—and I got there early so we could chip in with the preparations and then stayed to help clear up. Otherwise, it's unfair if the people celebrating have to do all the work. So yes, that spans half eleven to half six and there are at least a dozen people who can verify all or part of that time. The only occasions I was on my own was when I went to the loo and a couple of those times I'm covered if you'd take the word of their cat, who wouldn't leave me alone." He raised a hand in apology. "Sorry. This is no matter for flippancy, is it? All joking aside, I hope you get whoever did this, because murder's a foul business and I have nothing against Mark, so I promise it wasn't me." Foakes paused as Pru noted everything he'd said. "Do you really think his death is connected to Suzy lying about her condition?" His face was drawn, as though he'd been mulling things over and come to an unpleasant conclusion.

Robin said, "We can't rule anything out at present. It's a serious business, playing on people's emotions as she did, and it's not likely to be the kind of thing people forget about now she's dead. Hurts linger."

Foakes nodded. "What about me? Am I likely to face charges?"

Robin had been assessing that question, at the back of his mind, through the interview. "It's hard to say. If you've told us the truth, and nothing but, I doubt there'll be a criminal case. I'm going to feel duty bound to report what I've learned through the proper channels. You might get off with a knuckle-rapping."

"Surely it can't help anyone to rake this all up now? Suzy's parents would be devastated to discover the truth. What's the point?"

Robin wondered how many times such an argument had been used, resulting in no further action being taken. Feeling his hackles rise, he took a deep breath before replying, but Pru got in first.

"Can you imagine how people would react if they discovered a serving member of the Met Police had used that reasoning to try to cover up one of their misdemeanours? Especially if no action was taken as a result?"

"You're quite right, Sergeant." Foakes appeared suitably chided. "I sowed the wind, as they say, so I should expect whatever harvest comes my way."

"Dr. Foakes, I think you should count yourself lucky if the only harvest you reap is a warning from the GMC. Mark's dead and it's possible that whoever killed him did so because of Suzy. Maybe they thought he was involved in her death, or perhaps they believed he connived in her leukaemia sham." The latter possibility had occurred to Robin as he spoke. "It's conceivable the murderer could come to the same conclusion we did, assessing what they knew and deciding you must have been involved."

Foakes exhaled loudly. "Don't think I haven't had a similar thought while we've been talking. I'll be watching the news day and night to see if you've caught the killer, because I don't want to be their next target."

"Do you really think Foakes is at risk from Mark's murderer?" Pru asked as soon as they were back in the car. "Assuming he isn't the killer himself."

"I think we'll end up ruling him out. Easy to get your wife or parents to cover for you but a whole bunch of people stretches credulity." Robin manoeuvred the pool car's seat into position for him to drive the next stint. "As for being in danger, we shouldn't discount the idea."

"And what about the idea of Mark conniving in her medical fraud?" Pru grinned. "That blindsided me."

"Sorry about that. The thought came out of nowhere. The reality doesn't square with him trying to access her medical records, but I was more interested in what other people might think. They might find it unbelievable that he didn't know what was going on. If you share a bed with someone, surely you'd notice their body changing?"

Pru shrugged. "Unless that had all stopped because she said she was too ill. It's a possible motive for killing Mark, though. Foakes went through the same reasoning process as we did, about whether Mark could have contributed to Suzy's death, so other folk could have too."

"Conversely, you've got that strong chance of Mark getting into an argument with somebody he felt had helped her con him, even if he had no proof they'd done so." Not Foakes, though, if his story was factual. "We've got some options for our elusive motive, and they could equally be applied to an argument that turned fatally violent and a cold-blooded, planned killing."

"Foakes did admit speaking to Mark, after initially denying it," Pru pointed out. "It clearly got heated."

"True, but I suspect our pal the doctor coming clean about Mark ringing him almost counts in his favour. If he really does have an unshakeable alibi, then it can't hurt to tell the truth. Especially if he's suddenly realised he could be somebody's next target so has an incentive to help us all he can."

"Got a name in mind for this 'somebody'? I can't think of any other medical professionals we've run across over the last week or so. He might have suspected her GP, I suppose."

"Or maybe a friend, one who'd consistently backed up her tale or whom Mark suspected helped fabricate documents. Whether they actually did so or not." Revenge for perceived slights could be equally virulent as for actual ones. "I had another idea, in there." Robin, who'd still not started the car, jerked his thumb towards the hotel.

"Don't keep it to yourself, then."

"There's no way I can prove this, although we could follow a timeline of Suzy texting Foakes and comparing that to when Mark rang for an ambulance." Robin drummed the dashboard. "What if he left off doing it until the last possible moment. Making her suffer as she'd made him suffer?"

"I think you may have something there. Perhaps it wasn't simply that he wanted to hurt her. If he knew about the fake cancer, then he might have thought she was exaggerating again. Putting on a cough and reporting symptoms she didn't have. Until she became so genuinely ill he had to act." The sergeant paused. "I wonder who else she texted when she was feeling like crap and whether they realised there was a discrepancy between the time they were sent and when she was admitted."

"My thoughts entirely." Robin turned the ignition key. "When the chips are down, it's your nearest and dearest you usually turn to, despite what's gone on between you in the past."

A nearest and dearest who were just about the only people they'd interviewed who hadn't been able to furnish themselves with an alibi.

Chapter Seventeen

A tired and frustrated Robin and Pru got back to Abbotston an hour after their expected arrival time. A pile up on the southbound M40—at a long stretch between junctions—had caused them to divert, only to get snarled up in traffic after an accident had happened on the diversion route.

As the pair entered the incident room, Danielle immediately offered to make them both a mug of tea, while Ben broke open a packet of biscuits he'd had stashed away. He brought them over, with the air of a rescue dog bringing sustenance.

"You lot are treasures." Robin grabbed a biscuit before the offer got rescinded. "Custard creams, as well. The best. Give us a few minutes, then we'll all get up to speed."

Once he felt confident of speaking coherently and he'd checked Pru was likewise, Robin got the team's attention. "Long story short, Hanley may have caused his mother's fall but he's no longer a person of interest for Mark's murder. We're pursuing a new line of enquiry." He paused, unable to hide a grin. "I'm sounding like a telly copper. The next part's a bit straight out of a script too. We came up with the idea that Suzy may have been faking her illness."

A ripple of nods and "Guessed that" ran round the team.

"We were all confident that you'd have a good reason behind what you asked us to root out," Ben said. "We'd have done it anyway, even if it had been odder still."

Robin, temporarily unmanned by the confidence his team showed in him—his tiredness must have been affecting him in surprising ways—made his way over to the incident board so he could pull himself together. He tapped on Harry Foakes's name. "We fell on our feet with this guy. I'd say his role in the cover-up has been weighing on him, so it didn't take much to get him to confirm it. Pru, want to update people on that interview?"

The sergeant went into her usual, highly efficient precis of the discussion, picking out the salient points and ending with, "So, whatever Mark's actual role in Suzy's death, we want to know whether that's the key to his murder."

"First things first," Robin said. "Foakes's alibi. Any news on that, Ben?"

He'd asked that particular constable to deal with the issue because he could increasingly be relied on for subtlety, something Ashok wasn't quite on top of, yet.

"Yes, sir." Ben had his notes to hand. "I've been in touch with both his wife and parents-in-law. I did my best to assure them it was merely routine in such cases, but I'm not sure any of them believed me. Not like Foakes was a close friend of the deceased and the excuse I gave—that he'd been a key witness about Suzy's illness—didn't seem to cut much ice."

"He's going to cop some stick when he gets home, I suspect," Pru said, with a grin.

Robin grunted. "I wouldn't want to be in his shoes, but if that's all he gets, he can't complain. What did they say, Ben?"

"That what he told you checks out. He was at the in-laws' house all day, getting increasingly sozzled."

"Thanks. I've got to say I had no real hope it would turn out he'd been away for an hour on some pretence." Shame that the suspects in this case whom he didn't like could prove where they were and the ones he did like couldn't. "Which all means that we need to turn our attention back to Justin and Izzy Packer."

"On the principle that they think he delayed the ambulance arriving?" Ben asked. "Did they mention something about that when we interviewed them? My memory of that day's all a bit fuzzy because of the food poisoning. Last time I use that new takeaway."

Robin thought for a moment. "I think they said they wished Suzy had called for an ambulance sooner."

Ben nodded. "One thing, sir. There was no car at the Packers' house. If they don't drive, how could they have moved the Yaris?"

"*Don't* drive doesn't mean *can't* drive, young Benjamin." Robin, grinning, wagged his finger. "They may have elected not to have a car now, but they could have had one in the past and both of them might have passed their tests when younger. We know they're not your stereotypical off-grid type. One of them could have cycled to Kings Ride Woods but driven away, utilising that bike rack. And they'd be likelier to know about that being on the Yaris than a relative stranger."

Ben conceded the point with a nod.

"Do we get them in for questioning now, sir?" Ashok asked.

Robin had been wrestling with that question ever since he and Pru had emerged from the traffic jam. "I'm inclined to sleep on it and get them in tomorrow. We can leave ringing them until first thing so they don't have this evening to plan anything they haven't already planned, story-wise."

Danielle raised her hand, timidly. "Do you think there's a risk they'll do a runner?"

"Good point." Robin could tell she wasn't used to producing anything like a challenge to a superior officer. "I'd say there's not a great risk if they haven't already upped sticks. It's possible they could have gone to ground since Ben and I saw them and we haven't noticed the fact, but we've not done anything to spook them, have we? All our attention's been aimed northwards."

There'd been nothing much in the local media, either, apart from a few snitty remarks about lack of progress, but Mr. Cowdrey had dealt with those in his usual effective manner.

"If we make it tomorrow afternoon," Pru said, "we'll have the best chance of laying our hands on some supporting evidence, no matter how circumstantial. Suzy's phone records from the time she went into hospital, maybe?"

"It won't hurt to get on that trail. If we're right, we'll be needing them for the CPS. At present our level of concrete evidence is pretty well nothing." Robin was acutely aware that the Crown Prosecution Service would have their guts for garters if their case was based on nothing but speculation. "Ben, was there anything at Tumulus Gardens that could help us?"

"Not a scrap, sir. I kept an eye out for anything to do with Suzy, but there was nothing over and above what you'd expect." Ben shrugged. "He seems to have cleared out most of her stuff, although that's what a lot of people do when they're bereaved."

"Well, any bright ideas between now and when the Packers come in will be much appreciated. I don't know about you lot but I'm shattered. If I interviewed anyone now it would be a wasted opportunity, and I want us all to be on top form for that encounter. I'm hoping that what happened with Foakes happens again and that they realise the game is up, fold, and tell all." Robin yawned mightily. "Let's do anything that can't be left until tomorrow and come to the rest fresh in the morning."

He could have added that not only was he extremely tired, but he was in desperate need of a warm, comforting cuddle from his warm, comforting Adam and a lick from a bouncing, daft Hamish.

Pru, who was stifling a yawn herself, said, "Deferring until tomorrow works best for me too. This new hypothesis hangs together now but I want to sleep on it. Always a risk we'll wake tomorrow and one of us will have spotted a hole in our thinking large enough to drive a bus through."

Which was absolutely sensible and depressingly accurate. Come morning, the Packers might have become the least viable suspects and they'd be back to square one.

Thursday morning, halfway through a week that already felt interminable, Adam was awake before his husband, so he crept out of bed and across the floor, trying not to rouse him. His alarm wasn't due for another few minutes, and they could be precious, sleep-wise. Robin had been dog-tired when he'd got home Wednesday evening, grabbing a kiss and something to eat before flopping on the settee. He'd refused to discuss the journey back from Birmingham, vowing he'd never again travel on the M40, but had wanted to discuss the progress they'd made and the new hypothesis the team was working on. This was not merely because Adam had been the catalyst for the leap forward.

"We're all at the excited stage and at risk of missing some obvious hole in the logic. You're independent so the chances are, Adam, you'll spot it and, better still, you'll have no hesitation in pointing it out."

Adam had listened, asked questioned, and followed the logic, but he hadn't spotted anything obvious, apart from the lack of evidence. Even now, when he'd had the chance to sleep on it, he still couldn't think of anything that would bring Robin's house of cards down. And given how reliable Adam's unconscious tended to be at working on a problem, doing what his dad used to call "going through the card index of the mind while you're out like a light," then surely there was nothing obvious to be rooted out.

As Adam returned to the bedroom to get a hoodie to put on top of his pyjamas, he found Robin yawning and stretching.

"Sorry. Did I wake you?"

"I don't think so." Robin turned off his phone alarm. "The room was empty when I came to. No worries if you did wake me, because I haven't the time to lie around here today and there's no incentive if you're not available to lie here with me."

Adam ruffled his husband's hair. "As soon as your case is settled, we'll book a stay-in-bed morning. Send Hamish to one of our mums for a treat."

"Deal." Robin stretched again. "I'm glad I decided not to do the interviews late yesterday, because I feel almost human this morning, whereas last night I was like the walking dead."

"You certainly look and sound perkier today."

"A shower, a mug of tea, and a couple of slices of toast inside me and I'll be perkier still."

"I'll go down, let himself out, and get the kettle on. You'll probably get an extra lick from Hamish this morning because he noticed the state you were in yesterday." The Newfoundland had been particularly attentive and loving, to the extent of hauling his favourite blanket into the lounge and laying it at Robin's feet.

Robin rubbed his knuckles across Adam's hand. "I don't know what I'd do without you two. I come home feeling like crap, and when you've worked your magic I sometimes think I could take over the world."

"Please don't. I'm not sure I could live with a dictator." Adam headed for the door. "Save your efforts for being mustard in that interview room."

Robin snorted. "I'll do my best. I'm increasingly convinced that we've come to the right conclusion, but I can't help worrying about the lack of evidence. If you can find any in the teapot, put it to one side for me."

"If I could, I would."

As Adam fiddled about in the kitchen and waited for Hamish to finish in the garden, he puzzled over the matter of proving a murder when proof was so hard to come by. Not his problem, really, but what affected Robin naturally affected *him*. Anyway, it was always fun to tackle somebody else's issues, rather than your own. By the time Robin appeared, not only was breakfast ready but Adam had a couple of ideas to air.

"Feel free to tell me either to bugger off or to stop the whole 'stating the bleeding obvious' lark with this." He poured their morning cuppas. "Have you got any interactions between Mark and his in-laws that sound dodgy? A punch-up at the wake or whatever?"

"Not that anybody's reported to us, and I've a feeling they would if there'd been fisticuffs at the graveside. Christine Probert would have been all over it, for starters." Robin, lips pursed, buttered a slice of toast. "Hold on a minute, though. Izzy Packer told us she'd met Mark at some farm shop last autumn and he'd been surprisingly sweet and sympathetic with her. I guess we could explore that, because it might indicate he'd known then that Suzy's illness was imaginary."

"So, he'd have already realised they couldn't have prevented her having treatment?"

"Exactly. There may well have been more to that conversation than they admitted, because Izzy did say she'd got upset. I think she then moved the interview on to the topic of Mark himself, how he'd fallen out with his brother, so she may have been deflecting us. Now, wait a minute"—Robin waved his toast—"I'm sure she said Mark had been talking about how everyone always gave their sympathy to the person who was ill and didn't bother with the family around them. The story was supposed to also refer to a miscarriage she'd had—how it was *his* child as well as hers but people seemed to forget that. He might have been referring to her supposed illness."

Adam nodded. "And if Suzy relished the sympathy she got when she miscarried, she might have wanted to replicate it."

"Which led her ultimately into the fake diagnosis stuff? Could be."

"I'm sorry this idea's not particularly concrete."

"It's a start, though. At the moment I'll take all I can get." That appeared to include another couple of slices of toast and a banana, which Robin loaded onto his plate.

Adam, taking his husband's hearty appetite as a positive sign, said, "Then you can have this too. Again, it's not a lot and you've probably already thought of it. When you ring 999, isn't that call itself recorded and not merely the time and date?"

Robin tapped his forehead, sending a shower of toast crumbs flying. "Well, that shows you how knackered am I. Pru too, because it's the kind of detail she'd usually have jumped on. If we pin down the time and compare that to when Suzy was texting, we might have a clearer idea of what went on that evening. If I wasn't all buttery and jammy I'd give you a kiss."

"Keep it for later." Adam blew him one in return. "Actually, I was thinking that you could listen to what Mark said when he rang for the ambulance. Hasn't that kind of evidence been used to catch people out? I appreciate that if he did let something slip it couldn't have been anything so obvious that the operator would have become suspicious and made a note. But he might have made a remark that only has significance in light of your new theory."

"You, my genius boy, deserve more than one kiss." Before Robin could expand on the offer, Hamish jumped up, stuck his paws in his dad's lap, and thrust his head forward, evidently expecting his reward. "No, not you this time." Robin tickled the dog behind his ear. "I meant the other handsome, clever boy in my life. I'm lucky to have you both."

Adam smiled. "Leave the mush for later too, for when I can appreciate it. I don't want to arrive at school all teary-eyed."

Robin squeezed Adam's hand. "I don't want to go into a key interview in a state, either. I shall stiffen my upper lip rather than soften it for a snog."

"I'll do the same. I won't forget I'm on a promise, though."

"Quite right, too." Robin took another bite of toast. "You're on lots of promises. I'll deliver on every one."

Adam grinned and then took a swift drink of tea. He'd have to make sure he wiped any hints of lasciviousness off his gob before he arrived at school too. Otherwise, what would the parents say?

Chapter Eighteen

Thursday afternoon was crunch time. Nothing new had turned up so far that day evidence-wise, despite the best efforts of the team, apart from confirmation that both the Packers held driving licences. Ashok had identified a traffic camera on the cycle route from their smallholding to Kings Ride and was planning to scrutinise it as a matter of priority, while Danielle was on the hunt for the recording of the 999 call the night Suzy went into hospital.

Pru, Ben, and Robin reviewed exactly what had been said in the previous interview with the Packers, including the account of meeting Mark at the farm shop, so they'd be fully prepared. As prepared as they could be under the circumstances. Nobody had found an insurmountable flaw in the premise of the Packers' guilt, though.

As they headed down to the interview rooms, Robin said, "I'm still keeping an open mind. At present, it makes the most sense for Suzy's fake illness to be linked to her husband's death, but it's possible a better motive or culprit will turn up."

"As you often say, can you get better than the classic *family or friend*?" Pru smiled. "In an hour's time, you'll know."

"I hope you're right."

They'd put Justin Packer in one interview room and his wife Izzy in another. In Robin's experience, splitting a pair of suspects created several advantages, over and above the obvious ones of not having moral support to draw on or being able to ensure that each kept to an agreed tale. A witness or suspect spoken to confidentially, away from their cosy kitchen and the presence of their partner, might reveal information that they wouldn't otherwise.

Who would want said partner hearing about, for example, an alibi involving meeting a lover? The witness might also make a disclosure—maybe about domestic abuse—that they'd never dare do otherwise. There was even the possibility of previously agreed pacts being chucked out and one part of the duo being thrown under the bus to save the other. Robin had seen all those outcomes, and more.

He didn't expect to be seeing the "under the bus" scenario today, though. The Packers had struck him as a close couple and would surely be likelier to each admit being the guilty party in order to protect the other. Robin knew he should be entirely objective, but he couldn't supress every bit of humanity; he'd liked the Packers from the start, appreciating the way they'd helped Ben when he felt ill and the understanding attitude they'd taken towards their daughter. During their previous interview, he'd felt their deep pain and anger. His opinion of them hadn't changed yet, although his guess at the likely provenance of their pain—and what they might have done as a result—had shifted.

Once all the pre-interview formalities were completed, Robin said, "Mr. Packer, what we're about to discuss is no doubt going to be painful for you, but we have to get to the truth about Mark's death and the events leading up to it."

"I understand that." Justin, face drawn, kept his gaze fixed on his hands.

"We'd like to start with Suzy. We've had it verified that she'd had an early-stage melanoma removed, but we've also learned something much more disturbing about her medical history." Robin waited for any response from Packer, but the suspect remained quiet, his facial expression suggesting wariness rather than surprise. "Were you aware that she didn't have any other form of cancer and that all the business about her leukaemia and any treatment for it was faked?"

Unexpectedly, Justin began to weep. Mrs. Botterman, the duty solicitor who accompanied him, seemed as taken aback at the reaction as Robin was.

"I'll get you a drink of water," Pru said, while Robin paused the interview. She returned shortly with both a cup and a box of tissues, which the suspect took with thanks. "Danielle's outside. She has a message for you, sir." Clearly an important one, given Pru's tone of voice. Justin's glance flickered towards her, but his face was too grief-stricken to be readable.

"I won't be a moment." Robin slipped out of the room, to find the constable waiting.

"Sorry to interrupt, sir," she said, "but I checked with Ben, and he said you'd probably want to know this, ASAP."

"You can always interrupt us if what you've got to say is relevant to the interview we're conducting. Ben clearly thinks it is."

"I do too." Danielle's voice grew in assurance. "We haven't yet listened to the recording of the 999 call for Suzy, but we know it wasn't Mark who made it. No evidence he made any calls to the emergency services that night. Justin Packer rang for the ambulance."

"Bloody hell. I never expected that. Did Mark ring separately? Or Suzy herself?"

Danielle shook her head. "Only Packer. I suppose Mark might have been trying and for some reason couldn't get a solid mobile signal, but his house has a landline he could have used."

"It does. Is Sergeant Davis aware of this?"

"Yes. I told her in case you couldn't come out of the interview. Did I do wrong?" Danielle nibbled at her lip.

"Of course not. I'm not the kind of boss who'd resent her knowing something first, especially in these circumstances. As long as my team doesn't hold any information back from me." Robin gave the constable a smile and a thumbs-up. "If you get hold of the recording before I'm finished interviewing this pair, you and Ben listen to it and give me another heads-up if anything leaps out."

"Will do, sir." Danielle almost skipped off, beaming. Whoever had managed her in the past had clearly knocked her confidence. Still, dealing with her career development could wait: Justin Packer couldn't.

"Sorry about that," Robin said, as he re-entered the room. "The news was important and I'll explain why later. Are we ready to resume, Mr. Packer?" The suspect nodded and they restarted the recording. "We were discussing Suzy's supposed diagnosis."

"We were. You have no idea what that time was like for us, Mr. Bright. All the worry we'd had, all the guilt we'd borne that we could have done something if we'd got her to a doctor early enough." Justin took a sip of water. "Discovering that some people believed *we'd* prevented her getting treatment was bad enough, but then to find out it had all been a lie and she'd been the one fooling us . . ." The tears started to flow again.

"Would you like us to pause again?" Robin asked.

"No, let's just get on with it." Another sip from his glass. "Izzy and I have kicked ourselves so often since then. We should have realised things didn't add up, especially when Suzy kept looking so well. Thing is, she was plastered with makeup and wore the kind of billowy clothes she'd not normally have chosen, so we assumed that was all part of an act to cover up how ill she was, hiding bruising or weight loss or whatever. We'd never have guessed the makeup and the clothes were covering up the fact she was perfectly well. Not that we saw her much towards the end."

Robin glanced up sharply. "Why was that?"

"She said she didn't want us upset by seeing her so ill. We spoke weekly on the phone, which was more frequently than we'd done for a while. I'd assumed it was because she was nearing her end, but that can't have been. Maybe she was starting to feel guilty—if she'd lived, we might have been reconciled." Justin blew his nose, clearly trying to stem his tears. "When you and that other constable came to visit us, we told you about wishing we'd known she was ill and paying to get her help. That referred to the time we believed she had cancer, but it also applied to what we know now. Thinking of her being mentally ill, rather than physically, and the help she should have received for that." Justin glanced from Robin to Pru and back again. "She must have been unwell, mustn't she, to have done something so cruel?"

Unwell or unscrupulous. It wasn't unknown for a supposed victim to be the manipulative party, deliberately inflicting pain on others.

"How did you discover the truth and when?" Pru asked.

"After her death. It started at the first U3A meeting we went to, when we thought we should get back into the swing of things. A new person joined us, a retired nurse called Dora who used to work in the ward where Suzy had been treated. Was supposed to have been treated, I should say. We discussed her, naturally and Dora seemed perplexed. You see, the name of the consultant Suzy had told us she'd been under didn't ring any bells with her. We assumed we'd got the name wrong, so we got in touch with Mark to find out who the doctor was, so we could ask Dora properly. That's when it all came out." For the first time in this interview, Robin had the feeling he was being led along. When the suspect had spoken about his feelings, his words had come across as authentic, but now the detail felt laid on with a trowel.

"And this was definitely all after Suzy died?" Pru said.

"Yes."

"So," Robin cut in, "when your wife met Mark last October— at a farm shop, I think she said—he didn't tell her anything then?"

"Not so far as I know." Again, this didn't sound convincing. "You'll have to ask Izzy about it when you interview her, although I'm sure she'll tell you the same."

"I'll do that. Then I'll no doubt want to speak to you about it again." Robin feigned consulting his notes. "Suzy died of sepsis, as a result of Covid. That's not in dispute. What I'd like to know is why you were the one to ring 999 for her and not Mark."

Justin flinched at the question. Maybe he hadn't realised that emergency calls were recorded or—like Robin and his team—he'd not remembered the implications. "She texted us that evening, feeling desperate, so I knew I had to get her help and quick. I've done first aid courses in the past and they always used to tell us to get a couple of people to ring for help. Better that 999 gets three separate calls than you've only asked one person to try and they can't get through."

Which was true, although that wasn't an answer. "Why didn't she ring them herself? She had the use of her phone."

"She did but her text said she could barely speak. Throat like sandpaper." Justin's brow furrowed. "I assume she was telling the truth about her symptoms by then. She came across as frightened. In an awful state."

"And as far as we know Mark never tried to ring. You must have known that too."

Justin flashed a glance at Mrs. Botterman and then said, "Mr. Bright, my son-in-law was bloody feckless at times. When Suzy texted us, he was being as much use as a chocolate teapot. She said he'd gone to pieces entirely. Knowing now what we didn't then, I wonder if she was hiding the fact that he'd already got doubts about how ill she was. If he knew about the leukaemia and assumed she was faking how ill the infection was making her, he may not have realised that things had become serious. When she was little, I used to tell her the story of the little boy who cried, 'Wolf!' I couldn't have dreamed it would happen in real life."

The suspicion that Suzy was crying wolf again was a viable explanation for Mark not ringing for help, and one which put him in less of a bad light than the theory he'd known his wife was ill yet held off getting help. Was Justin now setting up a situation in which he and his wife could say, *Why would we have killed him? We know what he was going through.*

"Did you hold a grudge because Mark didn't get her help sooner?" Pru asked. "A few hours could have made all the difference to her chances of survival."

Justin shook his head. "I did feel angry at the time, but the hospital told us it might not have made much difference to her outcome. She developed sepsis and that was it. I suppose the person who told us that might have been trying to be kind. A little harmless lie."

"Mr. Packer," Robin said, "I'm not at all convinced you're telling us the whole truth. You spoke to someone at the hospital about Suzy's death, yet you never discussed her supposed terminal cancer?"

Justin flinched again. Robin was sure he'd identified a loophole in the Packers' pre-prepared story.

"Please answer the question," he insisted.

With another glance at Mrs. Botterman, Justin said, "I have no comment to make."

"Then will you comment on Mark's death? If you thought he'd—for whatever reason—not got help to your daughter quickly enough, that would give you a strong motive to get even with him. You have no alibi for his time of death, so did you meet him in Kings Ride Woods then?" That would leave the door open for the suspect to say they *had* met but he'd left the man alive, although Robin suspected the shutters had now come down. Justin would want to regather his thoughts, surely.

As expected, his reply was a curt "No comment."

"Then we'll recommence this when we've spoken to your wife. I *will* get to the truth, I promise." With that, Robin suspended the interview.

Once outside the interview room, Pru confessed she was in desperate need of a comfort break before she did anything else. "Effects of too much coffee, sir."

"Too much information, Sergeant." Robin would appreciate a similar break, though. "I'll swing by the incident room, then meet you back here. There's a couple of things I want to discuss before we see Izzy Packer."

When he returned, to find Pru seemingly much relieved, the couple of things had become three. "Nothing from the traffic cameras, yet, but Ben's hit on something," Robin reported. "When I first saw Justin, he reminded me of Robert Plant from Led Zeppelin. They were my dad's favourite band."

"I've heard of them," Pru said, in the same way she might have confessed to having heard of Neanderthals.

"Google him, like Ben did. He reckons I'm right about the resemblance. Anyway, he's just spoken to your mate Mr. Rashid, and he not only knows what Robert Plant looks like, he saw a bloke similar to him in Kings Ride Woods that Saturday. On a bike." Robin jabbed his thumb over his shoulder, towards the interview room where Izzy would be waiting. "There was a woman cycling with him, whom Mr. Rashid described as resembling a groupie. Not a very complimentary description, but he's got a point."

"I bet he'd pick them out in a lineup too." Pru pulled at her lower lip. "This 999 business, sir. I know it's only speculation, but do you think Mark not making the call was because he was feckless, suspicious, or being downright vindictive?"

"Short of a message from beyond the grave, we'll never know. I'm not sure it matters, anyhow, because it's what other people think his intention was that counts. I doubt Packer believes some of what he's been telling us, by the way. Seems like he was sticking to a script."

"Agreed. I'm sure he knew Suzy wasn't ill long before they met the nurse at U3A." Pru pulled at her lip again. "I've been wondering what Suzy would have done if the sepsis hadn't killed her. She couldn't keep up the pretence of being terminally ill indefinitely."

"Maybe she'd have taken a journey to Lourdes and then pretended she'd been granted a miracle cure." Robin shrugged. "Come on. Let's get the other side of the tale."

The start of Izzy Packer's interview mirrored that of her husband, except that her solicitor was a man called Dolby, who appeared rather uninterested in the proceedings. Robin used the same form of words, the same question about her knowledge of Suzy's illness—partly so she'd have no indication of what her husband had said—although the response he got was different. No tears, this time, just the same steely courage in the face of despair as Izzy had shown in her own kitchen.

"Yes, we did find out that Suzy wasn't riddled with cancer, apart from a minor melanoma. It cut to our hearts like a knife that our own daughter could do such a thing to her parents. I keep having to persuade myself that it wasn't some sort of revenge on us." Izzy paused, maybe having said more than intended.

"Why should she want revenge?" Robin asked.

"'Revenge' is perhaps a poor choice of word on my part." She ran her fingers in circles on the table, as though regathering her thoughts. "Maybe 'getting her own back' describes it better. She was always a rebel, in her own way—she hated our lifestyle, as you know—so anything that could have had a dig at us would have been up her street. But it can't have been that alone, because we weren't the only people she deluded. She must have been mentally ill, surely. Munchausen syndrome or something like that."

Robin now had severe doubts about such a diagnosis and would have plumped for Suzy being that old fashioned but useful term *wicked*. "*When* did you find out she'd been faking it?"

Izzy fingered the table again, the gesture suggesting she was weighing her options, given the intense look of concentration on her face. "We didn't know for certain until after she died, but we started to have an inkling when I saw Mark at the farm shop last October. I told you and your constable about that, when he had the upset stomach and needed help. Is he better?"

"Much, thank you. And you *did* tell us about seeing Mark, although clearly not everything." Robin smiled ironically.

"Can you blame me?" Izzy returned the smile. "What I said was the absolute truth as far as it went because Mark *did* talk about how everyone fussed over Suzy and ignored him. That was when he let slip something about the innocent suffering and not the guilty. He clearly was referring to Suzy, so I'm afraid I gave him a bit of the third degree about what he meant, and it transpired that he thought she wasn't as ill as she'd been making out."

"What was your reaction . . .?" Pru asked.

"After the initial shock? Feeling closer to Mark than I ever had. If what he suspected was true, then we were fellow sufferers, if that's not being overdramatic."

That point might need exploring further, depending on how the interview progressed, but for the moment, Robin wanted to drill down on the previous answer. "That's not the timeline your husband gave. He said you didn't know about the fake illness until after Suzy's death, starting with a conversation you had with a nurse at U3A."

Unexpectedly, Izzy laughed, smiling at her solicitor. "Justin's doubtless trying to protect me, the daft sod. I got very upset back then, not only at the farm shop, but for ages afterwards. I was so low I nearly did something very silly, although thank God I had the support from Justin to get me through. He's a good man, my husband."

"He just makes up stories about nurses called Dora?" Pru evidently didn't feel the same sympathy for Izzy as Robin did.

"No, Dora's real and if Justin told you we asked her about Suzy's so-called consultant, he's right, because we were trying to uncover the full story. If she'd involved real people on the medical side, for example."

"And had she?" Pru asked.

Izzy shrugged. "Not as far as we could tell, although that's not saying much. Mark played his cards pretty close to his chest and wouldn't tell us any of the details about what he'd found out or how he'd done so."

So the Packers didn't know about Foakes's involvement?

Robin said, "Given that you had your suspicions back in October, did you confront Suzy about them?"

"Would you have done, in the same circumstances? She was making less and less contact with us, anyway—all part of the pretence, I'd guess, because she'd have been worried we'd twig. We decided we'd bide our time, rather than jump in and risk her cutting all ties." Izzy shook her head, ruefully. "We knew she wasn't terminally ill, so we had time and space and could use that to see if she came round. We never suspected that time would be cut short by something else." Izzy produced a handkerchief, dabbing at her eyes.

Robin offered her a break, but Izzy insisted they carry on, which was a relief. She wasn't quite echoing what her husband had said and each answer felt like it was edging them nearer the truth.

A knock sounded on the door. Pru leaped up to answer it, but Robin intervened. "I'll go." He'd had an idea, prompted by the reference to their previous interview with the Packers, and he wanted the team to test it.

Ashok was outside bearing some pieces of paper in his hand, which he passed to Robin for perusal. A fuzzy printout of what must have been a still from traffic camera footage was accompanied by a note in the constable's distinctively neat hand.

This shows a couple of cyclists who look exactly like the Packers heading in the direction of Kings Ride at 11:05 on the Saturday morning Mark was killed. Google Maps says they'd have got from the camera to the middle of the Kings Ride Woods by 11:40.

"Brilliant. See if you can work the oracle with this." Robin asked the question his idea had prompted.

Ashok grinned. "I'll get onto that right away, sir."

Robin returned to the interview room, passing the paper to Pru with a satisfied nod before resuming his questioning. "Mrs. Packer, can we turn to the evening Suzy went into hospital with Covid? Who rang for the ambulance?"

Izzy paused a moment, clearly coming to a decision. "By the tone of your voice, you must know already that it was Justin."

Robin ignored the comment. "Why did *he* ring and not Mark?"

"I wish I knew. I mean, I wish I knew why Mark didn't ring. Suzy had texted us to say she needed help but he'd gone to pieces and was being as much use as a chocolate teapot."

"Those were her exact words?"

"They were not. She was too ill to make jokes."

Gone to pieces. Chocolate teapot. Those phrases made it sound as though the Packers had agreed the wording of that answer in advance, so they *must* have been expecting to be asked about the 999 call. Had Justin's flinch at the mention of it been less concerned with guilt at his own involvement and more about how the events of that evening gave them reason to resent their son-in-law? "Given what you suspected by then, didn't you speak to Mark about why he hadn't rung for an ambulance? Being useless doesn't seem a convincing excuse for his inaction."

Twin spots of red appeared on Izzy's cheeks. "What would have been the point? It wouldn't have brought Suzy back."

"Agreed, but most people wouldn't have been able to resist clearing the air," Pru pointed out.

"We're not *most people*." A hard edge had crept into the suspect's voice, one that matched the steely glint which had appeared in her eye. Perhaps Izzy realised how harsh she now sounded, because she followed up with a mellower "You learn to pick your fights."

"Like the fight you had with Mark the day he died?" Robin asked.

"I have no idea what you mean by that." The answer didn't sound convincing.

Robin turned over the picture and passed it across the table. "I'm showing the suspect a photograph from a traffic camera on the old Kinechester road. This was taken at 11:05 in the morning on the Saturday Mark was killed. Is that you and your husband?"

Izzy, a look of alarm quickly hidden, peered at the image. "What did Justin say about this?"

"Nothing, because we didn't yet have the evidence to hand when we interviewed him. Answer the question, please."

"That could be us. I know we said we were at home all day but we needed toilet roll—the cat had got into our supply and destroyed it—so we went to the shop in Kings Ride because they stock the eco-friendly type." Izzy pushed the picture back. "We went together because I'm increasingly nervous of cycling on my own."

Robin doubted Izzy Packer got nervous about anything. "Why didn't you tell us this in the previous interview, when we asked what you were doing that day?"

"We forgot. It was only a short run to the shop and home again." Izzy sat back, arms crossed.

"Do you have the receipt from the shop?" Pru asked.

"I don't ask for them. Waste of paper. I paid cash, anyway."

Robin studied the suspect for a moment. Was that fact a sign of innocence, given that a guilty person might have made sure they had a receipt to account for the journey? Although given that such an item would be time-stamped, it would have suggested a premeditated attack, with alibi pre-planned. "We have a witness who says two people matching your description were cycling in Kings Ride Woods around the time Mark was killed. Was that you and your husband?"

Izzy opened her mouth, shut it again, and then forced out, "No comment."

"Are you sure there's nothing you want to say?"

"No comment."

Robin picked up the picture and rose. "Let's go and see what Justin has to say about this. Interview suspended."

Halfway between the two interview rooms, Robin halted. "What do you make of that?"

Pru rolled her eyes. "We've been here before, haven't we? Two suspects with a pre-planned story, desperately trying to busk the bits they forgot to plan."

"Agreed. I'm confident we're getting nearer to the truth, though. The Packers were there in Kings Ride Woods, all right, but the challenge is linking them to the fatal blow." With a deep, calming breath, Robin headed to talk to Justin, still not entirely sure how he'd achieve his aim.

Once they'd recommenced the interview, Robin said, "You've not told us the truth, have you, Mr. Packer?"

Justin's expression of bafflement was clearly false. "The truth about what?"

"For a start, about when you first suspected Suzy wasn't as ill as she made out. Would you like to amend your previous statement?"

With an enquiring glance at Mrs. Botterman, one that got a nod in reply, Justin said, "Okay. I can't see how any of this matters, but when Izzy saw Mark at the farm shop last October, he said something that raised our concerns. By the time Suzy died, we were pretty sure the cancer—apart from the melanoma—was all an act, which is why we didn't talk to anyone at the hospital about her not getting the care she needed. I didn't say this earlier because it hurt at the time and it's worse now, given all the what-ifs we've had to ask ourselves every day. Are you satisfied now?"

"For the moment. About that aspect, anyway." Robin let his reply sink in. "Then there's this." He turned over the photograph, then pushed it across the table, with the same words—for the recording—about what he was showing the suspect. "At 11:05 in the morning of the same day Mark was killed, this traffic camera on the old Kinechester road shows two people who look for all the world like you and your wife cycling off in the direction of Kings Ride. When you assured us you'd been at home all that Saturday."

Justin squirmed in his chair. "We were rather stressed the day you interviewed us—with the shock of Mark's death and everything—and had completely forgotten we'd nipped out. And how embarrassing to have to admit we'd run out of loo roll."

"Oh yes, I suppose it is, if you use up the last sheet and you've forgotten to replace it," Pru said, with an innocent air that would probably fool the suspect but which didn't take Robin in.

Justin smiled, clearly relieved by Pru's response. "Quite. You feel such idiots that you hadn't stocked up, especially after the shortages during Covid."

Evidently the cat destroying the spares was part of the story that hadn't been agreed in advance. Robin pressed on, encouraged. "If you only went out to get supplies, why do I have a witness who says he saw you both cycling in Kings Ride Woods around the time Mark was murdered?"

With another glance at Mrs. Botterman, Justin shrugged. "He's mistaken."

"As the officer who interviewed this witness," Pru said, "I'd say there's little chance that he'll fail to pick you out in an identity parade."

The suspect sat quietly, no doubt weighing his options. Eventually he said, "I know this sounds bad, but try to see it from our point of view. We did go for a spin, after we'd been to the shop, because it was such a lovely day and the traffic wasn't as awful as usual on a Saturday. There's a nice trail through Kings Ride Woods which we've always liked. Using that doesn't make us killers."

"It makes you liars, though, so yes, it does sound bad. And I'm not sure what you mean by seeing your point of view," Pru continued. "What made it so essential to lie?"

"We were worried that we'd be suspected, but we have nothing to hide."

"Then why not be honest in the first place?" Robin was starting to lose his patience, having gone through a similar experience with Alex Hanley. "Our witness also heard somebody arguing in the vicinity of where Mark was found. We believe this argument led to his death. Had you and he arranged to meet?"

"No way."

Robin had heard every colour of a lie over the years and that sounded like one.

"Really?" Pru said. "Your son-in-law wouldn't ring for an ambulance when your daughter was desperately ill and you didn't at any point want to have that out with him? Look, we know you've been torturing yourselves ever since that evening trying to imagine exactly what went on. Mark at the end of his tether, perhaps, saying to Suzy, 'You told me you were too late getting medical help for this nonexistent leukaemia of yours; well, let's see how you get on without help for your real, live Covid.'"

"It wasn't that. It—" Justin shut his mouth with an audible snap, undoubtedly having let his tongue run on too far.

When Pru spoke next, her voice was no longer harsh and accusing. "Mr. Packer, why don't you just tell us what the argument with Mark *was* about?"

The suspect, without the merest squint in his solicitor's direction, and with an air of defeat, said, "We didn't accuse Mark of anything, I swear. Yes, Izzy and I have speculated time and again about why he didn't ring, but honestly, we came to the conclusion that we could understand any reticence on his part. We felt for him." That did seem to have an element of truth and echoed what Izzy had told them.

Robin's phone, on silent, vibrated with what must have been an incoming message. It would have to wait. "So, when did attitude that change?"

"About a month ago, when Mark got in contact out of the blue. We'd not seen him since the funeral and honestly expected that we wouldn't likely speak again unless we ran across him somewhere. We only had Suzy in common, really." Justin reached for his glass of water and took a long draught. "I don't suppose the wounds we suffered because of her will ever totally heal, but

Izzy and I had moved on a bit, trying to grasp what made her act as she did. So, the last thing we needed was Mark accusing us of having helped pull the wool over his eyes."

Honesty. No. One of the last things that Mark had written. Did it refer to his suspicions concerning the Packers?

"He alleged that you colluded with Suzy over her illness?" Pru asked.

"Yes and he said he had proof. That was the whole point, you see." Justin ran his hands into his long, straggly locks. "How could he have anything like proof, because we'd had absolutely nothing to do with Suzy's fake illness and we knew we hadn't."

Pru narrowed her eyes. "Can you state that for both you and Izzy?"

"Of course! Do you think I wouldn't know if my wife had been involved?"

"Then what gave Mark the idea you'd been tangled up in it?" Robin asked.

"I swear I don't know. Not even now. I can only think that he'd found some texts on her phone between her and us and misinterpreted them. If he'd become paranoidly suspicious after discovering she'd lied to him, he might see what he thought was there, not the reality." Justin put his head in his hands. "It's been a nightmare."

No doubt it continued to be. A nightmare in which the Packers were starting to give themselves away. But had Mark possessed anything resembling evidence?

You can do this. You're strong. The partly printed sheet from the wastepaper bin. Maybe it hadn't dated from the same time as the bills but was part of a batch Mark had printed off before his trip to see Tom.

It doesn't feel right.

It may not but you got it. Remember . . .

Words that were possibly innocent, definitely capable of misinterpretation by someone who wanted to prove a theory.

Pru said, "Mr. Packer, you said you don't know *even now.* What did you mean by that?"

If ever a suspect resembled a rabbit in the headlights, that was Justin Packer. "Eh? Only that we've not found out anything else since."

"What about after you'd had it out with Mark in Kings Ride Woods?" Another moment of inspiration hit Robin. "Following which, you took his car so you could search through *that* for his so-called evidence."

With an expression of alarm and a clasp of his hands, Justin said, "I want to talk to my solicitor. Privately."

"We'll give you ample time to do that in a moment. Beforehand, I need to check what could be another vital piece of information. For the benefit of the recording, Chief Inspector Bright is checking his phone." Robin at last read the message, which came from Ashok.

I've checked with the medic, as asked. She says the mark left from the weapon could be consistent with a rolling pin, as long as it's one without any pattern on it and with a level end, like a cylinder shape. According to her, the style is called a straight dowel. She's also a bit of a dab hand with baking so knows more about them than I do.

Robin showed the message to Pru, who raised an eyebrow. He put his phone back on the table, face down, then said, "One final question before I leave you and Mrs. Botterman to your discussion. Mr. Packer, I know that the local area is hardly downtown Detroit, but living out in the sticks as you do must raise security concerns. Do you or your wife carry any form of self-defence with you?"

"What do you mean?" Justin waved his arms. "We don't have a gun of any kind, not even for deterring the crows."

"We're not talking about a gun. Or a knife. Plenty of women keep something about them to protect themselves. Maybe something they shouldn't, but I'm not discussing the legalities or morality of that. A form of defence which they'd only get out and use if they felt under severe threat." Robin leaned forward, tapping the back of his phone significantly so the suspect would guess he was referring to what he'd been reading there. "Have you or your wife ever carried something you could use to defend yourself in a fight?"

The hands got clasped once more. "No comment until I've consulted Mrs. Botterman."

In the corridor again, Pru said, "I feel like a yo-yo or a tennis ball. The back-and-forth strategy feels like it's working, though. Each time we seem to be knocking another brick off the wall of lies. Why the rolling pin business, though?"

"It was from a reference, earlier, to the interview Ben and I did at the Packers' house. I remembered sitting in their kitchen and being struck by the array of baking stuff—I'm sure there were at least three rolling pins—and then I thought of the story Ben told us about his gran."

"Self-defence with a carving knife or a rolling pin?" Pru snorted. "I guess the average kitchen is full of potential weapons."

"Exactly. Mark's wound's consistent with a rolling pin having caused it. Justin's admission that he and Izzy were cycling through the woods around the time Mark died, on top of the catalogue of lies, is probably enough to get a warrant to search the house, kitchen included, but I want something stronger." Robin quickly consulted his phone, vainly as it transpired, in case another little gem had come through. "That bit about not knowing *even now* seems a dead giveaway. Implies they were in a situation where proof was discussed and he regretted letting slip the fact to us. Let's see what herself has to say."

Izzy Packer appeared calmer. Someone had fetched her and Dolby a hot drink, and they were chatting about keeping slugs off lettuces as Robin and Pru entered the room. The solicitor seemed much more animated now, although whether that was because of the case or the gardening tips, Robin couldn't say. He formally recommenced the interview. "We've spoken to your husband about you two being seen in Kings Ride Woods around the time Mark died. Would you like to tell us about it?"

"Who says we were there?" Izzy's air of calm hadn't lasted long. "This witness of yours?"

Robin smiled. "Not only him. That husband of *yours*."

Izzy's response took Robin by surprise. He'd anticipated a denial or perhaps an accusation that the police were lying and trying to frame them with false evidence. Likely, given the way the two interviews had gone, that he'd be presented either with tears or a brusque "No comment." Instead, Izzy began to laugh—nervous laughter perhaps, but plenty of it.

"What's so funny?" Pru asked, coldly.

"This situation. We're rubbish, aren't we, me and Justin? Justin and I. Whatever." More of the awkward giggles. "It's not easy lying when you're fundamentally honest people. We've tried to stick to as much of the truth as we could, because that's easiest, but we still get found out."

"Like your story about the loo roll?" Despite the seriousness of the situation, Robin had a sudden memory flash through his mind of Campbell playing merry hell with a loo roll all over the garden at their old house. Time for a deep breath and a refocus. "Justin gave a totally different account of why you ran out and needed to buy supplies."

"We didn't discuss that point. What a bloody mess." Izzy's increasingly hysterical laughter was clearly about to morph into tears. "There's no point in denying it. Yes, we were in Kings Ride Woods that day. Yes, we'd gone to meet Mark because he said he had proof we'd helped Suzy fake her illness and we wanted to put him straight that we'd had no involvement. We chose the woods because they were neutral ground and a convenient place to have a chat that wouldn't be overheard. I can see all of that's no news to you, so Justin must have said the same."

"Your husband *did* tell us that Mark contacted you because he thought you'd conspired in Suzy's deception. He didn't say that any meeting had taken place, but we'd already concluded it had and you've confirmed our conclusions exactly." Now Robin needed to hear the truth about what really happened that Saturday morning. "What proof did Mark say he held?"

Izzy, who'd blanched at realising she'd admitted something she might not have needed to admit, said, "He wouldn't tell us over the phone and said we'd have to wait until we were all face-to-face. I told Justin to call his bluff, because frankly what he said was a load of crap. You can't have proof of something that never happened, can you? Mr. Bright, I swear that we never colluded with Suzy, so anything Mark had got must have been itself misinterpreted at best or faked at worst."

"But you still agreed to see him?" Pru asked, pulling them back to the key point, rather than the nebulous matter of who thought what.

"Not me, so much as Justin—he wanted to clear the air. He was scared that Mark would start causing trouble for us by spreading tales or the like. Maybe going to the local press with the story. My son-in-law was a very angry young man."

"He had every right to be," Pru pointed out, "given the situation with his wife and the nightmare couple of years he'd have spent worrying over what turned out to be nothing. So, you met him in the woods. What happened next? Remember that we have a witness who heard a heated argument at the time."

"He—or she—would have heard Mark sounding off, then. Saying that messages he'd found on Suzy's phone proved that we'd been involved in her scam. Saying how the lot of us had broken his heart and how he got no support from his current family, either. He said he was off to see his *real* family and how they'd treat him properly, irrespective of them having rejected his mother." Izzy rolled her eyes. "It sounded like a load of nonsense, but he clearly believed it."

"But *two* voices were heard arguing," Robin said. "So, it couldn't have been Mark ranting on his own. Was it you shouting back at him or Justin?"

"Can't your witness tell a male voice from a female one?"

Robin couldn't decide if the response was sarcastic or a last grab at a straw. "Not when it's one that could be a tenor or a low alto. Plenty of women have a husky voice, Mrs. Packer. You included." He tapped the table. "Let's assume that at the time you both would have had enough of his accusations and both would have had a go at him. Suzy was the child of two parents."

That off-the-cuff remark got right under Izzy's skin in a way that prepared questions hadn't quite, given the way the colour flared on her cheeks. "Yes, she was, Mr. Bright. She was our little girl. And if you have children, you'll know how you don't stop loving them, no matter what they do and you don't stop fighting their corner even when they're gone."

"Any parent would feel the same." Robin nodded, slowly. "That day when you met Mark, you're admitting that you fought Suzy's corner with him? Or did you only fight your own?"

Izzy flung her hands in the air. "Okay, I admit that we argued. You know that because your witness heard us. We let Mark have his rant, thinking that if he got it all off his chest, we might be able to bring him to see how stupid his accusation was. But he went on and on, mixing up things about Suzy's illness with all sorts of stuff concerning his family. How he'd been let down on all sides but had suddenly found somebody he could talk to and trust. We had to stop him short, because we weren't prepared to listen to his crap."

"You said that?"

"We shouted it rather than said it, because it's difficult to talk to someone who's ranting away and not raise your voice. We told him he was being ridiculous about us being part of Suzy's deception. He didn't like being called ridiculous. Went ballistic."

This all seemed very thin as the rationale behind such a violent argument. Justin's slant on things would be vital in understanding what had really gone on.

"You say Mark erupted at being called ridiculous. Is that when you hit him with your rolling pin?" Robin asked. Izzy turned pale but didn't reply. "Or was it with some other weapon that you carry for self-defence?" Still silence. "Maybe it was Justin who struck the blow. As you say, he's inclined to protect you."

"He is, but I can fight my own battles, thank you."

"We should be able to tell from the forensics, when we search your house. Very difficult to hide every trace of blood or DNA on a weapon and harder still to explain away."

"I suppose it is." Izzy flicked away a restraining tap from her solicitor. "No, it's all right, Mr. Dolby. We've pussyfooted about too long. What's the point of keeping up the pretence—it's not like we have a daughter to live for now." She sniffed and set her shoulders. "Very clever working out about the rolling pin, Mr. Bright. Yes, I do carry one with me. They say the streets aren't safe for women these days, but if you'd been brought up in a rough part of London, like I was, you'd know that's nothing new. I've always refused to be dictated by people telling me where I can or can't go, so I've had a rolling pin of one kind or another tucked in my backpack for years, although I've never had to use it."

That sounded rather like a well-rehearsed speech, one no doubt aired often before when discussing the way women were treated. Robin shot an involuntary glance at the purple patterned backpack that Izzy had brought with her.

With a knowing raise of an eyebrow, Izzy shook her head. "Nothing in there today, Mr. Bright. I was anticipating being searched."

"The murder weapon's still at home, isn't it." Robin stated. "Washed and put away?"

Izzy nodded. "I once read a theory about the Holy Grail. How the legend was nonsense because when the last supper happened, the cup for the wine would have been washed afterwards—no doubt by the women—and put away with the rest to be used another day. I thought of that as I washed the rolling pin and stuck it with the others."

"Where we'll find it when we conduct that search?"

She nodded again. "I swear it wasn't murder, though. That implies intention, and we had nothing planned apart from clearing the air with him. I swear that I hit Mark in self-defence, and that story isn't going to change. I know you're not likely to believe me, given how we've arsed you about, but we both know there's no point in hiding the truth any longer. I'm sure you'll use your clever forensics to link us to the scene, as well as your witness and traffic cameras."

Robin's turn to nod. "It never ceases to amaze me what the team can turn up from the crime scene or from the car." He noted Izzy's rueful smile at the mention of the car but that could wait. He mustered up his kindest tones. "Best if you describe how it came to blows."

"It began when Mark had become incoherent with anger. We asked him where his so-called proof of our involvement was and he said he wasn't so stupid as to have brought it with him. Justin made the mistake of calling him a liar, that he'd be taking it to show his new-found family, and all hell broke loose. Mark went for Justin, lashing out with his fists, so I tried to fend him off. When that didn't work, I was so scared I grabbed my bag, got the rolling pin, and lashed out with it. I genuinely didn't think I'd hit him hard enough to kill him." Izzy's ashen face and trembling voice lent veracity to her words. "I must have caught him at the wrong spot."

"He had what's called an eggshell skull," Robin said, "so a lesser blow could prove fatal. That fact is no defence against a serious charge, though, as Mr. Dolby can confirm. So, you struck him. Didn't you try to get help?"

"There was no point. I crouched down to check his pulse and breathing, but he was clearly dead and beyond first aid. That wound . . ." Izzy shuddered. "I think seeing it close up sent us into a panic. Complete and utter *can't breathe and want to run away* panic. The only other time in my life I've felt that bad was when Suzy told us how seriously ill she was. Said she was." Izzy's eyes began to well, but she sniffed loudly and pulled herself together, as though this was a fence she couldn't avoid taking. "Justin seemed to have frozen to the spot, so I tugged at him and said we had to get away because there was nothing we could do for Mark. I spotted his keys hanging out of his pocket and knew he'd have the car with him because he'd said he was off on a trip. I told Justin that if there was any supposed evidence about us being connected to Suzy's fake illness, it would be in the car or at the house and if we had the keys, we could check both."

"As well as get away from the area quickly?" Pru asked.

Izzy waved her hand. "That was a bonus, when we spotted Mark still had the bike rack on the Yaris and after I realised that we couldn't openly search the vehicle there in the car park. So, we just loaded the bikes and set off. Nobody gave us a second glance—I guess it's the kind of thing you see there all the time—and when Justin crunched the gears because he was out of practice, I guess anybody would have thought we were useless old codgers who shouldn't be on the road."

Again, the resort to humour. Robin said, "What happened next?"

"We drove off and found a quiet lane so we could give the car a quick once-over. Nothing turned up, but he had a case and a bag in the boot, both with a sturdy travel padlock on. We had nothing to break them with, so we decided to drive past our house and quickly dump them there behind the hedge, where we could break into them later. Then we headed off to the car park in Kinechester, where we left the Yaris, having paid for a couple of days." She shrugged. "That was all Justin's idea and a clever one for the spur of the moment, I thought. It gave us breathing space and wouldn't appear suspicious."

A clever idea indeed. "What did you do with the bunch of keys?" Robin asked.

"We tucked them away under some rubbish."

"What about your plan to search Mark's house?"

Izzy shook her head. "We ditched that. Got cold feet after we dropped off the bags and decided we'd ridden our luck enough. The panic had eased and cold reality set in, so we wanted to get rid of the car as soon as we could and be done with it. We cycled home, opened Mark's cases, and checked them over."

Danielle would be pleased to see how close she'd been with her theory, despite having got the wrong cyclist.

"And you found . . .?" Pru prompted.

"Apart from his spare clothes and a pile of family history stuff? Nothing. The only things which seemed relevant were copies of some emails and texts between us and Suzy. With a warped mind it might be taken to mean we were helping her, but we were just trying to be supportive."

If that was all the "proof" Mark possessed—and Robin knew how people could delude themselves and see what wasn't there—then his death had been even more in vain than they'd suspected.

"Can we see these copies?" Robin said.

"I'm afraid we destroyed them. Along with as much of his stuff as we couldn't dispose of—we'd had one of those plastic charity sacks come through the door that very day, wanting clothes. Good timing for us." Izzy smiled, ruefully.

Robin supressed a groan. One of the constables might be having a thankless time following up who'd been distributing sacks in that area and where the goods had gone. Although there might be a chance of an easier piece of evidence to locate. "Did you donate the suitcases too?"

"No, we thought that would look too suspicious. As would deconstructing and burning or burying the things. We were going to wait a few months and then offload them in a skip somewhere, but transporting them on a bicycle's a challenge." Izzy snorted. "You'll find them in the loft."

Robin sat back to take stock. If all this proved true, and the Packers didn't suddenly decide to rescind their story, then getting the Crown Prosecution Service to progress the case would be a doddle—although what charge should they press on the couple at the moment? Manslaughter seemed the obvious one, if the fight with Mark had gone as Izzy said it had but something didn't add up. There had been no strange fingerprints in or on the Yaris, which didn't chime with a sequence of events which had allegedly been completely unplanned.

"When you go cycling, how are you dressed?" Any answer Robin got could be easily checked against the traffic camera picture.

"Eh? Sensibly, I'd say. We both wear trousers, a warm top, but no helmets because they give you a false sense of security. Fingerless gloves." Izzy stopped, maybe having made the same leap of logic that Robin had.

"If you were both wearing fingerless gloves on that Saturday morning, how do you explain the lack of either of your fingerprints on Mark's car?"

Izzy glanced at her solicitor. "We wiped everything down, naturally. We've read enough crime books to know we should do that."

"Then how do you explain the fact that Mark's prints were still there?" Robin said. "The car hadn't been wiped down. His prints were smudged in places where somebody had used the vehicle after him, wearing gloves. Gloves that covered their entire hand, which suggests they were prepared not to leave prints."

Izzy, evidently shaken, eyed her finger ends. "No comment."

Time to give Justin the opportunity to revise his statement, although first they'd need to get a set of house keys and put the Crime Scene team into action. While they'd need to corroborate what Izzy had said, they could also be on the lookout for anything that might support the theory that the attack on Mark was, if not pre-meditated, then seen as a possible outcome of the meeting.

With a shudder, Robin thought again of that welcoming kitchen and wondered if Izzy Packer had used the murder weapon to roll out the dough for the homemade biscuits he and Ben had enjoyed so much.

"Yo-yo time," Robin said, as he and Pru moved between rooms.

"Productive yo-yo, I'd say. If you can have such a thing." Pru's eyes were alight, clearly at the prospect of settling the case. "Am I wrong to feel a bit sorry for them?"

"I'd say not and you're hiding it well." Robin halted. "I'm trying to keep objective when I feel for both the victim and the killers. So many lies, so much hurt. I *think* Adam and I wouldn't have resorted to violence in such a situation but who knows?"

"I do, sir." She smiled. "You two are too decent to let yourselves get so wound up. You'd walk away, kick the car tyres, give Hamish a cuddle. He'd put you right."

"I appreciate that, Pru." The sooner she was made an inspector, the better for whichever force was blessed with her. He pointed at the door behind which Justin was waiting. "Let's hope this is the last bounce of the yo-yo."

When confronted with what his wife had said—apart from the detail of the gloves—a plainly weary Justin redid his statement, giving the police an almost identical story to hers. Although not so identical that it made Robin suspect he was being told yet another pre-planned lie, apart from one aspect. He pushed the traffic photo across the table for Justin to see, using the same words he'd used for Izzy.

"That's us, all right." The suspect's brow furrowed. "But you knew that from what we've both told you."

"We do." Robin nodded. "But there's one puzzling thing. You said you took Mark's car, drove it, parked in Kinechester, and wiped the touch areas. Is that correct?"

"Ye-es." Justin evidently hadn't spotted the trap. Would it spring on him as it had on his wife?

"Which is why we could find none of your fingerprints in it?" Pru asked.

"Correct."

Time for Robin to put to Justin what he'd put to Izzy. "So how can examples of Mark's prints still be there? Some of them smudged where someone else has been driving the car wearing full gloves, not the fingerless ones you can just about make out in this picture."

"No comment."

Back there yet again. Robin had been dreading such an outcome and the likelihood he'd have to remand both suspects in custody, leaving them to stew overnight while they waited to see what forensics turned up. He felt his phone rumble in his pocket, glanced at it—nothing important—and was struck by a last-ditch line of enquiry. Mark must have kept Suzy's phone, because he'd got Foakes's number off it, but the thing hadn't turned up yet. "What happened to Suzy's phone?"

Justin couldn't have recoiled more if Robin had struck him. "Her phone?"

"Yes. We know Mark had it, but where is it now?"

The dramatic effect of such a simple question proved horrible to witness. Robin had never seen a man disintegrate so quickly and so deeply into a rambling, blubbering mess. It began with Justin saying Mark had told him he'd kept Suzy's phone so he knew what they'd all been saying to each other.

"He was gloating about the night Suzy was taken ill. How she'd led him on for so long, making his life hell, and how he'd decided he'd give her a taste of her own medicine, especially as he was convinced she was putting on how ill she was. He wasn't being feckless—he totally refused to ring for help." Justin's eyes welled. "My girl, my baby, all I could think about was her."

"When you say that all you could think about was Suzy," Pru asked softly, "are you referring to the night she was taken ill or when you argued with Mark?"

Justin ignored the question; maybe he hadn't even registered it. "I still think about her all the time. Now, here, yesterday, at home. In the woods, on the road." He patted his trouser pocket. "She's here, with me. Always with me."

Robin glanced at Pru—she was obviously finding the remark as bizarre as he did, until the penny dropped. "Suzy's phone is in your pocket? Did you take it off Mark?"

"He shouldn't have had it." Justin scrabbled at his pocket again, alternately grabbing and stroking at what must have been the item in question. "It was lying in his car boot, like it was trash, when it's so precious. So precious." He paused, eyes wild and fixed on Robin. "You mustn't take it. There's nothing on there."

"Mr. Packer," Pru said, in her kindliest voice, "we'll need to look at it. We'll take good care of it, I promise."

"No! You can't. It's all I have of her. Please, I beg of you. You see, he took all the rest away." Justin turned to his solicitor, who seemed alarmed. "He *did*. Mark. He wouldn't ring. He wouldn't help my baby. He took her away from us. I couldn't bear it."

Robin felt torn between continuing—because it wouldn't take much to get Justin to say exactly what had happened in the woods—and his conscience telling him that the bloke wasn't totally in possession of his faculties.

Before he could say anything, Justin pressed on. "You don't know what it's like. You have your heart torn out, and then it's thrown back in your face. *He* was gloating, so I had to do it, for her sake. I had to stop him, shut him up once and for all. Now I've got her here." Patting his pocket again. "I'll always have her with me, now. You can't have her."

Mrs. Botterman raised her hands. "This interview has to stop. Now."

"Agreed." Robin formally concluded the discussion. "I'll get the doctor in to give him the once-over."

"I don't need a doctor. I need my little girl. My little girl . . ." The rest drifted off into semi-incoherence about Suzy and Mark and how unfair everything was, as though Justin's dammed off thoughts and emotions of months—years—had at last broken through and couldn't be held back. But the recording had stopped and the words would only be retained in the memories of those who were present.

Chapter Nineteen

Robin got home not long after Adam, although he wasn't wearing as big a grin as might have been anticipated, given the earlier message he'd sent about cracking the case.

"Got the pair of them bang to rights?" Adam asked, once he and his husband had shared a hug, a kiss, and a fuss of Hamish, who clearly didn't want to be left out of the fun.

"I hope so. They're remanded in custody while we search the house for the murder weapon and anything else that will help tie up all the loose ends." Robin ran his hands through his already messy hair. "We'll charge them tomorrow if we can pin down whether it's manslaughter or murder."

"Is that still in doubt?"

"Striking the blow itself, no. We've got two confessions, although they can be revoked. Mind you, if that happened, we've got a witness who's identified them in a lineup and various other bits of evidence coming together, such as Mark's suitcases in their loft. I'd like some further forensics for the CPS, let alone to convince a jury, in case they plead not guilty. It all hinges on whether it was self-defence, as they claim, or intentional, which is what I'm leaning towards." Robin snorted. "This'll make you wince. Izzy Packer says she hit Mark with a rolling pin that she routinely carried for self-defence. We've sent off every one of them from their kitchen for testing. It's enough to put me off homemade pastry for life."

"All the more for me and Hamish, then." However, Adam could tell that this was no joke. Something in the case continued to eat at his husband. "I *have* known women to put pepper sprays or an innocent-seeming item like a small, sharp pair of scissors in their bags so they can ward off an assailant, but I've never heard of carrying a rolling pin."

"Yeah. Doesn't ring true, does it? It's the bit about their gloves, though. They must have worn them when they drove his car, and we caught her out about it." Robin raised his hand. "I know, that'll sound like gobbledegook. Let me get changed and I'll tell you everything. It'll make better sense to me then."

"Glad to be of assistance."

Over dinner, with Hamish gently snoring near Robin's feet, Adam was given the fuller picture, meaning that everything, including the point about the gloves, eventually did make sense as promised. They'd reached Izzy Packer reverting to her "No comment" position before they broke off to head into the lounge for a drink of beer and a stretch on the settees.

"Where had we got up to?" Robin asked, as he made himself comfortable.

"You'd stunned Mrs. into silence and were heading to get a new statement from Mr."

"Okay. So off we went again, like we were on elastic between the two rooms. When we let Justin know that his wife had told us what had happened, he must have known the game was up, at least to some extent: neither of them would tell us the truth about the gloves. Then I had one of my *bright* ideas. Yes, almost as bright as one of yours when food's involved," Robin added, with a tickle under the dog's chin.

"Your dad can't resist a pun, Hamish."

"Don't listen to your other dad, boy. This was one of my crowning moments. No laughing matter, as it turned out, though." Hamish must have noticed how pale Robin had turned, given the way he snuggled closer. "I asked whether they'd found Suzy's phone among Mark's stuff. I thought Packer would simply give me an upfront yes or no, but he suddenly went to pieces. All sorts of stuff came out about the argument they'd had with Mark, which made better sense than it only being about Mark saying they'd abetted Suzy."

"I did wonder. I know people get in a spat about nothing, but that rang as untrue as the rolling-pin-in-the-handbag stuff."

"My thoughts exactly. Anyway, I'll spare you the details but Justin admitted the argument had sent him doolally."

"You reckon *he* struck the fatal blow?"

"I think it's possible. But before I could press him on that, he'd become so rambling I had to call a halt. All to do with keeping Suzy's phone on him all the time, so that he felt he had *her*." Robin shuddered, generating a pout of affront from Hamish. "Sorry, lad. Not a nice business."

Adam moved over to Robin's settee, where he lifted his husband's legs so he could sit down with them on his lap. This was the key to why Robin wasn't himself. "What happened next?"

"After I terminated the interview, I had a word with his solicitor. She was as shocked as we were at the change in him: verging on the temporarily mentally incapable, she reckoned, so it wasn't a case of compassion on our part, because anything he'd have said might have been inadmissible. That's nice," Robin added, in appreciation of Adam rubbing his legs. "I called a doctor to check him over and give him a sedative or whatever else he needs. We'll have him on watch overnight."

"That bad?"

"Yep. I guess if you've been dealing with one blow or another over all that time, it gets to you in the end. She doesn't seem so affected. Hard as old nails."

Adam sniffed. "I remember one Easter the Lindenshaw vicar at the time telling us that there was an old saying that the nails for the crucifixion were made by women blacksmiths because the male blacksmiths would have been too soft-hearted. It always struck me a bit harsh, although I guess in some instances it's perceptive."

"It is in Izzy's case." Robin stroked Hamish again. "Tell me something happy."

"Happy? Well, my new 'bestie' Ryan is hot on the trail still. He'd messaged me, because he knows how busy you are, and we had a quick chat not long before you got home."

"I thought he was Mum's client? He must fancy you."

"If he does, it's a vain hope." Adam chuckled. "Irrespective of that, his rationale's not unreasonable. He's come across a picture of the guy from Australia whom he thinks could be your grandad."

"Lutterworth Len?" The change of subject alone was clearly raising Robin's spirits.

"Lutterworth Dave. Ryan's given me his name now, on the principle that we could do a reverse search for the picture and find the text with it. Yes, same Christian name as your dad."

"Well, what do you think of that, Hamish?" Robin probably addressed the dog because the catch in his voice might give way completely if he faced Adam. "Does Ryan have a surname for him?"

"Ingleby. David Ingleby. And he says if he's not the bloke, it's the coincidence to end all coincidences because everything matches, date-wise, name of solicitors out in Australia, and all the rest."

"And all this from the name Brown and a tax treaty?"

"Ryan's probably got some trade secrets he won't reveal, like having the nous to go looking for obituaries. That was what set him on to Ingleby in the first place: a notice about how charity donations would be preferred to flowers, to be sent via his solicitor's office. Then Ryan found this picture on another genealogy site and apparently it came with some text, that'll make sense when you see it." Adam got out his phone, although he wasn't quite ready to show the photo. "I said Ryan's rationale is understandable regarding your mum, but it applies to you, as well. See, he had some pictures of your dad that your mum gave him to help his research. He thinks there's a strong resemblance."

"Meaning he doesn't want to risk upsetting her?" Robin, looking up now, nodded. "Sensible idea. I've got you to comfort me and she's on her own."

"Yeah, that's what Ryan said. He wants all of us to be together when he feels in a position to present everything, but it the meantime, have a gander at this." Adam passed over his phone, then rubbed his husband's legs again.

"I see your point." The catch in Robin's voice was back. "I don't think I'm imagining the similarity."

"Lutterworth Dave's got a touch of you, as well. Not the bra." The photo showed a float from a carnival, obviously with a sea theme and several of the men on it dressed as mermaids. The comment Ryan had highlighted from the site made a joke about how David Ingleby was perfect for the role, given the webbing on his fingers.

"I can see that resemblance." Robin continued studying the photo and text before returning the phone. "It seems he had a good life. I hope he did. Do you think his family took the opportunity to get rid of a black sheep by sending him down under? I guess there weren't so many hoops to jump through around that time."

"Possibly. And if he *was* a black sheep, then it's possible that journey might have been the making of him, because he seems to have done well legitimately. There could be some element of that reflected in his providing an inheritance for his son's family."

"Eh? Not with you. Probably me being thick."

"Or me not making myself clear." Adam patted Robin's foot. "Was Lutterworth Dave showing a bit of gratitude for the fact that if he hadn't been sent packing—whether for getting your gran pregnant or whatever—he might never have made a success of himself?"

"Making the best of a bad thing?" Robin produced the kind of smile he'd not worn all evening. "That *is* happy. Thank you." He shifted position—much to Hamish's disapproval—to hold Adam's hand. "Do you know why the thing about Suzy's phone really got to me? Apart from seeing a suspect go to pieces."

"No. Or maybe yes." Adam jerked his free thumb in the direction of their garage.

"Yep. Campbell's lead." It still hung there, although his collar had gone with him when he'd made his last ride with a wonderfully sympathetic and professional pet undertaker. The lead was their sole memento of the big fellah. "I could never throw it away. It's all we have bar pictures and memories."

"We'll cherish them all, then." Adam squeezed his husband's hand. "We'd never let it become an obsession, would we?"

"I bloody well hope not." Robin grinned. "I think I'm pretty sane to start with, and you two keep me from going off the rails.

What's so funny?"

"Robin Bright, your idea of going off the rails is a four pack of Stella Artois and back-to-back episodes of *Friday Night Dinner.* Don't ever change."

"I won't. Policeman's honour." Robin raised his other hand, earning another dirty look from the dog. "Given the state of certain forces, maybe that's not such a cast-iron guarantee. *My* honour, is that enough?"

"It was when we got married. It still is."

Hamish eyed them, such an expression of disdain on his face at their slush that they couldn't help laughing.

"I hope he never changes, either. So judgemental." Robin hugged the dog.

"Amen to that."

Explore more of the *Lindenshaw Mysteries* series at:
riptidepublishing.com/collections/lindenshaw-mysteries

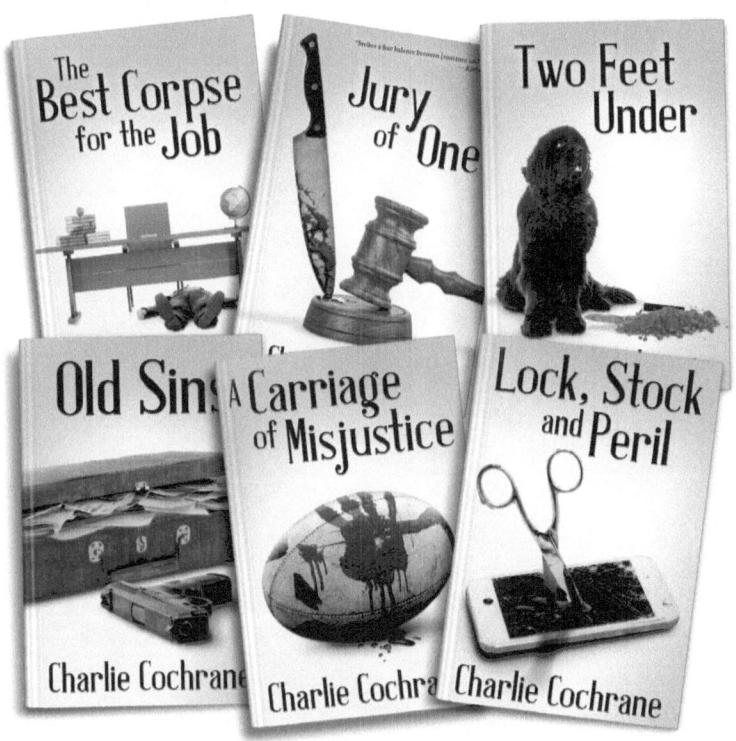

Dear Reader,

Thank you for reading Charlie Cochrane's *And Nothing But the Truth*!

We know your time is precious and you have many, many entertainment options, so it means a lot that you've chosen to spend your time reading. We really hope you enjoyed it.

We'd be honored if you'd consider posting a review—good or bad—on sites like **Amazon, Barnes & Noble, Kobo, Goodreads, Twitter, Facebook, Tumblr,** and your blog or website. We'd also be honored if you told your friends and family about this book. Word of mouth is a book's lifeblood!

For more information on upcoming releases, author interviews, blog tours, contests, giveaways, and more, please sign up for our weekly, spam-free newsletter and visit us around the web:

> **Newsletter:** riptidepublishing.com/newsletter
> **Twitter:** twitter.com/RiptideBooks
> **Facebook:** facebook.com/RiptidePublishing
> **Goodreads:** tinyurl.com/RiptideOnGoodreads
> **Tumblr:** riptidepublishing.tumblr.com

Thank you so much for Reading the Rainbow!

RiptidePublishing.com

Also by
Charlie Cochrane

About the Author

Because Charlie Cochrane couldn't be trusted to do anything grown up, she writes cosy mysteries. These include the Edwardian-era Cambridge Fellows series, the contemporary Lindenshaw Mysteries, and her 1950s Alasdair and Toby series where two actors play Holmes and Watson both onscreen and off. Multipublished, she has titles with Carina, Riptide, Lume, and Williams and Whiting.

Charlie is a member of the Crime Writers' Association, Mystery People and International Thriller Writers Inc, and regularly appears at literary festivals, reader conventions, and author conferences.

Where to find her:

Website: charliecochrane.wordpress.com

Facebook: www.facebook.com/charlie.cochrane.18

Twitter: twitter.com/charliecochrane

Instagram: www.instagram.com/cochrane.charlie2

Enjoy more stories like
And Nothing But the Truth
at RiptidePublishing.com!

Pressure Head	*Investigating Julius Drake*
Some things are better left hidden.	He'll have to stop pretending if he wants to save the day and get the boy.
ISBN: 978-1-62649-713-9	ISBN: 978-1-62649-448-0